MW01113406

RID OF RED

BY

JUD WIDING

PROLOGUE

THE NIGHT AFTER

RID OF RED

THE SEA HAD SOMETHING TO SAY. Or so it seemed to Officer McCall, shivering on the bluff, arms folded tight against his fleece jacket. The water was too dark to see from here – a deeper darkness than moonlight ought to have allowed – but he could hear it. The crashing exhale as it broke upon the toothy grin of the shore. The long, ragged inhale as it dragged itself back out. The sea was forever drawing its breath for more than just another chuckle around the sharper rocks. Yes, McCall was certain. The drink had more on its mind than the senseless click of pebbles tumbling in the tide. It was searching for words. Words to remind McCall, perhaps, that all those little pebbles had once been many-edged, and massive. How many waves had so reduced them, over how many years? To think of it was dizzying. Not the time itself, no. The waves. And their *patience*.

7

On second thought, McCall *could* see the sound. A stretch of unfathomable black, between the edge of the island here, and that pale yellow bruise of the mainland there. He could see the waters scoffing their way up the shore, in as much as he could see the shore disappearing, swallowed by the encroaching absence. As the sound rolled out, the shore returned. Changed, ever so slightly. In a way undetectable across even the whole of a human life. But give it time, and one day the mighty boulder upon which McCall now stood would be worried into nothing.

The sea, somehow, knew this. Knew the power of its virtue. Seemed eager to remind McCall of it, by tossing itself closer to him, ever closer, as the tide came in. Remind him of its patience, and the perfect knowledge that sustained it.

McCall refused to listen. Didn't care to look at the slow creep of oblivion any longer. Perfect knowledge? No thanks. Who would want such a thing?

He already knew more than he cared to. He knew that the sound was too wide for any of the kids to have swum across. He knew how many either hadn't tried, or just hadn't had the chance. Give it time, and he would no doubt come to learn just how many had tried and failed, managing one final glimpse of the old fishing town of Pitney before sinking down into the black. Too much to know already, that was. What good would it do him to know *more,* to know what final thoughts or memories had raced through their minds, what last words they'd tried to scream into the night, as their lungs filled with black perfection?

McCall shook his head slightly, and let out another trembling sigh. Hugging himself tighter, he took the opportunity to once again curse his choice to wear the fleece jacket. Normally his go-to garment, for the largely pleasant temperatures of summer in Maine, but then, he normally wasn't stood about on a moonlit shoreline for hours on end, so near the breaking surf. Had he known he'd be left to watch the bodi…the beach, he'd have gone for something waterproof. Something that wouldn't just slurp up every drop of water thrown against it. God, this thing was a sponge. McCall wondered if perhaps he might not improve his situation by just taking the damn thing off, but ultimately decided that what little insulation from the night it provided was worth preserving.

He'd also no doubt improve his situation by stepping back from the shoreline a bit. That would certainly save him having to look out on that sightless sound, keep his imagination from turning that depthless black into a canvas.

But, well, none of that was as bad as turning around.

Even here, looking out at the sea, steadfastly keeping his back to them…he knew they were there. Could hear the sheets, draped over top of them and weighed down with old stones, shuffling and snapping in the wind. That, too, rang of language to McCall. They, too, wanted to tell him something. Dreadful though the waters were, better to loose the imagination there, then to feed it the sight of countless sheets on a stony beach, cast in the loving relief of night. McCall knew that imagination of his would have no trouble at all tracing broken forms onto all those pale sailcloths.

While not exactly a *comfort,* Officer McCall felt a touch less alone out here, to think of how rattled even the thirty-year veterans had been by all of this. The way Chief Greider – who didn't exactly make a habit of visiting active crime scenes anymore – paced the southern reach of the killing fields and came out three shades paler than normal, the way he hollowed himself out before announcing they hadn't the man- or sea-power to evacuate the bodies all at once, they'd need to take them a few at a time, and someone would have to stand sentry here in the meantime…oddly, those memories were a salve to McCall. His was not a lonely horror. At least, he was not alone in feeling it. Even if he was very much alone on this island, with all of these bodies, waiting for more manpower to arrive.

If only he'd managed to spare himself those glimpses of the dead. For glimpses though they were, they remained branded in the folds of his brain. A girl of surely no more than ten or eleven, hair lovingly braided in a way she couldn't have managed on her own, with her jaw on her stomach; a boy perhaps half her age, with one of those ridiculous bowl haircuts most people get to laugh about when they're older, whose right shoulder had exploded with enough force to pull the bones of his arm from the sheath of his skin; a body upon whose age and gender McCall couldn't even speculate, who…well, perhaps that was illustrative enough. It was the glimpse of this last victim which had peeled McCall's gaze from the Earth, cast it into the waters, at that point still reflecting the sunset caressing the horizon before him. The eventide off the water was bright enough to burn his eyes, but better that than the bodies on the shore. The sunlight off the water, at least, offered the eventual reprieve of blindness.

Then the sun had set. And McCall was left here, alone, in the dark. With the bodies. Easily outnumbered by the dead, on this little island. Thirty to one, at least. Thirty being the *estimate,* reached before a formal search of the island had even been attempted.

He shivered again. Hugged himself still tighter. Felt moisture on his cheeks. What reach the sea had! A quick swipe under the eyes, though, revealed tears. Oh, he was crying. That was surprising. How had he not felt it coming on? Perhaps because he'd felt like crying for hours and hours. He'd just managed to hold it off until now. Assuming he hadn't been crying this whole time, without realizing it.

That boy with his shoulder blown off had reminded him of his nephew, Max. A nephew he saw only two or three times a year, a nephew he had nonetheless loved dearly. A nephew he had introduced to fingerpainting – apparently they didn't do that in his school. A nephew who, according to McCall's brother, only ate his vegetables when his beloved uncle asked him to. A nephew who had been killed by a drunk driver, in the middle of the day, just a normal day like any other. As all days were, until they weren't.

McCall's heart had broken at the news. For all the reasons one could imagine. He missed Max so much, grieved every day for the man he would never grow up to be. More than a few times, McCall found himself gripped by the impotence of rage. Found himself thinking that there was nothing he wouldn't do, to bring Max back. To make his brother's family whole again. To fix this one awful mistake, to put right a world that had gone irrevocably wrong.

There were so many bodies here, in the dark.

Someone behind McCall hummed. Tuneless, unbothered.

He spun around faster than he could unthread his arms to reach for his gun.

Twenty yards up the bluff, there stood a nine-foot tall man, hunchbacked and humbled by his own immensity, a thoughtful grin carved into the moondust soil of his face. He…McCall blinked at the tree and cursed his imagination.

That reprimand gave the humming a familiar form as well: vibration. A cell phone on silent, ringing. Of course.

McCall squinted back up the beach, where it climbed towards the tree line of the island proper, gathering stones as it rose, and saw the incoming call glowing from beneath one of those oh-so-thin sheets draped over the dead. Oh, no, not beneath – the rectangle of light it threw was too sharp.

The phone was in a hand. The hand was sticking out from underneath the sheet. As thought asking McCall to answer. *You mind getting this for me?*

12

Something about that patch of light hypnotized him, beckoned him. He had no desire to scramble blindly up the razor-sharp shoreline, his feet slipping and sliding off the rocks. There was always the fear that he might put down his boot, maybe even his hand, and feel beneath him something softer than stone…

But something about the light. The warmth of its banality. It called to him, yes.

So he scrambled. But slowly, carefully. Respectful of the fact that he was treading on ground that would soon enough be hallowed by the mayor, the governor, maybe even the President, if the body count was as high as the initial estimates indicated. Not that it was the eventual imprimatur of a career politician that demanded respect. No. What bowed McCall was a part in the clouds, a swell of silver moonlight, and the realization that the sea rolled up the shore black, yes, but it rushed back out red. That was the sort of thing that demanded respect for its own sake. McCall hoped that, by making this pilgrimage, he was showing it. In some fashion.

The nearer he got to the ringing phone, the more wary of it he became. He had the sense that it, too, was speaking to him, as had the sea. Had the sense that it wanted something of him. As before, he refused to listen to it…yet he continued his approach. For he was already in motion, and stopping was sometimes harder than the alternative.

It wasn't until he was standing almost directly over the phone, that he could recognize the face of a teenaged girl blazing brightly upon it. Above her face was the word

CHERRY, between two heart emoji. A real name or a pet name or an inside joke, McCall would never know. No matter; the picture already told him more than he wanted to know. The way Cherry was looking at whoever was taking that picture, with a small, unaffected smile, eyes wide and bright…that looked like love, or whatever storm of emotion and impulse passed for it between kids that age. Kids. She was a kid, Cherry was. A kid in love. As was the boy who had taken her picture, linked it to her contact in his phone. The boy beneath a blanket, on a pebble beach.

All at once, McCall realized that he was standing directly over the boy's body. Summoned by the light.

Light which revealed that the pebbles holding down the tarp had slipped; the boy wasn't as well-covered as he ought to have been. McCall could see, by the light of Cherry's smile, a baseball-sized cavity in the boy's head, tasseled with ribboned flesh where his right ear had been. That his phone was out of his pocket, gripped too tightly for death to prize free…God, the bullet had punched through the kid's head at precisely the spot he had intended to bless with his sweetheart's voice. Or whoever he had been calling. To tell them he loved them, maybe.

The phone stopped ringing. Cherry's face vanished. What remained of the boy's lingered.

Then, a moment later, Cherry was back. The boy had never left, of course. McCall feared he never would.

From further up the beach, McCall heard more humming. Ha, no. Another vibrating phone. Why did that keep sounding like a voice to him? Without quite knowing why or wanting to, he searched for the glow of this next phone. Even as the one at his feet continued to ring.

As though it had merely been waiting for him to turn his attention from the black of the water…the beach parodied life.

He heard music, he saw lights. The latter were hidden in pockets beneath the sheets, by ranges of sea stone; the former drowned each other in a soup of toneless incomprehensibility. More than a few of the phones, he swore he could see even from this distance, displayed faces. Smiling faces. The bright, smiling faces of loved ones clinging to the hope that their child or friend or first love or niece or nephew was still alive, was perhaps among the unhappy survivors who had been evacuated to the mainland. All of these little hopes, illuminating all of their worst fears. They didn't know yet. But McCall knew. And for a moment, he was gripped by the conviction that it was his responsibility to answer each phone, one by one, and tell them. Educate them as to the sort of world they lived in now.

The thought nearly knocked McCall backwards. His imagination thrilled to this new prompt: he saw himself dashed upon a crag, splattered on the black stones like the nearly two dozen kids who'd made it as far as the pebble beach here, but no further. Would his phone ring, though? No. There would be no familiar faces to illuminate the night for him.

McCall's heart rattled his ribcage, and he was quite certain he was about to be sick. He groaned softly, then once more crossed his arms across his sodden fleece jacket as he made a careful descent back down towards the water. Even where the rocks grew particularly treacherous, he kept his arms folded tightly against his torso. Somehow, he reached the beach unscathed. Somehow.

He found a rare patch of fine-grained sand, used the toe of his boot to clear some of the more aggressive pebbles from it, and levered himself down to a seat, arms still folded. There he sat, crossing his legs to match his arms, to watch as the obliterating tide inched ever closer to his knees. To listen as the water crawled across the stones, still speaking to him. To listen as the phones vibrated beside those bodies just up the shore. The killing field, still singing to him.

Part of the killing field, at any rate.

Someone sat down behind McCall.

He knew by the sound. The shift of stone. The hush of sand. The heavy satisfaction, the stillness. He knew the sound.

Even in that, there was a voice.

But he didn't turn around. He didn't have to. A nine-foot giant with the face of the moon cut an unmistakable figure, even when one couldn't see it.

Because that was what this new universe was missing, wasn't it? There was the black expanse of the sea, galaxies of hope, and constellations of grief. Yet it had needed a new moon. One that threw no light.

But, of course, a moon needs something to revolve around.

McCall didn't turn around. Refused to heed the voice of the elements, the call of this figure at his back. Gravity

16

was something that acted upon him. It was not something he could offer. Not here. Not in this place.

So, in time, the moon moved on.

After it left, Officer McCall somehow felt *less* alone. The sea seemed quieter, soft enough to let him hear the vibrations over his shoulder. Its gasping reach seemed further from his feet than it had just a moment ago. And it had lost its voice, no longer seemed to reach for words.

Odd to feel relief, out here. Fortunately, upon closer inspection, McCall realized he didn't.

He stood up, walked forward a few inches, and sat down again, arms folded all the while.

ONE

THE MORNING BEFORE

KIRA WAS SO ANGRY, she just stood in the middle of the room for about ten seconds, thinking about groaning or slamming a drawer or something, but not doing it.

Okay. Deep breath. There were only four cabinets in which the Bisquick could conceivably be: the two tall ones next to the fridge, the bottom one nearest the oven, and the one socked in under the knife block with the towel through the looped handle, that drawer where Kira used to sometimes find their cat Nova sleeping, back when Nova had been alive. Kira checked each one of these cabinets again, more carefully this time, all but emptying them out in search of the flapjack mix.

"Where the hell is it?" she mumbled at the cat-shaped hole in space under the counter under knife block.

Never one to accept the permanence of the material world, Kira went back and searched each of the cabinets a *third* time, before expanding her search to the drawers, in which the Bisquick *couldn't* conceivably be. And so it was: the familiar yellow box was not tucked behind the pots and pans, nor was it to be found behind the needlessly expensive glass bowls in which the flapjacks would have been mixed, nor indeed was it associating with the soaps and detergents under the sink. That last one provided a relief Kira found rather unearned, but alas, there it was. The relief. Not the Bisquick.

So, she wondered for a second time (silently, as she was vaguely aware of speaking to oneself as a habit to be broken), where the hell was it? She would have testified before any tribunal you like that she had purchased some goddamned Bisquick not four days ago, pulled it off the shelf at Hannaford, put it in her cart, walked it to the checkout line, plopped it onto the conveyor belt, paid for it, brought it home, retrieved it from one of her reusable bags, and put it…there, in the upper cabinet next to the fridge. Yes. The most logical spot for it to go. So why wasn't it there? She had no reason to doubt her memory; surprising Leigh with flapjacks on the morning of her big day had been on the metaphorical books for quite a while now. That she might have neglected a step as instrumental as *purchase the flapjack mix* wasn't just inconceivable, it was impossible. It was truly not possible.

As such, there was no contingency in place. Other than *eat what was already in the house*. So, what, Kira was going to send Leigh off with something as pedestrian as Honey Nut Cheerios on the morning of her trip to Pitney? That'd be stupid. No, today's breakfast needed to

22

be special, because the day was special, and the only part of it Kira was going to get to be a part of was breakfast. So it was important – it was *essential* – that Kira be able to make flapjacks for Leigh, just the way she liked them. With a splash of vanilla and almond extracts, not quite cooked through all the way. Were it blueberry season, Kira would have thrown a handful of those suckers in there too, but it wasn't, so she wouldn't. Put some extra-crispy bacon on the side, though, and that's it. Breakfast, the way Leigh liked it. One of the few things Kira felt like she still knew how to do for her fifteen-year-old daughter, without inexplicably embarrassing her.

Which was why it was so mission critical to find the fucking Bisquick.

She widened her dragnet, searching hidey-holes of increasing improbability with mounting urgency. For there was a ticking clock here: Leigh's alarm would go off in (Kira checked her phone) fifteen minutes. Hell. She'd wanted the flapjacks to at *least* be on the griddle by the time Leigh came down, ideally with bacon sizzling in a pan on the next burner over (she checked the drawers of Harlow's dry bar). The full sensory experience, sight and smell and sound (she checked the cabinets in the mud room). It was unacceptable that Leigh should come down to find her mother insisting *surprise, I'm going to make you flapjacks just as soon as I can find the fucking Bisquick* (she checked the toolboxes in the garage). Kira supposed she'd accept being in the process of *mixing* the batter – the whisking would kick up the scent of the extracts, the tines in the needlessly expensive glass bowl would provide sound, and the sight would be sufficiently evocative of the taste to come (she checked the crawlspace beneath the house). Okay (she checked the compost pile out back). That would be acceptable (she checked the…)

…

The recycling.

"WAKE UP," Kira advised Harlow.

"Hrn?" her husband wondered.

"Wake up, honey. I have to kill you now."

Harlow wiped his palm down his face, as though he were going to change his expression as his hand buzzed his nose. But he didn't, instead keeping his standard *just woke up* face, eyelids puffy, lips pursed like an orangutan watching a magic trick. Slowly, gravity pulled his head back towards the pillow. "Ooogh…just kill me in my sleep," he mumbled.

Kira smiled despite her frustration. "You used the fucking Bisquick. That was for flapjacks."

Harlow sighed mightily. "I…but…Iuzifu-"

"Can't understand you with your face in the pillow, my love."

He didn't lift his head, instead rolling it just enough to kiss daylight. "I used it for the chicken."

Oh. Right. The fried chicken that Leigh had asked for two nights back. Another of her favorite meals. That *had* been breaded, hadn't it?

Still…the *whole box*? It had been about the size of a cereal box. Kira wasn't much of a chef, but she didn't figure it took a whole box to bread three chicken breasts.

She presented this surmise to Harlow, who replied by farting and seeming startled about it. "I put it in the bag," he went on to explain, rolling over onto his side now. He retrieved his hands from atop his head and pantomimed holding the upper corners of a Ziploc bag. "I put the, uh, stuff in the bag and I shake it up." He demonstrated the shaking process. He gave another little toot, but had apparently been prepared for that one.

"So you used the whole box?"

"I guess. I don't remember."

"You knew I was doing flapjacks this morning. I told you about that ages ago."

"I forgot." He frowned. "I'm really sorry."

Kira sighed and glanced at the alarm clock over on her side of the bed. T-minus zero seconds until Leigh's alarm went off. Maybe. Leigh used her phone's alarm, which was linked up to the nuclear clock or whatever the hell, which her parents' bedside alarm clock was not. So give or take a few seconds, maybe as much as a minute or two. Either way, not enough time to run out and buy more Bisquick. The morning was ruined.

But of course, hindsight hissed, if she'd just gone and gotten the fucking Bisquick right away, instead of marching around the house in a huff…

She smiled unhappily at her idiot commitment to an impossible breakfast. Recognized it as childish, *certainly* unbecoming of someone just creeping into their forties. The mature thing would be to recognize what she *already knew,* which was that this didn't need to be a big deal. A meal was not a morning entire. But…well, letting things go had never been her strong suit. Oh, she felt herself more than capable of *forgiving* other people, if not the *forgetting* part. But looking past her own personal failings wasn't something she'd yet managed. In many ways, she considered her inability to make peace with her own shortcomings to be her greatest shortcoming of all, which she was of course not able to make peace with. Her doctor kept telling her she had high blood pressure, which Kira thought was an annoying thing to tell somebody.

Early in their now *twenty-three year* relationship (had it really been that long?), Harlow had identified this touchy tangle in Kira's brain, and in his usual way (well-meaning, unthinking), he'd gone ahead and just said, *you seem to have a hard time getting over stuff.* Kira's response had come in the form of lots of short words spoken loudly, accompanied by a pointing finger. Suffice it to say, *forgiveness* was something she'd learned, and honed through practice.

Twenty-three years with Harlow Trecothik. That was a lot of practice.

To face this latest trial, Kira closed her eyes and remembered the chicken. That had been something Leigh had asked for, in the lead-up to her big departure. So, the Bisquick had still been used for a specially-requested foodstuff. Wasn't that enough? Wasn't that what mattered?

And taking a step back: wasn't that a pointless question? What was done was done. There would be no flapjacks this morning. So why continue even thinking about it, trying to justify it?

She was still kind of angry, but at least she could stand back from that hot knot of batter in her heart and appreciate its pointlessness.

"It's alright," Kira told Harlow. "Just go back to sleep."

Harlow smiled a big, closed-eye smile, then rolled back onto his stomach and buried his face in the pillow.

Slowly, gently, Kira placed her hand on the back of Harlow's head. "Go to sleep, baby." She pressed his face into the pillow, gently. "That's right." Pressed a little harder. "Go to sleep, forever."

Harlow laughed into the pillow. Mumbled something in mock-terror. Hard to tell, but it sounded like it might have been, *it's just Bisquick!*

"It's never *just* Bisquick." Kira cooed. *"Sleep."*

Harlow laughed harder.

Kira smiled. Lifted her hand from her husband's head, gave him a soft squeeze on the shoulder, then got up and headed downstairs to intercept Leigh, and salvage what she could from the wreckage of breakfast.

KIRA HEARD HER DAUGHTER before she saw her. The undead shuffle of her slippers, scraping down the hall from the bottom of the stairs to the kitchen. *Shhk. Shhk. Shhk.*

She couldn't stop herself from imagining how Leigh's little face would have lit up, upon getting that full sensory experience of the…*God,* enough with the flapjacks, huh? She didn't want to think about them anymore. Which was why it was so annoying that she couldn't *not* think about them.

Finally, Leigh staggered out of that little hall and into the kitchen. Wearing an old tie-dye number as a sleepshirt. Kira smiled every time she saw it – Leigh had made that for school…or maybe for a summer camp or something? Hard to say. But she'd needed a white shirt to tie-dye on very short notice, and all the Trecothik household had to offer was an XL undershirt of Harlow's. At the time, Leigh had seemed close to crying, insisting the shirt was *way* too big, everyone would laugh at her. Kira tried to reassure her that, you know, one day everyone else will be too big to wear what they're making now. But you'll be able to wear yours for the rest of your life, if you want to. That hadn't made Leigh feel any better at all, but in the end, here she was, living the punchline of the story.

Not much of a story, granted. But so few of the memories that linger truly are.

"Ggwgloehgg," Leigh greeted her mother, as she staggered to the upper cabinet by the fridge, where, once, there had been flapjack mix.

Kira stewed in chunky resignation from across her bowl of oatmeal, as Leigh reached for the Honey Nut Cheerios. "Mornin'," she said. "How'd you sleep?"

"Pretty good?" Leigh speculated. She coughed into the air, flinched slowly, and offered a fake-sounding second cough to the crook of her elbow. The hand attached to that bent elbow was the one holding the cereal box, a box in which a few Cheerios had gone rogue and abandoned the bag. So as the crook-tendering tilted the box, the fugitive cereal circles slipped through the partially-torn top lip of the cardboard and pitterpattered to the floor. Leigh frowned at the Cheerios as though their flight from the box was a personal betrayal. Needless to say, she'd inherited her lazy pace of waking from her father.

Kira lowered her gaze to her oatmeal and kept eating. It was to her breakfast, then, that she asked "feeling good? Nervous?"

(It will be the small things like this that will most haunt Kira in the days to come. Moments wasted looking at her fucking oatmeal, when she could have been looking at Leigh. She'll wonder why oh why would she ever have looked away from her daughter, for even a moment, she'll wonder how on earth could she ever have taken an instant of their time together for granted, and she'll sit in the very chair she sat in that morning and she'll wonder, how can Leigh be gone, she was just here, in her tie-dyed sleepshirt, pouring herself a bowl of cereal?)

Leigh didn't answer right away. Kira glanced up and saw her daughter bowing before the open refrigerator, halfway to climbing inside, right hand holding the door open.

Oh, God. Was there something *else* missing this morning? The oat milk?

"Looking for something?" Kira inquired.

"Nooooo," Leigh replied distantly.

"There's oat milk in there?"

"Yep." Leigh regained her full height, lifting a carton of oat milk into view. She shunted the door to the fridge shut with her shoulder, plopped the oat milk on the counter, and retrieved a bowl from the cabinet to start assembling her ho-hum breakfast, so unworthy of the occasion.

Oblivious to her optimism, Kira imagined reflecting upon this morning some fifteen years in the future. Would Leigh's first day at the Firestarters feel so significant – so *epochal* – at such a remove? Probably not, but Kira felt that spoke more to time's slow erosion of import, rather than the magnitude of the morning itself. Because goddamnit, this was a big morning! Leigh had been attending Firestarters events for years now. She'd always been such an outdoorsy girl – Kira and Harlow had been fairly restrictive about screen time, and that choice appeared to have paid dividends – and Firestarters was southern Maine's premiere wilderness-shit-for-kids organization. Yeah, they walked right up to the edge of seeming like far-right survivalist-prepper pinheads, if it came to that, but Kira had done enough research to satisfy herself on that score. In the sense of them *not* being that.

Which wasn't to say they weren't still a bit backwards. *Very* backwards, in fact. In 2016 – hardly an auspicious year for empathy and inclusion – Leigh numbered among the first girls *ever* admitted to the Firestarters. Up until that point, the organization had managed to bullet-time various petitions and even lawsuits, by virtue of the fact that their ban on girls wasn't technically *official*. The fact that they finally caved spoke to either a change in leadership, or a solemn recommendation from their legal team. In either event, Leigh got her picture in a rotation on the splash page of the *Neirmouth Chronicle's* website, which publicity had absolutely rocked the then-eight-year-old Leigh to her core, stunning her into a wide-smiled silence for nearly a full hour. Over the years, she took part in various full- or half-day Firestarters activities, learning how to start fires (obviously), how to forage for mushrooms and edible plants, how to build a rudimentary shelter, all the sorts of things that were terrific fun as long as you were *choosing* to do them. She even learned how to shoot a bow and arrow, which remained Leigh's favorite day.

Firestarters, of course, offered overnight retreat options for the kids as well. Something Leigh had been interested in for four or five years now, which Kira and Harlow (but especially Kira) had balked at. "It's too soon," Kira had always told her increasingly frustrated daughter, year after year, forever dreading the day Leigh thought to ask, *for who?* Mixed blessing, that such a day never came: Leigh grew from a child who went red in the face and started shouting when you told her *no,* to one who prosecuted her case with uncanny composure and a comprehensive PowerPoint ("all of my friends are allowed to go" being one of the points she hit hardest). Last year, that had been. Oh, Harlow was won over at once, and, *enragingly,* turned to Kira and said "I think she should go," while Leigh was still stood in front of them. So much for a united parental front, huh? Kira balked yet again, but then night fell, and her traitorous brain made clear what the problem was. Not that she hadn't known; she'd just been able to avoid confronting it so effectively, for so long. Hint: *Leigh* wasn't the one who wasn't ready yet.

So this year, Kira relented. Leigh signed up for her first Firestarters retreat, a week-long "survival" stay on the snowglobe of Knot Hedge, that tiny island just off the coast of Pitney. Though maybe the air quotes weren't earned here: well-provisioned though the kids would be, Knot Hedge was a fairly barren little dwarf planet. A few acres of dense woods, besieged by sharp stones and pebble beaches. Leigh almost certainly wouldn't be in *danger* – there would be adults on-site, and the kids would all still have their phones – but she might struggle. Critical though Kira knew adversity to be for growth, she hated the idea of her beautiful baby girl *struggling* for a week.

On the other hand, of course, she loved to see Leigh proud of herself. And Leigh *was* proud. Kira was proud *of* her. For not only was Leigh attending the retreat – she would be *leading* it.

This year, in 2023, the Firestarters had finally admitted girls – *young women* – onto their leadership teams, a policy change effected in large part thanks to Leigh, and those comprehensive PowerPoints of hers. She (and, alright, a few others) had petitioned the organization's muckety-mucks, and made them see the light after all these years of having their heads firmly fixed in a dark place.

So, yes, by golly, this was a significant morning. However Kira would come to feel about it in ten, fifteen, twenty years, she decided, this would remain an enormous moment in Leigh's life.

As such, she urged herself to stay present. Don't fixate on how this will be the longest Leigh had ever been away from home. Don't sink into how empty the house will feel, without Leigh. Don't forecast the worry that might well keep you up, for at least the first night. She'd heard that quote – every parent has – about how when you have a kid, your heart lives outside of your body, you grow another heart that walks around without you, always something about your heart not being your own anymore. Kira had always understood that, and she'd certainly *felt* it before. But until this morning, she'd never truly, fully experienced the vulnerability of the sentiment.

The older she got, the more those pithy little pull quotes came to seem truer than all of poetry or philosophy. Your heart lives outside of your body, yes. How beautiful. How terrifying.

Kira looked up from her breakfast for a moment, just to watch her daughter pour her cereal, pour her oat milk. She thought of telling Leigh how proud she was of her, but didn't. That'd be too hokey. Leigh would just smile and roll her eyes, say it wasn't that big of a deal, something like that. So Kira didn't say anything.

(Of course she'll think of this tomorrow. Of course.)

HARLOW WAS RUNNING LATE FOR WORK, so he said goodbye to his daughter by grunting into the buttered English muffin he'd stuffed into his mouth, only to yank it free and kiss her on the forehead with his dairy-slicked lips and mumble something like "have fun this week!"

through his first bite. Then he was out the door.

Leigh waited to hear the garage door rumble open, waited to hear the grumble of Harlow's engine roll off as he backed out onto the driveway, waited for the garage door to groan its way back down. Then, and only then, did she lift her hand to her forehead and wipe clean her brow.

Kira only noticed what she was doing once Leigh redoubled her efforts with the sleeve of her sleepshirt.

Leigh noticed Kira's noticing at once. "Buttery," she mumbled, a shadow of a smile on her face.

Kira, too, smiled.

The two of them smiled for a time, eating their respective breakfasts in silence. Silence, of course, being an ample canvas for sound. For the periodic *slurp* of Leigh sucking the milk from her spoon, for the *splorch* of Kira dredging her oatmeal for another chunk of banana. What talkative meals they had. Hard to imagine flapjacks managing such a dynamic soundscape, eh?

"So, uh," Kira said, mostly just to fill out the empty space, "do you know what you're doing the first day?"

Leigh shrugged, bobbling her head from side to side as she finished chewing her latest mouthful. "I know I'm gonna help check in the kids."

"Cool. So you'll be the person with the clipboard there, that the parents check in with?"

"I don't know exactly how it works. I know I'll meet my troupe though. I have their names, but I obviously don't know them yet or anything."

Kira hesitated. "Oh. You have their names?" she

asked as casually as she could.

Not casually enough, it seemed; Leigh cocked an eyebrow defensively. "Yeah." Tendered in the tone of a dare.

"Hm," Kira said, nodding. Looking down at her oatmeal again. "Who, um…how did you get them?"

"Mr. Colson emailed them to me."

"…huh. When?"

Leigh put her spoon down in her bowl. Oh dear. This was now officially *a conversation*. "Is that bad?"

"It's just a bit strange for a grown man to be emailing you without at least cc'ing me."

"You signed the permission slip."

"I know that. But a grown man emailing a fifteen-year-old?"

"Mom."

Kira raised her palms in mock surrender. "I'm not saying it's bad. I'm just saying, it's strange."

"He emailed me about my troupe. It's not a big deal. He emailed me about my troupe, and he attached pictures of his penis."

Kira flinched so hard she scooted her chair a half an inch backwards.

Slowly, eyes diverted towards the ground, Leigh smiled. It was a big, unguarded, private smile. Not one Kira saw much of, now that Leigh was into her teenaged years.

"That's not funny," Kira insisted, her voice no doubt betraying the fact that deep down, she did think it was a little funny.

Leigh just kept on smiling, then got up and walked her bowl to the kitchen. Kira heard it go *thunk* into the sink.

"Dishwasher's dirty," Kira called, as she retrieved her phone from her pocket to fire up her various news feeds and invariably despair at the way the world was headed.

Leigh sighed loudly, but dutifully put her bowl and spoon into the dishwasher.

As her daughter tromped back up to her room, Kira turned to watch her go with, mostly, frustration. Should have been a lovely morning, this. Instead it was just… normal. Sometimes she couldn't wait for Leigh to grow up, at least get through these teenaged years. She wasn't as bad as the kids of some of Kira's friends, but she still wasn't the way she used to be. She didn't randomly come toddling over to Kira, wrapping her arms around her mother's thighs as best she could, to shout "Mommy!" Like she was just so happy to see her. Be a strange and worrying thing for a teenager to do, of course, but all the same, Kira missed it. Had loved it at the time, yes, but still hadn't appreciated it as she ought to have.

She tried to imagine what she was failing to appreciate about how Leigh was *now,* what she would kick herself for taking for granted in ten, fifteen years. Stood to reason there'd be *something.* The pride she felt for Leigh, maybe, certainly the love. But…well, it could be hard to see all of that, through the choke of foliage that was her *enormous* day-to-day frustration.

Watching one's child grow up was such a bittersweet thing, but still, all told…Kira was ready for the surly teenage years to live in the rearview mirror. She was looking ahead.

Always looking ahead, or else looking back.

SOMETIMES the hardest part of being a parent was *not* getting credit for all the ways you *weren't* bad at it. True, in any relationship, discretion must by its nature go un-rewarded, but for some reason – for Kira, at least – this had never really bothered her until she had Leigh.

A specific example. Yes, Kira absolutely *could* have spent the morning right on Leigh's heels, pestering her to *finish packing already,* because there was only one ferry to Knot Hedge per day and if she missed it, then, well, she would have missed it. That pestering was just the sort of thing Kira would have engaged in not two or three years ago, in fact. There was really no other way to wran-gle a child. But now, Kira had learned to trust that Leigh was capable of managing her own schedule. More to the point, Leigh certainly knew about there being only being one ferry a day, and nobody was more invested in her getting to the island than she. So standing around at ten minutes before they *absolutely* needed to start the fifty minute drive from Neirmouth to Pitney, with her empty suitcase still yawning wide open on her bed, that was an *informed* decision. Not how Kira would be doing things, were she in Leigh's position. But she wasn't in Leigh's position. Leigh was becoming her own woman, and for the most part had taken the responsibilities that came with that easily in hand. If this slowpoke approach to packing stressed *Kira* out, well, that was on Kira. So she didn't say anything to Leigh about it, and was very proud of that restraint, and then kind of disappointed that there was no way to communicate that restraint to Leigh, so she could appreciate how cool and lenient her mother was.

"Do you need help packing?!" Kira croaked in the door to Leigh's room, because that wasn't technically the same as telling her to *finish packing already.*

Leigh looked up from the open mouth of her suitcase, staring through the old wooden columns of her bed-frame, that four-post family heirloom in which Kira's grandmother *and* mother had been conceived (weird detail to pass down), which had been foisted upon Leigh because that was cheaper than getting a storage unit, and Kira hadn't been able to bring herself to get rid of it. Oh, how Leigh loathed that bedframe, made to look like a spooky shipwreck by the cruelty of a century. How violently it clashed with the rest of her room, all bright colors and moody lighting, largely courtesy of sponsored tchotchkes flogged by her favorite Twitch streamers. In fairness to Kira, Leigh had been a lot more excited about it when she'd first gotten it. In fairness to Leigh, she had been nine years old at that time.

Six years ago, Kira noted. God, she hated that her brain did that. Forever jumpscaring itself with the passage of time. So annoying.

Leigh planted her hands on her hips, and sighed. "We don't have to leave for ten minutes."

With a slight flinch, Kira returned to the present moment. "All I asked was if you needed help."

"No. I'm fine. Thank you."

"..."

"..."

"Just because we don't *have* to leave for ten minutes doesn't mean we *shouldn't* leave for ten min-"

"Oh my God, Mom. I can't pack when you're there."

"Okay." Kira slipped backwards out of the doorway, like Nosferatu having second thoughts. "I'll be downstairs. I'm ready when you are."

"I'll be down."

"Okay." With that, Kira turned and headed back downstairs. Waiting for Leigh. Ready when she was.

AS ALWAYS, Leigh was as good as her word. She came thundering down the stairs with ninety seconds to spare, suddenly all hustle. "Let's go!" she shouted, with a great big grin on her face. "I'm ready! Let's go!" Kira considered making a joke about how *she* wasn't ready yet, but didn't for fear that it might be received as passive aggression. That would have been a shame, because she was *fairly* certain that it wasn't. As she rose, she wondered if there might be a day, twenty or thirty years in the future, when Leigh would tell Kira that she had been secretly appreciating her mother's restraint all along. Then Kira reflected on all the things she hadn't said to her own mother, even towards the end, and she decided it was best not to nurture that into a proper hope.

So into the car and down the street they went, the interior of Kira's Ford Focus filled not with conversation but with a podcast. That was by Leigh's request; she was near the end of some true-crime miniseries, and wanted desperately to finish it up before heading to the island. Kira allowed it, because that was easier than getting Leigh to talk when she'd rather be doing something else, like listening to a murder podcast. Oh, she was absolutely riveted by these things, whereas Kira found them all more than a little ghoulish. So she just sort of zoned out, let the long winding ride out of their housing development in what was otherwise a fairly uninhabited small town – just one notch above an unincorporated township, really – slide past her like any other part of her life. Thinking dimly about how she hoped Leigh had a fun, enriching time with the Firestarters. Perhaps warmed by the pride she felt for her little girl, who had worked so hard to get herself into this position, going out to this island – and as a leader, no less. Certainly feeling no pressure to clarify these thoughts, either to herself, or to Leigh. Why bother? For all the anxiety she felt for her daughter's departure, she didn't for a moment doubt her return. What a fearful thought that would be, how unfounded. No way to live at all.

The drive to Pitney, then, was a shamrock smear of leaves lining the highway, signs naming any township in southern Maine you might (or might not) care to visit, leavened by Leigh's muted reactions to the podcast, which always brought Kira back to herself just enough to try to figure out what was happening in the story. No dice; every dramatic revelation on this podcast was followed by five or six seconds of ponderous, royalty-free music, which was always more than enough time for the world around Kira to once more reduce to pudding. She wished she could be more interested than she was. That might be something to talk about with Leigh, whatever the latest murder was, or whatever. She really did try. Oh well. Maybe someday Leigh would listen to more interesting stuff.

She did sit up a bit straighter as she took the turn-off towards Pitney. This was a stretch of road she couldn't entrust to muscle memory. Not to say she didn't know her way around – given the state of Neirmouth's grocery (take note: not grocery store, but *grocery*), Kira found herself heading to the Hannaford in Pitney at *least* once a week to do the shopping, along with anything else that needed doing. No, the reason she had to come online a bit more here was that there were actually other people sharing the road with her.

Even still, it was a rather mindless twist she took through the lazy sickle switchbacks comprising what was, for Maine, an uncharacteristically sharp descent down to a town. Granted, this wasn't the Alps here; each double-back of the road came softly enough that a passenger distracted by, say, the story of somebody who got decapitated very slowly by a weedwhacker or whatever, might completely fail to notice them.

So Kira determined, at least, by the reaction she received from Leigh, at her announcing that the island of Knot Hedge had slithered into view.

"There is it," came Kira's announcement, toneless and objective, in just the way that someone in a car driving past a field of cows will say *cows*.

Even in the corner of Kira's eye, Leigh's confusion

had texture. "What?"

"The island."

"Hang on." Leigh scooped her phone out of the central cup holder – where it had to live, as long as it was plugged in to the aux – and paused the podcast. "Ah," she added, as though only now seeing the island (which may well have been the case). "Yeah."

Yeah. That was as comprehensive a response as Kira could have expected. To be fair, *look at the thing* wasn't much of a conversation starter.

So they kept on driving. As Kira slowed for the next turn, Leigh reached tentatively for the phone. "Is it alright if we try to finish this episode before we're there?"

"Sure," Kira allowed with a shrug.

Leigh started the podcast back up. Kira zoned out again. And they drove on, drawing ever nearer to the island. An island which Kira had, despite making this drive literally hundreds of times over the years, never really *looked at* before. An island which, at least from this distance, looked a sight more bald and barren than the pictures in the metaphorical pamphlet had let on. Kira had never done the online dating thing, but she felt like she suddenly understood some part of the experience. The deception, the disappointment.

There were trees on the island, certainly, a lovely little oasis of green in the middle, mostly pines of foreign provenance from what she'd read. The main thing she noticed were the rocks, though. The rocks that wrapped all around the shore. Dark and jagged, they had an almost volcanic look to them. Roll back the clock far enough, and Kira supposed they probably had been volcanic. Then again, she knew nothing about rocks.

She did know the island was a lot farther from the mainland than she'd remembered, or realized. No reason for that to make a difference – call it another fifteen minutes on the ferry – and yet…

Kira made a point of keeping all of this to herself. Keeping silent, not interrupting the podcast, as they drove on.

LEIGH'S FRIENDS were all already there, because of course they were. *Everyone* was already there. Because *they* hadn't insisted on waiting until the last possible moment to pack their bags and hit the road, *Leigh*.

As one, Leigh's friends darted their heads towards the Trecothik car. Real *Children of the Corn* vibe, there.

Before the car had even stopped, Leigh was gesturing frantically to (and for the benefit of) her friends, mooning and mugging and emitting little involuntary noises of delight as she did.

Leigh's closest friend, Zoe Cottrell, whom Leigh had known since the second grade (and whose father had a way of standing just a *little* too close to Kira whenever Harlow wasn't around), returned fire with a similar display. Kira wondered if this was some sort of inside joke between them, or if she'd just forgotten what it was like to be that excited to see a friend. She'd long-since learned not to ask; Leigh wasn't fond of explaining herself. A trait she'd come by *very* honestly.

"Uhh-uhh-uhh," Kira sang, as she nosed the car along the pavement leading to the quay where the ferry was docked. She couldn't tell if she was supposed to be this close to the ferry with her car. It was all still concrete here, and she didn't see anything urging her to *STOP,* but there were also no barricades between here and the edge of the water, so…where was she supposed to park?

While the car was still moving at a crawl, Leigh popped the door and hopped out.

"Oh!" Kira shouted, dowdy despite herself. She couldn't wrangle her language until Leigh had *slammed* shut the car door, and gone dashing towards Zoe. "Careful!" Gah, no chance she heard that.

She frowned at the world just outside her windows. There was a very obvious parking lot back towards the entrance to the dock – a *paid* lot, she couldn't help but notice – but, again, nothing that explicitly indicated she couldn't be here. But there was no one else parked here. Which left her either a rule-breaker, or a visionary. When she'd never suspected herself to be either.

"Goddamnit," Kira muttered to herself. Looking back to that parking lot via the rearview mirror. Which was quickly obliterated by Leigh leaping into view, to open up the back of the car.

Cuh-CLUNG.

Leigh swung open the tailgate, heaving out her bag with both hands.

"Hey!" Kira called to her. Through the mirror.

Leigh returned her mother's gaze, in that little sliver of glass. "Yeah?"

"I need to go park back there. Don't leave, okay? I wanna say goodbye."

"We can say goodbye now."

"No, I wanna hug you, say a proper goodbye."

Leigh sighed, not bothering to hide her frustration. "I can't make them make the ferry wait."

"Well," Kira said, and then stopped herself. Thank goodness for that. Wouldn't have helped anything, to say *if we'd gotten here* earlier, *we wouldn't be having this problem.* "Let me just park then," she substituted for the unhelpful thing.

Sure seemed like Leigh had read the silence right, to judge by her face. All she said was "okay." Then she closed the tailgate, and went scampering off to be with her friends.

Kira watched her go. Watched Leigh rocket right up to Zoe, watched the two of them start bouncing with delight. Zoe, too, was part of this historic leadership team. Their joy was wholly comprehensible, understandable.

But maybe that matters more to you than them, the mean part of Kira's brain whispered to itself. *Maybe they're just excited to be away from home for the first time.*

Possible. Very possible. The joy she saw now on her daughter's face wasn't a million miles removed from the first time she'd watched Leigh get into a car without an adult in it. Just last year, this was: she'd gotten a small part in the school production of *Into The Woods*, and as such had fallen in with the musical theater crowd. Kira had found that a touch concerning – the theater kids she'd known in her day had largely been overearnest perverts – but then Harlow had revealed that he had technically been a theater kid in his day, by virtue of manning the light booth. Once the shock had subsided, Kira remembered that she'd actually known that about him already.

What she wouldn't put out of her mind so easily was the night – a Saturday night – when a car had rolled up to the curb outside the Trecothik house, and ejected an eighteen-year-old girl, who swiftly conquered the walkway to ring the doorbell, *ding dong.* Harlow answered, and assented to the girl's request, and the next thing Kira knew her daughter was scampering out the door, shouting "BYE!" just before it slammed shut. Kira made it to the bay window in time to see Leigh getting in to the car, a car which she could tell by the overhead light was packed to the brim with kids. Most of whom were older than Leigh, none of whom could have been older than nineteen. All laughing, all smiling. Just as Leigh was. Oh, she was *glowing,* gripped by delight in a way Kira hadn't seen in years. Did Kira take that a bit personally? Yes indeed. Should she have? Next question.

The car door had closed, and the overhead light had shut off, and the car had gone screaming off down the street.

"Uh, where the fuck is Leigh going?" Kira demanded of Harlow, who had already decamped back to the couch in front of the TV.

Harlow's head cranked towards Kira in stages, in the style of a clockwork boy. "She's going out with friends."

"Going out where?"

46

"They're her theater friends."

"Do you know any of them?"

"…like have I met them?"

"Do you know who they are? Do you know any of their names?"

Only then did Harlow appear to realize that he had done something wrong. Eyes wide, lips taut. "I think, uh…I think I heard Leigh call one of them, um… Molly?"

"Do you know when she's coming back?"

"Oh, yes," he said, turning a bit more towards Kira, "I did tell them to have her back by ten."

Kira said nothing to that. Just stormed upstairs to their bedroom, and looked at her phone angrily for a while.

If the joy she'd glimpsed on Leigh's face that night matched what she saw on it here and now on the dock, Kira supposed she had to concede that she too was feeling reheated feelings from that episode. A toxic little cocktail of powerlessness, and fear, and, hm, was that… the feeling of a rocket booster detaching from the shuttle, realizing what it should always have known, that its true purpose was to be left behind, to exhaust itself in the service of getting its charge past the atmosphere, then go plummeting back down to the sea?

Moments like these always occasioned a little drop of melancholy at the base of Kira's throat. Not a big wave, no, nothing she couldn't handle. Just a little *plonk*. Only trouble was, the drops came quicker and quicker these days. And, you know, drip enough drops on a stone, and soon enough they'll bore right through. Whatever *that* meant.

Kira sighed, threw the car in reverse, and wended her way back to that parking lot a ways away from the water. It was one of those lots without an attendant, just a machine at the gate, smooth and featureless save a single button and a ticket dispenser. Oh, and a little screen that tells you to PAY AT EXIT as it prints your ticket, then to HAVE A NICE DAY as the gate opens.

After parking and locking the car, Kira turned to hustle for the ferry, just as the Tuba of Gabriel rent the heavens.

BLOMMMMMP!

Kira flinched so hard she tweaked her neck. Goddamnit, that was loud! And goddamnit…that was the ferry!

She broke into a graceless little speedwalk, knowing perfectly well there was no point to it. Her view of the ferry chugging away from the quay was perfectly unobstructed.

How had they finished loading the damn thing up so fast? There'd still been a little sprawl of kids milling about on the dock, just a minute ago. *Teenagers.* Since when could a group of teenagers be maneuvered so quickly, with such precision? And shouldn't they have waited for Kira to check Leigh in, or whatever? Shouldn't she have had to sign something?

Silly. She'd already signed all the slips, and what was more, Leigh was part of the leadership team. Which meant, presumably, she was capable of acting on her own. More than capable. Didn't need Mom's permission any more. Those days were over.

Belatedly, Kira slowed to a walk, then a stop. Partially in recognition of the pointlessness, mostly because she was already starting to get a stitch in her side. God, she was out of shape.

She felt more than a few little *drip drip drops* in her throat. Pressed her lower lip against her teeth, to work that quiver out of it. All the while watching the bow of the ferry as it backed away, waiting and hoping to see Leigh appear on it, to wave goodbye. Knowing how unlikely that was. Knowing that, back when she herself had been sixteen, Kira wouldn't have broken away from her friends to go wave goodbye to her mom. It wasn't until much later in life that she came to appreciate how important that relationship was. Not until it was just about too late, in fact.

Kira waited until the ferry appeared no larger than her thumbnail held at arm's length. If Leigh popped out on the bow now, Kira surely wouldn't have been able to see her. But she wasn't going to pop out. Of course not.

Wow. What a bust of a morning. She'd wanted to make it so special for Leigh, and instead it had been… what other word fit, but *normal.* She'd wanted to wait until the last possible moment to hug her daughter, just before she got on the ferry, to say *have fun,* to reiterate *I'm so proud of you,* to send her off with *I love you.* How silly, she felt in hindsight. Why wait until the last moment? Why wait to let your daughter know how proud of her you are?

(This won't be the question that bothers Kira the

most, though it'll certainly be on the list. No, the one that'll really keep her up at night is, *when was the last time I told Leigh I loved her?* Not that she won't be able to remember plenty of possibilities, from the day or two prior. She just won't know with certainty which had been the *last* time.)

Drip drop drip drop.

Kira rolled her eyes at herself, as she headed back to the car. Best to just be happy for Leigh, that she was surrounded by friends, off to enjoy the prize for her pre-cocity. Best not to make it all about oneself, no?

"Yeah, yeah," Kira grumbled at the smooth obelisk standing sentry at the exit of the parking lot. *Three dollars* it wanted from her, for just a few minutes in the lot. And she wasn't getting out until she paid up. No grace period here then. Or maybe she'd spent longer than she'd realized, watching the ferry shrink.

IT WASN'T UNTIL Kira got home that it fully sunk in: she was staring down the barrel of full week of free time. She accepted this the way one does a terminal diagnosis.

When had she last had such a generous stretch of time entirely to herself? Dumb question, obvious answer: before she'd had a kid. Oh, since then there had been date nights with Harlow (back before Julie Snell from down the block had gone to college; what a reliable baby-sitter she'd been), solo evenings and even long weekend getaways thanks to a sleepover here or there, all those classic gasps of alone time one learns to sniff out in par-enthood. And, you know, this wasn't exactly going to be a week of vacation. Kira still needed to work (even if she did work from home, even if she did set her own hours). Nor would it be true alone time – she'd be spending a lot of it with Harlow. Which she was actually quite looking forward to, in the runny-gut stylie of someone about to do their first skydive.

Suffice it to say, having a child had changed their relationship. Indeed, the decision to *try* to have a child had been a shift unto itself. Kira could remember being in her early-twenties, talking to Laura, a friend from college who had already had two kids. Well, more apt to say Kira received from Laura an unprompted, dead-eyed monologue about how *essential* it was that she and Harlow establish the division of labor before the kid was even conceived. "It was the classic thing," Laura insisted. "I stayed home, and he worked, and he didn't see all the work *I* did, so he felt like it was fine to stick me with all the bills, balancing the checkbook, doing taxes…we almost didn't make it."

Kira took that shellshocked confessional to heart, and recounted it very nearly verbatim to Harlow that night.

"If we have a kid," she told him, "we need to commit to open communication. I d-"

"Totally."

"I wasn't done."

Harlow smiled and nodded. "Sorry."

Not the most auspicious start, but there were more pleasant omens to focus on. For some reason, the one that sprang most readily to mind – the one that astonished so many of Kira's friends, whenever it came up in conversation for whatever reason – was that Harlow always helped his friends clean up after a dinner party. Clearing table places, putting in time at the sink or the drying rack, just generally being quite thoughtful and helpful to the hosts. It was, Kira had long since learned, not a common trait amongst the male partners of her friends.

That wasn't a deciding factor in their having a child, of course. But it wasn't *not* a factor.

So after quite a lot of tries – a fun little euphemism for *non-stop raw-doggin'* – Kira finally got pregnant, and the line of communication with Harlow remained as wide open as one could want. The division of labor was equitable from the jump, tending a bit in Harlow's direction as the pregnancy progressed; Kira had a rough third trimester, one in which standing for long periods of time caused her tremendous pain, whereas sitting or lying down *also* caused her tremendous pain. In the end, of course, Leigh was delivered, and came home, and Kira and Harlow communicated. They were clear and honest and sometimes that wasn't easy, but honestly, a lot of times it was. Not the *having a kid* part, God no, nor the *getting all the shit done* part. But the *talking about how to try to get all the shit done* end of things, that ended up being a lot smoother than Kira had ever expected. Harlow was a good man, after all, and it probably helped that his friends were largely good family men too. If Kira ever felt stuck or down, it was never on his account. Well, mostly never. No relationship was perfect.

Indeed. Because all of that communication about

logistics – finding summer camps to enroll Leigh in and making that happen, working out what fun after-school activities she could and couldn't do based on Kira and Harlow's divergent schedules (pre-COVID, Kira had worked as a bartender at a sleepy, closed-by-summer-sundown sort of restaurant), to say nothing of keeping all the plates spinning and the lights on at home – turned Kira and Harlow's relationship into something of a non-stop negotiation over time and attention and resources. This was not to say their marriage was drained of love; far from it. It was simply that, well, love could be taken for granted just like anything else. And over the years, it became something akin to emotional WD-40 applied to points of real friction. Harlow insisted he couldn't take Leigh to her friend Madeleine's birthday party because he was supposed to go golfing, but that didn't strike Kira as a particularly strong excuse because she would be at *work*. Remembering that they loved each other was the first step to resolving the issue. Communication, though, was what *actually* resolved it.

Kira could acknowledge that it was probably silly to think of those things as separate. But that was how they *felt* to her. Ah, but that was just time, wasn't it? Cupid could only carpet bomb a couple for so long. The lovey-dovey shit had an expiration date. That was what every-body always said.

Privately – never once communicating *this* thought, no – she sometimes wondered if maybe that old heart-erupting sort of love she used to feel for Harlow hadn't simply faded with time. Sometimes she wondered if maybe her capacity to feel that feeling hadn't been completely augmented by the arrival of Leigh. Her daughter had gifted her with the ability to feel love more deeply than she'd ever thought possible, with the fine-print that everything else in her life would come to feel smaller as a result. If that was the case, that was a deal Kira was happy to have made, would have made a hundred times over. Not in the sense of having more kids, G*od* no – even at her most difficult, Leigh was a jackpot in the genetic lottery. Kira had no interest in cranking the lever again, running the risk of spawning a little psycho or something, a fear she hadn't managed to relinquish until Leigh was about fourteen (might have managed it earlier, had Leigh not started listening to those murder podcasts around ten or eleven). Just…Kira didn't mind that her heart was two sizes too big now. Harder to fill, but more room for everything else. Not for nothing, but ever since Leigh's birth, Kira became a much lighter touch on the waterworks. A sentimental car commercial featuring a baby growing up could reduce her to tears; seeing two old people smiling in a restaurant was all it took to occasion a stoic lip quiver, of the sort well-known to patriotic newscaster reporting on national tragedies.

All of this to say, though…Kira was looking forward to seeing if some alone time with Harlow – their first real stretch of uninterrupted time together since Leigh had been born – might not surprise her on that score. If maybe doing more than barking dates and places and times at each other like two air traffic controllers might leave space for some of that old sparky firework feeling. If not,

RID OF RED

that'd be fine too. Leigh would be back in a week, and everything would go back to the way it had been, and that would be perfectly fine.

But wouldn't that be nice? Even just a few fire-crackers?

Kira got home, and went into her home, and then she was home, and she had no idea what to do. Just around a third of her entire life, focused so intently on another person…she'd sort of forgotten how to occupy time that was entirely her own. What do people even *do*?

She pulled out her phone and looked at the time on it. Barely lunchtime. Harlow wouldn't be home for hours.

Instinctively, Kira wandered to the "office" – a tiny room on the first floor where she'd set up a desk against one wall and a big bookcase on the opposite, so that she looked smart on Zoom meetings. She sat down in her little wheely chair, which she hated, intended to replace with something unwheeled at *some* point (a deadline that worked for her because it never arrived), and opened the top drawer on the right side of the cheap prefab desk.

Her physical planner. Hundreds of sheets of paper, spiral-ring style, bursting with the multicolored tongues of scores and scores of Post-It flags that had all meant something at some point, packed with a year's worth of activity for Leigh, all rendered in the hasty, deranged script of those notebooks from *Se7en*.

She got as far as putting the planner on her desk, then stopped and laughed at herself. What was she doing? Trying to plan something for or about or around Leigh?

Yes, that was normally what she did in her downtime. But that wasn't what this week was about. This was a trial run for the empty nest. Give it two years, and Leigh would be going off to college, home for just the summers. Then she'd start her adult life, and she might pop back once or twice a year. Maybe she'd start her own family, or maybe she'd just get busy with her life, whatever career she wound up in, and once a year would be the *goal*.

Drip drop. Goddamnit.

Kira sighed and returned the planner to the drawer. Tried to not think about how this big, empty, quiet house was going to be the new norm, before too long.

Ignoring that loose-screw rattle in her oversized heart, Kira drifted out of the office, through the kitchen, to the room where the TV more or less devoured the far wall. That had been a compromise with Harlow, who had wanted a screen large enough to see from outer space. Kira didn't care for it, but she also didn't really care about it either way. A TV, for her, had become something on which to watch the first ten minutes of a movie, then the last ten minutes of the movie, or whenever it got loud enough to wake her up.

Since sleep was a rare and precious thing, Kira didn't want to retrain her relationship to that device just yet. So she wandered to the front door, opened it, and stepped outside. Ah, yes. Drink deep of the beautiful day. Perfectly suited for a lovely little walk around the block. Yes indeedy. That would fill some of the time until Harlow got home. Then, from there, they could work out what the week ahead might look like. The possibilities were endless.

No small part of the problem, that.

KIRA WALKED AROUND the neighborhood for four hours, at which point she returned home and checked the clock and realized that she had actually only been out for twenty minutes. Damn.

Eventually, the day dribbled towards dusk, and at the end of it all Kira was hard-pressed to account for how she'd filled most of that time. She'd had lunch, she'd tried to imagine Leigh getting to Knot Hedge and settling in to her cabin, hoped she was enjoying herself even now, then had a go at reading Her Book, which was how Kira referred to whatever book of the moment she'd chosen to look at in bed, dimly aware that all those dark little shapes on the page were words, then vividly aware of whatever that night's dream might be. Much to her surprise, she discovered that Her Book right now – which Her Bookmark was nearly two-thirds of the way through – was some book about trees or something. What? It was about how trees might be secretly conscious in a way we don't understand. Pretty fucked up to print a book like that in paperback, huh? Kira wondered if that was ever addressed in Her Book, but instantly made peace with the fact that she would never know. She returned it to the nightstand beside her bed, because no doubt tonight she would want to look at it again.

For the rest of the day, Kira worked. Set her own hours, so she did. She'd picked up coding not far into

COVID, not because she liked it or had a knack for it, simply because it was a way to work from home. It paid well enough, she was mostly freelance, and, you know, what else was she gonna do? That restaurant where she'd worked had closed, first temporarily, then permanently, and Leigh's school had gone remote, unlike Harlow's office (and there had been more than a few conversations about *that,* rest assured). At no point had learning how to code felt like a choice to Kira. But it was fine. It was a job and she didn't hate it, and she'd turned out to be alright at it, so whatever.

Such was the headspace in which Kira passed the day. *Whatever.* At least it kept the hours sliding along. At least it made her some money. The hours were the main thing, though. Keep 'em sliding along.

The muted *chunga-CRUUUUH* of the garage door rattling open came as a surprise. Wasn't that nice? The whole day, whittled away making money. What more could one hope for?

Kira had a hard time getting back into her work, knowing that Harlow was home, but that was fine. She stared vacantly at the screen, focusing instead on the sound of the garage door groaning open, followed by the pause of Harlow's Honda CR-V puttering in (the grumble of its engine was lost to her from this distance, but she was familiar with that endless whinny as heard from the kitchen), concluded then by the *chunga-CRUUUUH* of the garage door reversing course, rattling back down towards the ground.

The longer she looked at her screen, the more alien

everything on it seemed to her. Wow. She was coding. What a strange an unexpected thing for her to be doing with her life.

She heard Harlow step into the house, through the door that connected the garage directly to the kitchen. Heard the familiar *clunk* of his briefcase hitting the hardwood floor. Man of tradition, taking his briefcase to work, in his business suit.

Out she went into the kitchen to greet him.

"Hey," she said.

He turned to her, smile growing even as his eyes were still en route. "Hi!"

"How was work?"

"Oh, you know." He made *a face,* folding up the bags under his eyes and lifting his brow slightly. It was a face that Kira knew very well, one that said *literally nothing of interest happened today.* It was a face she saw a lot. He turned the face back into a smile and asked "what do you wanna do about dinner?"

"I figured we'd have something from out. But you can go change first."

Harlow nodded gratefully, and wasted not a moment in turning towards the stairs and hustling up to their bedroom. A point of simple compromise, this: Harlow always liked to get out of his business duds as quickly as possible. Prior to the exchanging of the how-was-your-day, even. Though Kira was often starved for human contact by the time he got home (since she'd started the remote work, anyway), it was no problem at all to wait another few minutes to look a human being in the eyes.

Behold: after another few minutes, Harlow came galumphing down the stairs, dressed in a T-shirt and that weird pair of shorts with zippers on the pockets he'd gotten at an Eddie Bauer or some place like that. "So," he said, "how was dropping Leigh off?"

"It was good," Kira said, with an eye on the clock. Just like that, the currents shifted: now it was she who wanted to push off the conversation for a moment; she was hungrier than she'd realized. "Real quick though, what do you want to do about dinner?"

"I thought you wanted to have something from out."

"Oh, definitely. I meant in terms of, do you ha-"

"Do I have something in mind, gotcha."

"Yeah."

"Um…not really, no. Did you?"

"Oh…not in particular. I'm just hungry."

"Okay. Cool."

"Are you feeling, like, pizza, or…?"

Harlow shrugged. "I feel like I would be happy with most stuff."

Kira felt herself getting a bit upset, but recognized that was probably just because she was so hungry. "Okay. I think we've got pizza in the freezer, or some of that leftover Indian in the fridge."

Harlow made that blank face he made when he wanted Kira to make a decision. It was always so annoying because he almost always made it when Kira wanted *him* to make a decision.

"Which one do you want?" Kira pressed.

"Either's fine."

"…*alright,* how about the Indian? Probably won't stay good for much longer anyway."

"Sure."

That decided, Kira retrieved the plastic containers of biryani left over from a meal they'd had in Pitney's finest (by default) Indian restaurant about a week back, then set the oven to preheating, which she kicked herself for not doing before they'd had that whole conversation. But then, she hadn't known what they'd be having until they'd had the conversation. But then, whatever leftovers they'd gotten out would have to be reheated, and the oven was always preferable to the microwave. But then…gah. All Kira knew for sure was that she was too hungry to do anything except make food.

As a secondary consideration, Kira wondered if a week out was too long for leftovers. Reheated rice could be a risk, hadn't she heard that somewhere? In trying to remember where she'd heard that, she forgot what she was trying to remember.

So she reheated their food, and they set the table, and they sat down, and they ate. By the second forkful – despite the spice – Kira felt human again.

Belatedly, *very* belatedly, she answered Harlow's question properly. "Dropping off Leigh was a bit hectic," she said, without preamble or segue.

Mouth full of chicken, Harlow made a noise that surely meant *oh?* As in *go on.*

"She went right up to the wire in terms of packing," Kira explained, "and the parking at the ferry was pretty confusing. So I ended up just dropping her off, and by the time I parked and got back to them, it was gone."

"The ferry was gone."

"Yeah."

"Oh, man. No big goodbye then?"

Kira sighed at her latest forkful, halfway to her face now drifting back towards the plate. "Nope. And honestly, my first thought was being bothered by that. Then a second *later,* I thought, *gosh, I hope she has fun."*

Harlow just nodded, tilting his head back to slowly guide a longer strip of chicken into his open mouth, not touching the lips at all, like a game of *Operation.*

Something about that displeased Kira tremendously. "Pretty shitty, right?"

"Ah…mhm," Harlow replied, pointing to his frenzied chewing, rolling his eyes and bobbing his head and spinning his finger around in the air.

Kira waited.

Eventually, Harlow swallowed and said "I don't think so."

Only then did Kira take another bite of her biryani. She shrugged and said "I don't know" with her mouth full.

"Seems like a fair way to feel, given the situation."

Now it was Kira's turn to nod and chew, nod and chew. She swallowed, then said "do you wanna do an overnight in Portland or something this weekend?"

Harlow opened his mouth to respond, then flinched, then smiled, nearly laughing. "Almost asked whether you were thinking Leigh would come with or not."

Kira smiled too.

"Yeah…yeah, that could be fun. Think we could find a place to stay on such short notice?"

"Oh, yeah." Kira pulled out her phone. "Maybe look in South Portland if the peninsula's too pricey…"

"Peninsula would be nice though."

"Oh, of course."

"Better walking."

"Right." Kira opened up Airbnb. Obviously not ideal – far from Portland though Neirmouth was, she was well aware of how problematic that service had become for the locals – but, hey, hard to beat the prices.

Harlow scooted his chair over to Kira, and together they ate and scrolled through Airbnb listings in Portland, thrilling to the view from the terrace on one, gushing over the full kitchen to which they'd have access in another. Cheap thrills, sure, but it was fun. Fun to look at all the different places they could stay, and imagine staying in them. Imagine all the different things they would do on their weekend together. Just the two of them. What fun.

In the end, they booked a spot in the Munjoy Hill neighborhood, right near the top of the hill. Third story with a view, easy street parking, walkable to the trendy spots on Washington Ave. What wasn't to like?

A little impromptu getaway. Kira couldn't wait.

Later that night, Kira and Harlow undressed and got into bed, fondling and rubbing and lightly thwapping each other with clueless determination, in the style of working out how to turn on a baffling European espresso machine. After ten long minutes of doing breakdance moves on the other person's pelvis and saying *how's this,* Kira finally said "maybe we should just watch a movie."

"Yeah," Harlow granted. "Sorry. I'm just a bit out of it tonight I guess."

"It's alright. I think I am too."

"What movie do you want to watch?"

"I don't know."

They went deep, deeper than ever before into the Netflix menu. Discovering movies that neither had ever heard of, that surely didn't actually exist. They all sounded a *little* bit interesting, but not really.

"Maybe this one," Kira suggested, as she looked over to Harlow, to find him extremely asleep.

She turned off the TV and then the light, and she tried to go to sleep. But it wasn't so easy for her.

THERE ARE LOTS OF THINGS, good and bad, about effectively working for oneself. One of the good ones was that Kira could, if she remained mindful of her deadlines and allocated her work time accordingly, take days off whenever she liked.

Kira woke from a deep but overly agile sleep on that morning, the first of this full week without Leigh, and realized all at once that she liked her day off *today*. Before her eyes opened, she worked out how that would scan with taking the upcoming weekend off while she was in Portland with Harlow. Sure, might make for some busy days in between, but she could cram a bit and make it all work.

She opened her eyes, giddy over the gift of a full day off with which she'd just surprised herself, feeling sharp and bright and optimistic and about as well as one could ever hope to feel, on what she would come to consider the last day of a life worth living.

At 5:12 AM, Kira rolled out of the now-empty bed, then made that bed. Pulling the sheets taut, tucking them in, then yanking out the wrinkles in the comforter. Hardly the most pressing task of the day, but habits were hard things to break. And every day since time out of memory, when Kira woke up, she made her bed. So that was what she did, and that was why she did it.

That done, she trekked downstairs. She said "morning" to Harlow, who was already fueling up for his pre-work visit to the gym.

"Good morning," her husband replied, chipper and bobbleheaded. "Got anything good going on today?"

"I'm gonna take the day off."

"Oh, fun. Much deserved."

Kira doffed an invisible cap, which she had never done before and hoped she never did again.

"Any big plans?"

Smiling softly, Kira sidled up to Harlow, gently placing a hand on his back as she reached around him for the oatmeal. "Not really. *Day off* is as far as I've gotten so far."

"Strong start!"

"I thought so too."

Breakfast was a languid and stress-free affair for Kira, and what a pleasant contrast to yesterday that was. She sat herself at the table by 5:38 AM with coffee, oatmeal, and (rare luxury) a cup of Harlow's orange juice which clashed with her coffee, but that was life. Harlow kissed her goodbye and headed off to the gym to do whatever it was he did to maintain his snowman physique. Officially on her own, Kira sat her laptop on the table just behind her meal and did a bit of inbox tidying. No work-related emails, *certainly* not on her day off, just marking junk mail as *read* and investigating a few sales and clearances that all turned out to have come and gone already.

As her first little treat to herself, Kira skipped the daily news podcasts she usually listened to. Hardly a day off, if she started it by cramming her head full of existential threats to the future of the human race. As she went upstairs to draw a bath (what extravagance! And why not?), Kira went ahead and sang out the bad news she knew those podcasts would have had in store for her. "Country flirts with fascism! Politicians behave badly! All forests are on fire, all animals are extinct!" By the top of the stairs, she felt quite gloomy indeed. Not to doubt the consolations of humor in the face of a terrifying future, for both herself and, more to the point, her daughter. No, Kira just didn't care for how her voice bounced around the empty house. At 7:07 AM.

(7:07 AM being the very moment that Leigh did a lap around the eight-bunk cabin, waking each of the younger Firestarters she would be overseeing for the whole of the week. She was able to whisper their names to them as she shook their shoulders; she had spent all of yesterday, and much of last night, repeating those names to herself, over and over. It was critical to her that her kids all felt comfortable here, felt welcomed. For that was how she, all of sixteen years old, thought of these eight-to-eleven-year-olds: *my kids.*)

The idea of a bath lost its luster once Kira got a good look at the tub. Bit gummier than she wanted to see it, this tub. They paid a woman named Phyllis to come clean their house every other week, and it had been near to the full two weeks since she'd come last. Hence the gummy tub, which led to Kira choosing to take a shower rather than a bath. That was fine, though. What was so extravagant about laying down right next to one's toilet, anyway? She laughed at that thought, but stopped laughing when she got a bit of shampoo in her eye.

On exiting the shower, Kira dried herself off and started to get ready. By 7:47 AM, she was dressed, having settled on the most comfortable, billowy summer blouse in her wardrobe, a modern white-and-orange floral pattern that went great with the blue jeans she knew she would regret wearing by noon. Now dressed, it occurred to Kira that she had nowhere specific to go. It was, in fact, in her opinion, a little too early to be fully dressed without a good reason. Damn. It'd be silly to get *undressed* again, only to get *redressed* later. *Damn.* Should have thought this through. Having a day off was harder than she remembered.

Committing to her mistake, Kira went ahead and be-grudgingly prepared her hair and face. She finished that up at 8:03 AM, then considered texting a friend to make lunch plans. How long had it been since she'd had *lunch plans* with someone? How fun. At 8:04 AM, she texted her friend Charity Capatonda. Well, Charity was the mother of one of Leigh's old friends Clara; that was how Kira had met Charity, at some school function or another. She'd turned out to be one of the few parents-of-one-of-Leigh's-friends with whom Kira had in any way clicked, such that they'd maintained a very loose kind of contact even after Leigh and Clara had drifted away from one another, as kids do. So…easier to just call her a friend, then. 8:04 AM, she sent Charity a text. 8:05 AM, she got a response: affirmative. Lunch was a go. Twelve noon, it would be. So much time between now and then!

(8:05 AM being quite a dull moment for Leigh, though not for lack of activity. Simply that the activity in question was standing under that enormous wooden frame pavilion known as 'central deck' despite its being nearer the eastern edge of the island, and staring up at Mr. Protolph, one of the head honchos of Firestarters, forced to endure his toothy bloviations welcoming the organization's first-ever crop of female counselors. Leigh couldn't help but recall how he hadn't been smiling nearly so much when she and a few of her friends had been pitching the board of directors to actually *allow* those female counselors. Much though she wanted to think of that as a sign of his changing his ways, she didn't buy that for a second. He embraced the new leadership team only because the alternative would force him to acknowledge he'd lost a fight. Leigh tried to content herself with the victory that her presence here represented, reached for the magnanimity necessary to soften the scowl she still directed at this man. Here, though, she fully embraced her age – her youth – which she so often sought to deny in the name of being an *adult*. In short: was a sixteen-year-old not allowed to hold a grudge? Wasn't that the best age at which to hold a grudge? The thought made her smile, which was good, because she hoped to hide both her malice and her boredom from *her kids*. Leigh snuck what she felt was a terrifically discreet peek at her watch. 8:06 AM. God, they had another forty minutes here, and Protolph was the only speaker.)

At 8:12 AM, Kira decided she would do something she rarely had time to do – she would read whilst wide awake. Could it be, that she would manage more than eight half-comprehended pages before falling asleep? Yes. She believed that it could be done. Not wanting to commit to a full book, though – after this week, she knew she might not have an opportunity like this again until Leigh went to college – she pulled a collection of short stories off the shelf. One of those collections with the grandiose name, something like *The Top Short Stories of the Year* or whatever. After flicking through the indices of a few volumes of this series, searching for a halfway intriguing story title, wondering all the while *how have we been buying these every year, I don't remember buying any of these*, she determined that all short story titles were stupid. So she selected a year at random – 2003, why not – and at the very moment 8:20 AM became 8:21 AM, she sat herself down on the couch and started, my goodness, *reading for pleasure*. She stuck with the 2003 collection until 9:34 AM, at which point she cut bait and time-traveled to the 2014 volume.

(9:34 AM being when Leigh and the rest of the leadership team crested a small bluff that marked the end of the *scenic route* to Crescenzo Point, the westernmost edge of the island. The scenic route (in truth, a slow, precarious trek along the stony coast) having been made necessary thanks to an *enormous* tree that had fallen across the more direct path through the woods, that path having a steep rockface on one side and a menacing drop on the other. As it was hard to imagine anyone bringing over an excavator or whatever would be necessary to shove that fallen giant off the path, Crescenzo Point was now really accessible *only* via the scenic route. Just why it was necessary to undertake such a perilous scramble along the rocks to reach the Point, itself a fearsome armory of sharp black stones all drawn on the sound, as though forever warning the mainland *don't you come any closer,* Leigh couldn't imagine. Could this be a kind of retribution from the top brass? Possible. No time to think on it though. Exhausted from the walk – sorry, *hike* – Leigh wiped the sweat from her brow, swatted the mosquitos away from her face, considered the hour of *leadership team-building* they were here to suffer through in lieu of eating breakfast with the kids, and could only think about how maybe there might have been *other* strides for equality she could have made, in lieu of *this.*)

10:19 AM. Kira's phone hit her with the double-buzz, just as she was starting to think *what a pleasure this has been, reading, and boy am I excited for lunch.* She checked her phone to see a message from Charity, wondering if Kira had anywhere in mind for lunch, and, thankfully, recommending a spot in the process. Gerry's Gas-Up, she'd suggested. Fine by Kira, and she texted Charity as much. They then spent approximately twenty seconds reaffirming via text message how much they were looking forward to the lunch, and how fun it would be, concluding with Charity giving Kira's final message a *thumbs up* at 10:20.

(The worst part of the *leadership team-building*, Leigh determined conclusively at the very same moment as the *thumbs up* arrived, was the so-called 'airport.' Wherein all of the Firestarters leadership team – ages sixteen to nineteen, worth keeping in mind – were dispersed in a loose jumble across the pebble beach of Crescenzo Point, trapped between the water and the rocks, forced by the *authority figures* to lock eyes with someone across the scrum, dash towards them with open arms, and embrace them as though they were a friend not seen in many years, greeted upon landing at the airport. Fine, if awkward, to do that with her best friend Zoe. But with people she'd never met? How on Earth was this meant to bring them closer as a team, all of this touching and presumption? Leigh asked one of the older counselors if they'd airported each other last year, when it was an all-dude leadership team they were building. He said *yes* with a quiver in his voice, as though fearful that a trapdoor would suddenly spring open beneath his feet, and only then did Leigh realize that he was actually quite cute, this guy. Then he and Leigh embraced, in the style of old friends meeting at the airport, and a storm of butterflies raged in her belly.)

As it was a beautiful day and Kira had nothing better to do, she drove the four (4) minutes from the nameless suburb in which she lived – just the sort of *all-these-houses-look-the-same* sort of new money development she'd promised herself she'd *never* live in – into Neirmouth center, such as it was. 10:44 departure, 10:48 arrival, 10:49 AM throwing the car into *park* in one of the spots at the top of the main street, such as it was. That left Kira with a little under seventy (70) minutes to burn. She walked up and down what amounted to the whole of Neirmouth's commercial sector, i.e. *the grocery,* a timber museum that was quite literally just Lynn Fallon charging you three dollars to come into her home and look at framed photographs of dead guys on her wall, a mercantile that was usually sold out of everything except baby chicks and insulated work gloves, and Gerry's Gas-Up, a coffee shop fashioned from a converted gas station. The conversion was less-than-entire; the business nook still reeked of gasoline, and sometimes there were stains on the floor that, assuming they were coffee, would have been the darkest roast Kira had ever heard of. But as was so often the case in places where the line cooks – in this case the short, white pony-tailed Gerry or his son Clint, who as of 2017 was missing part of his left middle finger for reasons never discussed – worked with cigarettes tucked behind their ears, the food at Gerry's was out of this world. Drive to Pitney and pay four times as much, you'd never find anything as good as the corned beef hash at the Gas-Up. And if sometimes Gerry or Clint had those cigarettes not behind their ears but bouncing from their lips, lit, flecks of ash visibly flipping out over the griddle…well, either that stuff cooked out in the end, or it was the secret ingredient that made the food so damn good.

Feeling it too early to enter the Gas-Up, Kira wandered to the blinding white gazebo, the upkeep of which was just about the only local application of her tax dollars that she could imagine (Neirmouth was too small to have its own police department; the ambulance and firefighting services were all volunteer). Inside the gazebo were two benches set across from each other, facing each other. Surely it'd have been better to have them facing *out,* Kira felt, so you could experience the view of, say, the main drag back yonder, or perhaps the park and the softball diamond just a little ways down the hill, and the little Lake Hirsch beyond, as opposed to just staring at whoever was sitting across from you. Well, the gazebo had probably been built when Neirmouth was a true small town, where everyone knew one another, would be delighted to sit in a gazebo and stare at each other. Built before Kira's suburb had been plopped onto the outskirts, in other words. No matter how remote, no matter the size, suburbs in America are not for making friends. You meet three or four of your neighbors, you learn the names of a couple more, then the rest you only notice once a year as you judge their Christmas decorations.

So Kira alighted on one of the benches in the otherwise-empty gazebo to do that thing she'd only come to appreciate in her mid-thirties, i.e. staring vacantly into space and listening to sounds and not really thinking about anything. At a certain point, a little squirrel skittered up to her. *Right* up to her. Climbing up onto the bench, still approaching. Might well have mounted her hip, had she not shooed it away. Damn thing must have been used to being hand-fed by folks who didn't know any better. Who didn't know any better than to hand-feed squirrels? It was by this question that Kira was fully consumed, at 10:52 AM.

(At the same time, Leigh felt her shoulders slacken with relief as the *team-building* drew to a close. She drifted over to Zoe but didn't say anything, because one of the lead adult counselors, a very muscular man named Trent who seemed to touch his face compulsively whenever he wasn't talking, was currently giving what felt like a very patronizing monologue about the principles of the Firestarters, directed almost entirely at Leigh and Zoe and the rest of the new crop. In that same instant, a man named Ruther Gully made landfall on Knot Hedge, having braved the sound in an old wooden dinghy with a thirty-year-old motor. No one at the docks in Pitney that morning would claim to have seen him depart – none of the survivors of Knot Hedge could claim to have seen him land. Yet reach the island he did, boot touching the rocks at 10:53 AM, as he leapt out of the dinghy, black duffel bag in hand.)

Having had her fill of frowning at a squirrel, then staring at nothing, followed by a good twenty seconds of wishing she had brought one of those short story books here, then a bit more walking around, Kira finally entered

Gerry's Gas-Up (11:53 AM), heading straight for the self-serve coffee carafes balanced atop the precarious slope of a repurposed car hood. An old green car, this had come from, and that was as much as Kira could say. Her first pump of the dark roast into a twelve ounce cup happened at 11:55 AM, just as Leigh and Zoe and the rest of the leadership team, no closer for all that embracing and trust-falling and other such bullshit, finally rejoined the campers, their *kids,* for a picnic lunch, just as Ruthger Gully gently placed his duffle bag on a patch of clear soil, unzipped it, made a palm-patting inspection of the trash bag he'd wrapped everything in, a bit of extra security to ensure nothing got wet on the dinghy ride over, and, being satisfied that all was dry, started to unwrap what he had brought.

11:56 AM, Kira waved to Gerry through the little window to the kitchen. Gerry waved back. That was about as intimate an interaction as they'd ever had, despite Kira's coming here semi-regularly for years on end. Part of the charm of the joint, she felt. She placed an order with Barbara on the register, who was almost certainly connected to Gerry in some way beyond mere payroll. A hard-living wife, or else a youthful mother. Or something else entirely. Barbara wasn't much for conversation either, so Kira didn't know. She sometimes wondered if Barbara could smell the suburbs on Kira. Responding to the question "what do you want?", Kira ordered a turkey club. Too late for corned beef hash, after all. 11:57 AM. The same moment Leigh took her first bite of her last meal, some cold store-bought potato salad, quite a far cry from the earthy, foraged fare the Firestarters had offered in years past. The same moment Ruthger Gully spotted his first Firestarters of the day, two of the seniormost counselors on the island hard at work setting up an archery range on the outskirts of the island, whom he watched struggling with the hay bales for quite some time, crouched on the edge of the clearing, where they would surely see him if they looked his way, only they never did.

Seeing Gerry starting to assemble her sandwich, Kira wondered if perhaps she ought to have waited until Charity arrived to order her food. Darn. It was too late to ask him to stop now, probably. Just as she had that thought, Charity arrived, so it was all fine. They hugged each other and said hello, and Kira made a joke of having already ordered, and Charity laughed gamely before placing *her* order. Not a few minutes later, they both had their food (Charity got soup, which ended up being served before Kira's sandwich), and their coffee, and they sat at a table by the window, and they started to catch up. "So," Kira opened, "how have you been?" She then took a hearty chomp of her sandwich, the toasted bread offering the most perfect, pleasing *crunch* one could possibly hope to hear. This pleasing *crunch* of the sandwich at 12:04 PM (at specifically the fifty-third second of that minute), coincided perfectly with the first report from Ruthger Gully's AR-15. As well as with everything else in the world that happened at four minutes and fifty-three seconds after noon that day. Indeed, there was more occurring at 12:05:31 PM than Kira Trecothik taking a cautious sip of her still-steaming coffee, or Charity Capatonda blowing softly on the spoonful of soup just in front of her lips, or Leigh Trecothik and Zoe Cottrell and the other Firestarters leaders glancing at each other nervously, all trying to hide their fear for the sake of *their kids,* the fear being that they knew full well the source of that *crack* still galloping through the dense woods of Knot Hedge (they had, after all, grown up in an era of active shooter drills). There was more happening than just the second and third shots from Ruthger Gully's semi-automatic ringing out so near together as to seem simultaneous, striking Anne Soleil and Baxter Greene in the archery range they were still constructing, a task which had served as a necessary step towards flirtation for the two, both as smitten with the other as they were timid in their own skin, the first bullet of the double-tap doing what Ruthger's first shot of the day couldn't, hitting Anne in the back of the throat and punching her larynx out onto the paper target in front of her, the other shot entering Baxter's torso above the right hip, cutting straight through his gut yet missing anything vital enough to kill him on the spot. Elsewhere, in that same second, old Doug Oberlein was stopped at an intersection that, as of three years ago, boasted one of Neirmouth's three count em *three* stoplights, still failing to grasp what that green there meant, foot hard on the brake as he waved the baffled Sheridan clan through their red light. There was also Kim Lentrap having a hell of a time distinguishing the weeds her auntie Isabel was paying her to pull from the young garlic shoots struggling for sunlight among them, which she knew she was *not* supposed to pull. In Pitney proper, there was a woman named Lisa Bart sitting in her basement, debating a legal name change prior to launching her campaign for city council-woman because while she couldn't figure out precisely how the attack would work, she didn't want to give her opponents the opportunity to run negative ads with some sort of *Simpsons* reference, which given the quality of the show's last decade-and-change could well prove devastating. There was also Donnie McCall, the officer who would this very evening come to stand sentry over bodies on a pebble beach, finally biting the bullet and starting Duolingo for French after at least five or six years of telling himself he would, not because he needed to know the language but because he wanted to, he'd always thought it would be fun to learn a new language, though he didn't expect it to be easy.

There was so much happening, during the thirty-first second of the fifth minute past noon. Everything was happening, as it always does, every second of every day, to someone, somewhere.

Another second ticked by, and everything changed, as it always does. Leigh Trecothik stole a nervous glance at her phone, despite knowing that Knot Hedge only got signal on the furthest edge of the island, towards the mainland. Ruthger Gully lowered his AR-15, noting slowly that the woman was still but the man was not, and perhaps that might best be rectified by the 98mm side-arm holstered at his hip. Kira Trecothik, noting that her coffee was indeed a drinkable temperature, took another sip. And a second later, everything changed again.

THE REMAINDER OF KIRA'S DAY OFF was a reminder of how bad she was at relaxing. After that swell lunch with Charity, Kira didn't even make it halfway home before falling prey to that familiar disquiet: *you're not being productive.* So she wound up doing a bit of work after all, her current project being troubleshooting an app designed by some kids half her age all the way across the country who, given all the equity they'd raised for this thing, really ought to have known how to keep the red-asterisk *required* fields on the sign-up page from resetting every time the user tried to submit their phone number, thus making the whole goddamned thing functionally inaccessible. But whatever, they were lazy and had plenty of cash, and Kira was happy to capitalize on the lethargy of what she made a point of refusing to consider *Leigh's Generation.* Leigh was about a half-decade younger than these kids, and that constituted a different generation these days, right? With how fast everything moved? Kira liked to think so, and so, she would.

After that she filled up her thermos with some water (she didn't drink enough, she knew) and took another stroll around the neighborhood, her route dictated by darkness, clinging to shade thrown by the old oaks lining the sidewalks. Not for the first time, she wondered how such a new neighborhood could have such great big trees in it. Sometimes she imagined these things being uprooted from some forest and imported at great expense. More likely, she knew, was that this had once been a mighty, wild wood, entirely leveled save those trees that suited the planners' blueprint. All in all it was a nice walk, one that carried Kira into early evening. She returned home having enjoyed her day mostly-off, yet *still* somehow feeling she had wasted it. See, this was why she didn't do well with free time.

After a quick survey of the cupboards and the fridge, to determine what might function as dinner this evening, Kira threw herself down on the couch and loaded up an episode of *Shark Tank*. Junk TV, for sure, but as it was a show in which people yelled amounts of money at each other, she could convince herself that she was learning something about business.

Halfway through the episode, Harlow came home.

"Oh, Jesus," he laughed at the unfortunate product just then being pitched, "what the hell is that supposed to be?"

"A better way to apply sunscreen," Kira called over her shoulder.

"Looks like it hurts."

Kira grabbed the remote and paused it. "Lemme start it over. One of the guys got in a bitchy little tiff with Harold, it was *amazing*."

"Sure. I'll get changed quick. Also, what do you want to do for dinner?"

"We've got some potatoes, I was thinking just baked potatoes."

"Nothing in them?"

"Yeah, like famine times."

Harlow smiled. "You said *just* baked potatoes."

"I'm obviously gonna put stuff in 'em."

"Well that sounds good to me. I'll get changed!" Harlow tromped up the stairs in his usual fashion; i.e. as though he weighed three times as much as he did. He returned not merely in a more casual getup, but in his full-on pajamas.

"Work sucked?" Kira intuited from the dress choice.

Harlow nodded, as he staggered over to the couch. Kira adjusted from a sprawl to an upright seat, clearing a landing zone for him to *plop* down next to her.

"You wanna talk about it?"

"Not really. How was your day?"

"Pretty slow. Tried to take it all the way off, but, uh, you know."

Another nod and smile from Harlow. "Got some work done?"

"Got *some* work done, yeah. Got lunch with Charity at Gerry's though, that was nice."

"Oh, great. How's she doing?"

"Seems like she's doing well."

"That's good."

"Yeah." Kira considered the remote in her hand, then said to it, "it's weird not having Leigh around."

"Huh."

Leigh recoiled slightly, repeating Harlow's *"huh"* with an ironic topspin.

Harlow smiled slightly. "I mean, she's only been gone a day. It's just like she's at a sleepover at this point."

"I know. But just, knowing she's gonna be gone for the rest of the week…it makes the house *feel* emptier."

"Well…hate to say it, but once she goes to college, you know…"

"I know, yeah. Yep." Kira adjusted in her seat, leaning against Harlow. "Aaaaah, I don't wanna think about that yet." She pointed the remote accusingly at the TV, and started the episode over. Not at all bothered about seeing all the stuff she'd already seen again. It was always better, watching stuff with Harlow. That, too, helped her convince herself it was productive.

After that, they made dinner, and then ate it. And then they watched another episode of *Shark Tank,* and then they went to bed. Both setting their phones to *Do Not Disturb* mode, silencing them and putting them down for the day not fifteen minutes before the texts and phone calls started flooding in.

Later, Kira would be haunted by her complete lack of maternal disquiet. Shouldn't she have felt some inexplicable dread, some omen of the anguish to come? She'd heard stories like that. Where the mother just *knows,* somehow, that something has happened.

That night, she felt nothing of the sort. She lay in bed beside her husband, and she was generally content, and it didn't take long for her to slip into a deep, untroubled sleep. Just one of many things for which she would never forgive herself.

TWO

BRAVE

EVERYBODY KNOWS you're not supposed to look at your phone right before going to bed, but apparently it's also disruptive to look at it right after you wake up, too. So Kira had read, in one of the innumerable articles she'd skimmed in the middle a sleepless night. All of which made such big claims in their headlines. *7 Steps To Perfect Your Sleep, Beat The Common Cold, Achieve Climax On Command, And Spit In The Eye Of God.* Gosh, across all the articles Kira had absorbed, she must have learned hundreds of ways to perfect her sleep. And you know what? A lot of them worked. It was just a matter of remembering to implement them.

This morning, Kira remembered. She stacked her vertebrae slowly, rising to a seat in the bed, her movement made viscous by a lingering dream. What had she dreamt about? In reaching for an image, she scattered the memory like dust motes in a beam of sunlight. She would have to content herself with the vague sense of satisfaction, then. It must have been a nice dream.

Scooting herself to the edge of the bed, Kira stretched her arms high over her head, arching her back slightly as she did, loosing a soft groan of release as her muscles worked out their overnight knots. In so doing, though, she lost her balance slightly, falling a bit forward and to the side in such a way that her hand accidentally grazed her bedside table, and in so doing, involuntarily took hold of her phone, and wouldn't you know it if that phone didn't wind up kind of close to her face.

Deciding that now was as good a time as any to check her email, Kira thumbed the button on the side of the phone.

The screen lit up at once. Showing her something she had never seen before. So uncanny was the sight, she quickly deduced that she was still sleeping, still dreaming.

Her phone was bursting with notifications. Not just push notices from various apps wanting her money. No, these were messages.

Charity C

iMessage (7) & Missed Call

Darren T

iMessage (12) & Missed Call

RID OF RED

And so it went. Kira scrolled and scrolled and scrolled, marveling at all the names. People she knew, people she hadn't spoken to or thought about in years, people whose number she didn't seem to have in her phone.

The further she went, the more this felt like a list of everyone she had ever known in her life. All reaching out at once. As she herself scattered like dust motes.

Kira looked away from the phone, then back to it. Recalling that text, apparently, doesn't stay consistent in a dream. Yet the text on the phone did. Even as she was so certain this wasn't real. This couldn't be real.

Whatever *this* was.

Her scrolling thumb gave out before she'd reached the bottom of the list. It went on forever. In trying to resume her scrolling, she accidentally opened the phone. Easy mistake to make; hers was one of the ones with the face sensor on the front. It had unlocked the moment she'd looked at it.

Just as she opened her phone, Kira got another message from Charity Capatonda. Mother to Clara, estranged friend of Leigh's. Yesterday's lunchmate at the Gas-Up.

This morning, sending yet another text to Kira. The content of which Kira could now see, by virtue of her phone being open. Courtesy of a cute little drop-down bubble from the top of the screen, Kira read: *I'm so sorry. If I can help at all just let me know.*

Kira stared at that message until it slithered upwards, off of her screen, to wait. Along with the seven other messages Charity had already sent.

Then she was once again staring at the home screen of her phone.

She was aware of having thoughts. None of which connected to each other. None of which were accessible, or comprehensible. Beneath those were feelings, thrashing about like cats in a sack. What were those feelings? Who could say. It was an awfully thick sack.

There was one certainty though. One dreaded by all humans, yes, no one ever wants to hear those two terrible words…but hearing them, even *thinking* them as a parent was so much different. What with one's heart living outside of one's body, and all that.

Something happened.

That was what all of these messages amounted to. *Something* had *happened.* And a lifetime's worth of loose acquaintances wanted to tell Kira about it.

She desperately did not want to hear about it. Would have given anything in the world, to skip it like a morning news podcast. But that wasn't an option. Her phone was once again humming with satisfaction as it received another message. Then another. Then another.

The one that tore the veil of willful ignorance came from her late mother's second husband Walter. With whom Kira was still exchanging Christmas cards. That was about the extent of their relationship these days.

She only saw his message at a glance. Until it snagged her gaze, like beef on a meat hook.

The words she saw were *still a chance she made it out.*

At that point, Kira dropped her phone. It fell between her legs, landing on the carpeted floor underfoot with an underwhelming *whump.*

She teetered back and forth a few times, finding each breath less and less up to the task of filling her lungs. Slowly, she looked behind herself, to Harlow. Still sleeping.

She wanted him to wake up. As distinct from *her* waking him up. If *she* woke him up, she would have to explain. She would have to say the words to him. *Something happened.* And he would ask what that something was. And then Kira would have no choice but to find out.

Still a chance she made it out. Kira's brain cooked itself through, trying to make that fragment mean things it couldn't possibly mean. Fighting desperately to steer it away from the only things it *could* mean.

Harlow wasn't waking up. Kira felt like she was going to explode if he didn't wake himself up, right now.

Finally, nearly blind for those unknowable emotions, Kira whispered her husband's name. Her voice reduced to an outline of human speech. The shape of a word, without content.

The man who answered to that word didn't stir. He remained as he was. Face buried in the pillow, a slight drool stain commemorating his passage through the deepest regions of rest.

She pushed herself a bit harder. "Harlow," she managed. Like a soft tread on dead leaves.

He fidgeted slightly, slowly, but otherwise stayed below the surface.

Oh, she was going to burst. Kira felt herself so wholly inflated by emotion, yet being unable to identify what that emotion was, she couldn't be sure how best to vent it. Crying or screaming or laughing or getting a running start at the wall and doing her best to put her head through it. Viable options, all of those, and there were more besides. But she didn't know how to release any of this. Didn't know how to release herself from it.

Kira reached out and touched her husband's back. "Harlow," she said again, whispered as forcefully as she could manage.

He flinched not at her touch, but at the sound of his name. Taking a deep breath and mooing unhappily, he peeled his head from the pillow, glanced around the room with baffled solemnity, as might Punxsutawney Phil with six weeks of the world's fate in his little hands, until finally finding Leigh sitting beside him, staring at him with what must have been a most unreadable expression. "Hrhn?" he asked.

"Harlow," Kira repeated. "I think…something happened."

Seeming a little less than fully galvanized by those words, Harlow struggled his way up to a seat, eyelids still fighting a losing battle against collapse. "What?"

For one deranged instant, Kira became certain that

something had not *happened.* It couldn't have. Had *something happened,* she would be crying. Someone would be hammering on their door and screaming. There would be police cars and helicopters. Other *somethings* would be fucking *happening,* things of greater gravity and impact than her sprawled-out husband squinting at her, in this silent room, in this silent house.

"What happened?" Harlow pressed. Finally starting to wake up now.

"I don't know," Kira struggled to say.

Her phone hummed again. Another message. Involuntarily, she dropped her gaze to read the message.

It was quite a long one. So much bloat. It could have been just two words long.

She didn't see Harlow get out of bed, but she did feel the mattress lift to fill his sudden absence.

THE ONLY WORDS SPOKEN for quite some time were supplied by Harlow.

"This isn't right," he repeated, shaking his head, as he stared at devices of ever-enhanced dimensions. He started reading messages on his smart watch ("this isn't right"), then graduated to a bit more active searching on his phone ("this isn't right," delivered with more force this time), before finally arriving at the slow, passive drip of the television ("this isn't right," whispered in the manner of a prayer).

Not knowing what else to do, Kira drifted after him all the while. She didn't want to know what messages Harlow had received, couldn't bear to keep pace with what he learned from his phone, was desperate not to hear what the television said…but more than all of that, she didn't want to be alone. Oh, she didn't want to be alone.

Harlow had settled immediately on MSNBC. Not local news, but national. That choice in and of itself traced the scope of the *something* that had *happened*.

The television showed them an aerial shot of the island of Knot Hedge. Showed them blankets on the pebble beach, untroubled by breeze, first drafts of the human form. The lower third of the screen was occupied by the word MASSACRE. Kira saw the word, and understood its meaning, its full significance. And she thought, *no, no, no*. That was all she could think, as the world before her reduced to colors and shapes without meaning. *No, no, no.* Feet on the ground, she was falling, floating, locked in, spinning off into the void. Wishing she would die, right there, right then. The only way to save herself from ever hearing the words, those few words that would bridge the gap she so desperately tried to preserve, between the word on the television, and the name of her daughter. Even though she knew. She knew. The knowledge alone was enough to kill her, yet she lived. *No, no, no.*

The world began to spin along a different axis. She stumbled, steadied herself on the arm of a chair, and then was upstairs. No memory of going from the living room to her bedroom. No awareness. Nothing. A privilege.

She looked down at her feet, and saw what she had been feeling. Her bare feet were wet, cold. The cuffs of her thin cotton pajama pants were likewise sodden, speckled with dirt, trailing a few long strands of grass.

This isn't right, she thought, wondered where she'd heard that before. Wondering what it was from.

As Harlow would later describe it to her (for she had no experience and little recollection of anything else that happened that day), after staring at the TV for a minute or two, Kira had simply turned and headed for the front door, mouth a thin, tight slash across a bloodless face. When hailed by Harlow, she was unresponsive, stepping out onto the front porch without a word. Setting off the house's security alarm in the process. *BEE BEE BEE BEE BEE BEE.* A shrill, deafening report. They always turned that alarm on before they went to bed. The world was so dangerous. You never could be too careful. How incredible it would seem, that the alarm hadn't been enough to bring her back to herself. It was so loud, so abrasive. Yet she kept on walking, Harlow being forced to linger in the house just long enough to shut off the alarm. With the time she'd unwittingly bought herself, Kira had apparently drifted down the gentle slope of the yard, across the street, and into the thin copse of Eastern Redbuds that made up the northernmost portion of the Bettington property. Kira would wonder if she recalled how unkindly Richie Bettington took to kids cutting through his property on their bikes, hoping to halve their time to Neirmouth center. How Leigh had come home crying one day after being read the riot act by mean old Mr. Bettington, and how Kira had vowed to give Richie a verbal hiding in return, but had never made good. She would wonder if she remembered any of that, would wonder if she spared a thought for Richie Bettington at all. How he might react to an adult cutting through his yard. Surely he wouldn't have minded. Kira wasn't on a bike, and she wasn't halving her time to anywhere. She wasn't going anywhere at all. She was just going, and the Bettington property just happened to be there.

Whether or not she did, in fact, wonder this *in situ* or not, she would never know. All Harlow could attest to was stumbling after her through the tangle of Redbud roots, gently turning her back around, and guiding her home again.

She returned home long after her body. Suddenly upstairs again, with the cold feet, the wet cuffs. She took the stairs to the ground floor in slow motion, following sounds – not voices, just sounds – towards life. The TV was off. Harlow's brother Martin, having high-tailed it up from Boston (his presence being an indication of just how long she'd been gone), was futzing about in the kitchen, perhaps thinking himself helpful. Jess Ross, proprietor of a farmstand on Vacation Boulevard (which was a delightful name for that unpaved little one-lane rutcut) whom Kira had befriended in the pursuit of fresh produce, was sitting in the seat by the window, dividing her attention between a crossword puzzle and Kira. Spotting sensibility, she lowered the puzzle to her knee and smiled sadly.

Kira fell to the ground and found the gravity, the impact.

TO BEGIN WITH, she cried. She cried when she heard the details of the massacre – how a man, a boy, a monster named Ruthger Gully, upon being passed over for the leadership position in Firestarters that he considered his due, decided that the only explanation for such an over-sight was that the girls, the off-whites, the most regret-table of Firestarters' recent inductions, had taken his spot. He had quickly convinced himself that Firestarters was merely the beginning, that the "Woke Coven of Savages and Feminists!!!", as his hundred-page manifesto referred to them (oh yes, of course he had a manifesto), were plotting a great replacement of the Anglo-Saxon race all across the globe. Thus, cutting the conspiracy off at the knees, nipping it in the bud, smothering it in the crib, became something of an ethical imperative for Ruthger. That wasn't to say it was a call to which he rose solemnly. No, he met his duty with the alacrity of its appointment, and testified to his enthusiasm in his confession. Because Ruthger had been captured alive. Despite all the guns on his person, despite all the lives he'd taken, he had been spared.

Kira had cried about that too. She cried when she, along with the rest of the world, watched the boy's giddy self-incrimination playing on a near-constant loop on TV, leavened only by footage of the atrocity sourced from the cell phones of the survivors and – more horri-fically – from the pre-murder moments of a livestream Ruthger had somehow been running from a GoPro he'd strapped to his forehead (this had been so important to him that he'd rigged the stream up on something comparable to a satellite phone), footage which was itself forever preceded by a perfunctory warning that what viewers were about to see, may disturb them. It was a caution offered in the same spirit as a schoolyard bully shouting "think fast" before launching a dodgeball at the back of someone's head.

Kira cried because she couldn't find her daughter in any of the footage, cried because she couldn't stop looking despite hoping desperately that she wouldn't find her. She didn't want to see Leigh's face warped by mortal terror. Yet she couldn't bear the thought of some part of Leigh, even just her image, existing out there alone. That was such a lonely thought.

Of all the unanswerable questions that plagued Kira, the one that stung her most was *did she suffer?* Hoping that the answer was *no* meant hoping that her daughter had died a quick death. It was in these moments that Kira felt herself touching true madness. Sometimes, she felt, courting it. Because wouldn't that be easier?

Then the word came down that Leigh's funeral would need to be a closed-casket affair. That was when Kira stopped crying and started screaming. She couldn't leave the house, couldn't stand on her own two feet anymore.

Every moment brought another memory of Leigh, often unprompted, always unbidden. She remembered those first three weeks of Leigh's life, spent as a science project in the NICU, weeks during which Kira and Harlow worried they might lose their daughter, and she remembered the moment she found out Leigh was ready to go home, remembered that feeling she felt as she took her little daughter in her arms, the way Leigh had reached for her and *smiled,* god, it was relief deeper than any anguish could ever be, or so she'd always believed. She remembered when Leigh was five years old, bouncing around the house for no other reason than she was young and life was all still so new, and Kira tried to rein her in by announcing she'd poured a cup of apple juice (just what she needed, more sugar), and Leigh halted on a dime, turned towards Kira, and shouted "Apple juice!", then ran towards Kira and wrapped her arms around her mother's legs for as big an embrace as she could manage, and shouted "I *love* you!" Even then, that unexpected affection had teared Kira up, for even then, she'd known it wouldn't be like that forever. Not having any idea how right she would be.

She remembered badgering Leigh to do her chores. Clean her room, make her bed, and at a certain age help mow the lawn, do her own laundry. She remembered all the times she'd sent a younger Leigh to bed without dessert, for not touching her vegetables, or for just being disagreeable at the table. She remembered the first time Leigh had shouted "I *hate you!*" at her, also at five years, same age as the apple juice episode, who could remember which came first, but what Kira did remember was that this outburst came after Leigh had been told she couldn't go to her friend's birthday party – impossible to remember whose party at this distance – for no other reason than there was no one to take her, it was a rare day when Kira and Harlow would both be at work, the babysitter scheduled to come for the day was too young to drive, and despite Kira's best efforts she couldn't find any other trusted parents able (or willing) to come all the way out (not even ten minutes out of their way) to this little housing development to pick Leigh up as they took their own kids to the party, and for that, Leigh had insisted she *hated* her mother, and despite knowing the day would come when Leigh would say those words, despite believing herself prepared for them, Kira felt something inside of her *snap* like a mousetrap, something that turned the edges of her vision red, something that made her say "well sweetie, I love you, but sometimes I can't stand you." Then Leigh had started crying, and then Kira had started crying. There were so many of those days, where the only experiences they shared were mutual frustration.

It wasn't all emotional uppercuts from deep storage, of course. Other recollections possessed her hourly, never once warning her that what she was about to see, may disturb her. These were the true agents of anguish, the ones with the most guile and bite. They closed the distance through Kira's blind spots; how many objects that daily familiarity had reduced to visual static suddenly leapt to the fore? The lip of the kitchen countertop that Leigh had always gripped and attempted to hoist herself over, arms at right angles, body stiff and straight and parallel to the ground, doing what her history teacher called "the fulcrum" (an impressive feat of strength which that teacher, whose name Kira couldn't recall, could be goaded into quite easily, thus wasting class time). The rectangular window onto the backyard that a very young Leigh had stood outside, imagining it a television screen from which to recite amusing, fanciful news reports that she had insisted were improvised but which Kira had always suspected were prepared, which was even more adorable. The chip out of the wall across from the door to Leigh's room, which had been knocked out when Leigh had decided it would be a terrific idea to bring her bike upstairs, and found her balance not quite up to the task of keeping the handlebars from knocking against the plaster.

Kira screamed, too, when the memories failed to elicit any emotion at all. Grief was memory was absence, and there were times when Kira wished to rid herself entirely of the past, saw no other way to endure the present. She lost her emotional proprioception, so overwhelmed was she by this numbing crush, found herself impossible to locate. She felt everything and nothing in the same instant. So she screamed in the hopes that her heart would take the hint, get with the program, pull itself together and *break*. In those rare moments when thoughts untangled themselves into something coherent, they formed a simple, plaintive appeal to whoever might be listening: *kill me, kill me, kill me.*

Senseless beneath the tsunami though she was, Kira still refused to enter Leigh's bedroom. Knew she wouldn't be able to. Too much certainty, perhaps. She would scream outside of it, trying and failing to touch something vital, knowing that everything lay on the far side of a flimsy bit of wood. Yet she would not touch the knob. Could not. And so: the seeking scream.

There, the setup. Here, the punchline: Kira's screams and cries tore up her voice, to such an extent that she was physically unable to speak at Leigh's funeral, incapable of addressing the smooth mahogany of the casket lid with anything other than dumb torpor. For this was not her daughter. This was a box. This was wood. This was varnish. But she could communicate none of this to the mourners, many of whom were just looky-loos, strangers who had come for no other reason than what the pundits (on real TVs, not windows onto backyards) called the "historic" circumstances of Leigh's death. Her murder. Her assassination. Wasn't that what it was, in a way? Wasn't the political nature of the killer's motivations enough to earn Leigh that awful distinction? The talking heads sure thought so. The Knot Hedge Forty, the dead were called. The body count rose only as far as thirty-nine, but the Knot Hedge Thirty-Nine wasn't quite as punchy, so the broadcast brainboxes rounded up, optimistic that somebody else would succumb to their wounds. The politicization of the Knot Hedge Forty was swift and intense, all sides converging on the survivors, the relatives of the victims, whoever they could find with enough perceived authority to lend credence to the validation all factions sought.

Kira always declined to take part in that process. She didn't want to hang around with the parents of other victims, as many seemed to. She didn't want to be interviewed, forced to devalue her own grief by weaving it into a Political Context. Kira hated guns, and knew that

Leigh had as well, yet she had no interest in weaponizing Leigh's death, turning it into a tool, no matter how righteous and correct the cause might be. Perhaps someday she would be able to match Harlow's enthusiasm on that score, join him on the phone with reporters from this or that rag looking for a quote not about Leigh, but about the thing that had killed her. Sixteen years of human life, to be forever defined by the means of their termination.

Days continued to pass, one after the next, just as they had before. Just as they always had. Kira watched them go by with something between envy and contempt, knowing herself to be left behind; time moved on, but Kira did not. They did not carry her, could not support the weight she herself carried. She remained trapped in each moment, the moment of first knowing, the moment of first hearing the words, the moment of being led into an identification room in the hospital, empty save two chairs, a table, and a face-down photograph. Not like in the movies, no gruesome remains yanked from a giant freezer, no, this was a simple photograph of Leigh's birthmark on her left ankle. That would serve as identification enough, it emerged. The identity of the body was not in question. This was a formality. So Kira had thought it best to be done with it, had flipped the photograph over as the chief medical examiner was still monotoning his way through the *this will be quite difficult* spiel, to see an extreme close-up of a birthmark that was unmistakably Leigh's, printed on a glossy sheet of 8.5x11 printer paper. Kira had asked why the photo was taken in such extreme close-up. The chief medical examiner had responded that they tried to avoid capturing anything that might prove upsetting in these images. Which, he didn't seem to realize, was a pretty fucking upsetting answer. Certainly seemed to imply that this little patch of ankle was the only bit of the body that wouldn't prove upsetting. Of her daughter's body. Leigh. Oh, god. Nearly five feet and four inches of promising young woman, still growing in every sense of the word. Cut down to a birthmark.

This was not something that time could carry off. This weight. This memory. It was an anchor, crushing Kira at the bottom of a deep, dark sea. Too deep for anyone to reach her, yet not so far down that she couldn't see the sunlight dancing across the surface of the water, untold fathoms above.

Eventually, Phyllis came by. The woman they paid to clean the house every other week. The first intruder into Kira's deep-sea desolation. It was too soon. Knowing Phyllis was coming, Kira hid herself away in her room for the entirety of Phyllis' time in the house.

That had been the plan, anyway.

The plan fell apart when Kira heard a familiar creak and hush from the hall. One she'd heard when a four-year-old Leigh had snuck out of her bedroom on Christmas Eve, at the unthinkable hour of 8:30 PM, in the hopes of catching Santa in the act. The one she'd so often heard follow just behind the doorbell, when Zoe or Maddie or another one of Leigh's friends swung by. The one she'd heard day in and day out, when Leigh was just waking up in the morning, or finally turning in at night, or running up to change her clothes, or popping in to grab the purse she'd left on the bed, on her bed in the room, in her bedroom. Her bedroom.

For a single instant, Kira's heart jumped. Leigh was back. Why else would she be hearing her bedroom door open?

Then she remembered. From her watery grave, Kira remembered.

Phyllis.

Kira *launched* herself out of her own bed, landing on her feet and hitting the door to the hallway shoulder-first.

She spotted Phyllis, kindly old Phyllis, stooped and skeletal Phyllis, with her hand still on the doorknob, one foot just crossing the threshold into Leigh's bedroom.

"STOP!" Kira shrieked.

Phyllis squawked in surprise, staggering backwards and thumping against the hall wall opposite Leigh's bedroom door, hard enough to rattle the family photos hanging from old nails.

"Oh," Kira muttered under her breath as she shook off her stupor and rushed forward to help poor old Phyllis (though keeping her head inclined, to keep from so much as glimpsing into Leigh's room). "I'm sorry, Phyllis. I'm so sorry."

"You scared the shit out of me," Phyllis grumbled as she pushed herself to her feet. Despite looking yonks beyond her sixty-some years, with grey skin and grey hair, Phyllis generally moved with the grace of a forty year-old. Not so as she regained the vertical now, though. Oh, how she struggled back to upright.

"Oh, god. I'm so sor-"

"You don't have to tell me," Phyllis snapped, though with genuine warmth in her voice. The sort of feat only a true Mainer can manage. "You don't worry about it. I'm fine."

"I'm…it's just…" Kira shook her fist in the direction of Leigh's bedroom. She opened her mouth, closed it, then lowered her fist. But she kept on glaring at the stark white door so like the rest in the hallway. Until the tears blotted them all out.

"It's fine," Phyllis reassured Kira as she took her employer in her arms. The first time the two had ever touched, surely. "I shouldn't have gone in. I'm not goin' in. You tell me when, I won't go in 'til then."

It was quite a lot of crying after that, a bit in Phyllis' presence, the rest back in her bed. Her bedroom. Kira's bedroom. At the bottom of the ocean.

THERE SHE REMAINED, sunken, until there arrived a more durable disruption. After two and a half weeks of grey, tuneless days, Harlow came home and shook her from the not-quite-slumber into which she'd settled. As she blinked, not so much taking in her surroundings as struggling to pack them into the overstuffed suitcase of her skull, she realized that she was not in her bed. She was downstairs, on the couch. Sometimes that happened. Being crippled with lucidity long enough to realize that she was not where she'd thought she was.

Harlow's face was all hard angles, made ridiculous

with concern. For an instant, Kira feared that *something* might have *happened* to Leigh. Then she remembered. In remembering, it happened again. It was always happening. It would never not be happening, never become something that had merely happened.

In remembering, she always hated whatever brought the memory. So often, it was simply an object, a scent, a play of light on the wall. Today, it was Harlow. Whom she loved. And yet.

The dissonance of these thoughts brought tears to her eyes. As did everything else these days.

"Hey," Harlow said, voice soft, as he sat himself on the couch beside her. "There's someone here."

Kira struggled to interpret those words. Who? Where? "What?" she asked.

"Um...she was just on the porch. I didn't know what to do. I'm sorry."

"Who's...what?" Kira slowly clawed her way to an upright seat, gripping the cushions of the couch for dear life as the world sought to shake her free. "What's going on?"

"Hi Mrs. Trecothik," said a voice that wasn't Harlow's.

Kira glanced past Harlow, back towards the front of the house. Everything appeared to be the same distance away from her. Far. Way out there on the horizon, Kira could see someone. A face she knew she recognized. An earlier version of her would have recognized the face.

The face reminded her. In remembering, she recognized.

"Zoe," Kira said. For the face belonged to Zoe Cottrell. Zoe, Leigh's best friend. Leigh's fellow Firestarter, a fellow member of that historic leadership group.

Zoe Cottrell. A survivor of the island. A survivor.

The girl looked terrified. Brow bunched like a fist, shoulders half-hunched. For one seasick instant, Kira could see her on the island. Terrified. And in seeing her, she saw Leigh. In her final moments.

Terrified.

Until that instant, Kira had somehow avoided truly considering not the fact of her daughter's death, but the experience of it. The fear of it. The *anguish*. And perhaps, at the end, the certainty. A whole life of possibilities, reduced to a single certainty.

For just a moment, Kira allowed herself to hate Zoe Cottrell, for forcing her to think all of these thoughts. Then the moment passed, and her heart broke for the girl. She had been through all that Leigh had, save the one last thing. Perhaps, through Zoe, Kira could come to some understanding of what Leigh had gone through.

And with that thought, Kira too was terrified.

None of them spoke. For quite some time.

Eventually, Harlow repeated "she was just on the porch." As though Zoe weren't standing just behind him, as though she weren't able to account for her own presence here.

And maybe she wouldn't – Zoe Cottrell was a Survivor, which had surely accustomed her to being spoken for, or else speculated about. Silence signaled shellshock; a reversion to her old garrulousness was clear denial;

even the exigency of appetite (or lack thereof) would no doubt be worthy of study to the armchair psychologists in Neirmouth. Kira imagined Zoe's expression to betray her frustration with once more being spoken for, before realizing that she, too, was projecting onto the poor girl.

Kira settled slightly, leaning against the back of the sofa. Dredging up words took real effort – and she could hardly remember what to do with them, once she had them in hand – but eventually, she managed to wheeze "how are you, Zoe?"

Zoe shrugged. She brushed a bolt of hair back behind her right ear. It was only then that Kira noticed the young woman was missing all but the thumb and forefinger of her right hand.

Needless to say, she'd had the full five fingers before Knot Hedge.

"How are *you?*" Zoe asked, keeping her eyes on her feet.

Kira shrugged too.

More silence.

Clearing her throat, Kira scooted to the side slightly, making room for Zoe on the couch. She gestured to the empty space, and nodded at the girl.

Zoe took an unsteady perch next to Kira, placing her hands on her thighs and bowing her head. Her hair rolled forward, shielding her face from Kira's view. As the girl once more swept it back to hook behind her ear, Kira was struck by a truly inexplicable, yet undeniable terror. As though she were expecting to see something other than Zoe's face come in to view.

The young woman cleared her throat and shimmied in her seat. "Um," she began. "I…" she sniffed and wiped a tear from her eye, but it couldn't be said that she was crying. At the moment.

This new kind of silence disturbed Kira. The silence of the last two weeks and change had been solitary; this communal quiet here was an altogether different beast. *How* it was different was hard to say, though. So it was lucky nobody was saying anything.

Finally, Kira put a hand on Zoe's shoulder. "I can't imagine," was all she said.

"Yeah," Zoe replied through a taut little grin. "Um…I just uh, I came here because wanted to tell you something. It's a good thing," she added hastily, with a nervous glance to Harlow, "and I should have told you sooner. But I, ah…it's just hard, I guess. I don't know. But…uh. Ah."

"It's okay." Kira glanced over the girl to Harlow. He was staring somberly at his knees, hands hanging limply at his sides. Looking absolutely gutted, as a taxidermy in progress.

Kira shivered.

"Leigh," Zoe continued, "this…ah, man. There's no way to say it except to say it, and it sounds kind of silly or something maybe, I don't know, but…Leigh saved my life." She winced, looking nervously to Kira, as though expecting to be struck.

An absurd expectation. Who in their right mind would react that way? Though, come to think of it, how *would* a mother react to that sort of news, given…everything?

Kira wondered this, because she had no idea. Her own reaction to it was just a hole. An empty hole, unfillable by words. And that's all Zoe had brought her, were words.

"…?" she finally replied. She didn't know what to say to that. Whatever she'd expected Zoe to say just then, it hadn't been that. What had it been? Who knows. Not that.

Turning to glance at Harlow, he didn't seem to have a much firmer footing than she. He met her gaze nervously, then returned it to Zoe. "Wow," he said.

Zoe looked from one Trecothik to the other, then mumbled "yeah."

"Thank you," Harlow mumbled. The gratitude of a six-year-old given socks for Christmas.

Clearing her throat, Zoe continued: "yeah. Um. Not just me, I should say. Me, and Maddie, and Nicole. She…" A deep sigh. "I don't think any of us would be alive if Leigh hadn't…"

"Hadn't what?" Kira demanded. A bit sharply.

Oddly, Kira felt herself more surprised by her own intensity than Zoe seemed to be.

Harlow seated himself on the arm of the chair flanking the sofa, on the other side of Zoe, one leg sprawled to the side, hands limply clasped over his hips.

"What did Leigh do?" Kira repeated, making a conscious effort to lower the intensity of her voice. Still sounding as though Gotham was doomed if she didn't get the answer.

"How did Leigh save you?" Harlow wondered, in a much softer voice, at almost exactly the same time.

Zoe's eyes darted between two points in space near, but not overlapping, the Trecothiks' faces. "Ah, I…I don't want to dig it all…to go over it again. If it's still too…I mean, of *course* it is, I just mean…I was just thinking, you should know, since, um, in case nobody told you." She took a deep breath, almost visibly centering herself. "I don't know who else would know what happened. I don't think anybody would. It happened so fast, and I just haven't heard anybody say it or anything. That, uh…Leigh was a, ha, yeah I mean, yeah…the word fits. Leigh was a *hero*. Which, I mean, that sh-"

"Zoe," Kira rumbled, in what she really hoped was a friendly rumble. "Look at me." The expression she offered the girl could have set off a metal detector.

"Okay, honey," Harlow whispered to Kira, from the far side of Zoe. There didn't seem to be anything else attached to those two words, which had never seemed more meaningless. Indeed, Kira couldn't be entirely certain he was talking to her.

All the same, he had a point.

"I'm sorry," Kira told the girl, patting her shoulder gently. "I appreciate you coming here to tell us this. That was really brave of you. I'm just…"

"I know," Zoe whispered.

Kira sucked in a breath through gritted teeth, then nodded and said "can you tell us what happened?"

Harlow frowned loudly, made a small round noise. The sound of a dog realizing that the ball had not been thrown, that it remained in the hand of the cackling master.

Kira looked at her husband. "If that's okay with you," she added. "I'd like to know."

Harlow took a rattling sip of air, and said "I would too" in a way that was nearly convincing.

She nodded at him, squeezed Zoe's shoulder softly, then asked the girl "is that okay?"

Rather than answer, Zoe inhaled deeply, and spoke quickly. "Alright, um, tell me if you don't want to hear anymore or something because, yeah." So rapid was her speech that her words melted into each other. "So. Yeah. Um. I mean, I guess you know basically most of what happened first. We were, me and Leigh, and Maddie, and Cap was there too, which I don't know if Leigh ever told you but that's what we call Morgan. Like Captain Morgan. He doesn't drink, that's why it's funny. It's not like he drinks a lot. None of us drink, really, it's not li-"

"I don't care," Kira interjected, as softly as one can when interrupting someone to say *I don't care*.

Zoe, for her part, seemed elated to get back on topic. "Right, right, obviously not. I mean, so, it was me and Leigh and Maddie and C...Morgan, we were down at the wire pen, I think it used to be for cows or goats or something but now it's just like a, like a place to hang out, and it's, there's a little garden that would have tomatoes or something but I guess it's too early for those and so, but yeah, that's where we were when it...when the..."

"Shooting started," Kira filled in with a whisper.

"Right. Um. The, yeah. He was…" Zoe gave a dry, almost perfunctory sniff. She sighed and lifted her hands, palms face down and spread as though resting atop a large overturned bowl. "He…" One of the hands tracked over the bowl, and in so doing, transformed it into a rise of earth. "He was over the hill. He…started, I guess, if you, anyway, he started near the beach. I bet that's in the news though, like, you could find out if you wanted. I don't know for sure. But he was definitely over the hill from the wire pen at first. We couldn't figure out what the sound was at first because, I don't know how to…it was like we were hearing the echoes, at first. Like we heard these thin, bouncy little sounds, and then the sharper one. So, you know, we were, at first we were just like, 'what's that?' Somebody, it wasn't one of us, me or Leigh or any of us, but somebody from one of the other groups was like 'gee, I hope that wasn't a gun.' Something dumb like that. We didn't laugh though. I think we all kind of already…it didn't sound good.

"Then, somebody started screaming. From over the hill. That was when we knew, you know, something's really wrong. Some of the older kids, like the counselors and some of the kids even, they just started running over. They didn't even look at each other or anything. Leigh wanted to go, I definitely remember that. She was like 'somebody might be hurt!' And I," Zoe chuckled and wiped her eye (using the lonely first finger of her right hand) at the same time. "I was like, '*you think?*' Fucking asshole. I was just really scared. I think I just sort of assumed, you know. And then anyway the gun started going off more and more. So that's when C…Morgan starts running *towards* it. Now even Leigh was saying like, 'what the f…' ah, um, 'what the fuck are you doing?' Then that was the last time…well," she tapped herself above the eye and winced.

"Anyway, we ran. Away from the hill, so, I don't know if you're super familiar with the way the camp area is laid out or whatever, but you've got the hill, and then here's the wire pen, and then on the other side, away from the hill, there's just a bit of woods. It's a pretty small island and there's a lot of rocks, so it's just the woods and then it's basically just rocks. And you can't really hide in the rocks. Maybe a few places. I don't know. But at the time we were all like, ah…you know, 'we have to hide in the woods.' So we're running and there's this big tree in the way. It's *big*, like, it fell over so maybe it died because it wasn't…but anyway, I don't know how it got that big in the first place. It was fucking huge. In terms of wide *and* long. And so we were like, 'shit,' and because of the way it had fallen on the path, where there was a drop on one side and a rock wall on the other, you couldn't get around it. We were gonna try, but then Nicole comes over, from down by like where the roots would be, and she's like, 'not gonna happen'. She's just shaking her head and she actually said 'not gonna happen,' like it was super casual. We're like, 'what?', because we didn't know she was there, but she heard us. She's like, 'not gonna happen.' Then the screaming behind us got really loud. The…guy, h-"

"You can say his name," Harlow allowed.

Zoe grimaced at the ground. "I don't want to."

Harlow ducked his head and frowned.

The girl took a deep breath and spoke slowly now, seeming to measure each word as it passed through her, as she passed it on. "That…piece of shit, he came over the hill. And there were still so many kids down in the wire pen, but he just starts shooting. It was awful. You could hear the bullets hitting the bodies. I think that was the worst sound. They were screaming, and everybody was crying, and then sometimes they just stopped suddenly which was awful too, but hearing the…just like these little wet smacks, and I couldn't stop imagining it. Like, the whole detail." She held out the two digits she still had on her right hand, pinching an imaginary bullet. "Just these little things, moving so fast they make this huge sound and just rip you up…" Zoe blinked at her hand, exhibit A, as though it had just made a very good point she hadn't thought of.

"So yeah. At that point we're like, *we've gotta get over this fucking tree.* Only we can't jump it because it's seriously that big. I know this sounds crazy, but, it's almost like *he* put it there. Like he buys his guns, he figures out how he's gonna get to Knot Hedge, but before it's time he goes a few days early and drops this tree that's blocking the main way to get away. Obviously that's not what happened, but, like…"

"I know exactly what you mean," Kira assured her, which was true.

"Yeah. So." Zoe swallowed, a dry *click* from the top of her throat. "We couldn't get over the tree. And the

114

guy's basically done with the wire pen. He's…we can hear him. His footsteps, I mean. He wasn't making any sound though. With his voice, I mean, we could hear his feet, but…yeah. I kind of feel like, that might have been…I don't know. If we'd heard his voice. It might have been better. Or, like…easier. If he was laughing or yelling at us or whatever. But he was just, like, dead quiet.

"So anyway, we're like, *we've gotta get over this fucking tree, or we've gotta find somewhere else to hide.* And Leigh says to us, 'I'll give you a boost.' She puts her hands out like this…" Zoe interlaced her fingers, palms up, and dropped them nearer the floor. "…and was like, 'go! I can climb it after you!'"

And then, the levees broke.

"So we went up!" Zoe sobbed. "We just let her… boost us up!" She gasped, but somehow managed to get the lid back on. "Maddie went first," she snuffled, "then Nicole, then I was last. They both jumped over, and then when I got on top of it, I turned around to help Leigh up. I put my hand down…" she silently proffered her right hand, missing those three fingers and the two outermost knuckles, to finish out the story.

"Did you see it happen?" Harlow wondered timidly.

Zoe nodded and sniffed.

"Well," he said, a bit too quickly, "thank you for telling us." He glanced to Kira, who kept on grimacing at Zoe.

She continued nodding and sniffing. "Yeah. I just… I'm sorry I didn't earlier. I just wasn't sure…I don't know. I felt guilty, I guess. Just going to somebody and s-"

"And telling them their daughter could have lived." Kira heard herself growl. A true outside observation. Locked in that deep red slithering in from the periphery of her vision, she watched her hands tighten around fistfuls of couch cushion, inferred a great contraction of every muscle in her body. Yet none of this was a part of her. These things were simply happening.

"Um…" Zoe stole a look at Kira's face, then returned her gaze to the floor. "I just meant making somebody relive something like that. Or live it, I guess. Since you weren't there," she added, with a bit more firmness than she'd yet brought to bear. "I'm sorry if this wasn't a good thing for you to hear. But…what Leigh did was really brave. And three of us are alive because of it."

But my daughter is dead, Kira just barely managed to keep herself from saying.

What she couldn't keep herself from *thinking,* though, was that Leigh could have lived. She was a nimble kid; however big this fallen tree was, Kira was confident her daughter could have found a way over it, to safety. She could have lived. She could still be alive today.

But instead she'd done a brave, stupid thing. She'd stopped to save three other girls. And that was why she was dead. That was the only reason she was dead.

What bravery, yes. Something of which a mother ought to be proud. Kira couldn't get there, though. All she felt – yes, she was starting to properly feel it now, to *experience* it – was rage.

Things didn't have to be as they were. It could have

been Leigh sitting here between Kira and Harlow, or perhaps sitting between Zoe's parents, recounting *their* daughter's final moment to *them*.

See how they like it, Kira caught herself thinking. It was such a red thought.

"Jesus Christ," she whimpered to Zoe. That served as a farewell as Kira rose from the couch, hustled back upstairs, threw herself on the bed once more, and wailed. A true-blue meltdown, this was, greater than any emotional eruption she'd experienced in the past two and a half weeks. Hard to say if this was progress or regress, as far as lamentations went, but it helped to bleed her mind of its red. She wondered idly where all that red went, which was a silly thing to wonder, she knew it was a silly thing to wonder. So she let the thought go, swept away on a current of something that might have been blood.

She would have cause to wonder, in time, if it wasn't all that vanishing red that brought her the moon.

THAT NIGHT, Harlow crawled into bed beside Kira without saying a word. His arrival stirred her from the half-drowse into which she'd sunk, once crying had become too demanding.

She shifted herself to face Harlow. He lay flat on his back, staring at the ceiling in wide-eyed fascination. Or perhaps horror. It was such a difficult expression to read. Particularly after he clicked off the light on his nightstand.

Kira studied the landscape of his profile. Tried to divine meaning from its rises and falls, its peaks and valleys.

Not that she needed to. She could simply ask him what he was thinking about. What he thought of their daughter's heroism.

So do it. Ask. Just ask. Just talk.

Say something.

Kira really did want to. But she couldn't. The words caught like fishhooks. Which made sense, given how far underwater she was.

Harlow's head lolled to the side, towards Kira. He had a go at forcing a smile, but surrendered the effort almost at once. Just as well. It had been a losing battle.

"She was a hero," he mumbled. Half interrogative, that was. Like he was reading an exam prompt to himself.

Kira just nodded.

Harlow took a deep breath through his nose, gave the ceiling one final glance, then rolled over to face the wall.

After a few more nods, Kira did the same. Towards the opposite wall.

THREE

GOOD GRIEF

"YOU REALLY DON'T HAVE TO APOLOGIZE," Zoe insisted for the fourth time. This time, at least, she'd finally taken the note to stop calling Kira *Mrs. Trecothik*.

Speaking of taking notes: "okay," Kira finally agreed. She rustled up a smile and hoped it was good enough to fool Zoe. No, she was not at peace with any of this. She never would be. Was she proud of what her daughter had done? Absolutely. Was she furious at the injustice of courage and compassion being the cause of her death? Absolutely. Was she misdirecting some of that rage at Zoe? Had done, and quite frankly, still was. Did this mortify and humiliate her in equal measure? Of course.

It was pure emotional overload. She couldn't process it, couldn't parse one white-hot tendril of feeling from the others. Relief came only in escape, in cessation. Numbness. Unfeeling. This was no way forward, long-term. She knew that. But it was the *only* way forward, in considering the journey from this instant to the next.

What remained clear, though, was that Zoe didn't deserve to suffer for Kira's cathartic constipation. Hence, Kira's calling the girl up and asking her to meet for breakfast (having that breakfast at *six in the morning* hadn't been her idea, but the Gas-Up was open and she barely slept anymore, so why not?). Hence, Kira's profuse apologies for her standoffish behavior, when Zoe had come to tell her what Leigh had done. Hence, Kira's slapdash smile, the one already slipping off of her face.

Zoe seemed satisfied by it, though. The apologies, the smile. If she wasn't, well, at least *she* knew how to fake a good feeling.

"I heard you on NPR," Kira said, picking up her coffee cup and lifting it just an inch or two off the surface of the table between them. "Sounded good."

Zoe shifted in her seat. "Thanks. That was, uh…that was scary. I was just trying to not think about how many people were listening. But they told me what they were going to ask, so I could prepare for it. The scariest part was starting." She glanced out the window, then grabbed her tea off the table and took a grand old swig of it.

Like a drunk killing their first round, was the first thing that came to Kira's mind. From the emotional snarl: a whip-crack of pure compassion for the life this girl was going to have to navigate.

"It was…fucking pointless," Zoe continued, staring at the empty cup in her hand. "Nothing's going to change. They kept calling, and I thought it would make a difference, so I said, sure, but…" She shook her head and put the cup down. "Everybody there just looked so…*bored*. They didn't care. We were just the people they had to record that morning." She sniffed, and her head jerked forward and back once, like a cobra with a nervous tic. "I felt like such an idiot."

"You shouldn't," Kira reassured her. "You tried. That's…a lot."

"I just…I get why you don't bother."

Another *snap* of affect, this time pure offense. A moment later, she forced herself to recognize that what Zoe had said was *not* a passive-aggressive swipe at what Kira still thought of as her *cowardice*.

Oblivious to the little drama in Kira's head, Zoe sniffed once, and then again, the second significantly juicier than the first. A clear indication that tears were incoming.

Oh, no. Kira couldn't handle that right now. Not because she was liable to join her – quite the opposite. Or something. "Don't cry." She grabbed the napkin she'd been using as a coaster, unfolded it, tore off the bit with the coffee ring, and passed the rest to Zoe. "Please don't cry."

"I just…thanks," Zoe honked as she took the napkin, "I feel like, I got this second chance, I, like, *oh God.*" She gasped, blew her nose, and squeezed her eyes shut. "Leigh gave me this life, you know? I just want to *do* something with it! I want to make sure this never happens again!"

"Don't do that," Kira growled. She could feel the red

slithering in again. Always when she least expected it. Struggling towards a more even tone, she added "Leigh wouldn't have wanted you to…do that."

Zoe did a bit more dabbing with the napkin (for all the good that did), then tossed it into her empty teacup. "I'm sorry."

Kira sighed. "It's alright." A flash over Zoe's shoulder caught Kira's attention: it was yet another ogler. She'd spotted more than a few already. Whether they'd recognized Kira as the mother of the dead hero, or Zoe as a survivor of the killings, it was impossible to say. And really, who cared. Neirmouth was a small town, and the massacre was big news; anyone touched by the latter had become, to no small extent, public property.

Kira was still frowning at the looky-loo when Zoe asked "how is Mr. Treco…um, your husband?"

Finally: the ogler made eye contact with Kira. They looked away quite quickly indeed, quickly enough to pull something in their neck. Hopefully. That would have been nice.

Another red thought. So many red thoughts.

"Harlow," Kira corrected, which brought her back. She smiled, this one coming naturally. "He's…doing what you did. He's in D.C. to do *Meet The Press*. Trying to change things."

"Oh. That's good. But I m-"

"Yeah."

"Yeah. But I meant, um, *how* is he doing? With…it? Like, overall?"

"Mhm." Kira glanced back over towards the looky-loo. They weren't looky-loo-ing anymore. "He's…" she cleared her throat and forced her attention back to Zoe again. "I don't know. To be entirely honest, I don't know."

"He won't talk to you?"

"…it's…ah, it's closer to the opposite, I'd say."

"Oh." Zoe shimmied in her seat again. "We don't have to talk about it, if you don't w-"

"I don't mind." Kira considered her coffee, but did not partake. "It's…" she shook her head. Felt the space around her eyes that ought to have been filling with tears just then. Yet nothing came. It was just the numbness now. Tether cut, floating off into space. Watching the world shrink into the black, wondering how long it would be before the oxygen ran out. Knowing it won't make a difference, in the end.

"Are you alright alone? In the house? If you need to be with someone, you could stay at our house, I'm sure my parents w-"

"That's very sweet," Kira blurted out, a touch sharply. "But I'm fine. Harlow's getting on a plane right after the taping, he'll be back tonight. I won't be…well, he'll be back soon."

Zoe nodded. "If you ever need to just talk to someone…"

"That's very sweet of you," Kira reiterated, her tone sharper still.

"Mhm." Moments of nothing. Then, "sometimes there's…nothing to say, I guess," Zoe ventured, just to fill the silence. "Nothing you can say. We don't have to say anything."

Oh dear. *Now* Kira could feel emotion sludging its way up from her gut. Thick, viscous loneliness. It really did turn that fast. "I miss her so much," she choked out.

"Me too. I can't imagine."

Kira reached out and took Zoe's hand. Recoiling slightly, as her fingers passed through the empty space once occupied by the rest of Zoe's fingers.

For one sickening instant, Kira wondered where Zoe's missing digits had wound up. Imagined them half-buried in the iron-rich soil of Knot Hedge, half-devoured by all the things that flock to rot.

Then Zoe flipped her hand under Kira's and returned the squeeze.

The next thing either of them said was "thank you." Kira, speaking to Zoe. But it was quite a long time before she managed that.

YES, HARLOW WAS OFF IN D.C. to put in his appearance on *Meet The Press*, along with a few of the other parents who had lost children in the mass shootings that had occurred since Knot Hedge (for there had been several in the intervening weeks, of course there had). As usual, Kira had opted not to go, and felt strangely vindicated by Zoe's account of her own media appearance. It was such a ghoulish exercise in futility, she felt. This parading of the bereaved before the Klieg lights to plead their ninety-second cases to stony-faced camera operators and a public largely watching their grief on mute while running on the treadmill, while waiting in the airport. Who in this country owned a television and *hadn't* seen the second-order casualties of gun violence, become so well acquainted with their agony and fury that the talking points couldn't be summarized before the bodies hit the ground?

Kira recognized the true color of these thoughts. She understood the impulse to *do something*, recognized the importance of the endeavor, appreciated that if one day the tide finally turned and the country adopted halfway sane gun control measures, it would be in no small part thanks to those who had sacrificed the privacy of their grief for the greater good. But she couldn't do it. She just couldn't. She would no sooner take part than board the ferry to Knot Hedge and search the ground for Leigh-shaped depressions.

Nor would she watch the program. Which, she noticed with an unhappy glance at the clock, was on right now. That was fine, though. She knew precisely what it would be. She'd seen the episodes her husband *hadn't* been on.

There would be footage, she knew. Glimpses of what the country had collectively christened the Firestarters Massacre (and there must have been more than a few head honchos at Firestarters with steam whistling out their ears over *that*). What better way to turn the emotional screws? Kira couldn't blame the producers, or whoever it was making the decision to replay the footage on a loop. Always carefully edited to imply, but never *depict*, the carnage. Kira sometimes questioned the wisdom of that. Maybe desensitization could best be combatted by pushing sensation beyond the threshold of indifference. Show the bloodshed. Show what these fucking guns were doing, to whom they were doing it. But then, she thought, eventually everyone will see on their own. There's a shooting every goddamned day. This will touch everyone, eventually. And it will be turned into ten minutes of air time, to fill the space between stories about a celebrity writing a memoir about how they did not enjoy filming a popular television show, and the latest flimflam artist demonstrating how to smear oneself with the weight loss algae they happen to be selling. It will never end. Never. Ever. End.

In lieu of watching TV, she lowered herself delicately into a seat at the kitchen table and stared at one of the naked patches of the wall opposite. A splash of cream-colored paint between the picture frames, cut by veins of reaching red. Only…no. Kira closed her eyes.

The red remained. Of course. This was simply what a mind looked like, mid-fracture.

Had she always had such anger in her? That was what truly astonished her, when she had the presence of mind to notice; numbness was just as likely – maybe *more* likely – to yield to blinding rage as it was to anguish. Why? She didn't believe in deities or destinies, which left her no Prime Mover to rage against, no plan to question the wisdom of. So what was she angry at? The stupidity of burning up with such a useless emotion only further enraged her. Which was how minds broke, of course. Surely. God, where was that numbness when she really needed it?

Shhh-NK.

Kira flinched. Returned her attention to the splash of unclaimed paint across from her.

The little shadows of the picture frames had bled out into the rest of the wall. No more definition. Just little blobs of dark. Kira blinked and looked at the clock. Discovered just how long she'd sat there, staring at the wall. Better that than watching *Meet The Press* though. And wasn't *that* an evergreen statement.

She blinked, shaking her head slightly, as that *shhh-NK* replayed itself in her mind. What had that been? Something inanimate, yet…in a way she couldn't quite describe, the sound sat in her memory like a word from a foreign language. A word spoken by a human voice, in a tongue she had studied many years ago, but since forgotten…

There, on the floor. A picture in a frame, face-down on the ground. Slipped its mount somehow, slid down the wall, landed on the floor, tipped forward. *Shhh-NK.* Mystery solved.

Kira stood up. Approached the picture. Stood directly over it, stared down at it. Hesitated.

This was a picture of Leigh. She knew it. She recognized the frame, had no doubt subconsciously noted the empty spot on the wall. The picture was one of Leigh when she was seven years old, standing on one of those paddle boards. Part of an outdoorsy day camp she'd gone to. Framed against the deep blue of the lake, the punchy green of the far shore visible in the distance. Smiling wide, hair dangling damp down to her bright orange life jacket. Not waving to the camera, but only because she needed both hands for the paddle, only because she wasn't yet steady enough on the board to risk a salutation. Otherwise, she would have, surely. At seven years old, Leigh was still waving at any camera lens that turned her way. She'd been so excited, for nothing in particular. Just….always excited.

Kira didn't need to flip the picture over. Didn't need to look at it again. She could see it now, as clearly as if it was in front of her.

It occurred to her that her memory of the moment *was* the photograph. She had been at the lake that day, of course. She had been the one to take the picture. Yet the years had eaten away at everything outside the viewfinder.

She wondered if this was what the future held for her. If, years on, she would forget everything of Leigh not immortalized in photos, in video, no matter how hard she tried to hold on to it. The thought ought to have mortified her, she knew. Ought to have dropped her to her knees, torn her in half. Yet, ah, here at last, the numbness was back. Sweet unfeeling.

So she risked it. She crouched down, grabbed the top of the fallen picture frame, and stood up. Held it out to rehang it on the wall. Hang it by the firm little thread that was still very much intact, hang it from the nail in the wall which was still very firmly in place. Curious. How had it fallen?

Pointless question. It had fallen. *How* was irrelevant.

She rehung the picture without quite looking at it. Didn't need to. She knew what it was.

In straightening the frame, her eyes grazed the image. Somewhat soiled the memory with the artifact itself.

And in that moment, the strangest thought occurred to her. The feeling of finally remembering the word you couldn't find earlier that morning. Of finally realizing what that song you heard yesterday was from.

Shhh-NK.

For a split second, Kira thought: *Oh, I remember what that means!*

And then she thought, *how ridiculous*. Even if it didn't actually feel ridiculous to her.

THUD.

Kira lifted her gaze, to a ceiling run through with more roots of red. Something heavy, falling over upstairs. Something very heavy indeed. Heavy enough to shake the walls. To rattle the rest of the pictures. They sounded like a skeletal little laugh track, in response to the punch-line of the *THUD*. God, that was another word Kira should have known. She fought to find a translation for it. *THUD*. Like one of those words that could mean hello or goodbye at the same time.

Oh dear. Things were happening out of order. The falling picture could have been explained by the heavy thing falling over upstairs. And what would have explain-ed the heavy thing falling over? Kira supposed she would find out shortly.

Without quite thinking about it, Kira drifted over to the stairs. Then up them. The whole journey was something of a blur. One step, then another, then another. Not so much looking for the source of the *THUD,* as searching for the meaning of it. Searching for a room without so much red crawling along its walls.

In a daze, she found a door. A door unlike the others in the hallway, unlike the rest of the walls in the house, unlike the world outside, for being unblighted by vines of seething dahlia.

The door to Leigh's room.

Kira stared down at the knob. The same unremarkable brass knob that had always been there. Dented slightly at that spot there, towards the hinges. Who could say what from. Who cared. It was just a knob, like the doors were doors, like the walls were walls. There was no red. She knew that. She wasn't *totally* nuts. She was un-nuts enough to recognize that seeing something, hearing something, *understanding* something doesn't make it true. Just as surely as she knew there was an inversion of that she was doing her best to avoid. More than one, maybe. Words were tricky like that.

THUD. It had come from in here. She knew. Even if the geography of that didn't make sense. Leigh's room was not directly above the kitchen. And yet. She knew.

Her hand moved towards the knob.

Her heart kicked into double-time.

Her ears rang.

She pulled her hand back to her side, and thought a silly thought, which became a terrifying certainty.

There was someone in Leigh's bedroom. There was some*thing* in Leigh's bedroom. Perfectly still. Making no noise. Yet she could feel the gravity of them, feel herself drawn forward, gently, insistently.

The more assured of this she became…it was the strangest thing, but the more assured of it she became, the less afraid she felt. The less *anything* she felt.

She returned her hand to the knob, no intention of turning it. Just something to hold on to.

Softly, she asked, "is someone there?"

Oh, how she hoped she received no answer. She would even have accepted a voice saying *no*. Any excuse not to enter the room. She wasn't ready yet. She would never be ready.

Ch-rrrrrrr….

A small noise from below. Downstairs. Just down the stairs, in fact. A noise far easier to identify than the others. It was the knob of the front door, turning. It was the creak of the front door groaning open, just a crack.

It was a voice. Clearer than the others. This was a language she spoke. It could not be translated. But it was something she could respond to, something she could heed.

Kira drifted down the stairs.

As she descended, the door came into view. Just the slightest bit ajar. Not as though someone had snuck into the house. No, this was how a door looked when some-one had just snuck out, tried to close it softly as they went, not gone all the way with it. In their haste, perhaps. This hypothetical someone who was leaving quietly, but quickly.

None of this frightened Kira. She could see, as

though through gauze, that it ought to have. Yet it didn't. She was back in the nothing now. In which everything was only what it was, incapable of implying anything, without any expectations to defy.

She reached the bottom of the stairs. Stepped to just in front of the door. Considered it. Considered the long needle of sunshine driving into the gloomy hall. Considered the delicate to-and-fro of the door, tossed by a breeze. Considered the wordless shush of the dogwood tree just outside the front door, fondled by those same mysterious gusts.

It was all just what it was, and nothing more.

Kira considered closing the door. Until she started to hear a song from the dogwood. Music, in the same sense that a door creaking open was speech. She wanted to hear more.

She opened the door.

Outside the door: Hamlin Drive. The street on which Kira lived. That made sense, she supposed, though here in the nothing, any vista would have made just as much sense. Overhead: the sun splashed about in a blue patch amongst dense cloud cover. Across the street: the Carters needed to mow their lawn if they hoped to avoid the wrath of Dan, and the HOA he wielded like a cudgel. On the sidewalk: a nine-foot-tall man sauntered down the street, hunched and crooked, yet fluid as a dancer.

None of that struck Kira as odd. The only thing that punctured her cocoon was the sound of a sniffle, *her* sniffle. It was wet. She lifted a finger and touched her cheeks. Oh, had she been crying? For how long? What a silly question. Weeks, of course.

The nine-foot-tall man reached the walk up to Kira's front door. He turned, and took it. Gnarled, graceful.

Not a man at all.

As he approached, Kira could see that this was something else. As in, something different from every other thing. Something that gave the impression that physics and literature were the same, and it was possible to have no use for either. Its face was moonrock, eroded by pressure and atmosphere over millennia into something one might mistake for human. A bit like seeing Christ in the grain of a 2x4, just as the beam was being swung hard at thine own eye. The moonrock head was mounted atop a frame stooped in impossible places, coiled at the crown, bolt-straight in the center, jutting back nearer the bottom. Arms nearly as long as Kira was tall dangled limply from high-set shoulders; it was a wonder the creature, the *thing,* didn't get its spindly legs tangled up in them. The illusion of its humanity was, Kira realized, largely perpetuated by its clothes. Not that it had clothes. Its body was a cairn of volcanic sputum, undifferentiated grey without strata or grade. And yet…it was lumpy in such a way as to seem arranged to parody clothing. A uniquely human idiocy, executed with a cynical, knowing wink.

The creature was nearly on the porch.

Through seafoam: Kira saw that she ought to close the door. Close it, lock it. Call the police or the Ghostbusters or Earth Science department at Bates or whoever. It was strange, she understood, to not be doing anything in response to the titan now taking the two steps onto the Trecothik porch in a single casual swing of the leg. But wasn't this just a strange world?

As it ducked to fit beneath the overhang, Kira got a better look at its face. She studied its eyes, and saw nothing. Not the *nothing* of philosophy or mathematics. Not the poetic *nothing*, the one some of the more theatrical journalists had described Ruthger Gully's eyes as displaying, as he was taken into custody after the massacre. No. This wasn't like that. Looking into the creature's eyes was like looking at a Halloween mask sprawled flat on concrete. Yet, she knew, what the creature wore was not a mask. There was no 'real' face concealed behind it. That protuberance with the vaguely human features was something closer to a hat. A funny one at that, something worn to amuse other things like itself, if such things could exist. However it saw, or experienced, or communicated, none of that happened through its moonrock face.

Yet clearly, it did see, and experience. It stopped, just in front of the ragged brown welcome mat on the porch, and curled itself upright in such a way as to make Kira feel seen. As in, observed.

Kira was finally starting to feel like she should be calling someone, going somewhere, doing something. Not just observing the fact, but *feeling* it. And were it the deep of a starless midnight from which this apparition had suddenly emerged, maybe she would have. But it wasn't. The creature came to her round about lunchtime on a sunny summer Sunday. Kira could hear a lawnmower running down the street. Birds waxing rhapsodic about some bit of birdy business from the dogwood. Just beside the devil on her doorstep, a butterfly struggled to decide which to the lilies in front of the bay window it wanted to land on. It was, in short, not the right time of day for visitors from eldritch realms.

So Kira stood where she was, stared at the rock, and imagined it a face. She wondered what it saw when it looked at her. Wondered if it was, in any sense, *looking* at her, or if it became aware of her through means she couldn't begin to imagine, presenting her the face merely to save her the unpleasantness of speculation.

Slowly, as though its long, two-elbowed arms moved not by muscle but by plate tectonics, it lifted one of its massive, tussock-knuckled hands, and it peeled its fingers apart, and it waved.

Kira, not knowing what else to do… waved back. The gesture suddenly felt alien to her. To greet someone, *anyone,* by wiggling an open palm at them. How strange.

The creature, rockface still pointed at Kira, lowered its hand. Stopped moving. Became what it so resembled.

While Kira mirrored it, in lowering her hand, she couldn't match its crazy-making stasis. Nothing had so perfectly embodied the opposite of motion as this thing. Even mountains moved, over time. Not this thing. Not until it chose to.

It chose to. Eye-shaped sockets still trained on Kira, it stretched one of its hands out towards the front door, then to the doorframe. Then it depressed the doorbell as delicately as one might boop the nose of a newborn baby.

Ding dong.

It wanted to come inside, Kira realized. It wanted her to want it to come inside. Not because it was playing by vampire rules – it could enter if it chose to. It could go anywhere it wanted, do anything. She *felt* this. Feeling beyond observation, beyond knowledge. She did not *need* to invite it in. But it *wanted* her to.

On the one hand, Kira saw no reason to invite it in. On the other hand, it would be rude not to. The creature had been nothing but polite thus far. Indeed, it was perhaps the patience of the creature that settled Kira on the hospitable course of action. It hadn't rung the door-bell a second time, hadn't stepped forward to menace her, hadn't expressed the least impatience. It knew that she knew – that she *felt* – what it wanted. It was happy to give her all the time she needed, to decide.

But make no mistake: a decision was necessary.

Don't you want to know why the mountain has come to you? The thought appeared in Kira's head. Impossible to say who had put it there.

An answer came to her swiftly. Less mysterious, who had come up with that one.

She opened the door.

The creature bowed further, folded to near ninety degrees at a point on its body that Kira could not imagine calling a waist (she got the impression that the creature could bend and rise, bend and rise one hundred times over, and never once fold in the same place), and brought its rockface to near eye-level with Kira's much more brittle visage.

Suddenly, Kira marveled at what power the moon had. Think of the tides. Shifting the oceans, with no more persuasion than its presence. Imagine it crashing into the Earth, imagine it soaring off into the void. The end of all life, in both cases.

Impossible, of course. As impossible as finding the moon on one's welcome mat. Not looking in any sense, and yet, apprehending.

Vcl-clck. The deadbolt of the door clicked in and out of its own accord.

Kira flinched, her eyes darting down to it.

Hfllfhcu. One of the dogwood's branches shook, its bark and verdure rattled by similarly unseen hands, chasing off a bird perched upon it.

Again, her gaze followed the sound, though this time she didn't jump.

Tuh-teersk. A knife, somehow having freed itself from the block, clattered onto the counter in the kitchen behind her.

She did jump at that. Didn't turn to look at the kitchen, though. She instead kept her eyes on the creature with the face of the moon, immobile through all that commotion. Yet the cause of it all. Of that, Kira had no doubt.

Silence reigned once again. Kira studied the ragged edges of the creature's faceless mask, more perplexed than petrified by its telekinetic display.

Then she gasped.

Memory, or perhaps something more elemental, remodeled those sounds into language.

Vcl-clck. Hfllfhcutuh-teersk.

The syllables hatched, a stone she'd never pegged for an egg, and birthed words. The sounds carried their meaning to the same degree as the hatmask was a face, a glancing similarity that Kira's mind was, through its own devices or, more probably, through the irresistible powers of this moon monster, able to make sense of. Or *compelled* to make sense of, in the latter formulation.

Thus, those sounds became syllables; the creature spoke through the modest manipulation of Kira's home.

It said, *I've come to clean the gutters.*

And so it was that Kira understood, ah yes, she had finally lost her mind.

Kr-CHRK. One of the narrow panes of glass mounted beside the door cracked.

HrrrrLRF-rr-hfrtr. The thin drawer in the table beside the entrance slid open and shut, shuffling about the contents inside. Kira was quite certain she heard something in there break – a soft, shrill *snap* – yet she knew that was just collateral damage. That wasn't part of the language.

A joke, the creature had said through the disarray. *I live for levity.*

Kira remained precisely where she was, as she was. Couldn't do otherwise. The creature seemed capable of pulling Kira's house down around her, if it so chose, if it only had enough it wanted to say. No doubt, it could tear her apart just as easily. Yet it didn't. Evinced no intention of doing so. Perhaps that was what kept her rooted to the spot. It certainly wasn't anything as simple as fear. Because she wasn't afraid. Whatever she was, it wasn't that.

The creature resumed its movement, padding through to the kitchen, its footfalls celebrating themselves not with the thunder Kira would have expected from such a ponderous giant, but with the dry hush of a predator creeping between cornstalks. Soft though they were, its steps were brisk and confident, as though it had been here one hundred and one times before. And who could say, maybe it had. It was so very quiet.

Reaching a spot on the floor like any other, the creature turned to once again present its hideous kabuki crag to Kira. As it had on the porch, it froze, studying her with whatever dreadful senses guided it through this world (and Kira couldn't stop herself from mentally emphasizing the word *this*). Then, it collected dust. Waiting for Kira.

She was slow to follow, but follow she did. Not bothering to go back to close the front door. A bubble from her subconscious, perhaps. Maybe she was wary without realizing it.

Entering the kitchen, confronting the creature waiting so patiently for her, her steps slowed, shoulders angling. One forward, one back. A sparring position, not that she had any experience. A better stance from which to bolt, not that she could manage more than a jog.

"Are you real?" she heard herself ask. "Is this…is this real?"

Gentle as snowfall, the creature lowered that face-shaped appendage down to Kira's level. It didn't need to pull anything else in the house apart to make known its intention.

Kira reached forward. Surprised to see her hand trembling. Fully *shaking,* in fact. Those tremors lessened slightly as her forefinger tracked closer and closer to the brow of the rockface before her.

Within inches of the creature's form, her hand hesitated. She could push it no further. She tried to imagine she was simply stroking the snout of a well-behaved horse, but that was just another experience she'd never had before.

The creature did not inch forward, did not initiate contact. It simply waited. That was what it did. Kira could feel the aeons rolling off of this thing. What terrible patience it had.

She forced her hand forward. Ended up pressing her finger into the creature more forcefully than she'd meant to. Less delicately grazing the pedal of a rose; more hammering a big red button with the word LAUNCH on it.

Kira only touched the creature for an instant before yanking her hand back, holding it against her chest, cradling it with the other hand. As though she'd burnt her finger on it. Which she hadn't. The creature hadn't felt like anything physical. Not hot, not cold. It was firm, she supposed, yet seemed somehow malleable. Like its form could be changed, but not by anything as pedestrian as force or pressure.

No, in touching the creature, Kira came away with two apprehensions. Both of which crystallized at once, firming into certainty.

One: this creature was real. Kira knew perfectly well

how the senses could deceive; she'd read the books, she'd heard the podcasts. She knew. And yet, to lay a hand on this thing was to feel its history. Something deeper, more unfathomable than could be known from any terrestrial formation. This was a tactile experience akin to seeing images of the cosmic horizon, those gasps of light taken in by the world's most powerful telescopes. It was understanding what it was she was confronted with, yet being utterly incapable of truly processing it.

The second certainty was no less paradoxical: this creature, Kira knew, was not alive in any sense of the term she would recognize. It wasn't even alive in the way that a tree was alive, that coral was alive. It didn't *need* anything. All living things *need*. This did not.

Yet it *wanted*. It *wanted* so many things. That, Kira could feel.

Wholly unharmed, Kira nonetheless rubbed at the hand that had touched this wanting thing, taking a slight step backwards as she did. Feeling her heart beating faster, hearing her breath ripping more forcefully through her nostrils.

Fear. Good. She was afraid. She was feeling that.

The thing lifted its decorative head back towards the ceiling. Then once again grew still. Waiting.

Kira tried to form a sentence, a single word, tried to make a single sound, but she couldn't. Her entire jaw had started to chatter, though the day was hot, so hot.

The thing waited. Reduced once more to geology.

"What…" Kira finally managed. "…what are you?"

Hww, water bursting from the sink faucet. *Mwww,* the

foam handles of kitchen implements squeaking against each other inside their drawer. *Tuh*, the scrunched plastic of a water bottle on the counter re-expanding. *Whh*, coffee grounds settling in the bag. *Nht*, a half-full glass of seltzer toppling over on the table. *Glg*, the seltzer gulping as it spread over the countertop, *plp plp*, dripping onto the floor. *Hmm*, the dishrag sliding off of its hook. Even as the entropy of the kitchen continued through minor displacements, the sounds stitched themselves into coherence.

Might keep in mind how brittle your home is.

There being no actual *voice* making this suggestion, Kira had no way of determining the spirit in which this advice was offered. "You can't speak without…breaking stuff?"

The inaction of the thing was its answer.

Kira nodded, fighting to swallow despite a sandpaper throat. Yes, that was probably a question that even the absolute ruin of her home couldn't fully address. Find simpler questions then, with shorter answers.

"Do you have a name?"

The monolith lifted one leg and swept it backwards, dragging the very tip of the foot along the ground, like a bull preparing to charge. *Oo-eesh*, the foot said, as the very tip of it carved a long furrow in the hardwood.

Uisch, the foot meant. Pronounced Oo-eesh, but spelled Uisch. How had this thing beamed orthography into Kira's head? Why had it bothered?

No *needs,* but such specific *wants.*

All of which – beyond the *want* that Kira know how

RID OF RED

to spell its name – remained a mystery. So she risked her kitchen, and asked: "what do you want?"

Though Uisch drew no air, it was capable of conveying the elemental essence of a sigh. But no, a sigh was expiration: this was something like the opposite.

Kira worked that out about the same time as her kitchen exploded.

Shelves tore from the walls and crashed to the ground. Dishes shattered, flinging shards of themselves into cabinets full of clanking, clattering dishware. A kettle without water in it whistled and shrieked. Ice shot out of the little drive-thru window in the freezer door. A spent bottle of wine toppled from the top of the fridge, cracking but not breaking.

Kira screamed, staggered backwards until she thumped against the wall, swinging her arms up to shield her face. She privileged protecting the eyes, and was glad to have done so as she felt her forearms slapped (but, by fortune or design, not *slashed*) by dishware detritus.

The cacophony continued even as the meaning behind it breached, still only hinting at its true immensity.

Your grief sings. I live to dance. To take, I gladly give.

The last of the mayhem lapsed into silence and stillness. As did Uisch. Leaving room for Kira to respond.

She reclaimed her full height, fragments of an elaborate plate (a wedding gift only ever used at holidays) crunching beneath the sole of her bare feet. She'd check for blood later. She'd move her foot off the shard, later. For now, her entire body trembled. She made no effort to still it.

So many things she wanted to ask Uisch. Yet the thing was right: this was a brittle space. Every answer would cost her.

Surely, Uisch knew that. Understood full well that what it had said only raised more questions, deepened Kira's despair at not yet knowing the answers.

It wasn't as though the maskhat this thing wore could emote, but Kira was suddenly certain that Uisch was laughing at her. Playing with her.

Loathing how pitiful she felt, Kira only just stopped herself from asking the creature if it couldn't help her fix what it had broken. Even to a question unasked, the answer came through inaction. Uisch took things apart. Putting them back together was for other people, if it was to happen at all.

She took a deep breath. "I don't know what that means. What you just said."

A refrigerator magnet clattered to the floor. Sounded heavy enough to be one of the custom-printed ones, with a picture of the whole Trecothik family on it.

A gift.

Uisch swept from the room, the swing of its dangling arms perfectly timed to slip back down the front hall without knocking knuckles on the doorframe.

Kira took another look at the kitchen. Its disorganization was actually quite mild, viewed with an objective eye. A few things crooked on the wall, a few more scattered across the floor. Yet Kira had never once allowed it to look like this before. She supposed *mild* was relative.

She turned to look down the entry hall, through which

146

Uisch had lumbered. Yet Uisch was nowhere to be seen.

Kira blinked, only then noticing the whisper of its eponymous footsteps climbing the stairs. How the creature had managed to race down the hall and mount the steps so quickly was the sort of mystery you figure out within the first fifty pages. So down the hall and up the stairs Kira went, self-conscious, in a strange and distracted way, about the heavy gorilla *thud* of her own footsteps.

The upstairs hall was notable for its lack of hunched, nine-foot psychic golems. Gone, too, was the vasculature of Kira's red madness. Which surely meant something; she'd puzzle over that after she finished playing hide and seek with an ambulatory fjord.

"Where'd you go?" she demanded. Keeping her voice low, for reasons beyond her ken.

From down the hall, she heard something scraping the far side of a wooden door, the sound seeming to blossom and wilt within the hollow-core flush. The shiver up her spine somehow conveyed that the scratch went against the grain of the birch veneer. It was a feeling she had no choice but to trust; Uisch had opened her mind to new means of communication, ones that bypassed language, that signified without even the need for living intention. Things could speak, grief could sing. This was Kira's world now.

But there remained some constants. A handhold on sanity. A fingertip grasp, in fact.

Kira couldn't open the door through which Uisch had vanished. The door it had closed again in its wake. So that Kira would have no choice but to open it herself.

She still wasn't ready. Yes, the door to Leigh's bedroom was like all the others in the house. But she couldn't open it. She couldn't.

"No," she informed Uisch, by way of pressing her face to the door to Leigh's bedroom. It was a flat, incredulous *no*, as though Kira were answering the question *if I carve a zucchini to look like a phone, can I get Wi-Fi on it?*

A crash from the past. *Come*, Uisch said from the far side of the door.

Kira shook her head. "No. Please, we…there are things in my room to knock over. We can sp-"

From the far side of the door: thump clatter bump. *For your song, a gift.*

"Please *stop!*" Kira mewled, flinching at the crack in her voice. "Leave her room alone!"

Silence from Leigh's room. For only a moment. Then: shuffle crunch. *Sing.*

Kira shook her head at the door, mouth agape. Not knowing what to say.

Until a voice from Leigh's room spoke for her.

"Mom?"

Leigh's voice. From just behind the door.

Kira *swung* the door open before she had time to fully process what she'd heard, what it could mean, how it could be possible.

Leigh's room was precisely as Kira had remembered it, yet utterly unlike the way she often thought of it. For all the times it had appeared behind her closed eyes in these past few weeks, for all the times it had overwritten her waking sight, it was always as a space being occupied by Leigh. Never once had she considered that it might truly exist without her daughter. Never once had she imagined what it might be like, to step in here, fearful of that unfillable void at its heart. Kira recognized the string lights snaking around the ceiling, the wall covered in clumsily-hung doodles and polaroids and poems and all the detritus of young friendships. In those blown-out little images on the wall, in scribbles at the bottom of the poetry, Kira could see the names of two of the three girls whose lives were the cause of Leigh's death.

Zoe. Maddie.

Oh, how desperately Kira wanted to tear everything off that goddamned wall. Take a running jump at it, knock the whole thing down.

No. That was red. Eating its way into the room. Leigh's room.

Kira staggered her legs, reaching out a hand to touch the doorframe, hold herself steady. She was blind for despair, for just a moment. Then she blinked the tears away, and saw something in that unfillable Leigh-shaped void.

Uisch. Standing. No longer angling itself towards Kira. Wholly disposing of the fantasy of that face.

It occurred to her that the red wasn't eating into the room. The vines were not snaking along the walls. It was simply the red of her own eyes that she was seeing.

Her voice too quiet to be heard outside of her own head, Kira asked, "is Leigh here?"

The frames on the wall twisted and shimmied, knocking into each other. The very foundations of the house trembled. Vowels and consonants. Syllables. A promise.

She could be.

Kira's response was of her new world, speech without living intention, grief with golden pipes. "How?" she demanded, without her knowledge.

Leigh's bedroom tore itself apart.

FOUR

WHEN UISCH UPON A STAR

KIRA SAT IN THE RUINS of her daughter's bedroom and wept. Not grand tears though, no garment-rending, throat-shredding lamentations here. Just a humble dew in the corners of the eyes, which never quite pulled itself together enough to roll down the cheek. It was fitting, that a different sort of anguish should have a different method of expression.

She can come back to you, Uisch had chuckled through demolition. *That little life you loved. I can give you that gift.*

Kira remembered the tears coming in earnest then, remembered choking on her gratitude. To have Leigh back, to have her beautiful baby returned to her…yes, she wanted that. She wanted that more than anything. And more importantly, she really believed Uisch was capable of giving her that gift. Hearing Leigh's voice through the door was undeniable. Certain like death.

No gift is free, Uisch had said.

Here, Kira recalled – dimly, as though across decades – falling to her knees and begging. Asking Uisch what it wanted, anything, she would do anything.

The song is simple. The little life you loved gave itself for three others. Take those lives, and I will return to you that one.

What had been Kira's first reaction to that offer, so plainly stated, as easily grasped as it was utterly unthinkable? At first, in truth, it was still only gratitude, in its most urgent form. Could the momentous nature of Uisch's offer have been, however briefly, fully eclipsed by need? Or it had it truly been in an instant devoured, to become a bother only upon provoking a sort of deontological reflux?

Who was to say. That was all complication. And like Uisch said, the song was simple.

Zoe, Maddie, Nicole. Three girls just about Leigh's age. Just kill the three of them, that was all. Just do that, and Uisch would bring Leigh back from the dead. What had been her reaction to that? She tried to remember. Tried and failed. Could only imagine. Had she been mortified at the prospect of murdering three teenagers? One would hope so, but she couldn't recall. Had she tried to convince herself, despite knowing better, that Uisch couldn't possibly be making that offer in good faith, might still have been a figment of her imagination, the consequence of a dramatic break from reality? Less likely, yet still plausible. But if not, had she felt the world fall away from her as she witnessed this casual rearrangement of the very laws she had believed governed the universe, a dotting of the once-firm line between life and death?

No. She was fairly certain – though still less certain than she was of the reality of Uisch and its offer – that the only thing she had felt as her daughter's bedroom collapsed around her had been relief. Oh, and hope. Hope being that voice in the chorus most ready to accept the offer, to do whatever was necessary. So hope, then, and relief, and frenzy, all crammed into two words: *that's all?*

Yes, it was all coming back to her now. She had felt those things, thought those words, and then the higher faculties had begun to rain on her lizard brain's parade. Questions of logistics, of confidence in Uisch, and ultimately (yes, this was both the largest and the *last* of Kira's considerations) the ethics of the proposition. End three lives for the return of one. Moral calculus didn't enter into it; this was ethical legerdemain. In no way, shape, or form did Kira have even a pegleg of principle to stand on in considering this proposition.

In a way, that had made it easier to consider. Cleaner, at least.

"I've lost my mind," Kira could remember mumbling, more hopeful than anything. "I've lost my mind."

You have not. Were I to return when the other one is home, he would see me. He would tell you. But his grief does not sing. He will not accept the gift.

"This…has to be some kind of monkey's paw thing, right?"

Uisch had bowed just a little bit deeper at that.

Explain, it said, by the Christmas lights unspooling onto the ground.

"I just…if I…*if* I did what you're asking, I want to know I would have Leigh back as she was on the morning of the…on the last morning I saw her. Healthy. Normal. Nothing wrong with her."

Of course.

Kira shook her head at that. It was all she could do in the face of such an impossible offer. Yes, *impossible*. Though it was no longer what *Uisch* was capable of that brought the word back to mind.

Now, sitting on the ground, shifting piles of dust and drywall powder with her feet, hand resting on the mattress slumped unevenly across a broken bedframe, Kira once more recognized a vanishing fugue by the sudden splatter of shadows taking jigsaw chunks out of Leigh's bedroom. What was left of it, anyway.

"Can you please just bring her back?" she dimly remembered asking, back when she was still on her knees, begging. "Please. Please. Something else. Anything else."

There is nothing else.

"Why not?" Ah, right. She remembered red crawling into her peripheral vision then. Remembered climbing back to her feet. As though to challenge Uisch. As though to threaten it. Might as well leap into the path of an oncoming eighteen-wheeler and shout, *you're gonna regret this!* "Why does it have to be that? Why are you doing this to me? Why won't you just bring her back? Why d-"

Your grief sings.

"What the fuck does that *mean?!*"

Be grateful.

And Kira despaired, for she was.

At that point, Uisch had been silenced. There was nothing left in the room to pull apart, nothing to unsettle into speech. Leigh's room had been obliterated. At which point, Uisch turned its pointless mug from wall to wall, and then, with no final fanfare…left the room.

All at once, Kira had collapsed back onto the floor.

Oh, here the memories were much clearer. She could even now *taste* how she had wanted to rise to her feet once more, harangue the departing demon (for, yes, that was what Uisch surely was, a multi-dimensional, non-denominational demon), ultimately bend it to her will. But she couldn't. She'd been stymied at the first step, by the roots she had put down. Thick red roots into fallow soil, drawing forth rot.

Now, on the floor amidst the detritus of what had been her daughter's private space, her sanctuary, Kira wept. But here, perhaps, was something the demon might call grounds for gratitude: she no longer wept out of despair.

These tears sprang from a place of hope. Awful, terrible hope. And worse than that, knowledge. The knowledge that she didn't have to feel this way anymore. She didn't have to live this life. It was now a *choice*, to languish on the ocean floor.

Leigh was gone, but not beyond her reach. And what made it so unbearable was that the way to get her back was so simple.

Not *easy,* of course. But simple. So simple.

Zoe. Maddie. Nicole.

Three lives for one.

What Kira felt now more than anything was envy for the life she had lived not one hour ago. Oh, there was such a terrible mercy to be found in the futility of grief. How sickening, that she should miss it.

Perhaps that, more than anything else, was why Kira wept.

SHE STARTED BY RECONSTRUCTING THE KITCHEN as best she could. Leigh's room had remained sealed since she was no longer around to open it, and there was no reason to suspect Harlow would come home and suddenly decide to pop his head in and check out how the dust was laying. So Kira shut the door to Leigh's bedroom and left it to its end-times disarray; she could get that tomorrow. Instead, she stretched a new trash bag out in the less grody of the two ninety-five gallon cans from the garage, and dragged it into the kitchen. That turned out to be not nearly as sharp an idea as it had seemed in her head – the can left a long viscous slug trail of something that looked like it might glow in the dark if given the chance. Kira cleaned it up at once, despite her certainty that there were rubber gloves somewhere in the house.

A broom sufficed to sweep up the broken dishes, the spilled sugars and spices. Their noises struck her ears as ambitiously pre-verbal, like an infant attempting to repeat words spoken by doting parents. Had Uisch attuned Kira to the secret language all things spoke? Or was she just going a little bit bonkers? The Looney Tunes solu-

tion was a compelling one, given how simple a matter it
had been to fold whatever the fuck Uisch was into her
worldview, how little skepticism she had felt prior to
accepting its existence, and its claims of being able to
reach into the realm of the dead and pluck out a soul as
easily as one snaps a ripe apple from the bough. She
supposed the toaster she was uprighting, the hanging
light she was standing on the counter to rescrew into the
ceiling above the sink, the stove grills she was resetting
into their grooves, none of this could be considered
evidence. It was unlikely (but not impossible) that she
had, in one of those woeful lapses of consciousness that
defined her mourning, torn apart her own living spaces.
This, as it happened, spoke to the increasing urgency
with which she tidied, as Harlow would be home from
D.C. by dinner tonight, which for him meant six on the
dot. It wouldn't do to have him coming home to a kitch-
en in chaos. How could she account for it? The truth (as
she understood it) could send Harlow off to place a call
to the boys from the funny farm, just as surely as vague
dissimulation could. So what then? Say she saw a bug and
got a bit carried away with a rolled up newspaper? No.
Better to clean as best she could, make some lame excuses for the dishware that had made good on its fragility,
and try to seem sane, even as she made a sober study of
the impossible. In all of its forms.

Butter, somehow liberated from the fridge, splattered
on the floor from its overturned tray, made adorable little
sqsh sqsh sounds as Kira slopped it up with a paper towel.
Or was it saying *yes yes*? To which of the many proposi-

tions swirling around Kira's mind was it assenting? Oh, it was crazymaking. Surely it was.

Zoe Cottrell's face appeared in her mind, as vivid as it had been earlier today, as she'd comforted Kira from across the table at Gerry's Gas-Up. The ache of her indomitable smile, the way her hair rolled freely out from behind her ear, the way she sometimes didn't get it all as she tried to tuck it back. With those images came the warmth of her hand, as Kira had taken it, held it, squeezed it ever-so-gently.

There was no way. To consider hurting her, *killing* her, was…it was *ludicrous*, like fretting over how many kilos of Mentos and Coca Cola she'd need to blow a hole in a battleship.

Her mind moved quickly, though, and the next question came at once: *What about the other two?*

One had been Maddie. Madeleine Encomb. Kira knew her. She couldn't quite picture her face – with a few exceptions, she really only knew Maddie as the girl standing in the doorway of the Encomb house, as Kira pulled up to the curb outside to drop Leigh off. But, well…she knew where the girl lived. The other one, Nicole Ligeti, Kira didn't know her. From the way Zoe described it, she wasn't among Leigh's friend group. She'd just been around to get a boost over the fallen tree. Nicole didn't mean anything to Leigh.

She'd be the easiest to do.

The thought snuck up on Kira, unwanted, uninvited. It was enough to send her crashing into the wall, sliding to the floor, fearing she might be sick on herself. Void her stomach of the breakfast she'd shared with Zoe. She'd be the *hardest* to do, Zoe would.

Kira closed her eyes. Tried to convince herself that she *was* crazy. Uisch had been a bad dream, some food poisoning, maybe. Yeah. That was why she felt sick. Undigested beef, blot of mustard. Like Scrooge said to Marley. More gravy than grave. Though Scrooge had turned out to be wrong about that, so bad example.

So accept it. Wrap up anger ahead of schedule, leapfrog over bargaining (*especially* over bargaining) and depression, stick the landing on acceptance. Leigh was gone. Gone too soon, struck down by an evil man, denied what would have no doubt been a long and promising life. It was Kira's greatest fear realized, the worst thing she could ever possibly endure. She couldn't believe it hadn't killed her. But for all that, it was what had happened. It was the way things were. So accept it. Leave it alone, and move on with what still remained of this life.

She saw their names in the closed-eye dark: Zoe. Maddie. Nicole. Yes, it was Nicole. The easiest of the three, in screaming neon.

"Fuck," Kira heard herself whimper. She tried to shake them away, those names, tried to think about something else, anything else. Her first kiss with Harlow, one of those both-people-rush-in-as-one smooches you almost never got on the first crack. Where was that? It might have been at the, hm, at the roller rink, or the bowling alley. It had been somewhere kitschy and unassuming. Maybe the easiest of the three.

No. *Click,* on to the next frame in the mental viewfinder. The view from the cash register at her summer job in high school. Clerking at some miserable health food café, she couldn't quite remember the name of it right now, but she did recall that her manager was fond of calling her job on the register *clerking*. He hadn't been nearly old enough to pull that off without it seeming like an affectation, but then again, he was the easiest of thr…

Kira finished cleaning the kitchen listening to one of the classical music channels on Spotify. She wasn't a huge fan of classical – a lot of it just felt like the baroque equivalent of endless, noodling guitar solos – but the unrelenting density of it was enough to keep her mind from wandering, at least for a little bit. That done, she opened the bottle of cheap white wine that had haunted the fridge for so long, poured herself a glass, chugged it, poured herself another, then brought the glass – and the bottle – to the couch.

She was awoken from a slumber she hadn't been cognizant of falling into (she didn't even remember making it to the couch, yet here she was) by the closing of the garage door.

Kira turned and narrowed her eyes in the direction of that sound. A tuneless, useless sound.

The door from the garage to the kitchen opened. Harlow stepped through.

Best she could, Kira threw on a smile. Realized too late that she was modeling it after the one she recalled seeing on Zoe's face at breakfast this morning.

"Hey!" Harlow called. Kira braced for the familiar *thnk* of his briefcase hitting the floor, only to be surprised by the more sonorous *thud* of his little carry-on suitcase. She found this sonic swap distressing, somehow.

As he entered her orbit, he added a "woah!", monstrous with mock-amusement. Presumably upon seeing the half-empty…alright, three-quarters empty bottle of wine on the table beside Kira.

What, Kira tried desperately to recall, would be the normal thing to do here? Certainly not throw her head back and scream until she passed out, which was what she wanted to do. Oh, how she longed to lose consciousness, for just a moment.

Instead, she squinted and stretched her hands up over her head, smiling distantly as Harlow came and blessed her knuckles with a clumsy kiss.

"You eat already?" he asked. "I'm starving."

"I could eat," she lied. "How was the thing? The Press?"

"It was…I don't know," he sighed. "I'm glad I did it. I just don't know, you know…I just hope it makes a difference. Even a little one. But, hey!" She heard something crinkling behind her head, turned to see what it was just as Harlow encouraged her to "get a load of this." It was a loosely shrink-wrapped wicker basket full of expensive-looking chocolates, nuts, and booze in a bed of shredded newspaper.

Kira blinked hard, trying to make sense of the easiest of the thr…the…ugh, the bounty. "What's that?" she asked.

"Gift bag," Harlow explained. "You go on these big shows, I guess they give you a bag of stuff just for showing up." He relayed this not with delight, but with an almost courtly disapproval. "I looked it up, look, this tequila here? It costs four hundred dollars. Four hundred for the bottle! And they just give 'em away."

"Since when do you drink tequila?"

"I don't. I'm saying, it's crazy. They just give it away."

Kira rubbed her eyes and nodded. She could tell him a thing or two about crazy, and considered doing so. Yet the echoes of Uisch's not-so-words still made merry in her mind.

His grief does not sing.

There was absolutely no universe in which she could tell Harlow about Uisch, no *omniverse* in which Harlow would sit and listen to the terms of its dreadful largesse with anything less than mind-sealing mortification. She couldn't exactly fault him for this – left to explain things with either *a nine-foot-tall barnacle visited my wife and told her to kill some teenagers to get her dead daughter back* or *my wife broke,* he would be all but compelled to select the latter. Still, it depressed her to be so certain as to the limits of her husband's trust.

But hey, the man's grief didn't sing. No arguing with that.

All at once, and only just now, it occurred to Kira that they never went to Portland. They'd planned that weekend, and they'd rented that Airbnb, but they hadn't made it. That would have been weeks ago.

Considering that hypothetical life felt like getting a glimpse at a parallel timeline. At a version of herself that had always feared slipping into *this* world, yet never truly believed that she could. Not really, deep down.

But there was a way back. There was a way to put it all right. It wasn't easy, but it was simple.

It was also unacceptable. So drop it. Embrace the world as it is, miserable though it may be. Look forward, and nowhere else.

Kira shook herself free of that thinking, then smiled at Harlow's eminently comprehensible bottle of tequila, which wasn't anywhere close to crazy no matter how much it cost, then lied and said "yep, pretty crazy." So many lies, in such a short period of time. Then she asked him again how meeting the press had been. Not because she wanted more detail, as Harlow had clearly assumed, but because she'd already forgotten that she'd asked him. She was thinking about other things. She was trying so hard to *not* think about those things. But of course, that never worked.

Not bad, Harlow told her. Not bad.

THE FOLLOWING MORNING BELONGED to a truly mighty hangover – not being much of a drinker, Kira had no real constitution to fortify her against the aftermath. By a few hours into the afternoon, though, Kira felt she'd freed herself from the mental flypaper enough to put in a few billable hours. The first work she'd done in weeks. In truth, she didn't need the money, didn't want the money, didn't care about money anymore. Her life was over; what use did she have for cash? All she wanted was something to occupy her mind. Keep her looking straight ahead, nowhere else. Unfortunately, this latest

gig was a layup, something she picked up off Fiverr helping some old biddie set up an online store to sell her
needlepoint. It was such an easy job that her mind had
the freedom to wander while she did it.

At intervals throughout the work, she would suddenly
find herself in a new window in Chrome, set to incognito
mode. She would later question just how mindless her
little extracurricular here had been, seeing as she'd had
the presence of mind to ensure it wasn't recorded in her
search history. The questioning would be conducted
without urgency, though; it paled in importance to certain other questions.

In the instant she caught herself there, mid-pivot from
paid scutwork to personal gumshoeing, it would always
take her a moment to piece together what she was doing.

She was usually doing something quite first-base. Typ-
ing *Uisch* into a variety of search engines, with a battery
of follow-up words in turn. *Uisch monster. Uisch offer. Uisch
devil. Uisch creature. Uisch folklore. Uisch reddit.* As though
there were a million and one results she needed to
narrow down. As though she wasn't coming up dry every
time.

There was no record of Uisch, anywhere. Which
could mean a few things. Most obvious: that she had,
indeed, lost her mind. Of *course* there was no record of
Uisch – it existed only in Kira's head. What else could
explain the lack of documentation? Not even a half-mad
post on some no-account Cryptozoology forum. *Anybody
ever heard of this Uisch thing?* Nothing like that. She tried
punching the word into various translators, searching for

different variations on its name in every alphabet on Earth. Nothing. Not a single goddamned thing.

Yet even this, Kira took to be a kind of evidence. The reason no one had ever mentioned Uisch to the world was precisely the same as the one that kept Kira from saying anything to Harlow: she was afraid, somehow, that if she did, Uisch would rescind its offer.

This was what it did, she assumed. Almost certainly had been doing all across time. It made unbelievable offers to desperate people, and in return, asked for what?

I live to dance.

This thing wanted grief. Not needed; *wanted*. This wasn't sustenance, of that Kira was almost positive. There was no frenzy in its request, no hunger. Too much patience. Excitement, perhaps. Like it was waiting in line for concert tickets.

Kira couldn't fail to see how imbalanced the exchange was here. In making one family whole again, three others would be torn apart. Net gain of two, grief-wise. Incredible return on investment.

It made her head spin, to think of how much suffering in this world might have been at the behest of Uisch. How much heartache had been *commissioned* by that patron of torment and woe. Could its stony hand be seen in the acts of humanity's greatest monsters? In concentration camps and genocides? Kira didn't think so. She suspected that Uisch favored the smaller, more personal exchanges. Not to keep off the radar, out of the historical record. Those things couldn't possibly matter to it. She just had a sense that it enjoyed small-batch, artisanal anguish the most. Felt enriched, knowing that its gift came a real cost to the recipient. The sort of cost from which the architects of mass slaughter are, by the very scope of their evil, insulated.

Assumptions. So many assumptions, all based more on *feeling* than reason.

"Fuck," Kira whispered to herself. What was she doing? What was she hoping to clarify for herself here? Even were she to find Uisch's LinkedIn, fully up-to-date with all of its dreadful little compacts throughout the fullness of time, along with a detailed explanation of what drove it to strike these deals, what would she gain from that? Nothing. Except, of course, putting more distance between this current moment and the next one. This moment, after all, was one in which she was horrified by the creature's impossible offer. Just absolutely aghast at it, yes.

It was the *next* moment she was worried about. A moment in which she might find herself a bit burned out on being mortified, might start thinking about Uisch's ultimatum a bit differently. And if *that* moment came… she could only imagine what the *next* next moment might bring. And the one after that. And so on. Unto the end of her days.

Kira slammed her laptop shut and was astonished to discover that the room around her had vanished. Night had fallen during her search, swallowed her home whole; the screen had been bright enough to keep her from noticing. Even if she had, though, she didn't think she'd have gotten up to flip the light switch. It was all the way over there, and she was so tired.

So she sat in the dark and stared at the ghost of the laptop screen seared into her retinas. It hung there in front of her, refusing to fade. Staring back, perhaps. So she, too, refused to fade.

Some minutes later, she realized that the afterimage had melted back into the darkness. She hadn't noticed it go, though. Couldn't be sure how long she'd been just sitting here, alone, in the dark.

"OH," Harlow said, as though he'd been practicing it in the mirror.

Kira frowned. Oh yes, she could just tell he'd spent the twenty (largely silent) minutes of dinner thus far thinking about how to say whatever it was he was pretending to only just now think of saying.

He cleared his throat, and said "by the way." He leaned back in his chair, reached his left hand into his pocket, then scooted the whole seat back and leaned a bit to the side for a better angle on his pants.

Kira watched this performance patiently from across the table. Dreaded whatever Harlow was fishing out, knowing how deeply onerous it would prove to be (why else would he have so evidently struggled to broach the subject, after all). But hey, it'd be a bit of variety, at least. Compared to all the other meals they'd eaten together these last few weeks, this one (thus far) included. Silence, dressed in the soft clinking of silverware against plates, periodically disturbed by some go-nowhere conversational sally, almost always launched by Harlow.

I got a new filter for the humidifier.

Oh, that's great.

The grocery in town finally stocked back up on brown rice.

About time.

Do you know why the window by the front door is cracked?

No idea.

So, sure. Tedious as the slip of paper Harlow yanked from his pants was liable to be, at least it would be a brief break from this awful, impenetrable quietude.

As he looked down at the page and did his best to tug it taut, Kira realized that it was some kind of flyer. At once, she longed for the silence.

"I, uh…" Harlow licked his lips and cleared his throat again. "I was going to say that I just, you know, came across this. Out and about." He turned the page around and passed it across the table to Kira. "But that's not… true. I went looking for it."

Kira stared at the piece of paper for a moment, as though she might be able to wait Harlow out on this one. When he made no motion to withdraw it, she leaned forward and pinned it with her forefinger, dragging it across the table to her.

As soon as she did, Harlow hooked the first finger of his extended hand and dug the knuckle into his ear, wincing as he did. Weird tic. Not one she'd seen before.

Slowly, Kira looked from her husband, down to the sheet of paper.

It was a full-sheet flyer. Printed from a regular old

desktop printer, one that needed a new ink cartridge. The right side of the page boasted a stock photo of a sad silhouette slouching on a bench, atop a hill, at sunset. Above the image: the words *HOPE AFTER LOSS* in thick, italic, sans-serif font, made gradient from pale blue to wet-sand brown via Microsoft Word's Wordart feature. Ah yes, the sophisticate's answer to Comic Sans. Above those words: the logo for St. Philip's Episcopal. That eerie clapboard chapel at the west end of Neirmouth, the one that looked to be held together by nothing more than the blinding white paint slathered across its rot-hollowed planks.

Or maybe it was steel-reinforced, under all that driftwood. Kira didn't know. She'd never been inside. Neither had Harlow, she'd have thought. A valuable lesson in assumptions, this was.

"I know you don't love the, you know, group grief thing," Harlow explained hastily, "but…oh, and I talked to the guy, he said it's not, like, a *super* religious thing. They're gonna talk about God's special plan or whatever for a little bit, which, trust me, I don't want to hear either. But then the bulk of it is gonna be just talking. People who have gone through stuff like we have, talking about what they're going through. And we'll have the chance to do that too, to talk about what *we're* going through. And I think that might be good for us."

Kira studied the flyer for another moment, then looked to her husband. "It's, uh…yeah. I mean." She placed the page on the table beside her plate, with just as much care as she used to choose her words. To avoid saying the ones that came most readily to mind, at least. "Yeah."

Harlow watched Kira, waiting for a follow-up thought that never came. "You're not interested."

"I…my concern is just that…it feels like that's just gonna…" She lifted a clawed hand and spun it around in front of her, fingers pointing down towards the table, as though frantically cranking a gear shift, "…keep us *here,* I feel like. That doesn't seem like the way to…to go."

"I hear what you're saying. But it can be. It can be the best way forward. And to be honest…we're already *here.* It doesn't…" Harlow paused, staring at the ceiling, one flippered hand hanging in midair before him. As he resumed speaking, the hand hopped forward. "It doesn't feel to me like we're going anywhere right now anyway. So I don't think it would hurt to try. What do you think?"

Kira shook her head, sighed. Wished so desperately she could talk to him now. Honestly. But alas, his grief didn't sing.

Going to this little grief-off would be healthy for her, she knew. Would help her accept what had happened, which she *needed* to do. She needed to embrace things as they were, to let go of that other possibility. Because it *wasn't* a possibility. She couldn't do it.

But all the same, a small thought yodeled through her skull. Hard to tell exactly what it was saying, yet she knew *exactly* what it meant.

She was brought back from the precipice of the *next* by Harlow clearing his throat yet again, shifting in his seat, and mumbling "I saw what…happened, to Leigh's room."

That focused things up: Kira let the flyer lie and zeroed in on her husband. *Shit*. She'd forgotten to clean that up. Should have done so when she'd been staring at fucking Google.

"I thought we weren't going in there," she practically whispered. Which was, sure, probably not the *best* possible response.

For just an instant, Harlow looked actively frustrated. Then he softened, and said "uh…um, I mean, I don't remember us ever saying that specifically."

"Yeah, it's, uh," Kira sighed, "sorry. I don't mean like you should feel bad about going in. I just, you didn't tell me, so I just…" She cycled through explanations for the wreckage of their late daughter's bedroom. Needed to be something plausible, that also completely absolved her of responsibility. So, alright, *cycling* wasn't the right word for it. More like toggling between The I-Saw-A-Bug Contingency, and…the truth. Neither of which Harlow was likely to buy. So Kira concluded by shrugging and saying "I don't know."

"I don't think there's any wrong way to grieve," her husband replied, reaching across the table to gesture limply towards the flyer. "I just talked to Father…well, I should back up, I was…" he sighed. Fought a quiver of the lip. "I was crying a lot in my car, and so, I one time had pulled over near St. Philip's. Not intentionally, you know, just, that was where I was when it hit. The…" he repeated his loose-fisted gesturing, this time directed towards his own face.

"Yeah," Kira encouraged him.

"And I just wanted to talk to someone. S-"

"You could have called me."

Harlow made a soft, indecisive *hmm* noise. "I didn't know if I could. We still haven't really…talked. Really."

That hit Kira harder than she was ready for. Largely because it wasn't tendered as an attack. God, she'd left her husband alone in all of this.

"I'm so sorry," Kira said, feeling the words catch in her throat. "I've wanted to. I just h-"

"It's alr…oh, sorry."

"Oh."

"You can go."

"I was just saying…I, it's…I haven't been able to…I don't…you know, what do I say? I've really wanted to say something, but I don't have anything. I don't feel anything. Except…" her jaw trembled. "…I'm, *so angry.*"

"That's something."

"It doesn't make any fucking sense."

"It's a stage of grief. It's really common."

"*You* don't seem angry."

Harlow took a deep breath through his nose. "I'm sure I will be." He smiled softly. "I'm still on denial, I guess."

Kira said nothing. He seemed like he still had more to say. And so he did.

He scratched at the side of his head. "I still think of things I want to tell her. Not even anything important. Just something I'll see and, and, I'll think, I bet Leigh would think that's funny. I can't wait to tell her about it.

The way I always have. I mean, something like how I was going by the baseball diamond the other day, and I saw this kid, this *huge* kid, in the middle of the field, doing wrestling moves on this other little kid."

Kira smiled, making a sound dangerously close to a chuckle. "What?"

"This *huge* kid – they're just in the middle of the field, nobody else around – but he had this other smaller kid like this," Harlow held his arms out in front of him, elbows hooked, fists touching, "holding this other little kid under the knees, so he was bracing the kid's shins against his own chest, and he was just swinging this kid around and around and around. I think it was all for fun," he clarified quickly. "I think it was all good, they weren't really fighting. But it was just…so weird." Harlow's voice drifted off, as the mirth melted from his face. "And I saw that and I thought, I bet Leigh would think that's funny." His voice had more or less perfectly flattened out now, his eyelids quivering but not blinking, gaze fixed on a horizon visible only to him. His version of crying, Kira knew. Her husband never let himself cry. "I don't remember right away. I get to sit with that thought for about five or ten seconds, before I remember."

For a flash – the briefest of instants – Kira saw *rage* in his eyes. Something she'd never seen in him, ever.

Her small, yodeling thought got a little bigger. She could make out a word now: *try*.

No. Let it go. He would not entertain the offer, and Kira wasn't capable of following through on it anyway. So *let it go*. Accept. Leigh was dead. She could never come back. Just accept it, goddamnit!

Kira blinked slowly. Nodded. "I don't know how we do this, Harlow." She reached out and tapped the flyer. With its faded stock photo, its trite questions *("what does it mean to accept the hand we've been dealt?")*, its uncited bible verses. "If you think this will help with the, the *acceptance*…do you really think this will help?" She cleared her throat, dissolving the knot therein. "I need help with that. That's…" She concluded the thought with a shrug.

"I think it will," Harlow finally answered.

"…okay. Then I'll try it. I'm ready to try it."

Her husband looked ready to cry again. Not that he would, of course. Instead, he lunged forward, taking Kira's hand and squeezing it softly. "I'm so happy to hear that. I can't tell you how happy that makes me."

Kira forced a smile. Yes, it made her happy too. She was happy that Harlow was happy. She was happy that she might have just taken her first step towards making peace with the world as it now was.

More than anything, she was happy she no longer felt called to explain what had happened to Leigh's bedroom. Though she would have wagered that Harlow wasn't failing to follow-up because he'd forgotten.

An object lesson in consequence, that was. Don't make a mess you can't clean up. Or at least cover for convincingly.

ST. PHILIP'S WAS precisely as run-down as Kira remembered it, and just as well-painted to boot. Brilliant white boards frayed and decaying at the edges, stopping just a few inches short of the dull stained glass windows. The steeple of the building looked to be canted towards the south, though surely that was Kira's imagination. Still, it was an unnerving state in which to meet an edifice, the architectural equivalent of covering a pimple with full clown makeup. Not the sort of hovel one imagines entering to *diminish* grief.

Harlow locked the car, circled around the back, and met Kira. He took her hand in his and smiled. "Still good with this?"

"Oh, yeah," Kira nodded, letting out a whoopie cushion's-worth of air. "Of course." She squeezed his hand.

He returned the squeeze, and the two stepped across the gravel parking lot towards the church, together.

Inside wasn't a *whole* lot better: entrants were greeted not by the grandeur one might expect of a chapel, but by a long, low-ceilinged brick hallway. Tall, narrow windows cluttered the exterior wall, bravely rebuffing nearly all of the light seeking to breach the hold. In the gloom opposite, three corkboards hadn't fared nearly so well against the onslaught of flyers for fund drives, bake sales, can donations, contra dances, and a host of other church-friendly activities, most of which, it seemed, had already happened.

Save one that Kira couldn't help but notice. A vigil for the Firestarters Massacre. Scheduled for next week.

Red, reaching out from all those holes left by long-gone thumbtacks. A candlelight vigil. To what end?

Kira fought to roll back her rage. Everyone grieved in

different ways. Best to get her head around that *now,* before she went into that room. With other people, and their other ways.

Eventually the hall got tired of itself and yielded to a stuffy little antechamber, sandwiched between a water-stained drop ceiling above and a dull blue carpet below. This new room swung off to the left, not that it made much use of the space: just a few lumpy brown chairs against the wall, and the threat of another hallway across the way. In front of that was an easel with a sign reading *GRIEF GROUP*, and an arrow pointing down this second hall.

Suddenly the church's disrepair struck Kira not as sinister, but as sad. It was such a fine line, wasn't it?

They followed the arrow down the other dumpy little hall, around a corner, and into a square room with squeaky linoleum flooring and wall-mounted light fixtures radiating a mustardy-green, the color of food poisoning. Kira immediately felt ill. She wondered if perhaps this room wouldn't be like the catchy jingle in a commercial to something like Uisch, so thick was it with human agony.

But hark, what bounty over yonder: past the circle of folding chairs (and the grief-stricken sitting on them), against the far wall, Kira spied a cheap folding table with boxed coffee and a plastic bowl full of donut holes. In the swampy din of this place, they looked like colossal rabbit scat.

"I'm gonna be sick," Kira mumbled to Harlow, as some of the ten-or-so congregants in the room turned around to smile at the two new arrivals.

He squeezed her hand. "We're here. Let's give it a shot."

Kira strangled a whimper, set her jaw, and studied the people who'd turned to ogle at her. The guy in a button-up and suit jacket definitely seemed like the one leading the meeting – he just had that air about him. Oh, and he had a Bible in his lap. Not a great sign, as far as the churchiness of the evening went. Next to him was an empty seat, then an older gentleman, not old but old-*er,* mid-50's maybe, and then another empty seat, then a young woman about Leigh's age. Two middle-aged women next to the younger girl were in the middle of a whispered conversation, having the decency to not turn and stare at the late arrivals (or maybe, having their backs to Kira and Harlow as they did, they'd decided it wasn't worth the effort to turn). Not so for the two middle-aged gentlemen next to *them,* as the circle started to loop back around towards the pastor. They sat with arms folded and legs splayed, cranked stiffly to the side for a better peek at the newcomers. Next came another woman about Kira's age, then a kid who couldn't have been older than about twelve (oh, for them to be here in this group…Kira's heart broke for them), and then finally one arrived back at the man in the suit jacket, with the Bible in his lap.

Kira didn't recognize anyone here – but then, St. Philip's was on the boundary between Neirmouth and Graham's Landing, a slightly more populated township on the way to Pitney. More to the point, she wasn't looking at any of them too carefully. Couldn't quite bear to.

What they were going through was not what Kira was going through. For them, there was no way out. For Kira…

The man in the suit jacket waved solicitously in the Trecothiks' direction, his smile warm and genuine, yet stringy with dehydration. "Welcome," he beckoned, in a soft, soothing voice.

Perhaps it was the lack of a clear summons, but Harlow remained where he was. It fell to Kira to lead the way towards the circle, towing him gently along behind.

The man in the suit jacket mooned at their approach, then glanced around the circle. No pairs of open seats directly next to each other. So he turned to the older gentleman sat nearest him and suggested "if you wouldn't mind scooting over," then gestured to the empty seat between them.

The older gentleman grunted, then heaved himself up and swung himself over to the indicated seat.

There. Two chairs open, between the older gentleman and the young woman.

"Thank you," Harlow and Kira mumbled as they tracked around the outside of the circle, the former speeding up a bit to take the seat next to the older gentleman.

"Oh my God," the young woman next to Kira gasped as the latter took her seat, like a newcomer to Jurassic Park getting a glimpse of their very first dinosaur.

Kira sighed. She'd really thought the days of being recognized as *the bereaved mother* were over. Come to think of it, how odd to be identified as such in a group where attendance was, by its nature, self-identification.

None of that helped her fight that sickly feeling. So she simply ignored the girl.

"Well, welcome," the man in the suit repeated, patting the Bible in his lap absent-mindedly. "Just to make everyone feel comfortable, maybe we'll take another quick run around the circle with names. I'm Martin." He pointed to Harlow. "You're…sorry if this is wrong, I'm terrible with names, but you're *Harlow*, if I recall."

Harlow seemed ashamed of the fact, ducking his chin towards his chest. "That's right."

Kira nearly asked Martin how he knew her husband's name, before realizing there was no need. The day Harlow had pulled over and spotted St. Philip's he must have come inside. When he'd first shown Kira the flyer for this, he'd started and abandoned a mention of meeting a "Father." Must have been Martin.

Martin, who was staring at Kira. Not unkindly, it had to be said.

Slow realization: everybody around the circle was looking at her. "Oh," she mumbled, glancing to that older gentleman between Martin and Harlow. "Sorry. I thought we were going around the…"

"After you," the older gentleman croaked.

"Ok. Thanks. I'm Kira."

The girl about Leigh's age next to Kira made a delicate hitching noise, like a tulip with the hiccups.

A cold finger ran up Kira's spine. A girl about Leigh's age…

"Name's John," the older gentleman grunted. *"With*

an 'h'."

All eyes in the circle slid from John, across Harlow and Kira, to the girl sitting to Kira's left. The girl who was about Leigh's age. At the grief support group.

"I'm Nicole," she practically whispered.

Finally, Kira craned her neck to have a good look at the girl. Her shoulder-length brown hair. The dim freckles on her cheeks. The faint splash of hazel in her otherwise dark brown eyes, vibrating with emotion as she turned anxiously towards Kira.

Nicole. The name flashed neon once more in Kira's mind.

The girl smiled nervously at Kira.

Nicole Ligeti.

The easiest of the three.

"Fuck," Kira couldn't stop herself from muttering, as something precious in her mind cracked.

And through the fissure, a small voice whispered, *here's how you could do it.*

FIVE

NUTS

RID OF RED

KIRA SPENT THE REST of the meeting trying desperately to focus. Focus on the hollow religious platitudes, on the wrenching glimpses into what the living death of mourning looked like several years on (only Nicole and one other person, the woman about Kira's age, were here as a result of the Firestarters massacre), on the reflections and observations that she would probably have found useful, had she been able to keep her attention on them for longer than a few words at a time. Focus on the world as it was. Accept it. Let the rest go.

Easier said than done. So much easier. Because this was such a terrible world, the one in which Kira found herself. The present was unfathomable suffering, drowning without the release of death. Whereas that other world offered light. Hope. It didn't feel hypothetical. She could see it so clearly now. She had a window into it.

The eyes of Nicole Ligeti. Every time Kira looked into them, she saw Leigh. Staring back at her. *Begging* her. Save me, Mom. Please. Help me, Mom. Please. Bring me back, Mom. *Please.*

She could hear Leigh's voice from down the hall. When she was three and she'd had a bad dream. When she was five and she'd fallen off her chair. When she was nine and had experienced her first trial run of real heartbreak. All those times Leigh had come running, calling for Kira, calling for *Mommy,* because Mommy was the only one who could make her feel safe, make her feel like everything was okay, who could make everything *be* okay.

It was unthinkable, that she should ever have turned away from her daughter when she came running. Refused to pick her up, refused to wipe the tears from her cheek, refused to kiss her on the forehead and never let go, never let her go.

Yet that was what she was doing now. Nicole Ligeti was sitting right next to her. Right now. To look at Nicole and see her as anything other than a window into a different kind of life was to turn away from Leigh. To turn away from her beautiful baby girl when she needed her mother most.

Kira tried so hard to steer her thoughts away from that. Fix her attention on what was happening in front of her. See, and accept. Look at Nicole Ligeti and see Nicole Ligeti. Accept that she was alive, and Leigh was not, and that was simply what had happened. It was just so hard. It was impossible.

In those rare pockets of presence, Kira noticed that she was crying. Silent tears, sliding down her cheeks. No one said anything, though she was fairly certain they hadn't gone unnoticed. The tears.

How nice, to be in a space where you could cry without drawing comment. Kira could see how such a group could be useful, and healing. For other people.

She tried to listen. Tried, but failed. All she could hear was the voice from the dark of the fissure, whispering.

The moment Martin announced the end of the evening, Kira leaned towards her husband (and so, away from Nicole) and hissed "I want to go right now, please."

Harlow nodded sympathetically, and stood at once.

A few of the other attendees drifted off towards the, for lack of a better term, *catering* on the table at the other end of the room. Harlow, fortunately, gave Martin a brisk and manly handshake, thanked him, and then returned to Kira to make their escape.

"Thank you," she rasped.

He nodded, all business. "Yeah." Started heading for the hall through which they'd entered.

Revealing, just behind him, Nicole. Standing there. Waiting to talk to them.

Kira locked eyes with the girl. Could only imagine the face she made. Hadn't the spare brainpower to read into the expression Nicole was wearing.

Taking leave of her manners, Kira turned away from Nicole, fully turned her back to her. "Do you want to get something to eat?" she asked her husband as she took his hand. As if she could eat. All she wanted was to start another conversation that Nicole would be too timid to interrupt. She hoped.

"Sure," Harlow granted, as Kira took the lead and tugged him down the hall. "What are you thinking?"

"I don't know," Kira replied, all forward motion, steadfastly ignoring any humanoid shapes sweeping through the edges of her visual field. "Anything. What do you want?"

"Uh…I don't know." They passed through the hall, back into the blue-carpeted room.

"Okay," Kira mumbled, risking a glance over her shoulder. Nobody there, thank god. No windows onto other futures.

She slowed down a touch.

"Okay," she repeated, the intensity dialed back.

"Maybe something we could take home," Harlow suggested. "I think I'd rather be home than out right now."

It was only then that Kira noticed the wet on her husband's cheeks. He'd cried at some point during the meeting too. Had let himself cry. She hadn't noticed. "That sounds great," she agreed as they passed into the entry hall, doddering past the notice-choked corkboard. "Maybe just pizza? Something easy."

"Sure," Harlow agreed. He hustled forward a bit to open the door for Kira.

"Thanks," she mumbled. "Yeah. Pizza sounds like the move."

"Yeah."

As they left the church and crossed the unpaved parking lot, Kira listened desperately between the crunches of their every footfall in the gravel, listening for the door shutting behind them. She didn't want to turn around again, but wanted to know if they were being followed. If she di-

A satisfying *k-thnk*. The door to the chapel closing.

Kira sighed with something like relief. "Maybe when we get back, we can w-"

Th-k.

The door opening again. *Swinging* open, in fact.

Kira spun around to see the easiest of the thr…to see *Nicole,* running towards them.

"Fuck," she whispered again. Seemed the only word she could manage, when confronted with the window.

Harlow had no reaction to Nicole's hurried approach. Seemed halfway to catatonic, now that Kira really took a good look at him.

Oh, Jesus. She hadn't even considered how he was doing, after all of that sharing.

Forgetting Nicole for a moment, *accepting* the inevitability of her arrival, Kira unthreaded her hand from her husband's and placed it on his shoulder. "This was good," she assured him. "Coming here."

"Mhm," he nodded, fresh tears pooling in the corners of his eyes.

She was about to say something else, when Nicole shouted "Excuse me!"

Once again, Kira felt like she was going to be ill. It took everything she had just to lift her gaze to the girl; a smile remained out of reach.

No way to greet her, Kira knew that perfectly well. She felt rotten about not being able to be more polite. But maybe that was alright. Keeping Nicole at a distance was the safest thing. If even the easiest of the three proved difficult, that would be…safest.

At that thought, Kira felt a warm, welcoming smile tear her face in half. "Hello, Nicole."

"Hi," Nicole replied, clearly trying to disguise the process of catching her breath, and doing a pretty poor job of it. "I just wanted to say, your dau-"

"Oh my God," Harlow marveled, sounding somewhat breathless himself. "Wait. Nicole, right? Are you… aren't you one of the ones she saved?"

Nicole swallowed, panted once, and nodded. "Yeah. She saved us." The girl turned towards Kira. "And Zoe told me you were…I hope this is okay, but she told me you were having a really hard time with it. Which I, like, totally get. I totally get it."

Kira frowned at Nicole. *A really hard time.* What poetry.

"Ah," the easiest of the three continued, turning back towards Harlow, "so, I wasn't planning on saying anything. But then I saw you both here, so…" she scratched at the side of her head. "I'm sure everybody has said this to you, but if you need to talk, or, if you *want* to talk, I would also…well, I'm, I'm around." She made a face of extreme displeasure in the wake of that word choice, then recomposed herself with a more measured breath. First she'd managed since she'd sprinted out here. "Might be good." She blinked hard, and shrugged.

"Might be nice."

"Thank you for the offer," Kira replied, a bit too quickly, and *far* too coldly.

Nicole shrugged. "Yeah."

"We were just about to get some pizza," Harlow told Nicole, *for some fucking reason.*

"And take it home," Kira added, only realizing why she felt compelled to mention that once she'd finished speaking. Oh, she should have kept speaking.

"If you wanted to join us," her husband offered before Kira had a chance to shut him down, "we'd love to have you. I think it would be nice."

Kira was prepared to interject with something to the effect of *I thought you wanted to go home,* but then she heard an echo of what he'd just said in her head. The way his voice had trembled on that last sentence cut Kira to the bone. *I think it would be nice.* He was holding it together, but only just. Kira might not even have noticed how near he was to unraveling, had she not known him as well as she did.

So pizza pie commiseration was something Harlow needed right now. And it seemed to be something that Nicole needed right now. What did Kira need? A way out. A way to stop thinking these thoughts. A way to stop thinking about…well, not to stop thinking about Leigh entirely, as far as the future tense went. Just, a way to… accept.

So maybe this actually was for the best. Get to know Nicole better. Build a relationship with her, such that it became unconscionable to even *think* about harming her.

So Kira said "yes," and tried to find that smile again as she looked through Nicole, saw only Leigh. "If you're free, you should join us."

"Yeah!" Nicole erupted. "I mean, that would be so great."

Harlow smiled. "Do you have a ride, or do you need one?"

"Oh, man, um…if you wouldn't mind." She pulled out her phone and spoke to it. "My mom was gonna pick me up, but she's…I feel like from these texts she's maybe…you know, not able to drive. Right now."

Kira felt a flare of anger on Nicole's behalf. The elder Ligeti had been spared an agony beyond comprehension. And what did she do to honor the fact that *her* kid was fucking alive? Get drunk and forget to pick her up from her goddamned *grief club?*

This was who Leigh had died for?

No. This is how red gets in. Bleeds in from the edges, before swallowing up the whole. To make room for the moon.

No. No.

Kira forced a smile, tapping into the reservoirs of compassion she knew she possessed, somewhere in there. "That's okay. We can give you a ride."

"Cool. Thank you so much." Nicole looked back down at her phone, then up to the Trecothiks. "Is it cool if I invite Zoe and Maddie?"

Compassion slipped Kira's grasp. Too quickly for her to do anything about it.

She'd heard the names perfectly well, but her brain

translated them at once: *the other two.*

Nicole unlocked her phone, already tapping and swiping her way towards bringing the three of them together. All three, together. "Since they, I mean, they knew her better, they might…"

"Of course," Harlow allowed. "That'd be wonderful."

Kira's lips pinched together of their own accord. She could hear her skull groaning, crushed beneath the deepsea pressures closing in from all sides.

She was about to be in the presence of all three of them, at once. Zoe, Maddie, Nicole. At a pizza parlor. With a kitchen full of cutting instruments.

It was as clear as day in her mind. She could excuse herself for the restroom, make a detour into the kitchen, grab a knife from the block, go back to the table. Stand behind Nicole's chair. Cut her throat. Count on the shock to keep the others in their seats, while she did the same to whoever was next. At that point they'd probably get up, whoever was left, but Kira was confident she could finish the job. Do what needed to be done. She could have her baby girl back, tonight. An hour from now. If that. The opportunity had just presented itself.

Oh, god. She wasn't ready. She wasn't rea-

"Does that sound good to you?"

Kira flinched. Turned to Harlow, who had posed the question.

She tried desperately to welcome the invisible vise crushing her head. Finish the job, please. Make this stop.

"Kira?" Harlow pressed.

With a heroic outlay of strength, Kira pried her lips

apart and made them shape the words "sounds good to me."

KIRA DIDN'T SPEAK. She couldn't. Could only stare across the table at these three young women, a bay window onto a better life. Zoe, Maddie, Nicole. Sitting right there. *Right there.* It was maddening, truly crazy-making, to be so close, and yet…Kira knew she couldn't do it. Logistically, easy as could be, yes. But in all the ways that counted, Kira knew now that she didn't have it in her. Which struck her as a weakness. She ought to have been able to do anything for Leigh. Not being capable of murder was letting her daughter down. It was failing as a mother.

And then, there was another thought. A silly and self-ish one. That being: if I kill them all *here,* I'll go to prison. And then I'll barely ever see Leigh anyway.

This, too, was an idea that formed with thorns, shredding up the high-speed hotline from the head to the heart. Why should *that* matter, what happened to her? What mattered, *hypothetically*, was bringing Leigh back. That was it. If Kira wasn't prepared to do *whatever* it took to make that happen…

But she'd already established she wasn't. She couldn't do it. So why did she still feel this way? Like she'd swall-owed molten lead, like there were beetles scuttling just beneath her skin? She couldn't stop grinding her teeth. Slowly but at full force. Loud enough to drown out the conversation in front of her. Harlow, talking to the girls. Not realizing that they were just obstacles. Unbreakable glass. He had no idea what was on the other side. He couldn't understand.

Oh, she was exhausted. She could have collapsed right then and there. It took such energy, playing Whac-A-Mole with a seemingly endless procession of homicidal thoughts, with heart-hollowing guilt. She wanted to collapse. She wanted it to happen. Please. Please.

Suddenly, the worst thing possible happened: someone put a big pepperoni pizza down in front of Kira.

She stood up without saying anything, and rushed to the bathroom. She made it, but only just. At long last, a purge. It hurt. It clarified nothing.

Kira tore some toilet paper off the roll to wipe her mouth, got up and headed to the sink, and ran the tap into an open palm. She threw that water back, swishing it around in her mouth. Pausing when she got a look at herself in the mirror.

She looked fine. Perfectly normal. Bit baggy under the eyes, maybe, but considering she hadn't bothered with makeup, and more to the point barely slept anymore, that was to be expected. Aside from that…she looked fine.

Certainly didn't look like someone whose entire insides felt like they were fermenting, whose assorted cortices were arm-wrestling each other to the death.

In an odd way, a very odd way…the placidity of her appearance seemed to clarify something for Kira. Something. Unknowable epiphany, by way of pepperoni pizza.

Bracing as though to lift a small truck, Kira forced a smile.

In the mirror, it looked so normal. Totally fine. Were

it not for those bags under the eyes, the way they made basins to store all the day's tears…you'd never know. To look at her, you'd never know.

Even as the smile faded, you'd never know how much Kira's own composure terrified her. How much like launching oneself off a mountain it was, to stop thinking *I couldn't possibly do it,* and to start thinking…*I wonder if I* could *do it?*

And wouldn't you know it, she had still more to give. She returned to the stall, and knelt before the throne.

ON HER WAY BACK to the table, Kira made a point of not peeling off to peek in the kitchen. It seemed safer that way. For someone who couldn't be entirely certain of their limitations anymore.

As she returned to the table, she could see concern on everyone's faces. Harlow, and the three young women with their guard down. Lucky them, the cutlery supplied by Big Skinny's Pizzeria was barely sharp enough to split a pie without dragging the cheese off. Surely not up to the task of human flesh. But it wouldn't be impossible to get the jump on those three, surely. And if she could manage that, she could have Leigh b-

WHACK. Another murderous mole, whacked back into its hole.

Kira put on a smile, like she'd practiced in the mirror, and she watched their concern multiply. Oh, wait. Too big. She dialed it back a bit, and made a sad shape with her eyebrows. Their concern melted into compassion. That was more like it.

"Sorry," she said, retaking her seat next to Harlow.

Before she could commit to any of the innumerable excuses zooming around her head, Harlow reached out and took her hand, and said "it's alright."

She returned the gentle squeeze he gave her, then noticed how easily their hands slipped apart. Pizza grease. A glance around the table confirmed her suspicion; they'd all started without her.

For some reason, Kira found this hilarious. Absolutely hilarious. Despite their unthinkable anguish, they were all still hungry for pepperoni pizza.

As funny as she found it, though, to look at her... you'd never know.

WHACK.

Kira flinched. Only noticing a sinister ideation bubbling to the surface in the moment it was cast back into the mire.

That, her dinnermates seemed to notice. Maddie, at least, looked at her slightly askance.

So, as Kira reached across the table to claim a slice of pizza for her plate, she returned Maddie's gaze and said "I think this is the first time we've actually spoken in a while, huh?"

Maddie smiled bashfully at that, scratching nervously at the tip of her nose with a finger no doubt slick with dinner. "Yeah. Sorry."

"Oh, no, I don't mean it like that." Kira stared at the slice of the pie she held aloft in front of her face, as though watching the heat peel off of it, even though it was cold. "You've just grown a lot, so fast. I couldn't really tell when I was just seeing you from the car. Any-way," she added, eyes drifting towards the table, "I was usually saying something to Leigh. I always felt like I had to. You're dropping your daughter off, you feel like you have to say something. Even if it's just *have fun.*" She shrugged, took a bite of her pizza, then boggled her eyes out and made *HAFHAFHAF* noises.

"It's still hot," Harlow informed her.

Now it was her husband who Kira wanted to murder. *"HAFHAFHAF,"* she grumbled, only just now noticing that everyone had slices on their plates, but no bites had been taken yet. Still too hot. How was that possible? She must not have been in the bathroom for as long as she'd thought.

Kira didn't care for that at all. Feeling lost in time like that.

"Ahf," Kira managed, as she gulped down the just-barely-chewed bite. "Oh, fuck." She chuckled joylessly. "Pretty sure I'm not gonna taste any of the rest of this."

"They bring it out *really* hot here," Nicole informed everyone.

"Yeah," Kira confirmed.

Zoe brought her slice – just plain cheese for her, must have picked off all the pepperoni – back up towards her mouth, and blew on it.

Maddie took up her first slice and ventured a careful little nibble.

Nicole, too, finally started in on her slice. Only after the other two young women already had, Kira couldn't help but notice.

Harlow surveyed the scene with the distant satisfaction of a man who had resolved that he would cry when he got home, but not now. Only after another nod or three did he fall to his meal.

Kira cleared her throat, eyeing her slice warily. Once bitten…

Harlow chewed his bite and put his slice down.

Nicole used both hands to gnaw on the end of her slice, like a woodland critter.

Maddie nodded as she chewed, finally mumbling "good" to everyone and no one.

Zoe huffed on her slice once more, then, satisfied that it was cool enough, took a bite. She ferried it to her face with a strange delicacy…but ah, of course, she was still getting used to life with only seven fingers.

It seemed to Kira that somebody really ought to say something. Ideally somebody who wasn't Kira. Because she had no fucking idea what to say.

Harlow to the rescue: "So," he said, "are you three looking at…" He sniffed, his voice going syrupy with emotion. "At uh, at…*hoo,* at colleges?"

The three girls just stared at their slices now. Ashamed, perhaps. Or just not up to staring their dead friend's father in the face, as he fought back tears.

Kira, for her part, was just as near to tears as Harlow was. For all the anger she felt, the omnidirectional *rage,* there was still room for other emotions. And the sight of her husband – her best friend, truly – in such a vulnerable state rolled her with profound, impotent heartache. Which in turn spun her back towards anger, at herself now, because the impotence of that emotion remained a *choice*. It didn't have to be this way. All that stood in the way w-

WHACK.

"Never too early to think about college," Kira agreed, "if that's what you think you want to do."

"I want to go to college," Nicole whimpered.

Kira blinked hard. Wished she hadn't learned that. Everything she learned about these kids made their dispatch feel less and less abstract. Brought th-

WHACK.

"That's good," Kira said. "Do you know what you want to do?"

Nicole shrugged. "I don't know. Something with the National Parks, maybe. I really like nature."

"You could do music, too," Zoe suggested.

Harlow wiped his nose with his sleeve. "Oh," he said, "do you play an instrument?"

"I play the flute," Nicole confessed. "Just as a hobby, though. It's not professional."

"Mhm," Harlow replied.

Nicole looked to Zoe and Maddie. "What about you two?"

Zoe took a deep breath. "I don't know."

"Really?" Nicole and Maddie asked in unison.

"Yeah."

Zoe shrugged. "I don't know if college is for me."

Maddie shook her head, somewhere between astonished and affronted. "But your grades are so good!"

"It's a lot of debt."

"That's true," Nicole allowed.

"But your grades," Maddie reiterated with long vowels, as though falling from a great height.

This time, a shrug *and* a sigh from Zoe. "Unless it's full-ride, which is almost impossible to get…I just don't know if I want to commit to that debt."

"Don't worry about that," Harlow announced. "We can help."

Regardless of where everyone was in the pizza-eating process, all slices returned to their plates, as all eyes hurried to Harlow.

"What?" Zoe asked.

"Yeah," Kira added, *"what?"*

Harlow looked towards, but not quite *at*, his wife. Realizing his mistake, clearly…but not backing down. "We had gotten lucky with…well, investment stuff, but we were able to put away money for…*boo,* for Leigh to go to school."

Kira reached under the table and put her hand on Harlow's knee.

Either he misinterpreted what she'd meant to be a *halting* touch, or else he was ignoring it.

"It's just sitting there," he continued. "We're not going to use it for what it was meant for. And," he went on, turning towards Zoe, "we know how close you and she were." To the other two, he added, "I'm sure we could contribute some to *all* of you. Enough to help."

"Do you mean that?" Nicole marveled, her voice a whisper.

"We'll talk about it first," Kira snapped.

"It's just sitting there," Harlow repeated, without meeting her eye.

"We'll *talk about it first.*"

Glancing quickly from one Trecothik to the other, Maddie mediated by saying "of course, you two would have to talk about it first."

Nicole just kept grinning at her pizza. "Wow!"

"Either way," an audibly disappointed Zoe granted, "it's a very nice offer."

"We'll talk about it," Harlow reassured the girls, gesturing to Kira.

That marked the end of Kira's pizza-borne peace of mind. The remainder of the dinner was spent *WHACKing* vainly at the red thoughts, as they poured in from all sides to bury her alive.

THE PLAN HAD BEEN TO WAIT until they got home, but Kira felt herself boiling over the moment they got into the car. Thank god Zoe had her parent's car, and whatever license was required to drive without an adult present (Leigh hadn't had the chance to get that): she was able to take the other two girls home. Lucky them; Kira was mad enough to have brained them all right then and there. Starting with Harlow, for good measure.

Kira hadn't even closed her door before she turned to her husband and wondered, in quite a reasonable tone, "the fuck was that?"

Harlow just blinked quickly at her. "What?"

"Offering to pay for them to go to college? What are you doing?" The tone had become unreasonable.

"It would be a nice thing to do."

"Lots of things would be nice things to do. Selling everything we own and giving the money to a food bank would be a nice thing to do! Setting up a booth in front of the bank and helping everybody file their taxes would be a nice thing to do! Lots of things would be nice! But we can't do all nice things all the time!"

"But this one isn't going to cost us anything!"

"It literally is!"

"No," Harlow shifted in the driver's seat to better face Kira, "look, we already put the money away. We were planning on spending it on…on Leigh, but, obviously… we weren't planning on using it for ourselves. It comes out to the same thing. That's what I mean."

Kira flapped her mouth at that for a bit, then crossed her arms and turned to look out the window. Struggling mightily not to say the thing she wanted so desperately to say. The thing about how Leigh might need that money someday. Might need it a whole hell of a lot more than any of those three girls.

Yet each time the words formed in her mind, they were *WHACKED* apart by the voice of collapse.

His grief does not sing.

"See what I mean?" Harlow pressed.

Kira shook her head. "You can't just…decide to give our money away without talking to me." She turned back to her husband. "That's fucked up, Harlow. I get that you wanted to do a nice thing for them, but that's fucked up."

Harlow deflated. "I'm sorry. You're right. I just got caught up, I guess. I…feel like we're kind of…well, I just want to make sure they have a good future."

"We're not responsible for them."

"I guess I get that…but there are cultures where, if you save somebody's life, you're responsible for th-"

"Leigh saved their lives. And I think that responsibility ends at death, don't you?"

Harlow flinched. Physically recoiled as he finally met Kira's gaze.

"The only reason they *have* a future," Kira pressed, "is because our daughter is dead."

"Don't say it like that."

"How else should I say it?"

"Just don't…you're saying it so…just please don't be so rough about it!"

Kira pressed on: "we don't owe them *anything*. Honestly…" Rather than finish the thought, Kira simply gestured from herself, to Harlow, towards the pizzeria, back to Harlow, back to herself.

"I just see it differently. I f-"

"Yeah, I know y-"

"Let me finish, please."

Kira waved at him, somehow both permissively *and* dismissively.

"The way I see it," Harlow grumbled, "Leigh…" his voice hitched. "She died to *give* those girls a future. I wanted to do it for her as much as them. To honor her sacrifice." He took a deep, trembling breath. "I thought we could do it for Leigh."

The more Kira tried to work out how to steer this conversation, the more she began to confront a host of concerns she really ought to have engaged with sooner. Logistical concerns. The standard logistical concerns one has, when trying to explain the resurrection of a dead girl to a world rightly wary of miracles.

Ah, fuck. Maybe Harlow's grief *didn't* sing, but, well…she'd have to get him on board eventually. When Leigh came back, he would have no choice. None of them would. So it was only a matter of time.

So, as long as she was careful, it might not hurt to try. Now.

She turned once more to look at her husband, still staring expectantly at her.

"Have you ever asked yourself," Kira ventured, doing her best to blast the words out of her face before good sense had the chance to run interference, "what you would do to bring Leigh back?"

Harlow used his whole hand to knead his face like bread dough. "Kira."

She said nothing. Waited for a proper response.

Eventually, he lowered his hand to look at her once more. "There's no upside to thinking like that. It's j-"

"That makes it sound like you have."

"Have what?"

"Thought like that. Asked yourself what you would do t-"

"No. I haven't. Because…there's no point."

"Well…" Discretion caught up and hid all of Kira's words away. She had no words. "Ugh." She rubbed her palms nervously across her neck.

"This is just part of the way we process grief. It's

bargaining. I *know* it's so hard to accept. Trust me, I'm stru-"

"But just…" Kira kept one hand on her neck, using the other to pump a soft fist in the air in front of her. "…listen, just…what if…I'm trying to think of how to… okay, what if, hypothetically, th-"

"Thinking in these hypotheticals is only ma-"

"Shut up."

Harlow did as asked, doing a predictably poor job of disguising his hurt.

"I'm sorry," Kira added immediately. "Just…I wanna finish. I let you finish speaking, so, I wanna finish speaking now."

Her husband offered a single, slow nod of assent.

"Right…" she took a deep breath. "Okay." Now both hands waved through the air in front of her, pointer fingers protruding from her fists. *"Hypothetically.* And just… eh…you know, *imagine* that this is, that what I'm saying could happen. Okay?"

Another wary nod.

"Okay. *Hypothetically*…what would…ah, how do I phrase this? What…" she snapped with delight at a bright idea, and immediately regretted doing so. "Oh, uh, what *wouldn't* you be willing to do to bring Leigh back, if you could?"

Her husband stared blankly at her, hands resting in his lap, legs splayed awkwardly so as to avoid resting his feet on the pedals. Groaning slightly, he turned to look out the front windshield, tugging absent-mindedly at the seatbelt across his chest. Always the very first thing

Harlow did, upon getting into a car, was put on his seatbelt. Her sweet, cautious husband.

Overly cautious, if it came right down to it.

Harlow folded his arms across his chest and delivered his answer: "I don't see what this has to do with the college money."

"Just, please…play along."

"Play along," he repeated, with startling contempt. "None of this is a game to me, Kira."

"Me neither. That was a bad choice of words. But, come on, ju-"

"I don't know. I don't know. Horrible things, maybe?"

Kira brightened. "You would do horrible things?"

"No, I *wouldn't* do."

"Oh, right. That's right."

"You asked what *wouldn't* I do."

"Yeah, I know."

"There." He flopped his arms up into the air and back down to his lap, knocking the steering wheel with one of his knuckles as they fell. "Ouch," he huffed under his breath. "There's the answer. I wouldn't do horrible things to bring her back. It wouldn't be worth it."

"Wouldn't be *worth it?*" Kira grunted, squaring her shoulders towards Harlow. "What does that mean? Wouldn't be worth it for *Leigh* to *live* again?!"

Harlow shook his head, the incredulous crunch of his brow casting shadows across itself, in the sickly orange of the parking lot lights. "What is this conversation? What the fuck are we talking about here?"

"We…ah…*you*…guh," Kira added as she auditioned responses in her mind that *didn't* make her sound like she'd fully lost the thread.

"I'm worried about you, Kira."

"I'm…oh my *god,"* she croaked in frustration. She felt her chest tightening. Red crawling in from all sides. Saying what needed to be said would have been so *simple.* Uisch, and its offer. Speak of them and be done.

The problem, of course, was that those things couldn't be taken back, once said. And Harlow wasn't liable to believe a word of them. Why would he? He'd have to be crazy himself to accept Uisch without seeing it. Without hearing Leigh's voice, from the far side of a closed door.

There was no way, she suddenly realized, to convince Harlow of the truth of what she was saying. Because he hadn't seen. He hadn't heard. So she would *never* get him on board with harming the three girls they'd just shared such a lovely pizza din…well, it had actually been a pretty glum affair all told, but they'd shared a pizza dinner nonetheless. Not that the sharing of the pizza dinner was what would have ultimately brought Harlow down against the rock demon's horrible *quid pro quo* (or *quid quid quid pro quo,* as the case may be). He just wasn't the type of man to make the difficult choices. The impossible choices.

The wrong choices, perhaps.

No, Harlow would be of no help. And it was only in feeling a hollow, trembling dread roar through, that Kira realized her subconscious had been having its own little conversation without her, as was its wont. A conversation about *woulds,* and *wouldn'ts.*

Which only brought a second, altogether different tsunami of terror down on her.

Kira offered one final sigh, then slumped down in her seat, scrunching her chin to her chest. "I'm sorry. I'm not making sense. Not thinking clearly. It's just so hard to accept."

Harlow didn't say anything.

Kira glanced over at her husband.

He was mugging at her, one hand on the wheel. No, not mugging. *Studying.*

She couldn't help it – she narrowed her eyes at him.

Harlow's glare darted away – reflex – then back to her. He licked his lips, shrugged, and, *finally,* turned the key. "It's okay," he practically whispered as he cranked the car into reverse and looked down at the little backup camera screen. "It's a hard time."

"It's only gonna get harder," Kira mumbled in reply. Hadn't meant to say that bit out loud. Fortunately Harlow deemed it unworthy of comment.

Apparently nothing else Kira said that evening was worthy of comment either.

KIRA MADE A LIST. That felt somehow the most sinister step yet, so cold and calculating, but it had to be done. She wasn't the sort of person who could retain reams of information in her meat memory; hers was a world of off-loading. And why not? She was never far from a computer, be it one for her lap or her pocket, and technological recall could sometimes prove more nimble and precise than her biological hardware at its best.

The best place to make said list would have been on a piece of paper, but the chances that Harlow might find it were too great. For in the two days since their conversation in the pizzeria parking lot, he'd grown suspicious, lobbing quite a few puzzled, piercing gazes her way. Always with the piercing gazes! Whether he was stalking into the room looking for his water glass (so he said), or whether they were sprawled out on the couch watching a movie, he would try to sneak in a gaze or two whenever he imagined Kira wasn't looking. She'd seen them all, though. Well, she couldn't say that. She didn't know how many she hadn't seen, by virtue of having not seen them. But she'd seen all of the ones she'd seen. Um.

Anyway. The list. No, the *looks*. As of that morning, Harlow had mostly quit it with the piercing gazes, but it was safe to assume the suspicions that had motivated them remained. Suspicions not that she was drumming up a pro/con list for murdering three teenaged girls, no, of course not. Such suspicions would be entirely unfounded. No cause for them to even occur. His concern, instead, was surely just that grief had shattered his wife. That she was wholly out of her gourd. This was not a suspicion that Kira imagined she would be allaying for him in the near future; her behavior was only going to become more perplexing as time went on. As she debated the deed, and perhaps drew nearer to the time of its doing, to say nothing of the *having done it*. Which was to say: when Leigh was back. Which, again, would be pretty fucking hard to square with Harlow.

Ok, so throw that onto the list. The list she didn't want to make on a piece of paper, nor on a spreadsheet (which would have been especially convenient from a formatting perspective, but she didn't like the idea of it existing in *the cloud*).

So, she opened a note on her phone (having set the device to airplane mode), sat at the kitchen table, and started thumbing out some preliminary thoughts.

The first word she wrote: *hurry*. Because the fundamental problem of bringing Leigh back from the dead was more dramatic than simply pitching a just-so story to Harlow. Namely: how could she sell this resurrection to the world at large? Granted, there was no footage of Leigh being shot, of the sort that some of the other parents had been forced to endure prior to the newest cinematic tragedy for the news cycle to make into a maypole. The funeral had been a closed-casket affair, too; Leigh's body had been too mangled to display. A bit of daylight there, perhaps, to argue that the body in the box hadn't been Leigh's at all? The birthmark on the ankle used to identify said body was compelling, certainly. It wasn't impossible, Kira supposed, that there might have been two similarly-branded ankles on Knot Hedge that day. It also wasn't impossible that there might have been a mix-up with the teeth or the fingerprints or whatever else they'd used. Maybe that was enough plausible deniability to say...what, Leigh had just been misplaced? Oops, lost in the shuffle for a few weeks there, but we've found her now, very much alive and just as confused as the rest of us.

If that had the least hope of flying, Kira needed to get a running start at it sooner rather than later. The longer she waited to bring Leigh back into the world, the more difficult it would be to account for her absence.

So, begin.

As she set up a *PRO* section and a *CON* section, struggling to thumb the cursor up and down on the stupid iPhone screen as she had a new idea for one section or the other. All the while, she tried to keep the real fundamental questions in mind. Well, it was a single question, posed in two different tones of voice.

That being: how could she do this?

First, how could she *do* this? How could she live with herself, how could she ever look her daughter in the eye, knowing what she'd done to make such a sight possible?

Second…*how* could she do this? How could she kill three young women, with all the space-age shit forensics departments could pull off nowadays, with all the cameras covering every inch of American life, and get away with it?

"Are you playing that game?" Harlow asked as he drifted into the kitchen and filled a plastic baggie with nut mix to stuff into his briefcase.

Kira looked up from her phone, stared silently for several seconds, then realized that she really ought to have just smiled and said *yes* rather than boggling blankly at Harlow, but there was no sense dwelling on what couldn't be undone. "Sorry," she finally replied. "No, I'm, um, I'm writing an email."

"Oh." Harlow swung his briefcase up onto the counter, but hesitated with his hands on the latches.

Go on, Kira caught herself seething. *Ask me who to.* She was ready and raring to go with a righteously indignant dress-down, along the lines of it being a friend he'd never met, and anyway, what's the big idea nosing into her business?

Alas, Harlow said nothing. He clicked open his valise, inserted the baggie of nut mix, closed the briefcase, and slid it off of the counter. "Well," he said, "have a good day today."

"You too."

"Love you."

"Love you…too."

And then Harlow was gone. Out the door from the kitchen to the garage.

Kira stared at that door as she heard Harlow start up his car, open the garage door *(chunga-CRUUUUH)*, back out, and close the garage door behind him *(chunga-CRU-UUUH)*. Then she kept on staring, her phone seeming to grow heavier in her hand by the second.

She loved her husband. He loved her.

Why had their saying as much landed not as a reaffirmation, but a reminder?

She glanced down at the list she'd plonked out while thinking of other things:

PRO:
get leigh back

CON:
have to murder three people
hard to explain how leigh is back
you will be a murderer
prison?
further tear apart community
harlow will not get it

That was as far as she'd gotten. Staring at the list only strengthened those thoughts milling about in the more civilized (and ever-diminishing) environs of her mind, as madness gentrified the rest; it was insane that she was still considering this. That she'd gone some way beyond mere consideration. Just look at it. One point in favor. Six against. Yet still, she considered..

Because, she reminded herself as she stared down at the list, *not all of these points carry equal weight.*

From behind her: a *shhw* and a *thump.*

Kira whipped around. Scanned the room to see what had fallen. What had spoken to her.

She saw nothing out of place. Nothing capsized on the counter, nothing face-down on the floor. Something inside the walls shifting, perhaps.

Patient in a way she'd only recently learned to be, Kira waited for the sound of the *shhw* and the *thump* to coalesce into meaning. Waited. Waited.

Waited.

Finally: *how.* That was what the sliding sound had said. Posing her own twice-over question to her. How could she do it? Yes, that was what her home had wondered. How could she do it. Join the club, home.

The *thump,* meanwhile, had simply been a *thump.*

MAKING A LIST helped to systematize her thinking. Daffy as all of this was, yes, quite insane, all of that…she needed to fit it into the rational scaffolding she would have used to make any decision. If this was going to work – if it could *ever* work – she needed to proceed with forethought and caution.

None of that helped assuage the sickness that had settled over her. The sheer dissonance of the enterprise. Knowing full well that what she was contemplating was an act of evil. Knowing her contemplation came from a place of true love. Oh, Kira had never been so happy that Harlow didn't work from home; she spent most of that day dry-heaving over the various trash cans scattered about the house.

With great effort, she strung together enough lucid moments to formulate a plan. That being: she needed to answer one of those two questions that her home had asked her. The how. Starting with the first one: how could she *do* this? Because if the answer turned out to be *she couldn't,* if it turned out she was just constitutionally incapable of harming another human being, regardless of what stood to be gained…well, that would simplify things tremendously. What a relief it would be, to simply drop all of this. Free her up to fully embrace the world as it was.

So spoke a perfectly rational mind. Complication came quickly, in the form of emotion. Of panic, of terror. How, exactly, was she supposed to prove to herself whether or not she would be capable of killing a human being?

In a way, she took her anxiety to be a good sign. The more she thought about it, the more certain she became that she *wouldn't* be capable of killing someone. A persuasive thought, that was, right up until Leigh's face reappeared behind Kira's closed eyelids. Shortly thereafter would come the word: *anything. Anything. Anything.*

The rational mind was eager to compromise. Start smaller, it suggested. Nobody learns to drive on the highway. Engage with the principle, but reduce it to its fundamentals.

See if you're capable of killing something *other* than a human being.

The thought became a resolution. Thusly resolved, Kira felt something like peace. That peace brought its own kind of anguish, harder to grasp yet no less harrowing.

Tonight. She would do it tonight. She would go out, and she would try to kill something. Just to prove to herself that she couldn't do it. Wasn't capable. Just to put her mind at ease. But what would she proof this out on? A squirrel, if she could catch one. A rabbit. Maybe someone's dog. No, not a dog. She definitely wouldn't be able to kill a dog. But then, wouldn't that be the best test? The hard case? Far too belatedly, it occurred to her that *human* really ought to have been the hard case.

She decided on a squirrel. The ones in the park were bold during the day. Came right up to you, in fact. As long as they were awake at night, she was confident she could lure one over with some food.

Tonight, she would go to the park, and try to kill a squirrel. Tonight. She would do it.

Oh, god. It wasn't just an idea anymore. It was a plan.

A few minutes before Harlow was due home, Kira checked herself in the mirror, just to be sure. Confirming that, to look at her, you'd never know. Was that the face of a woman determined to sneak out of her own house in the middle of the night and murder a squirrel? Wouldn't say so. That was just a normal woman's face there, with a soft smile and wet cheeks.

Dinner with Harlow was a blur. Hard to think of the food as anything other than something to sick up later. There was a conversation over the meal. What did they talk about? Kira couldn't be sure. She could hear in Harlow's voice that he was still a bit on-edge after their conversation in the car. Oh, that had been so stupid. She shouldn't have said anything. She'd accomplished nothing, other than putting him on-edge.

Uisch had tried to warn her. Should have listened.

Kira managed to get through dinner without any sort of disagreement breaking out. Phew. She didn't want Harlow turning an argument over in his head tonight. Didn't want him having a hard time getting to sleep. She couldn't sneak out to kill a squirrel, if he didn't get to sleep.

Couldn't sneak out to *attempt* to kill a squirrel, that was. Just to prove to herself she couldn't do it. Couldn't take a life. Any life.

But, came the whisper through the fissure, *what if you*

can?

No. Impossible. So put it out of your mind. Put it out of your mind as you sit on the couch next to Harlow and pretend to watch whatever is on the TV screen. Put it out of your mind as you get dressed for bed, as you go through the whole routine, as you put in your mouth-guard and say *goodnight* and lay your head on the pillow. Put it out of your mind as you listen to his breathing, waiting for it to get slow, heavy. As you wonder, *what if he's faking it?* Because he might be. He might have looked at you and known. Seen the face of a woman who was going to sneak out of her house tonight and kill a squirrel. Might have seen more than that.

He didn't sound like he was faking it. He sounded asleep.

Slowly, Kira rolled herself over to look at him. He looked asleep, too. She pushed herself halfway to upright for a better look. He really seemed like he was asleep.

So she got out of bed. Gentle as could be. Patient. Not rushing anything. Glancing over her shoulder at him all the while. Still sleeping. On his side. Facing her, of course. And if he woke up? Oh, sorry dear, just heading to the bathroom.

Locked and loaded with the lie, but no need for it; Harlow didn't wake up.

Kira snuck down the stairs, descending on tiptoes like it was Christmas Eve, feeling appropriately torn up by something that was not excitement, no, but nor was it a million miles away from that.

Moving quietly through the kitchen, lifting drawers

slightly to keep them from groaning in their runners, closing them first against the meat of her thumb to guarantee against any audible *thumps,* Kira fetched a little plastic baggie and filled it with something she thought a squirrel might like: some of Harlow's nut mix, which he took to work every day. A pang of guilt, at making him an unknowing accomplice. Oh, guilt already! She was torn between the delight at yet another indication that she wouldn't be able to do this, and disappointment at the same.

Before leaving the kitchen, she took one of the big knives from the faux-mahogany block on the counter. The knife she particularly favored for slicing onions and sweet potatoes. A knife that had been, as far as she knew, thus far wholly bloodless. Hadn't touched so much as a chicken breast.

At this, too, she felt herself washed in a useless broth of shame.

Treading slowly, carefully to the mudroom, she threw an unseasonably heavy coat across her shoulders, stuffed the knife into the right pocket, reached for the knob to the door which led onto the slab of concrete they called a back porch, unlocked it, and

"Guh!" Kira jerked, knob cranked in her hand.

The home security system. If she'd opened this door even an inch, the alarm would have gone off.

Poor planning. Overlooking the most obvious obstacles. Yet more indications that she wasn't cut out for this. Any of this.

Still, she snuck over to the little wall-mounted panel

by the door to the garage and deactivated the alarm, wincing bodily at the full-throated *BEEP! BEEP! BEEP!* that accompanied each touch of the buttons. Most absurdly, she caught herself in the act of priming the delayed reactivation they always used to arm it when they were leaving the house. Stupid. Were she not locked in this lonely, deathless midnight, she might well have laughed at her abject idiocy.

She paused once again at the back door. Trying to focus her thoughts, trying to think about anything else. Settling at least on the certainty. The knowledge. She could not do this. She could not kill a living thing. She would know this, and it would set her free.

She opened the door, and stepped out, and left the alternative behind. Because she truly didn't know what she would do, if it emerged that she *could* do this.

THE QUICKEST WAY TO THE PARK was to cut through Richie Bettington's yard. It was probably alright. Richie was probably asleep. And if he should somehow recognize that someone had – say it ain't so – cut through his yard in the night, he would no doubt assume it was one of those troublemaking neighborhood kids with their bikes. The sort of riff raff the home alarm systems were meant to keep out.

So Kira cut across Richie's yard, and then she followed a star that she could not see, even on this deep dark night. But she could feel it. Felt pulled towards it, compelled by it. So perhaps it wasn't a star after all.

She was shivering by the time she got to the park.

Even through that unseasonably heavy coat of hers. It wasn't all that cold, needless to say. That wasn't why she was shivering. Needless to say.

So don't say it.

Once in the park, she ducked her head, reached into the pocket of that heavy coat, and grabbed the handle of the knife. Just to feel it. The certainty of it.

The force of her grasp drove the blade into the bottom of the pocket, slicing through the fabric with an effortless little *slk* noise.

The entire knife plunged through the hole, with an enthusiasm that certainly implied the words *I'm freeeee!*, and clattered to the pavement just beside Kira's foot.

"Fuck," she grunted, as she snapped down and snatched up the weapon that was, at this moment, still only a kitchen accessory. Both of her knees popped, one on the way down, the other on the way back up.

Once she'd regained the vertical, she quickly passed the knife to her left hand and stuffed it into the left pocket, blade up. *Blade up,* she willed herself to remember. *Careful when you grab it. Blade up.*

She glanced around the park for witnesses. None. Just the loose arc of the paved path swinging from the eastern entrance to the northern, the two lonely lamps at either end doing their best to brighten the night, accomplishing little more than getting their light tangled in the branches of the sweetbay magnolias. A terrifically ominous scene. Ordinarily, she might have been frightened to be out here, at this hour, alone. As it happened, though, Kira wasn't fretting over what might emerge from the oily dark beyond the reach of those lights tonight. The knife probably had something to do with that.

Blade up. Don't forget. It's blade up.

Still, the shivering, without the cold. It wouldn't have made sense to say she wasn't afraid. So don't.

Say it.

"Come on," Kira encouraged herself. She took one step along the path, then another, then another, drawing closer and closer to the haunted little park benches filling the void between the two lamps. So charming during the daytime, facing southwest as they were, offering a lovely view of the softball diamond and, beyond that, a portion of Lake Hirsch, and the nameless woods beyond that. During the day. At night though, *now,* the benches gazed out upon blackness.

She glanced the other way, and saw the implication of that bright white gazebo through the gloom. Like the ribcage of some Bible-times behemoth. Cooked clean by the same sun that had shone down on her as she'd sat in that gazebo, the day Leigh died.

The beauty of that day came back to her, as though glimpsed through a keyhole. Taking a load off in the gazebo, because she'd gotten to town too early to go straight to Gerry's Gas-Up, to have lunch with Charity. What a different life that had been. A life she couldn't even recognize.

It occurred to her – and not for the first time – that when she'd been sitting in that gazebo, relaxing, enjoying the day, dimly anticipating her lunch in the way one anticipates something taken for granted, Ruthger Gully had probably already started shooting. Leigh was probably already starting to figure out what was going on. Wondering if she was going to die.

Kira gave the gazebo a wide berth. Another step, and another, and yet one more delivered Kira down the path that cut through the park, to a bench. One bench among several that became *the* bench the moment she sat on it. Carefully now, *blade up,* adjusting the knife in her pocket as she settled to avoid slicing herself. Unfortunately, she couldn't avoid the knife punching up through the down of the coat, the liberated tip nearly jabbing the underside of her left arm, having the *audacity* to glisten like the dorsal fin of a shark.

Glistening. In this light? At this time of night?

Kira made noises of tectonic displeasure, then pulled the little baggie of nuts from the pocket of her jeans. Much less problematic a pocket-filler, these nuts.

Like a bullet from the night, straight between the eyes: Kira remembered.

She remembered the day Leigh, all of ten years old, came home having learned something outside the normal curriculum: the art of the *deez nuts* joke. An art she treated more like a science, never actually attempting to assemble a joke for Kira, instead patiently explaining to her the concept and construction. *You have to ask someone if they have a CD or something, or something like that, then you say, 'see deez nuts!'* Leigh's visible frustration at her inability to assemble a *deez nuts* correctly was funnier, and more adorable, to Kira than any successfully deployed use of *deez nuts* could ever have been. Still, she'd had to put on a severe face and make clear that those sorts of jokes were *not okay.*

She snickered quietly over the baggie of mixed nuts, intuiting from the snottiness of her every sniffle that the tears weren't *just* from laughter. "Deez nuts," she whispered. That most versatile punchline of her middle school years. Like mother like daughter: Kira couldn't remember any of the setups at present. They'd seemed pretty funny to her though, back then.

She tried to hold on to that insignificant little memory, feeling it slip her grasp, watching it melt back into the black boil of her mind. Given ten lifetimes to do nothing but reflect on her daughter's life, Kira was confident she would never, ever have been able to pull that recollection up from the memory mines. Not without this uncanny context to conjure it.

Maybe that was another indication that she should just accept the world as it was. There was more of Leigh left in her mind than she realized. Given only *one* lifetime to reflect on her daughter's life, Kira would never want for new recollections.

No. That wasn't right. None of that was right.

Giggling a bit more nervously now, she opened the bag of nuts, and then didn't do anything. Just sat there, staring at the bag. Slowly, she lifted her gaze to the magnolia tree she could see from here. She knew there was another further to the east, but that one was lost until morning.

She reached into the bag and pulled out as much as her hand could hold. Then she tilted it over, palm up.

Presenting *deez nuts* to the gloom of the softball diamond before her with her right hand, she used her left hand to – with great care and effort – free the knife from her coat pocket and lay it across her left thigh. Didn't cut herself in the process, so that was good. *Blade up.* She'd remembered. A different kind of indication.

She pursed her lips, pressed her tongue the roof of her mouth, and made soft clicking sounds, holding the handful of nuts further out in front of her.

No reply from the nighttime.

Kira sighed. Really ought to have looked up when squirrels sleep. She supposed nothing was stopping her from pulling out her phone and checking now, but, well, she had nuts in one hand and a knife in the other. And she was here, on a park bench, in the middle of the night. It was too late for research.

"Here," she stage-whispered, before remembering that squirrels didn't generally come when called for. It was the food that brought them. Though, to be fair, she didn't know anybody who'd ever *tried* to call a squirrel over. Maybe they were all just waiting for an invitation.

To her right, overhead: a rustle among the boughs of the magnolia.

She glanced that way. Saw nothing. Clicked her tongue a bit more insistently. That seemed like a squirrel noise to her. Squirrely. Squirrelish.

Her right hand swung around towards the tree to her right.

Her left hand tightened around the grip of the kitchen knife.

The rustling intensified as the wind picked up. Ah, yes, it was the wind. Just the wind. Damn.

She let out a breath she hadn't realized she'd been holding and faced forwards once more. Heart hammering, forehead sticky with sweat…but that sickly feeling had gone. Somehow, being here, the whole enterprise felt less real than it had when she'd snuck out of her home.

Movement, directly in front of her. From that darkness of what during the day would have been the charming view, with the diamond and the water and the woods, but was now just a launchpad for skunks.

For yes, it was a skunk breaching the night before her. Heading her way.

Maybe ten yards from her. If that.

She lifted the knife from her thigh. Could she…? No. No way she'd gut a skunk without getting sprayed, and how to explain that to Harlow? She'd never gotten hit by the gland cannon before, but she'd heard it was more than just a quick bath could take care of.

"Back the fuck up," Kira warned the skunk, in something just above a library voice.

The skunk did not reply, because it was a skunk. It just kept on swaggering forwards, taking wide steps with its front legs, the back legs holding to a narrower gait.

Kira wondered if they all walked like that, or if this one had gotten injured.

Could she kill a half-busted skunk without getting sprayed? Like, *logistically?*

Even if she could, the skunk wasn't the dry run she

was after. She could trust herself to frame that as a kind of self-defense, however disproportionate. She needed to kill something that didn't spray, couldn't harm or inconvenience her in the slightest. Something innocent. Which, she reminded herself, the skunk still was. Skunks were just trying to survive like anybody else.

A squirrel was perfect. Ticked all the boxes. She needed a squirrel.

The skunk was definitely less than ten yards away now.

Kira was just starting to rise from the bench when she heard a scratching noise from beside her.

She glanced down to her right.

A squirrel had clambered up onto the seat next to her. A little baby squirrel, from the looks of it. Turning its head from side to side, eyeing Kira's handful of nuts eagerly.

Fuck.

She looked back to the skunk. Still heading her way. No particular menace or urgency to its approach. Just out for an evening stroll.

She glanced back down to the baby squirrel.

As much as she didn't want to get sprayed by a skunk tonight, wanted to just get up and go…she didn't want to do all of this again. The sneaking out of her own house, the prowling around town at ungodly hours. She wanted to finish this, tonight. Now.

Her eyes darted from the one hand, to the other. From the skunk to the squirrel. Back and forth, back and forth.

Slowly, she extended the hand with the nuts down to the squirrel. It recoiled sharply at her movement, but recovered just as quickly. Almost *definitely* a baby squirrel, she could see. About half the size of what she was used to, with big, curious eyes.

As it took step after cautious step towards the upturned palm, Kira's other hand lifted the knife from her thigh and, carefully, as smoothly as possible, arced it up and over her lap. Towards the baby squirrel at her right hip.

She risked a glance towards the skunk.

The big striped idiot had stopped. Seemed to be staring directly at her now. As though it was weighing its own *wouldn'ts* and *couldn'ts*.

Kira felt a tickle on her right hand.

She looked down to find the baby squirrel with both of its little paws planted on her first finger, using it to peer into her palm. Like a kid at the window of a candy shop. Or the way Leigh used to smush her face up against the glass of the claw machine game at the arcade those few times they took her there as a kid. "Leigh, don't do that," Kira had snapped each time, because the glass was no doubt dirty, and she wasn't about to waste fifty cents or however much the machine wanted to go through to motions of dropping a limp-grip claw over some cheap stuffed zoo animals that it would never pick up, never carry to the chute, never drop for a hopeful little girl who had yet to learn the dread virtue of cynicism. Oh, Leigh was always so disappointed at that. But she would peel her face from the glass and keep walking.

She had always been such a good listener. Wasn't quite as good at disguising the disappointment on her face, but hey.

The baby squirrel climbed up onto Kira's right hand.

Kira paused. Telling herself this was a final moment of reflection, of consideration. Knowing, deep down, that she was only waiting until the squirrel was in just the right spot to be grabbed.

Once the squirrel finally got into position, Kira stopped telling herself anything.

She clamped her hand shut, as quickly and powerfully as she could.

The squirrel made a choked little squawk sound, like a rubber ducky getting clocked by a heavyweight boxer. It squirmed, but couldn't get away.

The image of King Kong with a struggling Ann Darrow in his hand occurred to Kira.

She could read terror on its little squirrely features. More guilt now. Oh, it came on strong.

The illusion was spoiled slightly when the feisty, bushy-tailed Ann bit down *hard* on the meat between Kira's thumb and pointer finger.

"FUCK!" Kira screamed. She held fast to the little shit though.

And in squeezing, in seeing those tiny little eyes bulge open, the face of the baby squirrel became a window.

Thinking of nothing but efficiency, Kira lifted the knife, brought it to the baby squirrel's neck, pushed the blade into its furry little throat, and yanked HARD to the left.

The blade whispered through the critter's flesh, smooth as warm butter, and just as sticky. The blade split little veins and tendons, as the minor imposition of the fur caused the grip of the blade to rattle slightly in Kira's hand. It sounded like the first raindrop falling at the head of a downpour. Just a single, wet, isolated *splop*.

Sharp though the knife was, it didn't make it all the way through in one go. Too much gristle. The baby squirrel's head flopped backwards on a thin tongue of still-attached skin, opening like a PEZ dispenser. The critter's soft paws slapped and clawed haphazardly at Kira's skin. She could feel its little legs kicking in the air, rocking her hand a fraction of an inch from side to side.

Black blood bubbled up from the neck stump and ran down all sides of the baby squirrel's body, coating Kira's hand. Cherry fondue. Melted sorbet. Lick it up.

Kira didn't realize she was going to throw up until it was already happening. She tossed the nearly-decapitated baby squirrel into the dark, tipped herself forward, and managed to get *most* of the vomit onto the ground between her feet. Probably a few bites' worth of dinner hit her lap, though.

The pain of the squirrel bite came on quickly, a hot coal dreaming itself a forge inside her right hand.

She looked down at the wound. Covered in blood. Two shades of blood, one lighter, one darker. Impossible to say for certain which was Kira's, and which had been the squirrel's. Oh no, wait, the lighter blood was hers. She could tell because her hand kept pumping it out, one mouthful at a time.

RID OF RED

"Jesus…*sshhhhhhit,*" Kira hissed as she stuffed her right hand inside the zippered flap of her coat, like a gangster in a trendy nineties movie reaching for their gun, then slapped her left palm against the outside of the coat, doing her best to apply pressure through the padding. "Fuck. *Aaaah*. Fuck."

As she rose to her feet, the knife slid from where she'd lain it down on her thigh and clattered onto the pavement.

The skunk – coming on once more, slowly but surely – took a clumsy crabstep backwards, making a horrible, shrill buzzing noise as it did.

Kira froze halfway to standing. Hadn't realized skunks made noises. Especially not *those* noises, a shrill, silly chittering.

Regaining its courage, the skunk took another skunky step forward.

"GO AWAY!" Kira screamed at the skunk, bending to grab the knife off the ground again. She released her left hand from the jacket and stretched it towards the blade.

The skunk's sandpaper laugh only got louder. It had a joke it wanted to explain to Kira. The concept, the construction.

"SHUT THE FUCK UP!" She grabbed the knife, grunting as the wound on her right hand dragged across the inside of the coat, the edge brushing the zipper. "SHUT UP!"

The skunk's dry mirth stopped. As suddenly as if someone had hit pause. No trail-off. No echo. Just silence.

Kira glanced up to the skunk, once more locked up halfway between standing and not-so-standing.

She assumed what she *thought* she was seeing was just a play of light. Because what she was seeing was the flesh of the skunk's face bubbling, then slackening. A play of the light. It had to be.

Then its face peeled back from the nose in four thick folds, like a banana. And Kira determined that what she was seeing was *not* just a play of light.

She dropped the knife again. Didn't realize until she heard it *cl-clck* onto the ground. Even then, didn't crouch down to pick it up. She couldn't take her eyes off the skunk, as it…*unfolded* in front of her.

The now-exposed muscles of its face *plop plop plopped* onto the ground as the skunk – still alive – tried to stagger backwards quickly enough to outrun whatever the fuck was happening to it.

Kira, too, took a step back. As though whatever the skunk was going through might be catching. But, in truth, she already knew it wasn't. And that certainty kept her from running off, screaming to the heavens. Kept her instead just where she was, staring at a skunk spontaneously skinning itself alive.

The certainty, the *knowledge,* being that this was a message. For her.

The skunk's naked jaw opened in what would surely have been another terrible little skunk scream. But its tongue slithered out of its head, pulling a trail of viscera out with it. In silence.

Well, almost silence.

Whl, the tongue sighed as it settled into the grass.

Hlllf, the streamer of gore added.

Whhn, the skunk spake (at last!) with its dying breath.

Mffnnthn, its body concluded as it teetered, tipped, and fell onto the grass.

Kira knew for certain that she wasn't done being sick tonight, not at all, but now wasn't the time. She ducked down and scooped the knife off the ground, then shot all the way upright, shoving the knife into her left pocket as she glanced left, right, behind, *everywhere*, for a glimpse of the moon-faced demon she knew wa-

The knife slashed through the bottom of her left pocket – she'd thoughtlessly jammed it in *blade down* – and yet again it clattered to the pavement.

"Fuckin'…" Kira grunted as she crouched down. "Come *on,*" she added, as the knife seemed to skitter away from her grasping fingers. Finally, she snatched it up with her left hand, passed it to her burning, bitten right, wincing as she forced the blood-soaked fingers to grab hold of it, and once more tucked it into her jacket, this time keeping her right hand there to hold it against her chest, out of sight.

Blade up, she reminded herself.

She risked a glance down to find herself pretty well sodden with blood. Not enough to worry she was bleeding out, nothing like that. But more than enough to rule out passing under streetlamps on the way home.

"Where are you?" she whispered as she snapped her head this way and that. Looking for a silhouette. That familiar, hunched, dangle-armed form. In her search, she caught another quick glimpse of the skunk, its skull stripped clean, its tongue *oop,* yep, here came the sick.

She had the presence of mind to pull the knife out of her jacket before she doubled over, heaving what was left in her stomach out onto the pavement. This time there were tears, too. But hey, when weren't there?

Whl.

Uisch had spoken through the skunk.

Hlllf.

How fitting.

Whhn.

The sounds replayed in her mind.

Mffnnthn.

Yet their meaning was slippery. Were it not for the grisly impossibility of how those noises had been made, she might have written them off as meaningless. Sounds like any other.

Yet the unfolding left no room for doubt: Uisch was speaking to her. So she tried to understand. She tried.

Tried not to think of how often Uisch might have been speaking to her, without her knowledge.

Red overtook rationality. Made it harder and harder to think. Harder to focus.

Why didn't Uisch just kill those three girls itself? Apparently Uisch could fucking do that, if it wanted to. Clearly. Could peel open those three girls' faces, like lilies in bloom. So why make *her* do all of this? Why not take matters into its own enormous hands?

Because it didn't want to. Of course. It wanted *Kira* to

do it.

Ah. There it was. Meaning. Reached not through reason, but through red.

One life, Uisch had said through the skunk.

One minute.

"I don't know what the fuck that *MEANS!*" Kira raged at the night.

Hff.

That one hadn't come from her memory.

Slowly, Kira turned back towards the body of the skunk, sprawled at the very edge of the light. Halfway back into the darkness. Its front feet pawing vainly at the…

…

That movement wasn't Uisch speaking again.

That was just life.

The poor bastard was still alive.

Kira whimpered. No words. Just noise.

One life. One minute.

That was what it was telling her. The skunk was going to survive for a whole minute, like that.

Unless Kira intervened.

"I already fucking killed the squirrel," she mewled, her voice soupy with self-loathing and self-pity both.

The skunk bobbled its skull limply, eyes cracking and clouding as they spun frantically in their lidless sockets.

There was no way it could last a full minute like that. The amount of blood it had lost, the way it was *still* bleeding. No way. There was no way.

Just as there was no way a sadistic rock climbing wall

could bring back Kira's dead daughter. And yet.

Still whimpering, Kira strode briskly across the paved path, onto the grass, to the edge of the light, and up to the skunk. She considered using the knife, but couldn't imagine what vein she could open that would make a difference.

So she took a deep breath and lifted her foot, until it obscured the frenzied stare of this unlucky skunk whose only sin was crossing paths with Kira.

She showed it mercy with the heel of her shoe. It took a few tries, but success was, when it finally arrived, unmistakable. And it had arrived in less than one minute. By the heel of her shoe. What mercy.

Kira sat back on her heels and cried after that. But in time, some degree of sense returned. What brought her round, to some extent, was the sight of the gazebo. Now bringing to mind nothing but the glittering white of the skunk's skull.

Realizing suddenly that she might be seen here, she stumbled out to the darkness of the softball diamond, towards the lake, towards the woods, and cried out there.

KIRA DID INDEED AVOID THE LIGHTS as she sauntered home. The longer she walked on, the more the bite on her right hand tipped from mere pain into a kind of pre-agony. Well, it wasn't *so* excruciating as to meet the definition of *agony,* but boy howdy, was it on its way. And with the hurt, came worry. Could it be infected? Had the squirrel given her rabies? Did she need to go to the hospital? How much time did she have to get there before she turned into a weresquirrel, or whatever?

What if Uisch's *one minute* had been for *her?* What if that was all she had?! That couldn't be right. She'd been bitten more than a minute ago.

Peace of mind came at the cost of discretion: Kira pulled out her out phone – a little look-at-me rectangle of light in the abyss – and asked it "Siri, what do I do if I've been bitten by a squirrel?" As what she was suddenly certain would be her death sentence loaded, she glanced in as many directions as she could, as quickly as possible. Nothing to see, of course. It was just after three in the morning now. The chances of anybody being awake in sleepy Neirmouth – let alone being awake *and* looking out their window – were pretty low. Low enough for Kira to feel comfortable washing her face in blue light.

Apparently Siri felt the matter solemn enough to keep schtum: there was no *here are some results I have found for you* or whatever stupid shit it usually said. No, it said nothing at all, instead simply clogging the screen with articles carrying titles like "What To Do If You Get Bitten By A Squirrel" and "Do Squirrels Carry Rabies?" and, confess-ionally, "I Was Bitten By A Squirrel."

She kept the knife flush against her body beneath the jacket, using her left hand to turn the brightness on her screen down. It felt like a feat of coordination to scroll through her phone with her nondominant hand like this, but she managed it well enough to read as she resumed walking.

As she should have expected, she got conflicting ans-wers to her questions. Squirrels were generally clean, it seemed, and didn't necessarily require launching into the whole rabies protocol. So said some of the sites, while others urged the victim (not that she was the victim tonight, no) to seek *immediate* medical attention. There were blips all along the spectrum between those two extremes, as well.

The one point of agreement, though, was on the importance of cleaning the wound as quickly as possible. *Antiseptic and bandage* was step one in nearly every single response she read.

So she headed home, thinking only of the need to clean her wound. Such a blessing, that was; self-concern inflated to fill her whole skull, leaving no room for any other thoughts.

Save one, of course. Hard to recognize the substance of it, but easy enough to spot it in silhouette.

Head pounding with anything but guilt, Kira threaded her way through the dark spots, back to her house. Around to the rear, to that slab of concrete they called a back porch. Wincing with each step, by the end; the impact of her soles on the ground sent shockwaves up to her bitten, bleeding right hand.

She paused with her hand on the knob. Left hand, of course. Took a deep breath.

Full to bursting with mere thought though her head may have been, there were much more complicated machinations underway in her heart, in her gut.

"Okay," she steeled herself, as she cranked the knob and slowly, gently, opened the do-

BEE BEE BEE BEE BEE

The alarm. The fucking alarm.

Kira took two lunging steps through the mud room towards the kitchen, where the alarm console was, then stopped.

BEE BEE BEE BEE BEE

She hadn't turned the alarm back on when she'd left. She was sure of that.

BEE BEE BEE BEE BEE

Which meant it could only be going off right now if…

BEE BEE BEE BEE BEE

Down the short hall, she saw Harlow stride quickly through the narrow slice of kitchen visible from the mud room. Into view from the right, back out of it to the left.

BEE BEE BEE BEE BEE

She heard the console *meep meep meep meep* softly under the shrill alarm, as Harlow input the code to turn it off.

BEE BEE Bp.

Kira looked down at herself. Her coat run through with red. Slick in places, crusting in others. So clearly blood. Nothing else she could claim it to be.

Shit.

She pulled her knife-clutching right hand out from beneath the flap of her jacket, and stuffed it into her right pocket. Then remembered that pocket didn't have a bottom anymore.

Shit.

"Kira?!" Harlow called. Sounding quite anxious indeed.

Kira shifted the knife to her left hand just as she recalled that the pocket on that side was *also* fucked. Just like her.

Would Harlow try to have her committed? For coming home at three in the morning, covered in blood, doing a poor job of hiding a great big knife? Possibly. If he should happen to find out what had happened to the baby squirrel in the park, to say nothing of the skunk (even though that one had *not* been her fault): *very likely.*

Not knowing what else to do, Kira kept hold of the knife's hilt and plunged her hand into her left pocket, doing her best to strike a natural pose. Standing the way one stands, when one is just in from a brisk walk and is *not* holding a very large knife against one's body.

She cleared her throat. "Harlow?"

Thmp thmp thmp thmp, here he came, footfalls muted by the soles of his slippers. Still obscured by the wall of the little hall. She could just imagine the look on his face, though.

Or, more terrifying to think…maybe she *couldn't.*

She instinctively pulled her left hand a bit closer towards the center of her body. Hard to say why.

The tip of the blade doinked her skin. A rogue roll of belly fat she'd once told herself she'd get rid of. A long time ago.

Her skin didn't break, but Kira was fairly certain she'd see a mark there, whenever she shrugged off the jacket, lifted her shirt, and had a look-see.

All the same: it fucking hurt. More pain for the body. Less room in the head.

There was something to that, maybe.

Harlow came into view, arms crossed, gait stiff and

shallow. He took one look at Kira and froze. Arms falling to his sides, as his jaw flopped open.

Explain, a voice in Kira's head demanded.

How?

"Oh Christ," Harlow wheezed, as he rushed towards Kira, arms extended for an embrace.

She very nearly halted him by lifting her left hand along with the right. Just as the very base of the cutlery was sliding out of the pocket, she recalled herself and plunged it back in.

Halfway stabbing herself in the side as she did. Still not breaking the skin, but still stinging a hell of a lot.

She bit her lip, and managed to keep from yelping. Didn't fully manage to hide the pain, though.

Harlow quite clearly clocked her discomfort. "Get in the car," he ordered, with a confidence that didn't wholly suit him.

"I'm fine," Kira assured him. "This isn't m-"

"You need to go to the *hospital!*"

"This isn't my blood." Kira cleared her throat again. Hoped that her brain would supply the next sentence as confidently as it had that one.

"…wh…what?"

"It, uh…" she licked her lips. "There was…oh." Fuck. She shouldn't have said this wasn't her blood. Not that it'd have helped her to say it was. Fuck. *Fuck.*

Harlow just kept on staring at her. Waiting for an explanation. Clearly desperate for anything that would make sense of his blood-stained beloved.

"Um…I've…been going on night walks lately," was

where Kira went. "I just can't sleep."

"Have you been sleepwalking?"

"No, it's, I'll be *awake*, and then decide to get up and go for a walk."

Harlow said nothing to that.

"And," Kira continued, "um…I went out for a walk tonight, and, as I was walking, this, I heard this…just a really horrible sound."

Whl.

Hlllf.

Whhn.

Mffnnthn.

No.

She shivered. "It was like a…like a…dog."

Still, Harlow said nothing.

"And it *was* like a dog," Kira explained, warming to her fiction, "because…it *was* a dog. There was a dog… somebody had hit their car with…hit their…hit *a* dog, with *their* car. And I found it, on the road." She blinked twice, each eye out of sync with the other. "And it was…" she flopped her right arm up and let it fall back to her side.

As her right arm struck her flank, her belly fat jostled, sending ripples over to the left side. Forceful enough to wrap her skin around the tip of the blade.

And then a little further.

She felt the seal of her flesh *pop,* felt the leading edge of the knife enter her body. Felt blood immediately bubble forth, soaking into her shirt.

She winced. Couldn't help it. Ditto for the curling of

her upper lip, as she felt a new runlet of red dribbling down her tummy.

"…this is its blood," she concluded, fighting to iron out her voice. "The dog's blood."

Harlow was, for once, perfectly opaque. He didn't move, betrayed no reaction to what Kira had just said.

"It was a golden retriever," she mumbled.

"How did the dog's blood get all over you?" he finally asked.

"I was trying to save it," she explained, pantomiming cradling a dying dog as best she could with just her right hand. Realizing only too late that doing so called attention to how firmly her left hand was stuffed into that pocket. Not to mention the fucking squirrel bite on the top of her exposed hand. She once more dropped her right hand to her side, doing her best to gauge whether or not Harlow had noticed that wound. "I was, I tried to, you know, I tried to pick it up, when I thought it was just…I didn't know it had been hit by a car."

Harlow onboarded that lie slowly. Skeptically. Didn't seem to have noticed the bite on her hand. Phew.

"It was a golden retriever," Kira repeated, more firmly this time.

"Where was it hit?"

"On its body."

Harlow frowned. "Where in the neighborhood, I mean."

Kira sighed. "I don't know. It's dark. I'm not thinking straight." Recognizing an ill-gotten high ground a moment too late, she added: "are you saying you don't believe me?"

Harlow shook his head and made a meal of his next breath. While glancing down at the left hand locked in her pocket, it didn't escape her notice. "I'm just so worried about you. I *have* been. You're not yourself. And after what you did to Leigh's room, I just…so I woke up and saw you weren't here, and I, I've been sitting here for *hours,* so worried about you. Now you come home, wearing a…huge winter coat, *covered* in *blood,* not making any sense."

"It was a *golden retriever!*" Kira tilted forward slightly as she shouted, accidentally driving the hidden blade deeper into her tummy. "Ach!" she grunted.

A shock of pain ripped through her body.

She lost her grip on the knife.

It slid down her stomach, towards the ground.

She reached her left hand deeper into the not-so-pocket, slapping the knife halfway up the blade, pressing it flush against her body.

Had she caught it before the tip poked out from beneath the bottom of the coat? She tried to guess from Harlow's mortified expression. Guessed again. Again.

Harlow pointed to Kira's left flank.

She took a deep breath.

Felt her left hand slither up the blade of its own accord, until the fingers were wrapped around the grip of the knife. She felt the fingers tighten.

What am I doing?

She forced her hand to relax.

"And you're hurt," Harlow tutted.

"It's not my blood."

"I can see your hand, Kira. I can see your face. Stop lying to me. I'm trying to help you."

"My hand?"

Harlow made an unhappy shape with his brow, as he gestured towards Kira's right hand.

Damn.

"Oh, that? A squirrel bit me. And I didn't ask for your help."

"I know. That's why I feel like maybe I need to try harder." He paused for a moment. "A *squirrel* bit you?"

Kira's shoulders slumped slightly. Her chin drooped towards her chest. "Can I just go take a shower? Can we have this conversation later?"

Harlow thought about that. Then took a step forward. "I think this is a conversation that needs to happen now."

Kira noted the angle at which her coat was open in the front, and pulled the knife back along her oblique to keep it shielded from his view. "I'm fine, Harlow. I'm fine, and I'm *exhausted.*"

"And I'm *fucking terrified.*"

"Then…okay, just let me a take a fucking shower first. Can I do that? Or do you think you need to *help me* with that too?"

"…yeah, sure. Fine." He eyed her up and down, as though sizing her up before a fight. "But take off the coat. You'll track blood in the house."

Kira took a deep breath through her nose. Hesitated.

Harlow tilted his head at her slightly. "Just throw it on

the floor. It'll be fine there, we can mop it up later." And he stayed where he was. Watching her.

Goddamn him. She couldn't keep the knife hidden while she took the coat off. But she couldn't ask him to turn around. Tell him to go start the shower for her. That'd be too suspicious. And he was already so deeply suspicious of her.

Harlow was *deeply* suspicious of her. Which was to say, he didn't wholly trust her anymore.

She hadn't believed her heart could break any more than it already had upon losing Leigh…but this was a night of many surprises.

Kira did her best to reach her left hand deeper through the hole in the pocket, sliding the knife further around her back. Hoping against hope she wouldn't cut herself to ribbons.

Her hope was in vain. She felt the knife slice a thin cutlet of skin from her low back. But nevermind that: she got the knife tucked safely in her beltline, at her back. Relief outweighed even the pain of peeling herself like a potato. As long as the blade stayed there, stuck between Kira's back and her blue jeans, she could bear to lose a deli-style slice or two.

"I thought the night walks were helping me clear my mind," Kira babbled, hoping to distract him from the way her left arm was cranking into increasingly outrageous angles, "but I guess…maybe they weren't. But it's like you said, there's no wrong way to grieve, right?"

"I…" Harlow vanished down a wormhole of self-analysis, just as Kira had known he would upon hearing his own consolations turned against him. She felt bad playing his neuroses like they had a whammy bar, but well, you have to find ways to keep your marriage fresh, right? "I may have misspoken when I said that."

As Harlow's gaze tracked thoughtfully towards the floor, Kira finished setting the knife in her beltline, pulled her hand from her pocket, and shrugged her heavy winter coat off.

It made an unpleasant little *splat* sound as it hit the tile of the mudroom.

The knife shifted behind her, burrowing a bit more deeply, cutting off another helping of backmeat.

Kira blinked hard, and cleared her throat.

Harlow jerked back to reality. "There are some expressions of grief, I maybe should have said, that are more productive than others."

"Mhm. Yes," Kira drawled, "wouldn't want to waste time with that *unproductive grief.*"

Harlow rolled his eyes. "You know what I mean." With that, he turned and stormed back into the kitchen.

Quick as she could, Kira tore the knife from her beltline and scanned the room for a spot to hide it. She went with the first one to leap out at her, crashing to her knees and sliding the knife under the washing machine.

The blade made a shrill scraping noise as she pushed it under.

She heard Harlow's departing footsteps slow, stop.

"Hey," she called as she launched back up to her feet, not having anything else to say, simply wanting to capture his attention before he had time to think too carefully about that sound he'd heard. She hustled through the little hallway into the kitchen to find Harlow lingering halfway between Kira and the kitchen counter.

The one with the knife block, from which the largest knife was conspicuously absent.

Christ. It never ended, did it?

Hoping to close this horrible little interval out once and for all, Kira rushed to Harlow, buried her face in his shoulder, and let loose the waterworks.

Would have done, anyway. Only…nothing came. No matter how hard she tried. It seemed she was all out of tears. Left them all in the park, she had.

So she tried out a single synthetic sob, which sounded *far* too fake to her ears. Like the noise actors made in old westerns when they got shot. *AYCK!*

Fortunately, Harlow was just the sort to eagerly don the dunce cap of chivalry. He wrapped Kira in his arms and provided waterworks enough for both of them. "Oh, Kira!" he sobbed. *Sobbed*. When he so rarely cried, at least not in front of Kira. Oh sure, a few tears here and there, she'd seen him shed his share. He was a sensitive man, and he trusted her. So she'd seen tears. But the *sobbing* though, that he hadn't indulged in even after Leigh's death. At least, not that Kira had seen.

And yet, here he was, *sobbing*. "I'm so scared for you. I love you so much. It's okay. It's okay. We can get you help!"

That was something she'd push back on eventually, but now was very clearly *not the time*. "That's probably good," she placated.

Harlow pulled back, planted a hand on each of Kira's shoulders, and pouted down at her. "But no more night walks, Kira. Please. Okay? I was *so scared*, I didn't know where you were!"

"I mean…now you'd know, right? If I w-"

The pout wriggled.

"Okay," Kira agreed. "No more night walks. And no more trying to save dogs hit by cars, which is…well, anyway." She pressed her head to his chest again.

Once Harlow had done a bit more crying, Kira led him upstairs and tucked him into bed. Impossible not to think of Leigh, in that moment. The last person Kira had tucked in, before this. When was the last time she'd ever tucked her daughter in? Quite literally tucked her in, using her fingers to cram the covers underneath Leigh's little body, swaddling her in 500 thread count bedsheets? Best as Kira could remember, Leigh had been maybe six or seven. She'd had a nightmare. Or maybe she just hadn't been able to sleep. Something like that; she had definitely grown out of being tucked in fairly early, so these would have to have been extenuating circumstances. She'd awoken Kira – Mommy – and brought her in for a few minutes of drowsy consolation before, finally, the tucking.

Call it seven years old for Leigh. Kira liked the idea of it having been more recent than it probably had been.

One thing she remembered for certain was that she'd been aware of this final tuck-in being precisely that – the last one. Aware of the possibility, at any rate. Which was so rare. So precious, so beautiful, in a fragile, bittersweet kind of way. How many times had she done something, spoken to someone – told someone she loved them – for the last time, without knowing that it would, in fact, be the last time?

She stared down at her tucked-in husband for a few moments. Breathing softly, slowly. He appeared to have gone straight to sleep.

Kira turned and tiptoed to the bathroom. Closed the door behind her. Cranked the shower handle to *H* and undressed. Stood exposed before the mirror, watching her face slowly vanish as the glass fogged over.

Thusly obscured from herself, she was free to weep, for it was easy enough to imagine that she wasn't.

What she wouldn't have given to undo tonight. What she had done, what she had *seen*, and more than anything, what she was giving Harlow very good reason to think about her.

He thought she was losing it. Which wasn't entirely off-base…but not for the reasons he thought. How to make him understand how rational her insanity was? When his grief didn't *sing?* Any attempt to convince him would only serve as confirmation of his suspicions. If she was being honest with herself, she wasn't genuinely worried about him having her committed against her will – not yet, anyway. It just wasn't outside the realm of possibility that she could become such a disturbance to him that he might save himself the trouble. Pack his things, take his leave.

She stepped into the shower with her fist as far into her mouth as she could fit it, full-on sobbing. Oh, great.

Crying in the shower. How original, Kira.

If Harlow left her alone, all alone, she could well die. Her heart could crack open and dribble down her ribcage, and she wouldn't mind it one bit. Not one bit. She'd loved Harlow more than she'd ever loved anyone, until Leigh had come along. At which point, sorry Harlow, Kira's universe became one which revolved around her daughter.

Having the center cut out of her life hadn't restored Harlow to his former position. No, Kira had spent the past weeks drifting aimlessly through the void. Harlow had been a tether to that old world, though. Something to keep her from well and truly sailing away. He was the only person she could feel *anything* for anymore, even if that was sometimes frustration or even anger, more often it was love. Even if, lately, that had a way of looking quite a bit like frustration. Or even anger.

He wasn't just afraid his wife was losing her mind. He was afraid he was losing his wife. When everything she was doing that made him feel that way, she did for the both of them.

If she lost him because of all this…goodbye heart. Crack, dribble, dead.

Crrkk. The door to the bathroom, opening.

Kira paused mid-bawl, staring at the section of shower curtain between herself and the door.

Was Harlow coming in?

Or was that…

She waited, eyelids fluttering as the water rolled down her face, gaze fixed on the space in the mist where the door would have been. Waited. Listening for the voice of her husband, or else the message which had no voice unto itself.

She only noticed how hot the water was when her skin started to itch. It took about three full seconds for that recognition to translate into action: she reached out and turned the handle a touch towards *C*.

Harlow wasn't coming in. Hadn't opened the door. And the *crrkk* never hatched a greater significance. Either she'd imagined the sound, or perhaps the house had shifted ever-so-slightly in the cool of the night. Maybe something to do with the relative temperatures of the room, now that this one was so hot, while the bedroom was so cold. Something for which there was no doubt a perfectly simple explanation, that Kira had no access to.

Oh, but she did know what had caused the door to creak. *Not Harlow.* That was all she needed to know.

Coming home at three in the morning covered in blood wasn't the kind of thing one can easily walk back. No matter how much therapy she endured for Harlow's benefit, no matter how sane and square she could seem from this day forward, her husband would forever think of her as the woman who had, for however brief a time, gone bananas. No – nuts. He was probably thinking, *she's nuts.* And if she ever heard him say that out loud, she could reply, *deez nuts.* Ha. Ha. Yes, remember laughter? It went like this. Ha. Ha. Ha.

Would he ever be able to look past his wife having perhaps, in fact, she could concede, gone a bit nuts? Or would there be a little voice forever bringing him back to this moment, never letting him forget? Would that eat away at the foundations of their relationship, tear down everything they'd built, whisper their love into dust?

Assuming he still loved her. No reason to imagine he didn't. He'd just said he did, after all. Yet it was easy to imagine all the same.

None of this explained the tears, though. The bawling into her hands as now-lukewarm water cascaded down her knuckles, running red with the blood from her hands, only some of which was hers.

No, she was crying because there was a way to fix all of this. To make Harlow understand the *very good reasons* she had been behaving as she had. Reasons more compelling than grief, productive or otherwise

She couldn't simply *tell* him about Uisch's offer. But she could prove the truth of it. Oh yes. By bringing Leigh back. And in so doing, she could explain to him what it had cost. And he would have no choice but to understand.

Her life would have a center once more. Her best friend in the entire world would not leave her. *Could* not – for Kira knew perfectly well that Leigh had occupied the prime position in her husband's emotional orrery as well.

Suddenly, there were quite a few more bullets for the *PRO* side of the list.

Not that she would consult the list again. She'd forgotten most of what she'd written under *CON*. And it was probably best that it stay that way. Necessary, in fact.

Besides. Not all of the points carried equal weight.

She got out of the shower, toweled off, and realized she hadn't done anything more than stand under the water. No shampoo, no conditioner, no soap, no nothing. That was alright, she supposed. At least she'd gotten most of the blood off. The blood that wasn't hers.

She got a bit of the Neosporin from the cabinet under the bathroom sink, rubbed it on the bite wound – *delicately,* the fucking thing *smarted* – and covered it with a few crosshatched Band-aids. She was fairly certain there was gauze and medical tape somewhere in the house, but she couldn't be bothered to go find it at present. These would be enough to get her through the night. Besides, she'd know if they fell off. It wasn't like she was getting any sleep tonight.

She crawled under the covers beside Harlow, disrupting the tuck she'd so expertly effected for him. Why, she wondered, had she bothered to tuck him in? It suddenly struck her as an incredibly odd thing to do.

But that was what she did now, it seemed. Odd things. Like sneaking out of her home, skulking around the neighborhood, decapitating squirrels like some old Germanic fairy tale goblin.

Goblin deez nuts.

It almost worked. That was close to a proper joke. She turned her head into the pillow to suppress a little giggle, and she tried to think of ways to make it work. The joke. Because yes, while it had been a long time since Leigh had come home, delighted by this childish word game… there was still a chance she might still get a kick out of it. Whenever Kira had a chance to tell her.

She would have that chance, she realized. It was awful to realize, so awful, but it was beautiful too. Such beauty, such tranquility, in the silence of her conscience. A silence that held no matter how firmly she tried to summon to mind the image of a headless baby squirrel in a lonely park. She felt nothing. Struggled, indeed, to keep thinking of what she'd done.

It was so hard to linger on that, when she was so focused on making this joke work. For Leigh. To hear her laugh again.

SIX

THE BEST MEDICINE

REMEMBERING LAUGHTER wasn't always the easiest thing in the world for Kira – especially not once she'd awoken to discover that her unexpected night of (shockingly restorative) sleep had only strengthened last night's musings into a resolution. Be it resolved: Kira would do whatever it took to bring Leigh back. She was capable of doing it, she felt she had determined, and she *needed* to do it, for Leigh and for Harlow and for all three of them, so, she would do it. And as she knew precisely what that *whatever* actually meant…anyway, the laughter, yes, it was difficult to bring to mind as anything other than *the thing I used to do.*

And yet, a few giggles came freely and easily when Harlow came downstairs so soon after Kira had tucked him in, to announce that he had made an appointment for later that day with a couples therapist who specialized in grief. "Specifically our kind," Harlow added. Kira appreciated his pluralized pronoun, but there was no mistaking who these sessions were *really* for.

That wasn't what had prompted the laughter, though.

"That was fast," Kira remarked from her seat at the kitchen table, as she sniffed over the mug of coffee in her still-bandaged hand. Restful though her sleep had been, she'd forgotten to turn off the alarm on her phone, and she wasn't the type to be able to get back to sleep once she was up.

"Well, he had the openings."

"No, I mean, *you* were fast. In making the appointment. When did you call him, even?"

Harlow sighed and tilted his head like a disappointed softball coach.

No, not softball. Anything but softball. That called to mind the diamond, which called to mind the park, which called to mind the bench…

"Right," Kira continued. "I get it."

"Are you going to be okay?" He asked, stepping over towards the table. "I can stay home today if you need me t-"

"I'll be fine." She smiled at him. "Thank you. I can understand why you're worried. But…I'll be fine."

Harlow cleared his throat and nodded. "Well, if you need me…"

"I'll call."

More nodding, eyes rolling up and down in his head to keep his gaze locked on his wife. "Okay." He broke away and began the process of loading up his precious little baggie of mixed nuts. Kira was glad she hadn't eaten yet – not much of anything for the wave of revulsion she felt at the sight of that snack to work with. "So," he said, "I'll meet you at Dr. Mothers' office a-"

And here they were. The giggles. "Excuse me?" Kira managed through mirth.

Harlow paused. "The therapist."

"You found a therapist named *Dr. Mothers?*"

Thank god: Harlow cracked a smile. "Yeah, I know. Bu he was very well-reviewed online. And he had open appointments today."

"Hard to believe."

The smile repaired itself. "Just give him a chance."

"I'm going to," Kira snapped, a bit more defensively than she'd meant to. "It's just a funny name for a therapist."

"I know that. But it's a very serious thing we're seeing him about."

"Yes, I *know* that, Harlow."

Harlow threw his nut baggie into his briefcase and lifted his palms. *Don't shoot.* "Okay, honey. I'm just saying. We have to take this seriously." He shut his briefcase and threw its little latches. *Clck. Clck.*

Kira had nothing to say. She just stared at him.

He risked a timid little glance her way, then another. "What?"

Kira sighed and shook her head.

Harlow seemed to consider saying something else, but decided against it. "I'll text you the address," he said as he swung his briefcase off the kitchen counter. "See you there at three."

"See you there," Kira replied.

Harlow turned, opened the door to the garage, and shut it behind him.

Kira throttled her coffee mug, waiting for him to get all the way gone. Waiting as she heard the garage door rumbling upwards, the engine of Harlow's CR-V roaring to life and fading into a whisper as it backed down the driveway, the garage door rattling back down to the ground.

She shot to her feet and padded across the kitchen. Pressed her ear against the door to the garage. Just in case.

Nothing. Not that she expected him to have stayed behind. To have tried to trick her.

Just that…that's what she would have done, had *she* suspected *him* of something.

And better safe than sorry, of course.

Slowly, she grabbed the knob with her left palm and opened the door just enough to peek through.

Harlow was gone. Well, his *car* was gone. Kira supposed it was conceivable that he'd backed it out, then gotten out and hidden himself somewhere in the garage. Maybe in the wheelbarrow against the far wall, or even in Kira's car.

If he had, though, his car would have to be just sitting on the driveway outside.

So Kira ran to the front door to check. Not that she expected to see it. Just to be safe, rather than sorry. Because that was better. Of course.

No car on the driveway. *Obviously,* Kira chided herself.

The coast was emphatically clear, yet she still felt some unnamable sense of…something, as she hurried to the laundry room, plopped down onto her hands and knees, and peered under the washing machine.

The knife was still there. Again: *obviously.* Where would it have gone? Who would have taken it?

It brought her no relief from that feeling, though. That unnamable *sense.*

She reached for the knife with her right hand.

The squirrel bite scraped along the bottom of the washing machine.

"Gah, *fuck,"* she grunted, repositioning herself to have a go with the left hand.

It took a whole lot of reaching and straining – man, she'd really shunted it way in there last night – and she ended up pulling a muscle in her left shoulder in the process, but eventually, she managed to get a finger planted firmly enough on the grip of the knife to tug it towards her, until she could wrap the rest of her hand around it and pull it out from under the washing machine.

It made a dramatic *scccHING* sound as the dragging blade lifted from the ground. Kira held the knife aloft, as though it were a sword pulled from stone.

There was still black blood caked on the blade.

She glanced down the hall towards the kitchen. More-than-half expecting to see Harlow standing there.

But he wasn't. All together now: *obviously.*

She carried the knife back to the kitchen, took it to the sink, and frowned at it. Even if squirrels were *generally* clean, they were still gross. Would it be enough to wash this thing with soap and water?

Well, if it wasn't, she had a bigger problem on her hands. Namely, the one on her right hand. Which, come to think of it, was hurting a whole hell of a lot. Maybe moreso now than it had been last night. Er…earlier this morning.

She put the knife down on the kitchen counter and, slowly, with quite a lot of wincing, peeled back the soft clot of bandages on her hand.

Sticky little fuckers – they yanked the loose skin around the wound with them as they came up. She supposed that was on her. Should have been paying more attention to where the pads were as she'd slapped them on.

Doing her best to loosen up her jaw, she kept tugging, pulling off the Band-aid slowly, millimeter by agonizing millimeter. Until she hit the portion over the wound itself; seemed some blood had dried to the pad, was doing its best to graft with the bandage.

Kira took a deep breath, tightened the pinch of her left hand on the portion already pulled up, and *ripped* it off.

Tried to, anyway.

The bandage came most of the way off, tearing free of her hungry wound with an audible *hrrrk*. All that remained attached to her was a thin sliver of adhesive at the very edge of the dollar-store dressing. Could have easily finished the job, were it not for the shock of pain that had attended the *hrrrk*. That had been enough to knock her left hand off course.

"OH," Kira shouted, as her left hand flew free of the bandages to hover uselessly over the squirrel bite, "MOTHERfffffffff*FUCK!* Ah!" She slumped over the counter, staring straight down at the stupid finishing on the stupid counters. Made them look like they had little triangles around the very edges. Like tiny scraps of paper glazed onto the fucking…bullshit. Stupid.

That done, she ripped the Band-aid the rest of the way off her hand and crumpled it up to throw it in the trash, which was hidden in a convenient, stupid trash drawer.

She grabbed the handle of the tall, narrow drawer and pulled. Tossed the bundle of bandages in.

It drifted straight over the bin and slid easily into the space between the bin itself and the back of the drawer.

"Come *on*," Kira grunted, as she pulled out the plastic bin and reached in to grab the runaway refuse.

Just as her head was inches from being inside the bin, she froze. Her heart stumbled for a beat, then came back in double-time. The ghostly stench of bananas and fish lost its bite. She felt her whole jaw start to tremble.

The Band-aids weren't the only thing to have missed the bin, it seemed. Smushed into the very rear of the trash drawer, next to the tangle of adhesive, was the wrapper to one of those horrible protein bars Leigh liked. The ones that bent over backwards to seem like more than what they were, i.e. normal candy bars laced with whey.

They were absolutely bursting with sugar and preservatives and all sorts of shit, Kira had often pointed out to her daughter, but Leigh had never taken that under advisement. She'd wanted to cut down on her meat intake – not going full vegan, no, she liked hot wings too much for that, just cutting down – but still fretted about getting enough protein. And she was still young enough to not think twice about the other stuff. The sugar, the sodium, all that. So no matter how many times Kira said hey, maybe, just *maybe,* five and a half inches of Chocolate Chunk Chernobyl or whatever *X-treme* name they gave these fucking things wasn't the *best* alternative source for protein, Leigh would just smile and say "you're probably right, Mom. But I like how they taste."

Now, Kira stared at the protein bar wrapper, which must have been hiding behind the trash can for who knew how long. Well, at least a few weeks. Obviously. However long had it been since Leigh had absent-mindedly tossed the wrapper at the bin, not noticing it hadn't made it in. Or maybe she had noticed, but she'd been in a hurry and thought *I'll get it later,* and then forgotten. And then never had the chance.

"I'll remind her," Kira muttered to herself. And then she remembered.

And in remembering…she laughed. Chuckling to herself. Trying to smother the chuckles, which only gave them strength.

God. It was so funny. It was funny because, for the first time in weeks, Kira was able to think, *I'll have to tell Leigh about this,* without then catching herself, correcting herself. Because Leigh *would* be back. Kira had decided it. And because she would be back, it was just like Leigh was still at camp. Still at school. She'd be home soon enough. So rather than being sad, this could be funny. It was so fucking funny. Sure, Kira couldn't manage more than a nervous machine-gun chuckle, but that didn't change the fact.

She bumped the trash drawer shut by leaning against it and letting it guide her hip back to the counter, getting her first good look at the grisly business on the meat of her right hand as she went. Not chuckling anymore, but still feeling the ache of a smile on her face.

The bite on her hand was much smaller than she'd imagined it, based on how diffuse the pain had seemed. That tracked, given that she'd been chomped by a baby squirrel, not a full-grown beaver. Still, that good news was tempered by the bed of swollen pink skin in which the wound itself reposed. That didn't look good, to say the least.

Kira frowned at it and shook her head. She'd need to go to the doctor. No sense fucking about with an animal bite, whatever Siri had to say about it.

But that would make two different visits to two different doctors in one day. Which struck her as funny, and unacceptable.

"Too bad," she mumbled out loud. She reached into the sink to grab the knife, but paused with her hand hovering an inch over the grip. Curling her lip without realizing, she reached instead for the dish soap, and dumped several tablespoons' worth directly onto the knife.

Did she *need* to spend a full six minutes washing the knife, over and over and over again, even accounting for the way she babied her right hand? No, probably not. But maybe! There probably wasn't a *correct* number of scrub-a-dubs for getting rid of pesky squirrel blood; there was only *not enough*, or *too much*. Kira knew which of those extremes she'd rather occupy. So she scrubbed, and she dubbed, and she shouted rude words very loudly whenever soap slid directly into her open wound, which was quite often. At the end of six minutes, though, when she felt confident about having done *too much*, she toweled off the knife and stuck it back in the block, where it ceased to be a weapon, became just one kitchen implement among the others.

Kira stepped back and studied the knife, the block, the counter, the kitchen. It looked as it always had. As though nothing had ever happened. No baby squirrels harmed in the making of *this* happy home, no ma'am.

Knowing precisely what lay on the far side of this mirage was unsettling…yet strangely empowering. For one day soon, she hoped to be fully taken by the illusion of the innocent knife in the mahogany block. She hoped to forget which knife had done the deed, what the deed had been, that there had been a deed at all. She looked forward to her self-hypnosis, if for no other reason than it would be hers to see through whenever she chose. And she would simply choose to never do that.

She looked forward to this. To what awaited her, on the far side of doing the *actual* deeds. To the innocent knife, in the mahogany block.

WHAT WOULD DR. MOTHERS SAY, were Kira to share her latest insight with him in the moment she'd had it? Well, probably the same thing he'd said for most of the session thus far, a toss-up between "tell me more about that" or "interesting." Or maybe he'd have said something else entirely. He did sometimes do that, it seemed. And those *something elses* were, Kira could already appreciate, incredibly insightful. The guy's name may have been funny, and he may have even dressed in an unflattering Freud cosplay (complete with bald head, though his beard was orange instead of white, surely a source of great disappointment), but Dr. Mothers was no joke. By the end of their first session, he'd made quite a few startlingly incisive observations based simply on what Kira and Harlow had told him thus far. And Kira hadn't even said all that much; she'd spent most of the meeting picking at the more professional patchwork a *proper* doctor had done on her hand. It had meant a trip to Urgent Care – her GP wasn't able to squeeze her in – but Kira was glad she'd gotten it looked at by someone who knew what they were doing. They'd made her get a rabies shot, which had hurt like a *motherfuck,* and she would apparently have to get another dose in three days or so. Still, it was good to get out from under all of the anxieties that naturally come with being bitten by a baby squirrel you're in the process of decapitating.

Dr. Mothers just nodded after Kira told him all that (sans the decapitation bit). As though he heard the same from all of his clients.

Kira glanced nervously at Harlow. She'd yet to give

him an account, convincing or otherwise, of just how she'd managed to get bitten by a squirrel whilst attempting to save the life of a golden retriever that had been hit by a car. He didn't appear puzzled by this, though. He just seemed happy Kira had gotten the bite looked at.

"And how did you feel," Dr. Mothers wondered, "upon realizing that the dog had not survived?"

Kira tried to gin up some wet sentiment to really sell this response, but couldn't quite manage. So she settled for a shrug. "I was sad. But…you know, what could I do?"

"You stayed with the dog."

"Yes."

"That was something you could do. And you did."

"I guess so."

"Why *did* you stay with this dog, that you had never seen before?"

"…because…I don't know." Harlow took her hand. The unbitten one, natch. Kira just nodded at him. "I guess," she continued, turning back to Dr. Mothers, "…maybe it was like trying to be there for…"

Oh, hell. Here came the earnest emotion, bubbling up.

She lifted a preemptive hand to wipe the tears from her eyes.

Yet no tears came. Instead, she felt a smile.

She crushed that before it bloomed, hoping her raised hand had shielded her mouth from view, and let out a slow breath. "Like trying to be there for Leigh."

"Hm," was all Dr. Mothers had to say about that.

Harlow turned and looked out the window, in a way that didn't quite seem like he was being overwhelmed by the poignancy of, uh, hearing his daughter in any way equated to a golden retriever.

Probably should have given that one a *bit* more thought. Oh well. Lesson learned: leave the dot-connecting to the doctor.

She kept quiet for the rest of the session, answering what was asked of her but offering little more, until the end of the session, when inspiration struck. It wasn't the sort of breakthrough Dr. Mothers would have been happy to have had a hand in, not one bit. But she'd never have had it without him. So it was partially his fault, then.

What happened was Dr. Mothers said he'd like to see them again, biweekly if that worked.

"Does that work for you?" Harlow asked Kira.

As if she had any choice. "Biweekly like twice a week or once every other week?"

"Twice a week," Harlow and Dr. Mothers said in unison.

"…sure," she grunted, in the moment before the lightbulb went off.

Eureka came as they were scheduling a second session, for two days hence. Thursday, that was. How did three o'clock sound? Oh, that sounded great. Yes, yes, see you then.

"And I should just mention, in the event that my receptionist has not," Dr. Mothers added, in a tone that made clear some recent failure on this receptionist's part, "that I am quite tightly booked this week. So, regrettably, both of you must be here within five minutes of the start of the appointment, or else a small surcharge will be added to your account."

Kira cocked her head at that. Harlow had made it sound like getting an appointment with the good doctor here had been the easiest thing in the world. But this was not the lightbulb.

"Oh…you said five?" Harlow asked.

"Yes."

"That's…okay, yeah. We can do that." He turned and placed a hand on Kira's shoulder. "Right honey? Five minutes? We can do that."

Ding. Lightbulb. Even though lightbulbs didn't actually go *ding*.

"We're doing twice weekly?" Kira confirmed.

"If that works for you," Harlow answered.

"Tuesdays and Thursdays?"

"Sure."

"Can we lock in the time?" Kira wondered, hoping she sounded casual, having forgotten what casual sounded like. "Like, three o'clock is *our* time, and that's set in stone?"

Harlow looked to Dr. Mothers.

Dr. Mothers shrugged. "Certainly. You can schedule out up to three weeks." He gestured to the door. "Reception can help you with that."

"It'd just be easier for me to plan around that way," Kira babbled, struggling to keep her hand from migrating up to her chest. Christ, her heart wasn't beating anymore – it was *revving*, like a little stuntman was going to jump it over a canyon.

"Of course. Reception can help you with that."

"I appreciate that, Doctor."

Dr. Mothers smiled, and went so far as to open the door for the Trecothiks.

"HOW *DID* YOU GET THAT BITE?" Harlow pulled the question out of thin air, as the two lay on the couch, watching a documentary about orangutans or something. Kira hadn't been paying attention to it, and that question led her to believe her husband hadn't either.

"A squirrel bit me," Kira reiterated.

"Why would it have come up to you, though?"

Kira levered herself forward, tilting enough to enter Harlow's peripheral vision. Just so he could really *see* how much she didn't appreciate his tone. "Why are you fighting me on this?" She presented her hand. "You think I bit myself?"

"I'm not *fighting* you. Why do you think I'm *fighting* you?"

"Because you won't let it go."

"This is the first time I've asked!"

"Yeah, and still! There's nothing to probe here. A squirrel bit me, that's all."

"Which is fair to ask about. I've never met anyone who's been bitten by a squirrel. So I was just *wondering,* how it ha-"

"I was with the dog – which was a golden retriever – I was on the ground, and this squirrel just comes up, and I try to, you know," she swatted at an imaginary critter with her right hand, "I tried to smack him away, and he just, chomped me. That's it."

"Okay. That's all I was wondering."

"Yeah, I'm sure."

She was aware of Harlow leaning forward now, to impose himself on *her* peripheral vision, so she leaned back and welded her eyes to the TV. Watched one great big orangutan make brilliant little gestures to another great big orangutan.

She should have handled that differently. Played innocent and de-escalated. That was stupid. Red had gotten the better of her.

No sense dwelling on it, though.

Kira reached forward and grabbed the remote off of the table. Hit *rewind.*

Harlow said nothing.

"I missed the last part," Kira muttered.

Harlow shrugged. "I didn't say anything."

Kira crunched the *play* button hard enough to make her thumb pop. They rewatched the bit with the great big orangutans and their brilliant little gestures. She got nothing new out of it the second time.

KIRA SMILED AT HARLOW as he left for work. Last night she'd resolved to say *I love you* this morning, just to help smooth things out a bit (and, also, because she did), but found the words beyond her grasp now that the morning had arrived.

Not that Harlow said it either. He just smiled back – holy hell, Kira hoped her grin had been more convincing than his – and said "see you later."

Yes. See you later.

Kira sat and sipped her coffee. Appreciating a moment of peace. The final such moment, before she had to get started.

Oh, but who was she kidding. She'd gotten started the moment the lightbulb had gone off in Dr. Mothers' office yesterday. *Planning* was still a part of the process, after all. Maybe the most important part.

To that end…well, Kira would finish her coffee first. And she did, savoring each and every sip in a way she rarely took the time to do. Despite knowing each one brought her that much closer to the moment when she would go upstairs, pick her phone up off the bedside table, and text Nicole Ligeti. The easiest of the three.

That wouldn't quite be a point of no return…but all the same, she needed to think of it as one. Because return was going to be *very* tempting, she knew. She might well wish to return to this precise moment. Sitting at the table, sipping her coffee, staring vacantly out the window as the sunrise flattered her backyard.

A lonely moment, she reminded herself. In every sense of the word.

No. Return was not an option. She needed to move forward. The way to put her life back together lay in forward motion.

She took another sip, only to find her cup empty. Hadn't noticed the last sip even as she'd taken it. Oh well.

Kira gave herself another moment to sit, and stare. In silence.

"HA, HA" she said to Nicole Ligeti, because the girl had made a joke. She turned to the other two, Zoe Cottrell and Maddie Encomb, and said "ha, ha" to them as well, because that was what one did when a joke was made in company. Look at them all, having a grand old time here in the Peet's coffee shop in Graham's Landing, a setting which had been Kira's choice. It was, she decided, that last little ethical redoubt in her subconscious trying to scare the girls away from her. *Keep your distance! This lady's the kind of psycho who'll* choose *to go to a Peet's!* They didn't get the message, though, and so here they were. At a Peet's. All three of them, because at the last second Kira had decided that was the safest way to do it. Less suspicious. More likely word of the coffee date would get back to Harlow, but that was a risk she had to take.

But then, that was why she'd asked them to meet just outside of Neirmouth.

More to the point, she was counting on her husband's frustration to overwhelm suspicion. He'd sounded so *very* frustrated, after all, when she'd called him to say she wasn't going to make their second appointment with Dr. Mothers, scheduled for today, Thursday, at three in the afternoon.

"Kira…" was all Harlow had said.

"I want to," Kira had replied, "seriously, I really do, but…I just *can't* today." She hadn't thought of a proper excuse, so she just slathered the word *can't* in as much anguish as she could manage.

She needed *this* Thursday – today – free. So she could see what the easiest of the three would be up to some *future* Thursday, when Kira absolutely *would* be making her appointment with Dr. Mothers.

For now, though, today, on *this* Thursday, Kira was saying words and the girls were responding to them, and then Kira responded to those words. It didn't matter what was being said, and in fact, Kira made a concerted effort not to absorb any of their conversation. Zoe was saying something about trying yoga; Kira asked some question about that and deliberately tuned out the response. Maddie'd had an anxiety dream that had woken her up and kept her awake; Kira inquired after the dream, yet lost the response to her own visions of other worlds. And Nicole, well, Nicole was finally finding her way to telling jokes. After all she'd been through. Remarkable. Triumph of the human spirit. Something like that. Assuming the joke was any good, that was, which Kira couldn't speak to one way or the other. She hadn't heard it. She'd just laughed once she knew it was over. Ha, ha.

The only reason Kira had called them all together here was because at a certain point (right around ten, as it happened, as Kira had insisted she had some terribly important errands to run) the conversation would end, and she and the three girls would go their separate ways. Except they wouldn't *all* be separate. Ha.

Ha, as they rose to leave Kira ginned up some kind of conversational coda aimed squarely at Nicole, the sort of oh-that-reminds-me nonsense that can serve as a pretense for walking somebody to their car, just a glancing thought, because if it's too involved the other person, in this instance Nicole, is liable to stop walking so they can turn and listen to you, and then you don't get to see what kind of car they drive, you don't get to make a mental note of their license plate to write down in a note on your phone. The sort of thing that probably starts with "hey I was thinking," because whenever a conversation starts with "hey I was thinking" it's either completely unimportant or the beginning of an argument with your significant other. So Kira held the door open for Nicole and said "hey I was thinking" even though that was a lie, she wasn't thinking anything, she just trusted her brain to fill in the blank, the one big blank. Which it did. The brain filled in the blank but Kira didn't know what with. Something about a program on orangutans she'd watched last night. You might find this interesting, Nicole. You and only you, so let's wave goodbye to Zoe and Maddie, watch them both get in to Maddie's car (logging the make and model of that as well) and drive away. Kira and Nicole sauntered back to the girl's car (no doubt actually her drunk mother's car), a banged-up beater of a Toyota Corolla, fire-engine red (what other color would it be?) with a plate number that was hard but not impossible to memorize. Kira cleared her mind of language to make room for letters and numbers that meant nothing, though maybe this was unnecessary because what was the likelihood of her seeing sixteen red Corollas (Corolli?!) in a row, all binged and biffed in the same way (big dent in the rear, right on the word *Corolla*) and needing the plate number to know which was which, ha, no, that wouldn't happen (probably). Who knew. Stranger things had happened. Would happen. Ha.

Ha, she gave Nicole Ligeti a goodbye embrace, because that was where they were in their relationship, Kira and all three of the girls, they embraced at hello and again at goodbye. They had so much in common, after all. Ha.

Ha, Kira hustled back to her car and sat in it, watching Nicole pull out of the strip mall parking lot. She gave the kid a three-car head start and then followed her out, phone unlocked and open to the notepad on the empty passenger seat. It was as loud as a backseat driver, that electronic notepad, but all it said was *faster. Faster.* No, notepad. Down, device. Be patient. Kira led by example. She could be patient. She was patient. *Forget this*, the phone proposed. *Just call them up for one last coffee date. Poison their drinks. Have it done with. Quick and easy. Have your girl back.* No, no. That was all wrong. That was too obvious. Kira had been seen out and about with those three girls too many times. Granted, she wasn't especially known in Graham's Landing, but Neirmouth was nearby, and it was small, and people talked. And what was she thinking, she'd been out with the girls in Neirmouth too. Everyone in town knew what unified that older woman with the three younger ones. How would that look to them, if those three girls all suddenly carked it a few hours after a coffee date with the grieving mother? *Them* being the people of Neirmouth. *Them* being the world at large. Oh yes, and not only are those three girls all dead (from poison, any autopsy would no doubt show) but Kira Trecothik's got her daughter back. How would *that* look? It'd be weird. There'd be no way to cover for that. And she couldn't invite them to dinner at hers – Harlow didn't have what it took. His blood was too hot and his grief couldn't carry a goddamned tune. She wanted to act quickly, yes, she wanted Leigh back right now…but that wasn't the way. She needed to be careful. Clever. She needed an alibi. Which Dr. Mothers could well give her. Prescription: innocence. Perceived, at least. Ha.

Ha, at first it seemed like Nicole's Thursday was just chaos, just anarchy, just madness, like she went to the gas station whenever the fuck she wanted, like going to the gym was something that just snuck up on her, like being out of school meant the only constant in her life was being anywhere and everywhere except *in* school. This wasn't helpful. None of this looked like routine; Kira needed *routine*. She needed an anchor. Yeah, an anchor. Something to really sink the kid. Ideally around three o'clock. Which time came and went, with Nicole sitting alone in some trendy farm-to-table joint that had probably been aiming for Boston but was doing its best all the way out here. *Here* being back in Graham's Landing, after tooling around Neirmouth for a while. The hell was this kid doing? Kira watched her through the big front window, the girl just flipping through her phone, her face a blank. Impossible to read. Useless to write down, in the notepad. Like everything else today. Useless. Come on kid. Work with me here. Ha.

Ha, Harlow called Kira at just after 3:30. Kira didn't answer. She'd told him she wasn't coming. Why was he calling? To check on her? Try to catch her out? No. Let it ring. Say hello to my outgoing message for me. Ha.

Ha, things really turned around at four o'clock. That was when Nicole headed to the music store. The only one in Graham's Landing. She sauntered on in with a long, narrow black case. An instrument. A clarinet, maybe. Going in for clarinet lessons, maybe. A routine. Maybe. Ha.

Ha, but the music store was the hardest place for Kira to follow her, surprisingly enough. Her house would have been so much easier. The Ligeti family lived on a pretty busy (by Neirmouth standards) side street called Barber Ave that looked like it had only ditched cobblestones in the last five years, after there'd been a sale on shattered pavement. Easy as pie for Kira to slide the car into the ample street parking on the avenue that intersected Barber, rack her seat down and back, and wait. Case the place, wasn't that what they said on cop shows? *Stake*, her notepad corrected her. *A stake out.* Yes, alright. Ha.

Ha, but Kira hadn't seen any routine attached to the family home. Whereas Nicole had business at the music store. But the music store was harder. In terms of following. In terms of closing the distance. In terms of doing the deed. Ha.

Ha, the music store to which Nicole Ligeti had come on this Thursday at four (she actually arrived just *before* four, what a punctual young woman) was called The Conservatory, which seemed pretty fucking presumptuous seeing as it was in a sad little gulch below sea level, next to the parking garage for the Graham's Landing Shopping Plaza (mostly empty storefronts now). To get to the Conservatory you had to head towards the parking garage but turn *before* you get to it, then drive down the slope into the concrete pocket only just large enough for four parking spaces and the store. The Conservatory. Yeah right. No way to follow Nicole down there without being seen. So Kira tried parking on the top story of the garage and peering down to keep an eye on the Conservatory, but that was too exposed. She could just tell. So the Conservatory was where she lost track of Nicole. The good news was there was only one way in, one way out. *Bomb it.* No. Bad call. Just for a whole bunch of reasons, bad call. Though the sheer disproportionality of that approach was sort of amusing, in its own tremendously improbable way. Ha.

Ha, but who cared about the clarinet lessons. Kira didn't even know if it was clarinet, she just sort of decided that it was. It was conjecture of the sort she made no allowance for in the rest of her plotting. Because yeah, that was what this was. Plotting. She was plotting. She was plotting out Nicole's life, which at first seemed like chaos anarchy madness but yielded comprehensible patterns in the grand scheme, i.e. the days that followed, which Kira also spent following Nicole, trying to tease out a routine, see if maybe there was a better day to do it than Thursday, a better time than four, a better place than the Conservatory. See the easiest way to do it, which was what mattered. All that mattered. Nicole was a homebody most times, unless she was sneaking out the back door of her house without Kira seeing, but the latter didn't think so. Maybe a ladder out her bedroom window? Climb in, gut her in her sleep. No. Ridiculous. Occam's razor, baby. Cut it down to size: the girl woke up when she woke up, fucked about in her domestic situation, and two days out of every three left just a little before noon to go to the gym. Two on one off, like she was gonna bc a goddamned bodybuilder. Yeah right. Stringbean like her? Yeah right. Good on her for trying, though. Oh, but Kira just wanted to grab her by the shoulders and shake her, tell her to cut that fitness shit out and focus on doing fun stuff. Make these days count. Her time was short, and so was she. Ha.

Ha, in the evenings Harlow would ask Kira about her day. And Kira would say she'd had a good day. And Harlow would say he had too. And that would do, because it was better than sniping at one another, better than being dissatisfied by everything the other person said or did. Better than either of them saying what they thought of the other just then. Ha.

Ha, on gym days, the afternoon started with a smoothie at the gym, which Nicole was invariably sipping as she stepped out the door. Always always always, across the days Kira watched her, Nicole left the gym with her lips on the straw. The smoothie color changed but the sip-timing never did. Amazing. Poison the smoothie? How? Bad idea. Drop an anvil on her head? Tee hee. Good one. Not really. Too messy. Where does one get an anvil, in this day and age? Not the point. Non-gym days saw Nicole eating lunch at home. Probably. Conjecture. What happened in her own home was Nicole's problem. Her parents' problem. Where were the parents? Coming and going. Kira saw them but didn't register them (beyond that one detail she knew of the girl's mother, by which Kira couldn't help defining her). Were she to register them, she might have second thoughts. Might empathize with the world she was about to take from them. The exchange she was about to make. She couldn't afford that. Second thoughts. No. Only first thoughts here, please. Ha.

Ha, gym, groceries (Nicole did the family's shopping, interesting), clarinet. Sometimes lunch with friends. More often lunch alone. Sometimes crying. Alone. Poor girl. No drinks; she was too young. At least not in public. Too bad. That might be somewhere Kira could intercept her. A bar. Slip some strychnine in her drink. Where does somebody get strychnine? Same place as the anvils, hee hee, ho ho. The fact that her mind invariably returned to poison made Kira immediately distrustful of it. Its intuitive nature made it obvious. Besides, she wasn't a chemist. She wasn't a botanist. She didn't know shit about poison. Which meant searching. Which meant a search history, the kind you can't erase by clearing it in your browser. Which meant a lead. Which meant detectives. Then it all falls apart. Oh dear. Oh no. No poison, then. But where? How? Gym, groceries, clarinet. Sometimes lunch. Always dinner at home. Nicole was a fucking introvert. Introverts, Kira decided, were the hardest types to kill. So much for being the easiest of the three. Not that Kira had any frame of reference. She hadn't stalked the other two. Not yet. So maybe Nicole *was* the easiest of the three. Didn't matter. She would be the *first* of the three. Kira had a whole notepad full of the girl's life, as glimpsed over a week and a half. She had to be first, so Kira could delete the note. Or at least, clear it and get started on the second. Ha.

Ha, one night Harlow read part of the note over Kira's shoulder. She'd been looking at it while he was home. Stupid. Careless. Then Harlow was suddenly standing right behind her chair, asking Kira what she was writing down. She could tell from his tone of voice that he was suspicious. For some reason. What reason did he have to be suspicious? Besides *some*. At any rate: she locked her phone at once and told him it was a dream journal Dr. Mothers had recommended she keep at the end of their meeting on Tuesday, when Harlow had been in the restroom. Kind of embarrassing, silly, haha. Private stuff. Harlow respected this because he was a good person, and he had no idea that his wife wasn't. Ha.

"Ha," she said, "speaking of, would it work for you if I called Dr. Mothers and asked to move our appointment this Thursday to four o'clock?"

"Why?" Harlow asked.

"I…want to take a yoga class in the afternoon."

"Oh. You do yoga?"

"I thought I'd give it a try." She forced a smile. "A friend recommended it to me."

Warmth flickered across Harlow's face. The main emotion it occasioned in Kira was *nostalgia*. "Sure. I think that'd be great. I hear yoga is great."

"That's what my friend said," Kira validated him. "She said it was great."

"Great. Yeah, if it works for Dr. Mothers, I think that's…cool."

"Great."

"Yeah."

Ha.

Ha, ha.

Ha.

THE CONSERVATORY was located in more or less the center of Graham's Landing. What might euphemistically be called a "working class" neighborhood, which in this part of the country, at this time in history, simply meant "not suburbs." Lots of old row homes with tiny, untended lawns, peeling and rotting in the shadows thrown by abandoned factories and mills that would have long since been converted into luxury condominiums, were it not for the fact that, well, who wanted to live in Graham's Landing? Even gentrification couldn't be bothered.

Dr. Mothers' office, meanwhile, was ambiguously the crown jewel at the northernmost point of Graham's Landing, and/or stuck to the undercarriage of Neirmouth. It really was right on the line between the two. The office building from which Dr. Mothers worked was a tan, three-story stucco dump a block and a half from the hospital. If the directory in the lobby was to be believed, he was but one of the many, many doctors who worked out of that building. Kira wondered if any of them had silly doctorates, like in arts or theology. The idea of an oncologist sharing a wall with a musicologist tickled her. Something for everyone here. Tee hee.

At any rate: the distance between the Conservatory and Dr. Mothers' office, according to Google Maps, was just under three miles. And Google Maps had no reason to lie. So just under three miles it was. 2.8, to be precise. Be precise. Precision was going to be key here.

Kira spent all of Wednesday getting very precise indeed.

She didn't want to start from the parking lot of the Conservatory – didn't want her car seen in there, ever – so she typically began double-parked up on the street from which the turn-off to the parking lot slithered down the hill. Starting the stopwatch on her phone – such a versatile little gizmo, how did we ever live without them – she waited until twenty seconds had ticked by to throw the car into drive. Twenty seconds seemed a reasonable amount of time to allot for getting out of the parking lot and back to her car. Twenty seconds from the time the deed had been done. That seemed reasonable.

When the stopwatch hit :20, Kira gunned it. Not running red lights, not rolling through stop signs, not driving more than two or three miles above the speed limit, so perhaps not quite *gunning it* in any recognizable sense. But still, she was gripping the steering wheel *quite* hard, and clenching her jaw tightly enough to send pain cascading down her neck, as she explored the many ways to get from the Conservatory to Dr. Mothers' office. There were obviously no highways between them, but she did have some choices to make regarding whether she would stick to the more residential side streets, or try her luck on the main commercial drag for the middle portion of the drive. Slightly faster speed limits there, but more traffic. Jaywalkers, parallel parkers. A bit too unpredictable, she found – she made the drive three times on that, and clocked times all around eleven minutes, as opposed to the eight she could manage on the residential streets.

Three minutes' difference didn't sound like much. But three was practically five, and five minutes after four was when Dr. Mothers would tack on his lateness surcharge. In other words: it was when he would *notice* her lateness. It was when her time of arrival would be *formally recorded,* in a way that could be scrutinized later, should some person or persons think to do so. Which would really hurt the alibi she was so painstakingly assembling.

As she drove, she had the conversation in her head, over and over: *You're telling me a girl was killed across town? How terrible. I'm only just hearing about it now, having been at a therapy appointment when it happened. You can call my therapist to confirm; Dr. Mothers, he works in…yes it* is *funny, isn't it?*

It was all down to minutes. She was counting on the cops having some difficulty in establishing an *exact* time of death for Nicole; she was counting on no one being able to say *exactly* when Kira had arrived at Dr. Mothers' office. So three minutes, to one in Kira's situation, was… not zero. Blastoff.

Kira made the drive at least fifteen times. Maybe more. It was almost the entirety of her Wednesday. The day before Thursday. The day before.

Most of the journeys did little more than reinforce Google Maps' estimate of an eight minute drive. On the residential streets. She did, however, make a few key discoveries regarding alternative routes which, all taken together, could shave nearly a minute off of her transit time. Turning off of Gouldman Drive before the four-way stop and taking Lisbon over to Clementine was good for just under ten seconds, on average. Dodging the curve of May Street by, counterintuitively, taking the ambitiously named Highview over what was really just a very small hill, that could knock off another fifteen seconds or so. Falmouth Ave, she discovered, was best avoided entirely. Hard to say exactly why, but both Winthrop and Harrison on either side reliably saved about five seconds. Curious.

The most substantial change Kira found, though, one that knocked the drive from the Conservatory to Dr. Mothers' office down to a mere *six minutes*, was moving the starting block.

She'd found the spot almost by accident. Spotted it on her way back from an especially discouraging test run. A splash of green down on the far side of the Conservatory parking lot. Something to be investigated. From the far side.

Lo and behold: there was indeed a far side. Accessible by going past the turnoff to the Conservatory lot, past the Plaza parking garage, and around to the left. Took a bit more finding than that, in fact, but Kira was determined, and so, she found it.

The far side turned out to be a side-street called Lanier, an especially dismal streak of two-story row homes presiding over wild grasses and old auto parts, guarded by hip-height chain link fences. Kira frowned at them –

more *nostalgia* – then turned her attention to a particular pedestrian alley which branched off of Lanier, which alley could be followed to a set of uneven concrete stairs, which heaved one into the parking lot of the Conservatory, from the side opposite the entrance for cars. It was one of those quirks of urban planning that one so often took for granted, when one had the luxury of doing so. The high concrete wall of the parking garage formed a solid wall to the alley on what was now Kira's left, while a waist-high lip damming the dying lawn of whoever lived in that spooky-ass duplex there constituted the right side. It was a ramshackle haunt, that duplex, the sort with a deck covered in rusty bicycles. Theoretically, Kira's greatest risk of being spotted came from whoever lived there. But people who covered their deck in rusty bicycles weren't the sorts of people who spent a lot of time looking out their windows, were they? Kira didn't think so. She sure hoped not, anyway.

She did the drive, and marveled at the time. Six minutes. Incredible. She high-tailed it back to Lanier, and once more studied all the homes with an eyeline on that little alley, the one that cut through to the Conservatory lot.

There were a lot of windows on those homes. And a lot of homes.

So the risk of being spotted was quite a bit higher, if she started here. Run through the alley and into the parking lot. Do the deed. Run back out. Risky. Riskier than creeping down the hill on the other side of the lot, she thought.

But that was what masks were for.

And, again, just to really draw a line under it: *six minutes*.

Kira did the drive twice more, from Lanier Street to Dr. Mothers'. Just to prove to herself that this was the spot. That this was the way it would happen.

She did indeed prove it. Twice more.

So she drove home. It was starting to get dark, after all. And despite herself, she was getting hungry.

THERE WAS NO WAY HE COULDN'T HEAR IT. *Feel* it. She was leaning flush up against him – he was in a cuddly goddamned mood tonight, it seemed, and had wanted to watch some ninety-minute, bubblegum nothingfilm he'd heard bigged up on a podcast or some shit. Who knew. Kira had no idea what it was called, who was in it, what it was about. She wasn't aware of much at all, beyond the hammering of her heart. It seemed powerful enough to shift her bodily with each beat, to blast a tiny puff of air from her nostrils.

So how the fuck was Harlow not commenting on his wife being racked by a million little kick-drum hiccups? He'd spent the past few weeks doing little more than *commenting*. On how she seemed, on what she was doing, on what he thought she was thinking. True, most of these judgments were ones that never rose to the level of language. Kira simply intuited them from the slope of his brow, the tilt of his head. But the fact that he *did* verbalize some seemed to vindicate her suspicions that there were still more he *wasn't* verbalizing. Somehow.

The further into the night she found herself, the more her gut began to revolt. She was trying so hard not to think about tomorrow. Thursday. Oh, she felt like her stomach was collapsing in on itself. This was beyond the sensation of needing to throw up. This was having a black hole buried in one's viscera, just behind the navel.

Harlow's body felt perfectly motionless against hers. Against her rockin', knockin', *ba-bump ba-bumpin'* body. She wanted so badly to look up to his face. See if he had one of those little *comments* swirling around his noggin. She'd be able to tell. By his face.

So look.

She peeled her eyes from the television and tilted her head back, stretching the front of her neck as her chin cranked up up up. Finally, Harlow's face came into view. Upside-down, from a low angle. But easy enough to read.

His features were slack, his eyelids ever-so-slightly drooping. The classic mien of a man watching a movie by which he was vaguely amused, but not engrossed.

Not the sort of expression one wears whilst nursing suspicions that one's wife might be nuts.

Harlow blinked himself out of the narrative, then turned to look at Kira. A veritable landslide of small emotions ripped across his face, each impossible to parse in what little light the fifty-five inch screen threw off, yet each clearly distinct from the others.

Some looked friendly to Kira. Loving.

Others, not so much.

"What?" Harlow asked.

"Nothing," Kira replied. She'd wanted it to sound

gooey and romantic, in an *I just wanted to look at you, my love* sort of way. It came out more as *what, I'm not allowed to look at my goddamned husband?!*

"…" She could see the questions on the tip of his tongue. Practically see the words scrolling along behind his eyes, like subtitles in search of a better scene.

Are you alright?

What's wrong?

Do you have something you want to say?

She wanted him to ask her. Just ask one of those stupid questions. Not because she was locked and loaded with a response. No, she didn't know *how* she would answer such a question. She just knew he wanted to ask it. Knew he *needed* to ask it.

So fucking *ask.*

"What's wrong?" There. That was the question. Too bad Kira had been the one to ask it of him.

Harlow narrowed his eyes slightly. "You were…looking at me…?"

"I don't know," Kira grunted, sitting back and returning her attention to the TV.

"…what don't you know?"

She blinked too hard. Jerked her head forward slightly. Her neck whispered *crck* into her skull. "Can you just let me watch the movie?"

Harlow's chest rose and fell slowly. "If you want to talk, we can always turn it off."

Like the world's most tragic magic trick – *alakazam!* – she had tears in her eyes. Running down her cheeks. So she just kept on staring at the blot in her vision that she knew had been the TV, hoping that Harlow would do the same. "I appreciate that," she croaked, and meant it.

She reminded herself that this was all about love. Tomorrow was about love. Reclaiming all of the love that had been bled from her life.

Had to keep reminding herself. It was so easy to forget.

That night, Kira couldn't sleep for the smile on her face. It was hurting her cheeks. She couldn't stop doing it, couldn't force herself to relax. Tried desperately, and failed. Even as the tears came and went, came and went through the night…she couldn't shake the smile.

Couldn't stop thinking, *it's all about love.*

SEVEN

TWO THINGS A HEART CAN DO

THURSDAY drew upon Kira by inches. It was a creeping dawn, one she could hear dragging itself across the ceiling, sliming ever nearer until it was dripping its poison onto the center of her forehead.

She couldn't sleep. How could she, with such a black slug of a day pouring over her?

Eyes wide and dry, she rolled onto her side and looked at Harlow. Beautifully lit by the scythes of sunrise cutting mercilessly through the blinds. He was asleep, Harlow was. Out cold in his usual posture, arms thrown up over his head like somebody had just scored a touchdown. Snoring that light, raspy snore of his. It was cute, largely because it wasn't that schooner-through-fog bleat of which oversized adenoids rendered him amply capable. Kira reached out and placed her hand on his chest, felt it rise, fall, rise again. That was how she liked to think of it. Rise, fall, rise. It would have been just as accurate to say fall, rise, fall…but no. No. Rise, fall, rise.

This is about love, remember. Remember it like laughter. Don't forget.

Rise, fall, rise. That was Leigh's trajectory too. Just as soon as Kira got out of bed, got the day started. Did what needed to be done, to help her daughter rise from the dead.

Thinking of it in those terms got Kira off the mattress in a hurry. She rushed to the toilet, doubled over it, and summoned what little of last night's dinner she'd managed to get down for review. Boy, what a rough couple of weeks for her esophagus.

Quiet though she tried to be, Harlow heard her hurling. The snoring stopped, little footsteps taking their place. Then, when those ran out, a polite rap on the bathroom door. "You okay, hon?" he asked.

Kira stifled a gasping sob, ripped off a fistful of toilet paper, and dabbed carelessly at her chin. "I'm fine," she insisted. Only that wasn't true, was it? This seemingly unprompted bout of sickness might not strike Harlow as inherently suspicious, but if he should discover that Nicole was murdered later that same day…would he put two and two together?

There's no way he won't, her paranoia hissed.

There's no way he could, another part of her insisted.

There's a chance he might, a still more persuasive lump of grey matter decreed. And so it was. Maybe he would, maybe he wouldn't. Either way, he might.

All she could do was act as normally as possible for the rest of the morning. Ensure Harlow had nothing else upon which to hang suspicion.

"Sorry," Kira mumbled. "I think I got food poisoning."

Harlow's face slumped into a mask of concern. "From *my* cooking?"

"Either that," she added, remembering laughter, "or I'm pregnant."

Harlow did not laugh. Did something close to the opposite, even. His mouth and eyebrows snapped into rigid slashes of disapproval.

"Sorry."

"It's okay."

"Bad joke."

"It's okay."

She tossed her bundle of toilet paper into the toilet and tore off another. "Could you make me some toast?" she asked him.

"…yeah," he replied, after a thoughtful pause. "Of course." And off he went, to make her some toast. When Kira fancied him out of earshot, she bent back over the porcelain and made a bit more room for breakfast.

"SO WHAT DO YOU HAVE GOING ON TODAY?" he asked her over toast, which he was eating out of some kind of condescending solidarity. Or maybe he'd just smelled hers and wanted some. She wasn't feeling especially charitable about other people's motivations today.

"The usual," she replied.

"Oh." He nodded, yanking off a piece of crust and dipping it in the strawberry jam dollop at the three o'clock position on his plate. "Been a lot of that lately."

Kira glared at him.

He had the good sense to avert his gaze. "I mean that in the sense of…you deserve a break. A mental health break." He stuffed his toast into his mouth.

Boy, *that* almost squeezed a full-on guffaw out of her. She kept things down to a simple "mhm," though.

Harlow swallowed loudly. "Maybe not the best time to ask, but do you know what you want for dinner? I can pick something up."

She did her very best to put on a game face. *As normal as possible.*

"Maybe tacos," she smiled normally, as her stomach collapsed like a neutron star.

"Tacos!" he squawked. So she wasn't the only one putting on a game face. Couldn't be easy, breaking fast with a nutcase. "Sounds great to me."

She grinned and shot him a thumbs up.

His face fell, ever so slightly.

She frowned at her toast.

After a half an hour or so, he left. She remained. Sitting. Waiting for the morning to end, for the afternoon to arrive.

Her toast somehow got colder than room temperature.

SHE LOADED EVERYTHING she'd need today into the trunk, slammed it shut, then opened the garage door. She was behind the wheel with the car door shut before the garage door had finished chundering its way up. Her right hand swung around her and grabbed the seatbelt. She pulled. It *chunked*. Didn't move. Caught, the way seatbelts catch. The way they always seemed to catch, when you were fresh out of patience. Like they could smell frustration.

Well, the joke was on the seatbelt. That wasn't frustration that Kira reeked of. She had patience aplenty.

Hand steady, head clear, heart calm, she loosened her grip on the seatbelt. Let it slide a few inches back into whatever horrible little warren the seatbelt lived in. Pulled again.

There. Smooth as butter. It slid right out. Kira passed the clicky bit to her left hand, and slotted it home at her right hip. Excellent. Step one completed. Safety first. Always.

She planted her hands at ten and two on the wheel in front of her, then checked her rearview mirror. Not that there would be any obstructions behind her – it was her driveway, by golly – but, you know. Safety first. And second. Safety *always*.

She threw the car into reverse, and puttered back out of the garage. Slow, slow. Take 'er easy. Safety at all times.

When the car was fully out of the garage, she spotted her neighbor Christine in her garden. In Christine's garden, that was. Christine was in Christine's garden, kneeling on a filthy pillow, elbow-deep in the dirt. She wasn't looking Kira's way – didn't seem to notice her at all, in fact. But all the same, Kira didn't like that Christine was out. Didn't like that Christine was, however peripherally, seeing Kira leave. She could help somebody put together a *timeline.* She could be a *witness.*

Oh, but didn't that describe everybody who saw Kira, from here on out? Everywhere she went today, she would be making people *witnesses* without their even knowing it. Hopefully. If all went well. If they *should* end up realizing that they were witnesses to something, well…

"Oh, FUCK!" Kira shouted. She slammed the brakes, cranked the car into park, then swung open the door and dashed back into her house. Her car being the sort with a remote key, and the key being in Kira's pocket, her car began to *BEEBEEBEEBEEBEE* at her as she dashed away with the vehicle's favorite little rectangle.

She let it *BEEBEE* to its not-so-heart's content as she plowed through the door back to the kitchen (glad she'd forgotten to set the alarm as she'd headed out), thumped her way to the counter in four loping strides, and yanked the sharpest knife from the mahogany block. The one she'd washed so well. Hello, old friend. Almost forgot you. Wouldn't *that* have been something?

She jogged back through the garage, empty now save for the incessant *BEEBEEBEEBEEBEE* of her hopelessly needy automo-

"Hi Kira!" Christine called, just as Kira stepped back out onto the driveway.

FUCK.

Kira switched the knife around to the right side of her

body. Away from Christine.

Christine just kept on smiling and waving. Squinting and holding one palm over her eyes, too. So she hadn't seen the knife. Thank Christ.

Careless. Kira was being careless. This did not bode well.

But hey, at least she was finally close enough to her car again to make it shut the fuck up.

"Hi!" Kira returned, waving with her free hand.

"Beautiful day!"

"Yeah," Kira agreed, as she swung around to the passengerside of her car, opened the door, and put the knife onto the seat, "sure is!"

"You have a good one now!"

"You too, Christine!" Kira hustled around the front side of her stupid, noisy car, popped the door, and piled inside.

She threw the car into reverse and backed it down the drive. Her hands slid along the wheel, already halfway to glazed in her palmsweat. She felt her heart not merely in her throat, but as a tight, pulsing band *around* it, like she was being throttled by a metronome.

For some reason, she coughed twice. That was weird.

What the fuck was she doing? She hadn't thought any of this through beyond the drive to Dr. Mothers'. It had been an idea for so long. Now it was a thing. It was a thing she was doing. She was forgetting her knife, getting very nearly rumbled by her ride. This was fucked. This was fully fucked.

Still, she backed out on to Hamlin, cranked the automatic shift from R to D, and observed the speed limit. Because it had been an idea for so long. Now it was a thing she was doing.

About ten yards before the first stoplight of the journey, she put on her seatbelt, and returned her hands to ten and two.

HAD THE CAR ALWAYS BEEN THIS HARD to drive? It seemed like every twist of the wheel was either too hard or too soft, each depression of the gas similarly bound to extremes. Take a twelve-year-old raised in an underground bunker and throw them in the driver's seat, they wouldn't have had much trouble outperforming Kira just then. Right now that was alright, she supposed. She'd left herself plenty of time to get to Lanier, that side street behind the Conservatory. When it *wouldn't* be alright was during the getaway. When it was critical she manage that six minute transit. She supposed being a *little* (as in, less than five minutes) late for her appointment with Dr. Mothers wasn't the end of the world…but punctuality certainly strengthened the alibi.

With Christine having seen her, and Harlow having his default set to SUSPICIOUS, Kira needed as powerful an alibi as she could manage.

Therefore: she needed to get her shit under control. Now.

She pulled up to the next stoplight and came to an obedient (if jerking) halt. Guide me, oh Red one. She squeezed the wheel until her knuckles popped. Took long, slow breaths in and out through her nose.

In…

Out…

In…

Out…

In.

It only now occurred to her that if it came to the point where someone was asking her for an alibi, then…

She opened her eyes.

The light had turned green. Abandoned by the red!

She looked into the rearview mirror.

There was a car behind her. They were just sitting there, had been for an indeterminate amount of time. They weren't honking. They were just sitting there.

Kira squinted through the rearview, through two windshields. It was some old lady peering out from behind the wheel, *grinning*. A satisfied, toothless smile. So big Kira could imagine the old lady's dentures had popped out, were rolling around the seat well. A second smile at her feet.

What a strange expression on her face. It was one of pure, unadulterated happiness. Like the old lady had just broken out of a retirement home and was burning rubber for Vegas.

That was always an option. After. Skip down, let everything die down…then come back and finish what she'd started.

The thought put a toothier grin on Kira's face, for just a moment. Then she remembered she hadn't started anything yet. She still needed to start.

She frowned and puttered towards the next red light,

two blocks ahead. *Guide me.*

KIRA DROVE PAST THE TURN-OFF to The Conservatory, past the Plaza parking garage next door, and around to the left. Down onto Lanier Street. With the homes, and the yards, and the fences. And the alley, of course. That quirk of urban planning.

Kira checked the clock. 3:39 PM. Shit. That might be too early. Or maybe not. Ah, but here already was a variable she hadn't thought enough about: for the two weeks she'd watched the girl, Nicole had arrived at the Conservatory just about five minutes before four o'clock. But two data points did not a pattern make. She could be late today. *But,* Kira didn't want to get all kitted out and linger around the alley for fifteen minutes, drawing attention to herself while she waited for the kid to show up. *But,* she couldn't exactly wait in the car. There was no way to see the parking lot of the Conservatory from here, and even if there were, the distance would be too great to cover before Nicole made it in inside. *But,* it would take time to get everything on, to get herself ready, so she couldn't wait until Nicole showed up.

"Goddamnit," Kira grunted. She swung out of the car (having turned it off first, no more *BEEBEEBEE-BEEBEEs* today) and stepped around towards the back. All the while keeping her eyes firmly fixed on the alley.

A warm, humid breeze sighed from the mouth of that alley. Sure, maybe that was just her imagination. But she knew for a fact it wasn't. Even though it could have been.

Just as she placed her hand on the trunk of the car to open it, she heard someone laugh. A distant, carefree titter.

Pure reflex: Kira *yanked* her hand off the car. Jerked her head to the left, the right, forward, over each shoulder. She didn't see anyone.

But she could still hear voices. Teenagers, maybe. Somewhere nearby. Just nattering away, how teenagers did. Kira knew all too well how teenagers could natter.

Further up the street, she saw a middle-aged guy walking his dog. A coffee-and-cream coated pitbull. With clipped ears, Kira noted unhappily. She hated to see pups so disfigured, the natural flop of their ears ironed out into two little devil horns. *Cruelty without purpose*, she tutted silently to herself.

Still shaking her head, she tried to open the trunk of her car. As usual, though, the damn thing didn't open. It was *supposed* to open without being popped from the inside, as long as she had the car's *precious* little key next to the rubber bit under the handle, but this car had never done that. So Kira had to trek back to the driverside door and press the appropriate button.

This time, she ignored the disembodied voices from nearby and opened the boot. Empty of everything save a tarp lain along the bottom, and the garbage bag.

Another thought, unbidden: *her head is in there. Somehow, Nicole's head is in the bag.*

A wave of revulsion nearly sent Kira headlong into the bushes to purge herself of toast, the only thing she'd managed to gag down today. She held strong, though. It was too late for that. It was too late and too early. There would be plenty of time for that later. After.

But then, there would be two more to do *after,* wouldn't there?

Ooh, how tempting those bushes looked.

No! Kira slapped herself in the face.

She glanced up the street. Towards the man walking his dog.

He was staring down at his phone. Not looking at Kira. Not having seen her slap herself in the face.

She glanced over her shoulder.

Nobody behind her. To glance into the trunk. To see the tarp, the garbage bag.

Shaking her head, she fought the squeeze of her stomach, the tremor in her chest, the unmade-balloon-animal feeling of her limbs, to unstring the band from her wrist and tie her hair up in a ponytail.

Somehow, that helped. Putting the hair up felt like a step forward.

Ok. Deep breath. In, out, in, out.

It took two tries with the hair tie. The first time, she didn't get as much as she wanted in the ponytail. Too much hanging out on the sides. Liable to flap into the face, while she was running. Which she would be.

Second time was the charm, though. So she bent down and unwound the neck of the black garbage bag. Reaching in, she was fully braced to feel the soft tickle of human hair, and couldn't help the *whoosh* of relief she felt as she touched the familiar leather of her gloves.

On went those gloves. Thin, black. Definitely a bit

shady-looking, she supposed, but nothing one would give more than a passing glance. She hoped. Hope not being enough, she gazed sharply from side to side, over each shoulder. Which was *very* shady-looking. Fortunately the dogwalker was still boggling at his phone, and she didn't see anyone else to comment unfavorably upon her shadiness. She could still hear those voices though. Could hear, but not see, those nattering teenagers. *Witnesses.* Where were they?

No. Focus. Shadiness was borne of reticence. If she looked like she was doing something she shouldn't be doing, that was shady. As long as she moved confidently, with nary a glance this way or that, then she wouldn't look shady. Stood to reason.

Confidently, then, as assuredly as she could, she yanked the full-length poncho, of the deepest blue she could find, out of the garbage bag in her trunk. It was an attention-getting color, yes, but that was kind of the idea. Well, that and keeping the blood off her clothes. But the other virtue of it was that, should someone spot her, the things they would probably remember of her would be *blue poncho* and *black mask.*

Because yes, here came the mask. A pitch-black balaclava, lumping at the back as she folded her ponytail underneath, leaving no flesh exposed save the eyes and mouth, the former of which Kira subsequently covered with a pair of cheap convenience store sunglasses, the latter with a blue face mask left over from the teeth of COVID (twisting the elastic bands, naturally, to send her breath out the sides rather than through the top to fog her sunglasses). Face completely obscured, form fully devoured by the poncho. She was, if she said so herself, pretty fucking suspicious right now. While she supposed it wasn't technically a crime to walk about dressed like she was trying to work swing for Pussy Riot and The Weather Channel at the same time, there was no way in hell anybody spotted her and didn't keep a *very* close eye on her, perhaps calling the police for something more than moral support.

Nerves won this round: as she closed the trunk of the car, Kira glanced up Lanier Street.

The man walking his dog was looking straight at her.

Kira froze.

The man's pitbull, until now fully captured by the smells coming off of the post for a sign which had some *very* precise ideas about when one could and could not park on this street, joined in the staring contest. Eyes locked on Kira.

More than anything, Kira was proud of herself for keeping upright; her legs had gone mushy, just two unbaked baguettes in a pair of pants.

Well, pants *and* a poncho. And a mask and gloves, though those weren't covering the legs. They were covering the not-legs. A fact of which she reminded herself, along with all of the other things. Forgetful Kira. Always needing to remember that, for example, her identity was fully concealed. Even if that man with the dog lifted his phone to, for example, film her, there would be no way to identify her from those images.

So she tried to act confident. The way one does, when

one is out for a stroll in one's favorite poncho, with one's favorite balaclava, accessorizing with one's favorite leather gloves.

Casual as could be, she lifted her right palm towards the man, fingers hanging loose. A salutation, the way the kids do it!

The man had no free hands. A phone in one, a leash in the other. Still, he gave Kira a slow nod. Chin ticking upwards, then back down again. Rise, fall, and then nothing. Another form of salutation.

Excellent. This was normal. As long as one did not hope to extend *this* to cover Kira's heartrate, or blood pressure, or whatever intestinal overdrive was currently shredding her guts to confetti.

She took one last deep breath, turned slowly on her heel, and lurched into the alley. As soon as she knew she was hidden from the dogwalker's view by the side of that house with the bicycles on the porch, she crouched down, keeping low, hoping that the lip of concrete could obscure her partially or wholly from whoever might be in the aforementioned house.

At the risk of looking *shady,* she stole a glance up at that rotting old duplex. At windows hung with thin, ratty curtains. Couldn't have done much to keep the light out, Kira figured. They were also just the sort of curtain someone might be able to peer straight through without moving them aside. No way to know if someone wasn't doing just that, wasn't watching her, probably impassively, that was how Kira imagined them, watching *impassively* as a hunched blue ne'er-do-well crept through the paved pedestrian alley beside their dreadful house. God, how she hated them. Whoever was watching her through the windows. The *witnesses*. Assuming they were there, of course. Assuming.

A gust of wind tousled the tall weeds climbing the low concrete wall. It carried the voices of those unseen teenagers clearly enough to make comprehensible the word "told," and *only* the word "told." The larger context was lost as the afternoon returned to stillness. Which was fine by Kira.

As she neared the end of the alley, the parking lot of the Conservatory appeared as a widening cavity above five concrete steps. It put the pavement, the lot, and the whole of the Conservatory at hip-height with Kira. A strange, infantilizing approach. One which gave her pause. Just a second of pause, though. Just long enough for her to realize she wasn't sure why she was having a pause.

Okay. Pause over. Kira took the last few yards to the stairs at a jog and prayed for Nicole's punctuah *FUCK!*

Nicole was punctual alright. Her car turned onto the ramp down into the Conservatory parking lot just as Kira scaled the second step from the top. Which was also the moment she realized she'd *forgotten the fucking knife again.*

To hell with staying low – she turned around and full-on sprinted back to the car, chopping the air as best she could from beneath the poncho. A strong counterargument in *favor* of discretion presented itself just as Kira stumbled out of the alley and back onto Lanier: any witnesses might have a hard time identifying her through the poncho and the mask, but if they saw her mysterious blue personage ducking into a car – which, in accordance with state law, had a license plate on the front *and* the rear bumpers – and popping back out to hurry a great big knife over to what would soon be the scene of a crime, well…nothing, actually, because the man with the dog was gone, and Kira didn't see anyone else. Had *he* seen her car? No way to know. So she stumbled back into a sprint and all but launched herself at her vehicle.

Kira grabbed hold of the passengerside door. The car shouted *BEEBEE!* and happily unlocked itself. Swinging the door open, Kira ducked inside and retrieved the kitchen knife from the well of the passenger seat, where it had fallen at some point on the drive over here. Her angle of retrieval was a bit awkward; she ended up slashing the fabric on the front of the seat. Whatever. That meant the knife was sharp.

Sparing no thought for appearances now, she slammed the car door and dashed back into the alley. The bicycle house passed her by as a smudge in her periphery. The tall weeds against the concrete? Forget about 'em.

The shrubbery on either side of the stairs at the far end obscured Kira's view of the parking lot, and would do until she was beginning her ascent into it. What, she wondered, would she do if Nicole were talking to someone there? Would she kill them both? She'd never seen more than one person in the lot at once, but there was a first time for everything, wasn't there? Wasn't she about to prove that?

Her fear proved academic, thank Christ: she flung

herself up the steps to find Nicole futzing about with something in the trunk of her car. Alone.

New problem, spotted in mid-air: Nicole was facing the stairs Kira had just taken at a leap. Not looking directly at them, but facing in their general direction. The sound of Kira's feet hitting the pavement was sure to draw the girl's attention. Granted, if she glanced up, she would see a black-headed, blue triangle rushing towards her, with about twenty yards left to clear. Which might just be disorienting enough to keep her still. Or maybe not. Still.

No time for calculation: Kira hit the ground hard, pumping her legs as powerfully as she could.

Nicole lifted her eyes. Kira knew this only because of the gasping sound the girl made — Kira herself was running too quickly to visually register her as much more than one fleshy blur amongst grey.

Animal instinct: Nicole took a step backwards. Away from Kira, towards the Conservatory.

Couldn't let her get away.

Stop her.

A moment of grisly inspiration led Kira to shout, in the friendliest voice she could muster between wheezes (albeit one dropped as low as she could manage): "Hi Nicole!"

Addressing her by name had the desired effect. Nicole stopped moving. Palpably perplexed by the geometry goblin barreling towards her, who had hailed her as an old friend traveling at speed. If Kira wasn't very much mistaken, she even saw a confused, hopeful smile cross the girl's face. Realizing she was the butt of a good-natured prank, feeling so relieved.

And then Kira made contact.

The two fell to the ground, Kira leaping on top of Nicole.

Nicole's head *thwacked* against the concrete. The sound was thundering on either end but delicate in the center, the sound of a single egg cracked open on the edge of a glass bowl.

A toneless, plaintive sigh escaped Nicole's mouth.

Kira slapped her left hand over Nicole's face and leaned on it.

She plunged the knife hard into the girls' stomach. A thin *clck* rattled up the handle – the blade hitting the Nicole's spine.

A planet collided with the side of Kira's head. No: the girl's fist, bunched and far more powerful than it had any right to be. Colliding.

Kira staggered off the kneeling perch she'd taken up over Nicole's sternum. Despite a grievous wound to the gut, the sprightly young gymrat capitalized on Kira's imbalance, pushing her up and off.

Keep hold of the knife was all Kira could think. That was, emphatically, a bad sign.

Worse: "HELP!" Nicole shrieked, her voice cracking as she struggled to get her feet under her. "GILLIAN! HELP ME!"

The door to the Conservatory swung open. A woman, presumably Gillian, poked her head outside, her mouth a perfect circle of astonishment.

With another frantic, vain kick, Nicole set to scrambling towards the Conservatory on her hands and knees. Leaving a runner of deep red two inches wide as she went.

Now or never, Kira realized. She could finish this, had to finish it. It was simply a matter of trusting that she'd thought it all through. Enough to let her get away with it.

So she was in *deep* trouble, then.

She launched herself back up to her feet, stumbling slightly as the toe of her shoe dragged on the pavement.

Nicole was about a third of the way to the door to the Conservatory now. Lucky for Kira, that tear in the kid's tummy was slowing her down considerably. The blood left in her wake was turning black now.

Kira followed that trail at pace, tightening her grip on the knife as she did.

"NO!" Probably-Gillian screamed from the door.

Nicole turned, and so took the second stab in the right side of her lower back. The blade didn't penetrate far, once more halted by something tougher than skin. It didn't seem to slow the kid down. She just screamed louder, thrashed more violently.

The girl twisted around to face Kira once more. Punched twice at the hand holding the knife. Connected both times.

"Stop!" Kira shouted. Not because she thought Nicole would listen. Just reflex, pure and simple.

Nicole froze. Locked eyes with Kira.

Kira froze. Returned Nicole's terrified gaze.

The girl had recognized her voice that time.

Kira wrapped one gloved hand around Nicole's neck, used the other to tilt the blade sideways and jab it into the girl's already-opened stomach, once twice three times, as hard as she fucking could, *thack thack thack,* each time feeling another bit of anatomy popping like a needle-pricked water balloon, seven eight nine times, screaming herself hoarse as she lost count of the stabs, as Nicole's swinging arms lost their precision, then their force, then their movement all together.

"AAH!" Kira heard herself cry, probably because *no* had already been taken. That was what she wanted to scream. *NO* as she pulled the blade from the cavern of the girl's belly for the final time, and some unidentified organ came tumbling out with it, apparently cut free from the body in the assault. *NO* as the red in her vision guided her hand, lifting the knife up to the side of Nicole's neck and jabbing at her jugular once, twice, then three four five times at an angle up into her skull. *NO* as the red receded and it was just Kira, all Kira, no one but Kira. *NO* as she pulled the knife hard to the left. *NO* as the blade once again *clicked* against bone.

At the latest *click,* Kira paused.

This was a mistake, she suddenly realized. This was the wrong choice. It was bad. It was evil.

It was done.

Kira pulled the knife back to herself. Staggered through a one-step retreat.

What remained of Nicole crumpled over itself and slumped backwards onto the ground, landing heavily on the pavement. Landing in enough blood to make for a tiny little *splash*.

Aowuh, Kira heard her mouth say. It was a noise that had come from some deep-down part of her body that had never spoken before, was never meant to speak.

The knife slipped from her hand. Hit the paved lot with a *clatter-click* that was by now familiar to Kira.

She squatted down, picked it up, and rose once more, never taking her eyes from the girl's body. Her body. *A* body. It wasn't Nicole's anymore. Nicole didn't exist. Had existed for a few years, sure. But no longer did. Because of Kira. The thing on the ground there was just a, a, a thing. A thing with dull human eyes staring up at the sky, sure, a thing with a human mouth locked into a terrified gawp. That didn't make it human though. No. No. No.

Go. You have to go.

Kira pulled her eyes away from the *thing* and up to Gillian.

The woman from the Conservatory, whatever her name was, had her phone to her ear. She gasped at Kira and disappeared back into the music school.

Another rattling hiss emerged from Nicole's mouth. Trees shuddering on a gustless winter night.

Kira ran.

She took the alley at a sprint again, nearly taking a header down the steps, stumbling her way past the concrete lip with the lawn on top. Then she did fall, rolling and landing on her shoulder. On the hand with the knife. "Ah!" she cried in anticipation, but as luck would have it, she'd avoided stabbing herself. So much for karma. She pushed back up to her feet and rushed toward the car, immediately spotting a problem she hadn't anticipated.

Two, actually.

The idea had been that she would kill the girl quietly and cleanly enough that she could slip back to her car, pop the trunk, throw the bloody outer garments in over the tarp she'd lined it with, and be on her way. But the screaming had brought the bicycle bumpkins out from behind their thin curtains, and onto their balcony. They'd watched Kira's clumsy *exeunt*, and they, too, had their phones out. Both of them, a man and a woman. One calling, one filming. Why the fuck did they have so many bicycles, if it was just the two of them?

Didn't matter. The good news was that the bicycle house had no clear view of the part of the street where Kira was parked. The bad news, the second problem of a duology: the unseen teenagers were no longer just voices carried on the wind.

There were four of them, standing just about fifty yards from Kira's car, gathered around the tallest of the group, who had his phone out. Always the phones. With their cameras.

But they weren't staring at the phone. They were simply arranged in a way that implied they *had* been. No, now they were looking up. Their attention drawn by all the screaming, and now the sprinting blue poncho monstrosity.

Which meant Kira couldn't take off her poncho

before she got in the car, lest her regular outfit be seen and relayed to the police. To say nothing of her face. Which meant she was either going to sit her bloody ass directly onto the upholstery of her car, which was as good as stitching a *Killed My Daughter's Friend* merit badge onto her forehead, or, what, she was gonna fetch the tarp from the trunk and drape that over oh *FUCK AGAIN.*

This wasn't a duology. It was a trilogy.

The car.

Her license plates.

Why hadn't she covered them the first time she'd clocked them as an issue?

What the fuck had she been thinking?!

The teenagers could be dispatched easily enough; Kira lifted the knife and ran towards them, screaming as loud as she could.

As one, the four teens turned and ran away, as fast as *they* could.

Okay. One problem down.

Kira ran back to her car, around to the driverside, grabbed the handle *(BEEBEE!* the car chirruped), threw open the door…ah, *fuck it,* no time to worry about the bloodstains or the upholstery or anything. She plopped into her car, cranked the ignition, and threw it in to reverse. She just needed to get gone before anybody else showed up, with the presence of mind to clock her plates. The car itself was anonymous enough. Granted, most Ford Focuses were not driven by a woman wearing a blood-covered poncho *and* a full balaclava *and* sunglasses *and* a face mask, surrounded by smears of gore. But glimpsed through a windshield, those dark stains could be anything, right?

She didn't have time to worry about it. She took a screeching U-turn across the whole of Lanier, the nearest to an action hero maneuver she'd ever managed in her life, then hauled ass to the intersection. She slowed for the stop sign, but ultimately rolled through it, turning right onto Paper Mill Road.

It took a few blocks to realize she was going too fast. The speed limit was 25. She was doing 40.

Straining with herculean effort, she eased the brick of her right foot from the gas. Getting her seatbelt on while the car was moving proved no easier. Gasping, drenched in sweat, but finally observing all the proper rules of the road, Kira disassembled her above-the-neck disguise. The glasses, then the face mask, then the balaclava. Her eyes were certainly wet, but her face wasn't. She tried to look at herself in the rearview mirror, but couldn't quite manage.

It was done. She'd done it. What had she done? She'd done something unthinkable. So stop thinking about it. And the doing of it. Which she'd done. Fuck. Fuck.

Her breath was the loudest thing in the world. She couldn't quiet it down. It was just nonstop. Who breathed that loud? It shook the Earth and rent the heavens. It was distracting. She couldn't focus. Where was she going? She was supposed to be going somewhere. She had to go somewhere. That breath. That breath. That breath.

Now where was that whining noise coming from?

She'd have to get the car looked at. She hoped nobody had looked at the car. She unclicked her seatbelt and fought the poncho off at a red (guideme) light and threw it in the well of the passenger seat, with the knife. There was blood everywhere. Jesus Christ. Including…

GODDAMNIT.

On the seatback. And now, on the back of her shirt.

Which was when it all came back to her.

The plan, the stupid fucking plan, had been to go see Dr. Mothers right after the kill. Have that be the alibi. She had hoped to kill the kid quietly, and count on an imprecise time of death to overlap with her appointment with the doctor (and her husband, natch). Tertiary benefit: she'd even have been able to unload on the poor doc, indirectly. Obviously she wouldn't *confess*, wouldn't tell him what she'd done, but she'd imagined she could at least cry a bit, vent her new trauma in a way that made it seem like the old trauma, and not have him think, wow, this doesn't seem right. It had seemed like such a brilliant idea. It had seemed like the smartest fucking idea anybody had ever had.

JESUS. She just wanted the breathing to stop. It wasn't even hers anymore. She was its.

That was out of the question now. The plan. The six minute drive to the appointment. She had blood on her person, blood in her car. So much that it had stopped seeming like what it was. Like when you say a word too much. Blood blood blood. Blood.

How do you hide blood? How do you disguise it? How do you bury it?

322

A new thought birthed itself. As they always do. The human mind is little more than a midwife. If that.

Behold: how does one disguise blood?

Why, with more blood, of course.

KIRA DROVE HOME QUICKLY BUT CAREFULLY, obeying every traffic law on the books and a few others besides. Being pulled over was the obvious danger, one that persisted no matter how carefully she drove. What if somebody back on Lanier had seen her car, and called it in to the cops? Hell, the dangers didn't stop there. If someone at a crosswalk should look into the car, and see her sitting bolt upright at the wheel, hands at ten and two, seatback splattered with red…what would they make of that? If that wasn't quite grounds for this hypo-thetical person calling the cops and telling them about the interesting thing they'd just seen, the more proactive Samaritans might well see fit to take down her license number, just in case. Oh, and as long as Kira was cata-loging dangers posed by her dash back home, she might as well reflect upon the fact that she wouldn't know if any of these were coming to pass until they were well underway. Even if she made it home unmolested, there was no way to know if or when she might hear a humorless *knock knock knock* on her front door.

Pop. Kira's eyes shot to the rearview mirror. The fuck had that been? Oh. It had been her tooth. She had been clenching her jaw so tightly that one of the rear bottom teeth on the right had cracked. Her tongue caressed the fissure. It was sharp and cold. Her breath whistled through it. That damn breath.

However minor a reprieve it provided, swinging the car into the garage (with nary a glimpse of Christine) and clicking the door closed soothed Kira. It was just soothing enough, as it happened, to let her fully grapple with the next steps she'd charted out on the way home.

She rose from the car and surveyed the interior. A bloody silhouette matted the upholstery of the driver's seat, one she knew cast a long shadow across her back. The mask on the passenger seat reposed in crimson. Beneath it, the poncho in the well slumped into itself, with a relief Kira so deeply envied.

And then, of course, the knife.

Kira reached over and grabbed the poncho, turning it inside out and throwing in the mask and, ah Jesus look at the wheel, the gloves. She hefted the azure bundle this way and that, spotting for red. None. Just blue. Ok. She stuffed that all back into the garbage bag, then lay it gently on the concrete floor of the garage, ran inside, and grabbed a second garbage bag. The latter swallowed the former. Kira tied off the mouth and frowned at the lump. That would do for a hot second, in terms of minimizing leaks. But she needed to ditch it, in such a way that it could never come back to bite her. How? Where?

Later. Should have thought about that earlier, like so much else. Oh well. She could worry about this later. For now, she had to go about establishing her innocence. Well, first she had to fabricate it. *Then* she could establish it.

Her right thigh hummed. *Vrrr-vrrr.* Not the thigh: the phone against it. In the pocket. She pulled it out and was the precise opposite of surprised to see Harlow's name on the screen. Calling to see why she was late for the appointment. After she'd asked for it to be pushed back. After she'd promised she'd come. Which she'd meant to. That had been the goddamned plan. Shit.

Not now. She couldn't think about this now. Back into the pocket went the phone; to voicemail went her husband. Presumably.

She ran the black bag upstairs and put it in the one place Kira figured Harlow would never expect her to be squirreling things away: Leigh's room. Still a shambles, the room was. Harlow had given Phyllis permission to go in and do a bit of tidying, but Phyllis assured Kira that she wouldn't do that until Kira herself gave her say-so. Oh, she was so very glad she hadn't given said say-so, as the bundle of poncho mask gloves *evidence* went in the back of Leigh's closet, behind the hanging shoe tower thing. That would be safe for a day. Particularly when said day was still just getting started, as far as incident went.

Vrrr-vrrr. Another call from Harlow. This one somehow felt more insistent than the last. Even though that wasn't possible. The urgency of the phone's vibrations didn't change with the mood of the caller. Don't be ridiculous.

Pausing halfway down the stairs, Kira shook her head and answered the phone. "Oh, Harlow," she groaned, "I'm only just noticing the time. I'm so sorry."

"This isn't okay," Harlow grunted from the other end of the line.

"I'm *sorry.*" She resumed her descent. "I got carried away with what I was doing, and I lost tr-"

"And what was that?"

"What?"

"What are you so engrossed by that you missed *another* appointment?"

She tried to let the swing around the banister and towards the kitchen inspire a similar swing into defensiveness. Much to her surprise, that move proved more difficult than usual. "I was cooking. For *us.*"

"…are you serious? Why are you c-"

"Yeah," she snapped, as she charged back into the garage, "I was. I was trying to do someth-"

"You're breaking up. I can't hear you."

"I WAS TRYING TO DO SOMETHING NICE!" she shouted, as she grabbed the knife from the passenger seat of her car, and ferried it to the kitchen.

"Well coming to the appointment would have been fucking nice!" Uh oh. Harlow wasn't one to get wound up like this. "You can't keep doing this!" he practically shouted. *"I* can't keep doing this! I'm trying *so* hard, Kira, but you ke-"

"Oh, *fuck,*" Kira gasped, before getting to her new alibi: "I cut myself cooking!"

"What?"

"You distracted me," she improvised, "and now I'm bleeding! I have to go!" She hung up on Harlow and stuffed her phone back into her pocket, trying not to think too hard about where Harlow had been going with that last train of thought. He couldn't leave her, god-damnit. Not with Leigh already on the way back to them. One third of the way back. He *couldn't*…no, leave that for later.

She took the knife to the sink and washed it off as best she could. Lay it on the drying rack, not that it would be there long enough to get much drying done. Now came a moment of true decision: what was the most plausible thing for her to have been trying to cook? A peek in the fridge narrowed her options. It'd be a stir fry. Plenty of chopping there. Onions, broccoli, some carrots. It'd go wrong on the onion. Yeah. Those could be tricky little buggers, especially once you'd already cut them up enough to violate their structural integrity. They had layers, right, everybody loved talking about onions in terms of their layers. But those layers cursed the hum-ble onion with a catastrophic tendency towards collapse. That was probably a metaphor. A different sort of onion metaphor. How about that, *Shrek*, you slug-faced bitch? How about it?

She chopped up the carrots, went to town on the broccoli florets…then pulled the onion over to the cut-ting board. Closed her eyes. Breathe. In, out, in. Rise, fall, rise. Yikes. Ok. This had to be done. This was the only way. She was committed. She'd already sprung the lie on Harlow (who was calling her back, unless the *vrrr-vrrr* in her pocket was of the phantom variety). Oh, and she was also committed by virtue of the fucking blood in her car.

Why did she have so much blood in her car? Because

she killed someone? No, don't be ridiculous. It had been a stir-fry accident. She'd cut herself cooking and tried to drive herself to the hospital, squirt squirt, lo and behold, a repainted interior.

Necessary. That was what this was. Necessary.

Breathe. In. Out. So loud. Why so loud?

"Huuuuh," Kira whimpered. She placed her left hand flat on the chopping block, palm down, fingers splayed like a starfish that had just gotten run over by a flounder. Had to be the left; she was a righty. She cut with the right. She got bitten by squirrels with the right. Whereas there weren't that many things she used her left fingers for, right? Especially not the little ones. Ah, well, work. She typed with all eight fingers *and* both thumbs. No henpecking for Kira, no ma'am, no sir. So that would be a pain. They could probably just reattach the finger though, right? If she had the ice ready to go, throw it in there, drive it over, hold it up and say *hey look what I did*, they could fix it. Right? That wasn't uncommon, right?

So it wasn't even like this would be a permanent disfigurement. Disfingerment. Ha, ha. No, this would be a temporary digital divorce. An ephemeral finger-flaying for a favorable future. Phew! Ok. Relax. Just do it. What are you waiting for?

Did it make sense to say that her left hand was looking at her? It felt that way.

VRRR-VRRR!

She jumped as her thigh trembled. Goddamn, Harlow. Give a girl a break!

Hey, here was an idea: what if she didn't cut the

328

fingers *off* off? At least, not all the way? Even if they could reattach the fingers, it probably wasn't going to be a good-as-new sort of deal. Maybe in the future you could cut off your fingers and get new robot digits, or a new arm entirely, but these would be doctors tending to her with today's technology. Needle and thread, fix her up like a popped button on a corduroy jacket.

Aaah…she didn't want to lose a finger. But where else to cut that was plausible, as far as onion-cutting accidents went? *Wow, I don't know what happened, I was cutting onions and getting teary-eyed and next thing I knew the knife was three inches into my shoulder.* No. That was dumb. It had to be the hand.

Stop thinking about it! Just do it!

Her fingers trembled. They were scared. *They* were scared? *She* was scared!

Don't be scared. This is…

Fair. That was the word that came to mind. This was only fair.

Kira grimaced and brought the knife down, almost all the way to her skin.

Almost. But not quite.

Fuck.

She put the knife on the counter and paced the room. She was wasting time. With every second she allowed to pass, with every moment that rushed to fill the gap between her hospital intake and…what had happened in the Conservatory parking lot, her story got that much weaker. Contemporaneity was to have been her alibi. If that was even a word. It was definitely a thing. Things don't have to be words to be things. And hey, *alibi* was a word. Oh, when did the girl die? Gosh, sounds terrible, but I was at Dr. Mothers' office then. Only swap that out for the ER now. It still worked. Still served as an *alibi*. So there.

She needed a fucking alibi. Not having one meant going to prison. Going to prison meant that those other two girls stayed alive, which meant Leigh stayed…not alive, which meant Harlow was going to leave, and Kira would die alone, in prison.

Oh, and it meant that Nicole Ligeti had died for nothing.

So hey, how about that. It was for Nicole, to make her death meaningful, that Kira closed her eyes and brought the knife down. So she told herself.

Until words failed her entirely.

Oddly enough, the first sense to report on the experience was *hearing*. She *heard* the wet, plosive *slap* of the knife plunging into her skin like raw chicken breast.

Didn't *hear* the blade clicking against the chopping block, though. Huh.

Then red lightning shot up her arm, filled her vision.

Ooooh, that didn't feel like her finger she'd hit.

She opened her eyes and looked down at her hand, palm to the table, knife a few inches into the back of the paw, angled up just below her bottom knuckles. The way knives get stuck into wedding cakes, just prior to the first cut.

Kira wanted to scream for the pain, but she ended up screaming for relief. Here came the blood, to wash away the blood. The blood, the blood, the blood.

Boy, but there was a lot of it, wasn't there?

SHE WAS ALREADY A LITTLE LIGHTHEADED by the time she got to the car. Peeling the towel from her wound, she flapped her hand around the interior, sprinkling and smearing gore over top every drop that had once been Nicole's. Would that be enough to frustrate a motivated CSI crew? Probably not. But it was better than nothing.

Oof. Planting a hand on the top of the door, Kira tried her best to steady herself. Her breath had left her, it seemed. She sought its comforting concavity, longed for its stabilizing rhythm. Where had it gone? It wasn't here. It was somewhere else. Where?

Forget it. She had to get to the hospital. She hadn't planned on losing quite *this* much blood, *this* quickly.

Her finger slid off the garage door opener button. She reached up again and took another jab. Ah, *there* we go. The door rattled upwards. Kira put the car into reverse and stepped on the gas. Carefully, carefully, she backed out onto Hamlin. The street split and crossed itself. Kira at the crossroads. Hee hee.

Crank it into drive, then, and let's go! Kira gunned it. Whoops, forgot the seatbelt. That would have been bad! Safety. Safety when? Eventually.

Kira buckled her seatbelt and looked up just in time to see the oak tree roaring towards her.

She *slammed* into it. The front of the car accordioned in on itself, pushing the whole of the dashboard towards Kira, as inertia shot her forward to meet the steering wheel. Her chin *cracked* against the twelve o'clock position. Only then did the airbag deploy, landing a cushy uppercut right in the chops.

She felt no terror, no shock, no pain. She simply observed all of this as though it were happening to someone else. So, maybe that was shock.

An instant later, everything that had rushed together now fell apart. The axles underfoot creaked as the car jounced, finally settled.

Then all was quiet, so quiet. Just the hiss of the crumpled-up engine in front of her, an unidentifiable *ding ding ding* from somewhere along the dash.

The crash, Kira noted as she pawed the fast-deflating airbag away from her face, hadn't been that bad. All things considered. She hadn't been going much faster than twenty-five. Probably. All things considered, Kira was totally fine.

Until the heavy bough that had been loose ever since a lightning strike six years ago snapped off the tree and *crunched* onto the roof of the Focus, caving it in.

After that, she was still totally fine, all things considered. She looked at the log now sitting in her passenger seat, at the snarl of glass and metal in which it rested, and she laughed. Laughed and laughed and laughed. This seemed like it would do the job. How could she have killed a kid in town? She was too busy losing a fight with a stir-fry and crashing into a tree. Ha. Ha. Ha.

It took some time, but she did stop laughing eventually. Which gave her a chance to hear this Thursday afternoon – evening, almost – slithering in through her new, sudden sunroof. Birds chirping. Wind in trees. A lawn-mower in the distance.

It sounded quite a lot like the morning Uisch had first paid a visit, now that she thought about it.

Yet Uisch wasn't here. There was nobody here. Just Kira. Alone. Waiting to see who would find her. How long it would take. She certainly wasn't about to call for help.

Distantly, she noted that if she'd hit the tree just a few inches to the right, that massive branch would have landed on *her*. Surely killed her.

Yet that didn't seem possible. She couldn't die yet. She still had work to do.

Her eyelids got heavier, as the world outside started to melt.

Vrrr-vrrr, her phone reminder her.

The towel on her hand soaked through within minutes. It felt as though everything vital in her was leaking out through that hole in her hand. Her senses, certainly. Those were going.

Kira didn't try to hold on to them. She didn't mind them leaving. She would call this rest. It was the only rest she could ever hope to have again, in this life. By losing her senses.

By the time somebody came to help her, they were more or less gone.

EIGHT

SOMETHING SMALL, EASILY BUILT

HARLOW TORE INTO THE HOSPITAL, not quite making a scene, but fully prepared to start banging on the reception desk and shouting *I'm looking for my WIFE!* if his more reasonable approach didn't get results.

"Lucky for everyone it did," he smiled limply from beside Kira's cot.

"Mhm," she smiled at him. *Lucky,* there was a word. One the surgeon, or doctor, or whoever it was had said to her quite a lot. She'd been *lucky* she hadn't hit any critical nerves in her hand with that knife; with time and physical therapy, she wouldn't lose any mobility at all. She'd been *lucky* that tree branch hadn't landed on her; the consensus among those who'd seen the damage was that Kira would be comatose if had, and that was the best-case scenario. And finally, she was *lucky* to have such a doting husband. So said everyone who'd seen how often he'd called Kira's phone while she was still out, how quickly he'd come once a nurse had answered it and told him where his wife was.

Kira forced a smile for her husband, whom she was lucky to have. Amongst other things.

Harlow grabbed her right hand – softly, avoiding both the half-healed squirrel bite, and the fresh bruise it had gotten from *thwapping* into the dashboard when Kira had hit the tree – and wept. Quiet weeping, the sort where the inhales were louder than the exhales, but weeping nonetheless.

Not the next move Kira had anticipated.

"Did you…" Harlow asked through a hundred little gasps, "did…you…?"

Kira hoped he didn't feel how cold her hand went. Was he about to ask her about Nicole? No. There was no way he could have put everything together that fast.

She would be *so* pissed if he had.

"Did you do this to yourself on purpose?" he finally asked, nodding to her bandaged left hand.

She ran into relief like it was an oak tree. Very nearly laughed. "What?"

"Did you hurt yourself on purpose? I'm so goddamn-ed worried about y-"

"No. Obviously no-"

"Yeah, it's *not obvious to me,* Kira. That's the problem. I'm…" he took a *very* long breath, in and out. "I'm *so* tired of worrying about you. I'm trying as hard as I can to support you." He pointed to himself. "But I'm not strong enough."

Oop. So long, relief. Hard to believe you were ever here at all. "What does that mean?"

An even *longer* breath. "You keep getting hurt. You're behaving *so* erratically. I have no idea what you're doing for most of the day, I have n-"

"You never did before either."

"Well it didn't seem like a problem before!"

"There's no *problem*. You d-"

"No problem?!"

"You don't need to keep *tabs* on me."

"Ordinarily, one hundred percent. Of course. But you're coming home bleeding at four in the mor-"

"I told you, there w-"

"There was no dog, Kira! Stop lying!"

"Don't accuse me of lying!"

Harlow presented an upturned fist, and began ticking off his fingers. "I called animal control, I called the police station, I even called literally a *number* of vets, not just the one in town but all around the area too. *Nobody* knew anything about a dead golden retriever. And they *all* told me, stuff like that doesn't happen a lot around here. They'd have remembered."

Kira shimmied herself upright. Best as she could against these deflated-whoopee-cushion hospital pillows. "You're fucking fact-checking me?!"

"Kira! You're *lying to me!* About coming home *covered in blood!* You don't have a fucking leg to stand on!"

That...was a fair point. So Kira pivoted to what she could privately acknowledge *in situ* wasn't much of a defense. "Harlow, that was like *two weeks* ago."

"Yes. It was. And *today*, you're in a hospital bed, after slicing your hand open and driving your car into a tree."

"After a…I had a knife accident."

Harlow just made a resigned *"huuuuh"* noise, and shook his head in short, quick swings, each one dropping his gaze further and further towards the ground, until his chin was practically on his chest. "I had the appointment today. Without you. Dr. Mothers and I discussed…some potential next steps. We were going to wait until Tuesday to discuss them with you, but…given what's happened, I th-"

It wasn't just the hands that had gone frosty now. Kira was having a hard time feeling any of the bodybits not called *torso*, and even that had set to trembling. "Next steps for what?"

Keeping his eyes pointed towards the ground, Harlow said "I…*cannot*…give you the kind of support you need. And it's not fair to either of us th-"

Kira crunched as far forward over her legs as her hamstrings would allow. "Are you trying to have me fucking committed?!"

Her husband lifted his gaze, but clamped his eyes shut before they met Kira's. "Not *committed*. There are perfectly reputable inpatient facilities designed to help people suffering li-"

"Yeah, with lobotomies!"

"It's not that kind of place!"

Kira recoiled. "You have one in mind, then?"

"Dr. Mothers…" Harlow scratched aggressively at the back of his head. "He has a place in mind. It's a beautiful campus, he showed me pictures. In the woods in Vermont, *incredibly* peaceful. They can help y-"

"…trying to have me committed," Kira whispered in disbelief, to herself as much as her husband.

"They can help you there." Once more, he reached out for Kira's hand. "You don't w-"

Kira snatched her hand away. Remarkable she had enough control to do so, given that she couldn't feel the damn thing anymore.

Harlow sighed. "You don't want to feel like this forever, do you? To *live* like this?"

"It won't be forever," Kira heard herself mumble.

"What?"

"…I'll get better."

Harlow didn't say anything to that.

This was bullshit. Her husband wanted to lock her away in a looney bin. Wanted to interrupt the work she was doing. Which she was doing for *both* of them.

But it was happening. It was the way things were now. And the sooner Kira acclimated to a world in which her husband saw her as a liability, the better.

More than anything, she needed to play along. Needed to walk out of here on her own recognizance, as it were. Needed to tease out what little trust Harlow might yet have in her, just long enough to pack a bag, grab whatever cash she could, and slip out the back door. She wasn't all that confident in her ability to stay *off the grid* for any meaningful period of time…but she felt she could do it long enough to finish the job she'd started with Ni…with the easiest of the three.

No. Give the girl her name, at least. Nicole Ligeti.

Thinking the name called to mind the face. The face on the body on the ground. Seeing that again did nothing to Kira. Made her feel nothing. For the face was a window. Made so much clearer for having the life stripped from it.

Kira would finish her work, and Leigh would be back. And Kira could bring her to Harlow. And he would understand. And the Trecothiks would be back together. Everything would be how it had been. Before.

So Kira took a moment to get into character, preparing for her finest performance yet, then said "can I see the brochure then, or whatever?"

Harlow looked just about ready to cry. From relief, this time. A moment later, he did just that. Cried.

Kira watched him.

HE SEEMED SO MUCH LIGHTER, once Kira had agreed to consider the funny farm. Practically *floated* through the hospital, through the garage, all the way to the car.

It was only here, trudging along beside him as he struggled to keep to a normal walking pace, that Kira had considered how heavily she had been weighing on her husband. She knew for a fact that to even *consider* sending her away would have broken his heart, all things equal. He moped like a goddamned puppy every time she needed to go away for a week or so for one of those insufferable techie seminars. Hated seeing her go, he did. So for Harlow to be *this happy* about his wife's ostensible openness to fucking off for an indeterminate amount of

342

time, perhaps forever…Christ, how much had he suffered on her account in these past weeks?

Weeks, she reminded herself, as they stepped out of the elevator on P4, where Harlow remembered he had parked (though he couldn't remember *where* on P4). It had only been a few weeks, and already, Harlow was looking to be rid of her. That was a bit quick to be reaching for the nuclear option, wasn't it? To want her committed?

Yeah, it was. So *fuck him.* She felt terrible for how much extra pain she had introduced into his life, but she was doing it for a good reason, and also *fuck him.* These three incompatible-but-not-contradictory thoughts took up residence in her mind, bickering like sitcom roommates, before she'd fully settled into the passenger seat of Harlow's Honda.

Harlow threw himself in behind the wheel, clicking his seatbelt with the alacrity of someone midway through a musical number. "Are you hungry?" he asked. "We can stop and get something to eat."

"Would you mind starting the car?" Kira asked, gesturing to the air vent on the dash in front of her. She was neither hot nor cold – she just wanted Harlow to stop looking at her with that face. That…*excitement.*

"Oh…yeah." He pressed the little button and turned the car on.

The A/C belched to life, then throttled back to a low hum.

Kira stared out the windshield, watching someone walk to their car by themselves. In the dark. Dangerous, that. There were crazies out there. She sucked her upper lip into her mouth, then popped it out gently. "I just wanna go home. I'm tired."

Harlow considered that for a moment. "Sure. Sure thing, honey." He threw the car into reverse, swung his right hand behind Kira's headrest, turned towards the back of the car, and *screamed*.

The car jerked to a halt.

"What?" Kira gasped. She turned in her seat.

In through the rear window peered a lunar mask, near flush to the glass but not fogging it, certainly not. Attached to the mask was nine feet of concrete, parodying the human form.

"Oh," Kira said.

"Jesus," Harlow whispered, chuckling nervously, "that scared the shit out of me." He turned to Kira, then immediately turned back to Uisch. "Is that like a cleaning robot or something? Like in a grocery store?"

"Aaaah…not quite."

Uisch stepped out from behind the car, swinging around to the passengerside.

"It's walking. It's *walking.*" Harlow hissed. "What the fuck is that?"

"I honestly don't know," Kira replied at a normal volume.

Uisch persuaded the door to the backseat open. Ducked its head. Climbed in to the car.

Kira had a single instant to imagine that watching the behemoth struggle its way into the car would be amusing, but she ought to have known better. Uisch poured itself in through the aperture. There was a dreadful ease to the motion, undertaken with the same brainmelting grace of an octopus crawling into the mouth of a jam jar.

It struck Kira as somehow profane, that such an infernal beast should be capable of grace.

She swung around and pointed directly at it. "Don't talk!"

"The fuck is going on?!" Harlow whispered, staring at Uisch in the rearview mirror.

Kira turned back to her husband. "It's gonna pull the car apart if it talks. That's how it talks, it destroys stuff. We need to get it something to destr-"

Kht. The axle popped.

Hwoo. The engine sighed.

Rrf. Something shifted in the back.

Rrss. A vital bit in the undercarriage groaned.

Ddt. A drop dripped from one of the vents.

Kira looked to her husband. Frozen with his eyes on the rearview, white-knuckling the wheel like he was spinning out of control on a mountain pass without guardrails.

That wasn't fear of the unknown on his face, though. That was the sort of fear you could only get from true comprehension.

"You understood that?" Kira asked him.

"It..." Harlow swallowed hard, an audible *gulp*. "...asked you to move your seat up."

Kira nodded and racked her seat forward. "Better?" she asked over her shoulder. "Not out loud!"

The tectonic groan of impossibly long legs extending

would do for assent. Harlow shook his head at the windshield. His eyes darted towards, but not wholly to, the rearview mirror. "Jesus Fuck." He snapped his head to Kira. "You know what that is? What's happening?"

Kira thought about that, then rubbed her palms roughly across her face. Christ, but she wasn't prepared for this conversation. Living in hiding until she could take out the other two kids had been a nutty plan, but it struck her as infinitely preferable to what she was about to have to do.

Which was; tell Harlow the truth.

Swept by sudden anger, Kira swung around and actually *snarled* at Uisch. "The fuck are you doing here?! I'm doing…" she glanced nervously at Harlow. "…I'm doing the thing!"

"The *thing*," Harlow repeated for himself, as though it would make more sense in his voice.

Whhhh. The A/C revved.

Llll-eff. Something inside the glove compartment shifted.

Whhn. Harlow's hair tousled of its own accord. He ducked, and swatted vainly at the air above him.

Mn-TUH. Something heavy snapped off the underside of the car and slammed onto the floor of the garage.

It was all Kira could do not to leap into the backseat and strangle that goddamned rock monster. *One life,* it had just said. AGAIN. *One minute.*

Kira planted her hands on either side of her face. "What the fuck does th-"

k-PROP-mt. The sun visor on Kira's side snapped off,

bounced onto the dashboard, then slid into her lap.

A promise.

"A *promise,*" Kira repeated, taking a page from Harlow's book of befuddlement. She spun even further around, swinging her right hand around to grab the headrest of her seat. "I never know what the fuck y-"

Unbidden, Harlow put the car in reverse and backed out of his spot as carefully as one can with only the back-up camera.

Kira slid halfway back into her seat. "Where are you going?"

"To get it something to destroy," he replied quietly, as he finished backing out of the spot (the car bouncing softly over whatever had fallen off of it) and put the car in drive. "Please buckle your seatbelt."

Kira offered his stubbly right cheek a shallow nod. With one final glare at Uisch, she lowered herself the rest of the way into her seat and buckled her seatbelt.

She had the distinct sense that Uisch was laughing at them back there. It made no sound, tore nothing else off of the car. Yet there remained the sense. Disembodied mirth, hanging like an odor.

As they nosed out of the garage and passed beneath a streetlight, the dew in her husband's eyes sparkled.

"Are you okay?" she asked him.

Harlow gave a robotic "heh" and swiped at his eyes with the back of his hand. "I don't know why I would be."

"Well you know," Kira mumbled through a taut smile, "I hear there's this great place in Vermont that'll hel-"

"That's not funny," Harlow snapped. He frowned and took a right turn at a crawl. His eyes again flitted towards (but not to) the rearview mirror.

Kira begged to differ, but said nothing to that effect. And hey, it wasn't as though the joke had been wasted.

It sure felt like Uisch had gotten a kick out of it.

FAILING TO COME UP with any places that could be safely spoken to ruin, both from a practical standpoint as well as an ethical one (e.g. the wing of the elementary school currently under renovation would have been ideal, but for the fact that Kira didn't want that on a conscience already heavy with indignities visited upon youth), Harlow drove them to a 24-hour Wal-Mart Supercenter.

He ferried them there with such purpose. Kira looked her question at him. To that, he only gestured for her to get out of the car, as he unbuckled his own seatbelt. "Wait here," he snapped to Uisch as though it were a hyperactive child.

The maskhat did not smile, certainly not. But it *seemed* to.

As they left the car, with Uisch sitting inside it, Kira started to giggle. *Should we leave a sign?* she wanted to ask Harlow. *'Don't worry about Uisch, the A/C is running and he has his favorite toys?'* She didn't ask him that, though, because he wouldn't have laughed.

Uisch would have laughed, she was sure.

Once inside the store, Kira and Harlow grabbed a large cart and ran laps, looking for the ideal cross-section of cheap and breakable. They wound up in the toys section, swiping every overcomplicated, million-pieced geegaw they could find off the shelf and piling it in.

"I don't know if we need this many," Kira offered once the box pile crested the plastic blue lip of the cart. It was the first thing either had said to each other since they'd left the car. "We can just rebuild them after they come apart."

Harlow didn't say anything to that. He just kept grabbing and tossing, grabbing and tossing.

They ended up spending nearly three hundred dollars on board games and bullshit. All so Uisch could speak. As the cashier *beeped* each box over the barcode reader, Kira watched Harlow with great interest. *Beep*. Wondering what thoughts were swirling about beneath the scowl frozen on his face. *Beep*. Wondering if maybe the past few weeks hadn't been enough to get his grief in tune.

Beep.

They returned to the car, Harlow regaining the front seat, Kira (much to her husband's evident horror) slipping into the back seat behind Harlow. And so, next to Uisch.

She was struck by Uisch's odor, which was a lack thereof. *Eau de Absence*. It didn't just not smell like anything; it smelled like *nothing*. The nearer she got to it, the more even the quotidian stinks of Harlow's car were lost.

Movement caught Kira's eye: Harlow, adjusting the rearview mirror. So that he could see her. The band of Harlow's eyes slashed through the night, like he was wearing it for a mask. Just prior to doing something awful, say.

Tap tap tap.

Kira looked to her lap. A long promontory Uisch might have meant for a finger bounced impatiently off the topmost box. Jenga, the most obvious choice. Syllabically limiting, perhaps, but that was what some of the others were for. "You want that one?" she asked.

Uisch nodded from the waist. One of the waists, anyway.

Using the hefty box of an infinitely more complicated game called *Chicken Fingers Chicken Thumbs* as a foundation, Kira opened the Jenga box from the top, overturned it, and slid the pre-constructed tower out.

Immediately, blocks slid and slipped from the box, thumping to the carpeted well, thudding onto the *Chicken Fingers etc.* box, clacking against each other as they fell.

Supple work, Uisch told her. *How*, and then the tower fully collapsed.

Kira frowned at the blocks on the floor, then turned to the back of Harlow's head. "Can you help me here?" After the sentence was done, she looked to his eyes in reflection.

Those eyes simply stared back at Kira for a long, long second. Then they vanished, as Harlow cranked himself around and sent back a grasping fist, reaching for whatever Kira might hand him.

THEY DIDN'T BOTHER OPENING *Chicken Fingers Chicken Thumbs* — the box was big enough to host four Jenga towers. Harlow was tasked with keeping two more going in the front seat, a responsibility to which he set himself with a remarkable sort of anti-alacrity. Kira had suggested they just take the games back to their house, but Harlow had grown animated only in squashing that idea. "No fucking way that thing's coming back to our house. No way." And so, they sat in the parking lot for the Wal-Mart Supercenter, assembling Jenga towers as others collapsed, and in so doing, spoke.

Supple, Uisch repeated. *The doing.*

"What the hell's that supposed to mean?" Harlow snapped into the rearview.

"I think it means I covered my tracks," Kira ventured, "right?"

Tracks, it laughed through the blocks. *I don't know tracks.*

"Then what do you mean by supple?"

Danceable.

Kira shook her head at Uisch. Didn't know what else to do.

One life. One minute.

"What is it *talking about?*" Harlow demanded.

Kira paused as she bent to scoop fallen blocks from beneath the driver's seat. Slowly, she rose again, shooting her eyes to the mirror. Harlow's eyes were closed tight.

"Harlow, I promise I'll tell you everything but I need you to…just…wait." She looked to Uisch. "Why do you keep saying *one life one minute?* What does that mean?"

A promise. A reward.

God, that un-stench of delight was only getting stronger.

"Reward for what…?" Harlow wondered under his breath.

"Harlow, shut the fuck up!" Kira tilted towards Uisch. "I'm not playing this game anymore! Just tell m-"

You are. You live for the prize.

"What prize?!" Harlow shouted.

"The fuck?" asked Leigh's voice.

The voice came from Leigh.

Leigh was sitting in the front passenger seat.

In an instant, all that numbness diffuse through Kira's body ignited. She was feeling, she was *present* in a way she didn't think she'd ever been before.

Her entire body suddenly shaking uncontrollably, Kira stared at her daughter. Leigh. Alive. Sitting in the front passenger seat of the car, diagonal from her, sitting *in* it, the weight of her depressing and stretching the fabric, her hand leaving a warm fog on the window as she pressed it against the glass, her eyes alive and searching.

"Oh my god," Kira whispered. "Leigh."

Harlow just stared, unblinking, recoiling slightly from his daughter.

Leigh spun in her seat to face her mother. "Mom?" Nervously touching the base of her own neck, she turned to her father. "Dad?" Looking back to Mom. "How did I…I was…" her lips moved soundlessly, her eyes scanning the floor, as though searching for words amongst the blocks, seeking and finding. She lifted her gaze to meet Kira's and asked her "am I dead?"

"Oh God!" Kira lunged forward, knocking what

remained of the Jenga towers off her lap. The blocks clattered to the floor, soft like laughter. She wrapped her daughter in her arms, fully expecting to find her incorporeal, a mirage to be reclaimed by the concrete desert outside. But no matter how hard she squeezed, Leigh remained obstinately real. Kira could hear her daughter's heartbeat, the same heartbeat she'd heard through her doctor's stethoscope sixteen years ago. And here she was, listening to that same heartbeat weeks after it had been silenced. Or some days before it would begin again. Yes. That one.

Kira leaned back and turned to Harlow. Unmoving. Unblinking. Tears pooling along his lower eyelids.

"Mom!" Leigh cried, grabbing at her mother frantically. "I died! I think I'm dead! I don't know what's happening!"

"It's gonna be okay," Kira told her, planting her hands on Leigh's cheeks. "Look at me. Listen. It's going to be okay. Are, um…where are you? Where do you go, when you're…when you're not here?"

The blocks on the floor rearranged themselves, clatter clatter laughter.

"What do you mean?" Leigh asked. "I don't know what you mean!"

"It's okay," Kira wept. "It's okay."

"Dad," Leigh gasped, extending her hand. "Hold my hand."

Harlow blinked. That was the extent of his movement.

"Dad! I'm scared! Please!"

He shook his head slightly, then reached out a hand and grabbed Leigh's. "I love you so much."

"I love you too," Leigh replied. "Mom. I love you."

Kira tried to return the sentiment. *I love you so much.* But despair sat in her throat like concrete. She couldn't speak.

And then Leigh was gone.

Kira tipped forward, mouth drawn wide in a silent scream. Nearly faceplanting onto the center console of the car. She caught herself, in as much as the impact didn't hurt. She didn't lever herself back upright though.

Rebuild was all Uisch had time to say, with what little remained of the towers.

Kira did lean back now, glaring at the cavities in Uisch's mask where eyes might have gone. Though the longer you looked, the less like a face it seemed.

Rebuild, recommended the seat well.

"I am," Harlow growled from the front seat.

Kira snapped out of it, and joined her husband in fishing as many blocks as she could reach from the well. Joined him in rebuilding something to be immediately destroyed.

One minute. A reward. You are welcome.

"There was no way that was one minute," Kira whimpered. Despite knowing how quickly time could pass.

Two lives, one day. Three lives, one life. For as long as she may live.

Even as Uisch spoke, Harlow continued to rebuild. Even as the towers toppled themselves, he rebuilt, pausing only to wipe an arm across his face.

Can I have a ride back to my car? Levity. I have no car.

The towers *exploded*, spraying blocks in every direction. Cackling clatter from all sides. Kira yelped and shielded her eyes. Harlow, she couldn't help but notice, did neither.

In a maddeningly ordinary motion, Uisch reached for the door handle and popped it. The door opened, and Uisch slithered out, once again fluid as a dancer. It closed the door gently, gave a slow, final wave, then slouched towards the wooded dark just beyond the lot lights.

Kira watched Uisch melt into the black, a full moon made new before her eyes. That was a way to think of it. Full made empty was just new. So Kira looked at the newness of the front passenger seat. So new. So fucking new.

Leigh. Here again, and gone in an instant. No, sorry, gone in a minute. For one minute, she'd seen her daughter again. Touched her. Alive. Only to be – how else to say it – killed once more, by Uisch. For no other reason than it still wanted more from Kira. And now, from Harlow.

What was death, to Uisch? Just a delicate membrane, through which its enormous hands could pass at will? It was dizzying to imagine.

She hated the demon's freedom from finality. Yet she could not hate the demon itself, not entirely.

One can never hate the giver of such a precious gift.

Clck. Clck. Clck. Words without meaning. Just noise.

Kira turned to her husband.

Harlow was still rebuilding, rebuilding the towers. His

eyes didn't appear lost, as Kira had imagined they might as she leaned around the seat to get a look at his face. He instead wore an expression of such singular focus that Kira was afraid to disturb him. A part of him might snap off.

Oh, god. As sunken with shock as she felt, as disturbed as she was at having her daughter dangled in front of her like a gold star in grade school…Harlow had it so much worse. At least Kira had made something like peace, with living in a world of stony fiends and their infernal contracts. This was *all* new for Harlow. So new. So fucking new.

She dug deep, and found a quiet kind of anger she believed might pass for strength.

"Hey," Kira ventured softly. "It's gone. Uisch is gone."

Harlow rebuilt.

"Let's go home, baby. I can explain…some of that."

Harlow rebuilt.

"I can drive. I probably should. You don't seem…"

Harlow rebuilt, rebuilt, rebuilt until the tower was too high to stand.

THE MOMENT THEY GOT HOME, Harlow marched upstairs, collapsed onto the bed, and fell asleep with his face buried in the pillow. Kira didn't bother asking him to wait up, just listen to her. She'd spent the car ride home auditioning a dozen overtures to the impossible conversation she needed to have with him, but never managed to get much further than some variation of *please don't freak out*. Which was a ship that had already sailed. Long-gone over the horizon, that ship. So long. See you on the flip side.

The conversation could wait, then. It was probably best that it did.

Fine then: Harlow went upstairs, and Kira took her time in following, doing her best to clean up the blood she'd left in the kitchen earlier that day. The blood that had dried to the knife, the chopping block, the counter. Some of it came off easily enough – a few bits would take bleach and elbow grease, though. The dish towel hanging off the cupboard handle under the sink was certainly ruined. Too run through.

It was the strangest thing, but she was having a hard time remembering where all this blood had come from. Why it was here. With effort, she could solve that mystery. By remembering what she'd done, not even twenty-four hours ago now. A lifetime ago.

Eventually, Kira trudged up the stairs and into the bedroom. She removed her slumbering husband's shoes for him, listened to his breathing long enough to ensure he wasn't going to suffocate himself in the pillow, then settled in next to him.

After a concerningly refreshing few hours of sleep, Kira stretched, once again checked that her husband was still breathing, then descended the stairs with the determination that she would talk to him when he woke up.

The news beat her to it.

She had anticipated, albeit dimly, that Nicole Ligeti's murder was going to be all anybody in the greater Neirmouth area could talk about today. A stabbing murder in broad daylight was, suffice it to say, a sight more dramatic than the town's usual goings-on.

What Kira hadn't quite counted on was a *national* spotlight.

She'd heard it first as a brief, ninety-second piece on the *Up First* podcast. It began with Steve Inskeep reminding the listeners where they'd last heard talk of a town in Maine called Pitney – and how interesting, that though the Ligeti murder had happened in Graham's Landing, Kira caught herself thinking of it as happening in Neirmouth, while the world at large had folded it in to Pitney (on second thought, not that interesting). For a single sphincter-clenching instant, Kira expected to hear her own name mentioned on the podcast. Followed shortly by a knock at the door. Either the police to take her away, or the chamber of commerce to commend her for really putting Neirmouth on the map.

Alas, after ninety seconds the *Up First* team lost interest in the story, so Kira switched on CNN. They were, to put it mildly, much more singularly focused.

At around the fifth reiteration – for those just joining us – that yet another tragedy had struck a sleepy pocket of southern Maine, it started to feel like a rather colossal oversight on Kira's part not to have anticipated this. The Firestarters Massacre had been good for a solid three days of wall-to-wall coverage, and Ruthger Gully's eventual trial was, despite being some indeterminate time in the future, still the subject of much chop-licking amongst the talking heads.

The massacre was fresh enough in people's minds that Nicole Ligeti could still be defined by her survival of it. Even now, it seemed she always would be.

Kira, much to her embarrassment, got fully sucked in to the breathless coverage delivered *LIVE* from a dog-pile of reporters square in the center of the Conservatory parking lot, a decision she found rather ghoulish, while at the same time granting that boy, she was one to talk. How long she sat there listening to well-quaffed action figures overenunciate the words "still so much we don't know" was tough to say, beyond *too long*.

Which became apparent to her when she heard Harlow's voice say "that's what you did" softly, from a few feet behind her. Not quite a question, but not a statement either.

She cranked herself around to see her husband standing on the threshold between the kitchen and the living room. Arms limp by his sides.

In that instant, she saw Leigh in him. Back when she was surely no more than two or three years old, standing in the doorway to Kira and Harlow's bedroom, informing them that she had had a nightmare.

Made sense. Leigh was half Harlow, after all.

Slowly, buying time to think of what the fuck she should say, Kira reached for the remote and muted the TV. That done, she twisted around once more to look at Harlow. Trying not to see Leigh. Not trying hard enough.

"Do you understand what that thing was saying last night?" she finally asked him. "Three lives, one life? Did you understand?"

"I think I understand now." He pointed to the TV then, and said nothing else. So, yes, he understood.

Kira nodded. Once more wrestled with language. Finally settled on: "I just want Leigh back. That's the only thing I want."

Harlow loosed a trembling groan, swaying slightly as he did. He teetered to the wall, leaning against it, then sliding down until he arrived at the ground, sitting crookedly on his ankles.

"I know this is a lot all at once," was all Kira could think to say. "Seeing Leigh without expecting it. Not that I expected it either, but it was at least…anyway. I'm so sorry. I kn-"

"You don't sound sorry," Harlow sobbed at his lap.

"…I *am*. I've just had time to process…all of this."

"You murdered a little girl."

"*Little*…she was a *young woman,* Harlow. She wasn't a little gi-"

He threw his head back, showing Kira a face he had never shown her before. Were it anyone else…well, she might have tried to put something a bit more substantial than a recliner between that face and hers. Something like a door, maybe.

"That doesn't fucking matter!" Harlow shouted.

"It matters to me."

He opened his mouth to respond, then closed it again and shook his head. Stopped the shaking only to glance past Kira to the TV. His chin trembled.

Kira followed his gaze, turning back to the broadcast.

To see one Mrs. Ligeti weeping in front of a micro-phone-studded podium. *MOTHER OF SLAIN GIRL SPEAKS,* shouted the lower third of the screen.

I have to speak? was Kira's immediate thought, before remembering. Ah, yes. There was a new *mother of slain girl* in town.

She wanted to cry. No, scratch that: her *body* wanted to cry. Wanted to shriek and scream and wail, shake her fists at the sky and perhaps smite her thighs. The whole woe-is-me routine.

Her mind, though…her mind knew better than to heed the body. Down that path lay paralysis. Self-des-truction, perhaps. Neither of which were acceptable.

There was work to be done yet.

Kira turned back to Harlow. "This is what was sup-posed to happen." She rose from the chair and crossed the room towards Harlow, approaching him cautiously, as one might an armed landmine. "It's horrible. I know that. It's fucking horrible. But…" she pointed vaguely towards the TV. "…those girls were supposed to be the ones. Not Leigh. *They* w-"

"They," Harlow repeated, spitting the word out.

"The other two girls Leigh sa-"

"I know. I know who you're talking about." His atten-tion drifted from Kira, off to the empty space behind her. "What I can't understand is…well, I can't fucking understand any of this. I can't…Jesus *Christ,* Kira, you *killed* a person!"

"I know."

"You *murdered* a human being!"

"Yeah, I fucking know."

"You can't…" He buried his face in his palms and groaned again.

Kira finally reached him, lowering herself to the floor beside him. She considered reaching out and placing her unbandaged right hand on his shoulder, but decided against it. Hard to stop thinking of him as a landmine.

She gave him about a minute to sob quietly, then said "that thing you saw is called Uisch."

"I don't care," he wheezed at his feet.

Kira took a deep breath in through clenched teeth, and glanced off towards the TV again. Now there was a man with a suit standing at the podium. *DEPUTY CINARA: FBI TO ASSIST PITNEY PD IN HUNT,* announced the lower third.

Her body fell to bits.

Oh, Christ. The fucking FBI. They were going to catch her. It was already over. She was so fucked.

She couldn't breathe. Couldn't hear anything other than a high-pitched ringing. Couldn't see anything past the merciful dark eating in to her vision. Couldn't *fucking breathe.*

Until her mind reminded the body how. In, out. Rise, fall, rise. In that order. It was simple, the mind insisted. Everything seemed simple. Her mind felt clear. Clear as could be.

And sharp, too.

She reached out and placed a hand on each of Harlow's cheeks. Tilted his face towards her. "Harlow."

He showed her that face again. The one that'd really

look best on the far side of, oh, maybe *two* doors.

"There's only one thing worth focusing on here. *Leigh deserves to live.* She's a survivor."

"She…" Harlow choked, then cleared his throat. "She *wasn't.* She was a hero. Because she died saving those girls."

Kira withdrew her hands, placing them in her lap. "It wasn't supposed to be that way."

"What does that even mean?"

"We have the chance to fix this. And I…believe me, I *understand* that this is…fucked. But, it's, it's all we have."

"…"

Kira shrank into herself, noticed she was doing it, and commanded herself to re-expand. "If we don't…finish this, then Nicole died for nothing."

"…"

"You can't just not say anything. You have to say something."

"Do you hear yourself?"

"Yes, I hear myself. I know how it sounds. I know."

Harlow chewed on his lower lip. Threw his head back and, that's right, groaned. So much groaning this morning.

"This isn't hypothetical," Kira pressed. "We can get her back."

"By killing two more kids!"

"Young women!"

"I fu…look, we got to tell her we love her last night. She got to tell it to us. That's closure. So let's just let that be the end."

"Closure? She was terrified, Harlow. She was so scared. You're happy leaving her there?"

"Where?"

"A place that scares her!"

"She was scared because as far as she knows, she got shot in the woods and wound up in the parking lot of a Wal-Mart!"

"You don't know that."

"From what she said? I think I do." He scratched his right eyebrow with the nail of his left thumb. "Unless, what, you think she's somewhere right now? Where do *you* think she is?"

Kira pinched her lips shut. Truth be told, she agreed with him. She didn't believe Leigh was *anywhere* right now.

No sense telling the truth, then.

Harlow reached out and placed his hands over Kira's. "I miss h…look at me. I miss her. So fucking much. If I could have her back…there's a lot I would do, to get her back. But there needs to be a line."

"There is."

"A different line."

Kira frowned. "Let me tell you what I think you're thinking. You tell me if I'm right."

Harlow neither nodded nor shook his head.

"You think I don't know what I'm doing. Like, in terms of understanding how bad what happened to… what I *did* to Nicole was. *You* think I don't understand that I'm putting her parents in the same position we're in, or that I'm planning to do that two more times. You

364

think I've lost my mind a little bit or something. And maybe you think that if you can just make me stop, and slow down, and really *think*, I'll come to my senses. Is that close?"

Harlow stared at her…then, slowly, nodded.

"Ok. Listen to me." Kira took a deep, rattling breath. "Believe me when I say, I know exactly what I'm doing. I thought about it, for a *long* time. I had to get myself to that place."

"…"

"Leigh is the most important…just, yeah, that's actually it. She's the most important to me, full-stop. There's not a lot I wouldn't do to bring her back."

Harlow studied his wife's face. Every inch of it save the eyes, it seemed. "Would you kill me?"

She steadied her eyes on his. "If it would bring Leigh back, yes."

"Would you kill yourself?"

"…" Kira felt her upper lip twitch.

"Wow," Harlow chuckled mirthlessly. He pushed himself up to his feet.

"Don't say *wow*," Kira grunted as she followed him back up to bipedal. "Yeah, of course I would. If it w-"

"You had to think about that one."

"Yeah, that's a big thing to say yes to!"

Harlow stepped into the living room and sat across from the TV. The press conference was over, it seemed. Back to the studio, to hear everything said in the press conference repeated with fifty percent more intensity. "Didn't seem like killing me took quite as much thinking," he muttered.

"You...you'd...brought it up earlier!" Kira followed him into the room. "So I thought about it then! When *you* brought it up!"

"What? When did I bring it up?"

"I don't remember!"

Harlow sat on the sofa. "I just...can you...I need to think, Kira. I need some time."

A perfectly reasonable request, Kira knew. Given how dramatic a shift his entire world had gone through in the last eighteen-or-so hours.

Still...she couldn't wait for him to catch up. There was a *hunt* on for her. She needed to know whether or not he was going to be a part of it.

She needed to know *now.*

So Kira sat on the arm of the chair next to the sofa and said "the poncho and the mask, the stuff I wore when I killed Nicole, it's all upstairs in a garbage bag, in the back of Leigh's closet. Covered in Nicole's blood."

Harlow struggled to maintain eye contact, his gaze repeatedly drifting towards the floor.

"I say, let's get that out of there. Today. Right now. Where do you want to take it?"

It appeared to be more than Harlow could manage, to meet Kira's boggle-eyed glare.

"Do you want to take it to the police?" Kira listened to herself, to the graceful fury in her tone, as one might hear someone speaking from the next room over.

Harlow finally lifted his face once again. He didn't look angry. He didn't even have that hangdog insouciance from moments ago.

He looked afraid. Afraid of Kira.

He had asked her if she would kill him, if she had to.

She'd said yes.

So why *wouldn't* he look upon her with abject horror? Particularly when she was no doubt returning the gaze in kind?

It occurred to her that Harlow might have interpreted her question as a threat. Which wasn't how she'd meant it.

She cleared her throat. "I just want to be clear, I don't mean th-"

"No," Harlow croaked. "I don't want to take it to the police."

"Well," she said through a pained smile, "I'm very glad to hear that." She pushed herself back to her feet. "So, then…where *should* we take it, where nobody will ever find it?"

"Please, Kira…I just want to sit. I need to think."

"You can think in the car. I'll drive."

He looked up at her. "Where are we going?"

"That's what we need to figure out." She reached out, presenting an upturned palm to her husband.

He pondered it for a moment, then sighed, and met it with his own hand.

Kira tightened her grip, pulled him to his feet, and lead him across his line.

THE SOLUTION, hit upon by Kira after about twenty minutes of brainstorming (the most ludicrous suggestion being Harlow's "hide it in wet concrete at a construction site", which he zipped up with a hasty "nevermind"), was less concealment than deconstruction. Laboriously, Kira set about pulling the blood-spattered balaclava apart, one thread at a time. Fortunately for her unskilled hands, the wool was thick and not especially well-wound to begin with. The resultant tangle of synthetic fiber was tucked into a plastic CVS bag and taken, along with the poncho, gloves, facemask (though *not* the sunglasses – those could be washed), and painting respirators they'd bought during a mask shortage early in the COVID crisis, and a small camping stove, to a point of relative seclusion in the woods. Four hours later they returned home with a Giger-esque gobstopper of wool, leather, and melted plastic, a monstrosity which was marinated overnight in a half-full can of paint thinner, and the next morning deposited into a dumpster outside of an Applebee's three and half hours away, in Rhode Island.

Foolproof? Probably not. Kira was clearly no criminal mastermind. Exhibit A: the eight-stitch gash across the back of her left hand. Exhibit B: as the dealership appraised her tree-smushed vehicle to determine the cost of repairs, Kira responded to their questions about reupholstering the interior by asking if she could keep the old, bloody seatbacks (nobody there called the cops, as they all believed it was her blood, but the manager did come over for a nervy one-on-one with Kira). Yet she was smart enough to know (or dumb enough to hope) that there was no reason for anyone to suspect her, so in this case, perhaps good enough would be just that. Still,

Kira stayed on her toes over the following weeks, her heart rate skyrocketing each time she heard sirens or saw blue and red gumdrops twinkling in her rearview. No knocks on her door, though.

Which wasn't to say it was all quiet on the home front. Or rather, it *was* all quiet. That was the problem.

Harlow had almost entirely stopped speaking to her. Whether he had been robbed of speech by incredulity at what his wife had done, by rage at having been made an accessory after the fact, or by horror at what she was yet contemplating, well, Kira couldn't say, because Harlow wouldn't say.

It wasn't something she could get used to, living in this well of cutting silence. Having questions of what he'd done that day answered with an averted gaze and a shrug. Watching biweekly as even Dr. Mothers struggled to wring much more than a stray syllable from him. Meeting those hopeless eyes that seemed to daily recede further and further into his skull and knowing, from cruel experience, that saying "I love you" would bring no light to them.

It shattered her anew, each time she launched some conversational volley into the void. Yet she continued to try, not because she was tenacious but because she kept forgetting. Each time she looked at him she saw the man with whom she'd gone on a long camping trip years and years ago, laying atop blankets in the back of the dull red pickup they'd borrowed from a friend of his who'd been overseas for the summer, parked at a campground in southern Nevada somewhere, their legs dangling out the back of the dropped tailgate, high on weed they'd bummed off the hippie who'd helped them with directions back at the turnoff, staring up at the stars, giggling at the funny voices they were each doing for the other, not saying anything particularly witty or interesting, but laughing because they were high and in love and the evening was cool and the sky was clear and everything was still new.

It was to that man from the back of the pickup that Kira would say "I heard somebody drive by listening to *Midnight at the Oasis* today. You know that song? By Miriam…Maria…M-somebody. I haven't heard that in years." Just to make conversation. Just to talk.

It was a different Harlow who received those words. Not the man from the pickup. Someone much, much older. Impossible to say, if this man had heard the song *Midnight at the Oasis* recently, or ever. Impossible to say if he knew who M-somebody was. Impossible to say if this man had ever looked up at the stars, ever been in love at all.

What made this silent treatment truly excruciating was that Harlow made no effort to avoid her. They still ate dinner together. They still watched TV together. They still slept in the same bed, though he was careful not to touch her (the only real difference from the previous weeks of bereavement being the *care* put into the chastity*)*. Harlow's daily routine had, in fact, changed very little, if at all. He simply went about his usual business, in complete silence.

It was a bit like living with the sort of teenager Kira

had, as a younger woman, worried her future children might grow up to be. Which naturally called Leigh to mind in a most unwelcome way, though on that score there were even more unwelcome calls to screen.

"Ah," Kira huffed at her phone as it once again buzzed Zoe Cottrell's name at her. Both she and Madeleine Encomb had been calling Kira intermittently in the weeks since Nicole's murder. The first call had come the day after; in retrospect, Kira knew she should have just answered it. But, you know, she just hadn't been in the mood to cry about Nicole with the two young women she had designs on next. Go figure. So she let it go to voicemail, and was pleased to see that none was left. Then when the next call came two days later, she hadn't picked it up simply because she hadn't wanted to make up some reason for not having answered the first one. And so it went with each subsequent call, Kira fully aware that each kick of the can only sent her further into a blind alley, at the end of which would surely be a tense, awkward reunion. Unless she could manage to avoid them until it seemed the right time to eliminate them, which probably wouldn't happen until she could satisfy herself that she didn't need to worry about Harlow turning her in.

She couldn't manage it. The avoiding, that was.

The alley reached its end when Kira was doing a bit of work (despite the horror show her life had become, the bills never stopped) in a sleepy coffee shop just outside Portland. Bit of a drive, but that was the point; she'd taken to avoiding public spaces in and around

Neirmouth if she could. Too many condolences from too many strangers. She'd been expecting a call from a client any minute, just a quick touching-of-the-bases to clear up what the fuck they'd meant by the third-to-last line of the project brief, which encouraged Kira to *let us know if you see ways to maximize potential for machine learning in exhibitional capacities, and/or leveraging our fundamental business model to optimize our informational frameworks.* She blamed that sentence for, well, quite a lot. But she especially held it responsible for lulling her into the empty-headed daze from which she thoughtlessly snapped up her ringing phone, to greet the caller with a bright, chipper "hi."

Silence on the other end.

Kira frowned, then pulled her phone back from her ear and *very quietly* whispered the word "fuck" to herself.

It was Zoe on the other end of the call.

Kira put the phone back to her ear just in time to hear the girl say "sorry, I…wasn't ready to talk, I wasn't expecting you to pick up."

Now it was Kira's turn to be silent. She glanced around the shop, small and oddly angled in the back behind the counter, populated by just a guy reading a book, two old biddies giggling about something at a table in the other corner, and a scruffy younger man with a massive camping backpack slumped at a table against the far wall, charging his phone in a wall outlet but not looking at the phone, just staring at the table. Thinking about something far away.

"…Mrs. Trecothik?"

Kira blinked. "I'm sorry, I...I wasn't ready to talk to you girls just yet. It's so hard," she continued, starting to hit her stride, "so soon after I'd lost my daughter, to lose one I was...starting to think of...as another...daughter." Alright, so she wasn't *delighted* with where that sentence had taken her. But at least it had been something to say.

"I'm so sorry," Zoe replied, meaning every word, particularly that last one. "I hadn't even...I shouldn't have called so much. I'm sorry. We just tho-"

"It okay," Kira assured her, leaning back in her chair, crossing her right leg over her left. "I should have realized that you girls needed someone to talk to. Someone who could understand. I was being...selfish. I w-"

"No, you weren't, and we rea-"

"Listen, I'm busy right now, but maybe we could..."

Kira let that sentence die before it had a chance to chart its own destiny.

Was there a way to take them both out at once? Hurry Leigh back rather than dragging the whole thing out? Not for nothing, but there was no way Harlow could keep up the silent treatment with Leigh back in the house. Would her return solve everything in one fell swoop? Of course not. Would it *help*, though? Absolu-

"It's not that *we* need to talk to you," Zoe explained. "I mean, it's not that we don't *want* to, but, I mean, we'd *love* to, only if you felt like you, um, wanted to, though, but, um, w-"

"Maybe we could arrange some time to talk," Kira's sentence finished itself, without consulting her. That was alright though. Innocuous enough.

"…yeah. Yeah, that'd be great. But we also wanted to just let you know the detective wanted to talk to you."

"…"

"Hello?"

"Hm?"

"I think the signal cut out there."

"Yeah." Kira uncrossed her legs and recrossed them with the left on top now. "Yeah, it's going in and out. Um…who…why…why does the detective want to talk to me?"

"She came and s-"

"What detective, also? Zoe? What detective?" She pulled the receiver of the phone away from her mouth – she could hear her breath thundering back into her ear.

"Oh. Her name is…hang on, I have the card…it's in…hang on…"

Kira took a second look around the coffee shop as she listened to Zoe rummage around what sounded to be the toolbox of auto mechanic. She was, for just one moment, *absolutely certain* that everyone in here was listening to her. Watching her, from the corners of their eyes. The scruffy young fella wasn't *really* thinking about something far away. The guy with the book wasn't *really* reading it. Those old biddies were having a lull in conversation at such a *suspicious moment*.

The moment lasted no longer than any other moment, which was to say, for a beat, also known as a tick. Then it passed. And Kira accepted that, no, these people were not listening to her. They were thinking, reading, chatting.

"…have it in here…just a…sorry…"

"Oop," Kira announced, "bad signal." She hung up, rose from the chair, scooped up her laptop in one hand and her bag in the other, and made her escape.

Slightly more dramatic than she'd intended to be, as she dropped her laptop while trying to open the door, and then dropped her bag while bending over to get the laptop. Lucky her, though: nobody rose to help her. Nobody even looked.

KIRA COULDN'T STOP looking off towards the front door. Every time Harlow's fork *clinked* on his plate, every time an especially brawny gust made the house creak — really, every time Kira's brain tapped her on the shoulder and whispered *heard from the detective yet?* — she would jerk her head hard to the left.

The detective had wanted to speak to *her*. So where was she, then? Why not find Kira directly? Surely this detective wasn't relying on a couple of bereaved teenagers to schedule the appointment for her.

But why *wait*, though? Why not just call, or knock on the door? Unless the detective was somehow *suspicious*… unless, oh, for example, someone who knew a bit too much for their own good had picked up the phone and called someone they really shouldn't have…

Kira frowned down at the mediocre meal she'd picked up on the way back from her afternoon of aimless driving. Bahn Mi from a hole in the wall in Graham's Landing called *This One's Bahn Mi*. Their food wasn't much easier to stomach than their name. Oh, but that wasn't fair.

Nothing was fair.

She glanced up at Harlow, sulking across the table. What else was new.

He cranked his chin up far enough to meet Kira's gaze. "What?" he asked. Not aggressively. With genuine interest.

Kira had nothing to say yet. So she said nothing.

NINE

OH, THE HUMANITY

PARANOID THOUGH THE DAYS (and especially nights) were, desperately though Kira wished her husband would say something, *anything* to her (if for no other reason than it might help her work out how wary she should be of him), impossible though she found it to begin even wringing her hands about doing the next of the three while trailing so many goddamned loose ends from the first...hey, it wasn't *all* bad.

The Finkerts clan, from whose property tilted the oak tree that had been struck by – and subsequently struck back at – Kira's car, weren't in the least bit angry that Kira had driven onto their lawn and smashed into their tree. Far from it; they were planning on suing the township, whom they had alerted to the oak's loose branch multiple times over the six years since it had been half-severed by, as they saw it, "The Lord's Fury" (the were a pious bunch). And not only were they planning on suing the township – they wanted to cut the Trecothiks in on it! Without even having to name Kira as a plaintiff! "But I hit the tree," Kira pointed out. "The tree kinda hit me in self-defense."

"They'll settle," Archie Finkerts insisted. "Trust me."

Well, that suited her down to the ground, and wouldn't you know it if a few weeks later Minnie Finkerts wasn't knocking on Kira's door with a personal check for two grand.

"They settled!" Minnie giggled.

"That was fast," Kira marveled in monotone. She had the presence of mind to not ask how much the *full* settlement had been.

The unexpected little windfall at once suggested itself as a kind of…not solution, no, it wouldn't *solve* any of Kira's problems by any means. But it was just enough to potentially buy her some breathing room. Create the conditions in which certain stresses could be…dialed back.

She made the pitch that very night: "Minnie came over with a cut of the settlement for us," Kira told Harlow about three seconds after he'd come home from work.

Harlow put his briefcase down, flush against the side of the kitchen counter, and nodded.

"Yeah," she continued, as though she'd been met with an enthusiastic *Gee, how much was it for, sweetheart?* "It was for two grand." She followed him as he turned and drifted down the hall to the stairs. "So that got me thinking, because that's a, you know, that's a chunk of money, so maybe we could have a kind of, I don't know, like a, um…" she hesitated slightly as she about-faced around the banister and followed Harlow up the stairs, "maybe we could try to do the Portland thing again? Maybe even go for the same Airbnb. I think we're in shoulder season now, so it won't be as crowded as it would have been, if…it just won't be that crowded, I don't think."

Harlow kept his head down as he puttered into their bedroom, undoing the tie around his neck as he crossed the threshold.

Kira halted in the doorway, folding her arms and leaning against the frame. Made a study of his silence.

He sniffed and wrinkled his nose as he shimmied out of his jacket and untucked his shirt.

She felt her chin quiver.

Harlow huffed his way through a series of tiny rapid-fire exhalations as he unbuttoned his shirt. Not the sort of thing one would have been able to hear, had the room not been so deafeningly silent.

Kira took her time with a much deeper, *much* louder sigh. Until:

"Why don't you just leave?" she suggested, in the manner one suggests going apple picking at some point in the next month, just as Harlow was slipping his belt off.

He paused as he was about to toss his belt onto the bed, holding the swaying strap of leather out at arm's length, staring at the buckle as it swung in quickly-diminishing arcs.

"I'm going to assume you haven't called the police," Kira hoped she sounded confident in saying, "and you're sure as shit not enjoying being here. I'm not saying I *want* you to leave, because I don't, but…I don't understand why you haven't. And I'm *really* trying to understand."

Harlow had a go at swinging the belt towards the bed. It flailed well enough, but didn't generate any meaningful momentum. He made a more concerted effort to give it some motion, turning his wrist to send the buckle at the end of the strap forwards, back, to, fro…

"I'm trying to *fix this,"* Kira added, not doing a great job disguising her frustration, not really caring to. "I'm trying. What are you doing? You're not doing anything. You're doing *nothing,* Harlow. While I'm over here *trying,* like a dumbass."

Satisfied by his work, Harlow released the belt just as the buckle neared its bedward extremity.

It soared through the air. Splatted against the side of the mattress. Thudded onto the floor.

Kira only realized she'd been staring intently at the buckle – hypnotized by it – as it settled on the carpet. "What do you want, Harlow? Do you want to leave? Do you want to…what? What do you want?"

Harlow glanced her way, then slugged over to the bed, about-faced, and sat himself delicately down on the edge. He planted his elbows on his knees, and his face in his hands.

Kira remained precisely where she was. Standing in the doorway, leaning against the fr-

Her husband wept. Shoulders heaving, tears leaking

382

out from between his fingers, *boo-hoos* booming in his cupped palmed, the whole deal. It was more emotion than he'd shown in just about a month. Since he'd seen his daughter. Almost a month ago now. Jesus.

She would not have admitted it under pain of torture, but in that moment, Kira had the thought: *I liked it better when he didn't cry so much.* If for no other reason than she had no idea how to react when he did.

Safest course of action seemed to be to unfold her arms, step gingerly into the room, and sit on the bed beside Harlow. Which she did. The mattress beneath her bucked with each of his sobs.

She reached a hand out and placed it on his shoulder.

He stopped crying at once and spun towards her, *slapping* her hand away with a swift backhand.

"Hey!" she snapped.

"I don't want you to touch me right now," he sulked.

"Don't fucking slap me!"

"I didn't slap *you,* I slapped your hand!"

"You sl…my hand is a part of me!"

"When people say *slapping someone*, that means their face. I di-"

"Where does it say that? What fucking spousal abuse handbook did I forget to read?"

"Oh, come *on.*"

"Don't slap *any part of me* ever again."

"Okay. Yes ma'am. Gotta toe the line, since we both know you could *kill me* if you wanted to."

"Oh, *you* come on now."

Harlow turned and boggled his eyes at Kira.

"Alright," she granted. "But that was *your* hypothetical."

Returning his gaze to the carpet, Harlow leaned back and scratched at his chin. "What *I'm* trying to understand," he finally murmured, "is…did you change? Or were you always…" He gestured contemptuously to her, from head to toe and back up again.

"Willing to do anything for my daughter? Yeah, I changed into that. The day she was born. You're dodging my question, Harlow."

"What question?"

"What do you *want?* If you could snap your fingers and get exactly what you wanted, right now, what would it be?"

"I would want to go back to before all of th-"

"I mean *realistically.*"

"Wha…what do you mean, *realistically?* You want to bring our daughter back from the dead!"

"But we can do that. We can't go back in time."

"Then why did you have me snap my fingers to get what I want?"

"I said *snap your fingers* because that's the expression. It's just a thing people say. But you have to want something you can actually get."

"Well…I can't get what I want, so…I don't want any-thing, then."

"So what *do* you want?"

"…I just said, I don't want anyth-"

"But you also said…okay…list-"

"The thing that I want and can't get is to go back to

before all of this happened, befo-"

"I know. I get it. Listen. Stop talking. *Listen.* You have to want *something.* Otherwise you wouldn't fucking *be here still.* Right? So, do you want me to go to prison? Do you want to help me finish this, and get Leigh back? *What do you want?!*"

Harlow shot to his feet and took a tiny little lap of their bedroom. "I don't know, Kira! I don't fucking know!"

"Well, how about this, I want you to stop being so…*sullen,* because, I mean, I *get* it, but also, I'm…I can't live like th-"

He spun around, pinched his fingers together into a little pre-explosion chef's kiss, then flipped the gesture over and jabbed it Kira's way. "You know why I haven't been talking?"

"…*no,*" she replied, "I *don't.*"

"Because…*I don't know what I want.*"

"That d-"

"Do you understand what I'm saying to you, Kira?" The tears were threatening an encore. "You're asking me to take part in murdering two more gi-"

"I never technically asked you to take p-"

"Let me finish! You asked me, fine, you asked me to look the other way while you killed two more girls, or however you want to phrase it, but that's what you've asked from me…and *I don't know what I want.* That's so fucked up. That I don't know how I fucking feel about you *murdering two more girls.*"

Hello again, tears.

"Because I want to see Leigh again," he continued. "I want to spend a day with her. So badly. More than I've ever wanted anything." He choked on a breath and coughed it out. "But I also don't want anyone to get hurt. I don't want to *kill* someone, just to spend one more day with my daughter."

Kira opened her mouth to say *our daughter,* but caught herself in the nick of time.

"And I guess you've been through all of this already, and you…you made your choice, clearly. But I hate having to go through this alone. I'm so scared, and confused, and I'm just…" He quit pacing. Stood a bit straighter. "I need to make *my* choice. But it doesn't feel like I'm ever going to be able to. I haven't figured a single goddamned thing out since…the car…I can't *think* straight."

Kira waited until she was certain he was done talking, then crossed her arms and shrugged her shoulders up by her ears. "What are you choosing between?"

Harlow rubbed at his eyes. "Yeah. Of course. What does this mean for *you."*

That was an easy little snipe to ignore, mostly because Kira couldn't really dispute it.

"I don't know," he answered belatedly.

"Not ruling anything out, though?"

"I don't *know."*

"What *do* you know, Harlow?"

"I know that I don't love you anymore."

Kira only recognized the little spasm that ripped through her body from the way the mattress jerked beneath her. "That's a terrible thing to say."

"Well, I've spent a few weeks *not* saying it, and you didn't like that either."

She wiped at her eyes. There weren't tears yet, but there would be. Yes indeed. Her nose was already plugging itself up in anticipation.

Harlow, standing stock still now, watched her. He seemed coiled, but not to attack. More to dive for safety at a moment's notice.

Kira swallowed. It made a loud, soggy, cartoonish *a-GULP* sound.

"I don't hate you," he added quietly. "But I just don't love you anymore. I can't love someone so…selfish."

Taking another deep breath, Kira nodded and wiped at her eyes. Feeling tears this time. "I did it for us," she croaked. "For our family. It was always about all of us."

Harlow grunted. Hard to say what he meant by that prehistoric noise. If anything. Reinventing language, he said "what if I told you that I wanted everything to just stop, now? I didn't want to turn you in, but I *absolutely* didn't want you to kill either of the other two girls? Would you respect that?"

Kira scowled up at him. "Yeah," she sneered, after a pause. Knowing a bluff when she saw one. Trusting that this was nothing more than Harlow wanting to win an argument. "You tell me you *absolutely* don't want either of them hurt, and we'll call it. How about that. Tell me right now you're happy to not even *entertain* seeing your daughter ever again, and that'll be that."

One could not help but notice that Harlow failed to say any such thing. Or any thing at all. Which just went to show, he *didn't* know a bluff when he saw one.

Kira jutted her chin forward, turning her head slightly to aim an ear directly at her husband. "Hm? No?"

"I told you," he growled, "I'm...*debating*, between the tw-"

"I think you want *me* to do it." Kira sniffed, and pawed at her eyes again. "I think you're *waiting* for me to do it. So you can see your daughter again, and feel like you didn't have to do anything *untoward* for the privilege."

"No," Harlow responded, just a *bit* too quickly, "no, I'm carefully deliberating th-"

"You *just* told me you felt like you haven't gotten any-where on this in weeks."

"I'm trying to be as *perfectly rational* as possi-"

"You're a coward."

Harlow flinched. "Better that than a, a fucking psychopath."

"You're *really* lucky I'm not one, baby."

"...is that a threat?"

Kira heaved herself off the bed and stood, then took a step towards Harlow. "No," she replied, trying to cover her tears with bluster, stepping closer still, "it's a remin-der. Of how incredibly lucky you are."

Harlow took a step back, lifting his hands defensively. "Don't touch me." Fear cracking his voice. *Terror.*

Her husband was terrified of her. The man she loved, even still. Terrified.

She hated this. Feared that there was no going back from this. Dreaded whatever state of affairs was yet coming their way.

And, deeper down, from that venomous redoubt that thrilled to vindication and triumph and saying *I told you so*…Kira had to admit, there was some portion of delight here. The masochistic satisfaction of picking at a scab.

She hated to admit it, and yet she would. Because it would be dishonest to deny it. And dishonesty was for cowards.

Slowly, she reached out a hand towards Harlow's face. An open, upturned palm. Lover's caress, incoming.

Harlow gawped at it, recoiling slightly, hands rising to shoulder-height. "Don't…" he warned.

"Or what?" Kira wondered gently.

"I'm *serious.*"

"Or what, honey? What?"

Vrrr-vrrr. Kira's phone, buzzing in her pocket.

She halted her approach and dropped her hands. Didn't reach for her phone, though. She just frowned up at Harlow.

Vrrr-vrrr.

Harlow stared down at her pocket. Glanced back up at her face. Back down to her pocket. "You don't want to answer it?" he asked.

"Probably a telemarketer."

"Seems late for a telemarketer."

"Time zones." She waited for the next *vrrr-vrrr* to end, then narrowed her eyes at him. "Is there someone you've been expecting to call me?"

"I just asked you if you wanted to answer it."

Vrrr-vrrr.

"Yes," Kira replied, "but in a knowing way."

"No it wasn't."

"It was."

"It wasn't a *knowing way.*"

"It *was.*"

Vrrr-v. Kira's phone gave up mid-vibration.

"If it's important," she insisted, "they'll leave a voicemail."

Vrrr-vrrr.

Kira and Harlow both straightened up at that one.

Because that one had been *Harlow's* phone ringing.

"See who it is," Kira ordered.

Harlow obliged at once, stuffing his hand into his pocket and pulling out his iPhone. He squinted down at it like a *Law and Order* day player grimacing at a headshot. "I don't recognize the number."

"What's the area code?"

"207."

Kira frowned. Didn't narrow it down; 207 was Maine's only area code.

Vrrr-vrrr.

"Do you…" Harlow lifted his phone towards his face, but gingerly. "…do you think it's…that *thing?*"

"Uisch?"

He flinched slightly at the demon's name. "Yes."

"No." A smirk flashed across her face. "Why would Uisch call you on the *telephone?*"

"I don't know. Why would Uisch ride in my car?"

Kira granted that point with a bobble of the head.

Vrrr-vrrr.

She pulled out her own phone. Checked the number

of her missed call. It began with a 207 area code. She read the rest of the number to Harlow, and he confirmed that it was those same nine digits burning across his screen.

Vrrr-vrrr. Then nothing.

They looked at each other. Reunited, at last, in confusion. The sort of confusion born of ignoring the obvious.

RRRRRIIIIIIIING!

The phone rang. The *house* phone, the landline downstairs, on a small desk just around the corner from the door to the garage.

RRRRRIIIIIIIING!

A relic that nobody actually hoping to speak with a human would ever call.

RRRRRIIIIIIIING!

Kira padded slowly out of the bedroom, down the stairs, through the kitchen, and to the table upon which the ancient technology gathered dust. After a mood-ruining sneeze, she lifted the receiver to her ear and spake the word: "Hullo?"

"Hello," a forceful voice Kira had never heard before snapped directly into her ear, "am I speaking with Mrs. Kira Trecothik?"

Kira gave the question serious thought. "Yes," she concluded. "That's me."

"Excellent." *Click*, the phone announced, at precisely the moment the doorbell said *ding dong*.

Slowly, Kira turned to Harlow. He'd followed her downstairs, and was now standing expectantly between Kira and the front door. Giving no indication that he was about to turn around and answer it. Kira nodded at this and walked past him, to the door. She touched the door-knob on a second *ding* and twisted it on the attendant *dong*.

"Oh," a woman on the porch said with a start, "sorry about that." Hers was the voice Kira had just heard on the phone, now upgraded to having a body all its own to ride around in. *Upgrade*, as it happened, may have been overstating the case. The woman on the porch was short and squat, with short grey hair framing one colossal crow's foot of a face. The thin jacket she wore boasted a felt badge insignia sewn into the left breast.

Kira took this in impassively. Hand still on the door, and so blocking the path to entry, she smiled warmly at the officer of the law. "That was you on the phone."

The cop nodded. "Ma'am. Detective Dresselhaus. Apologies for the phone calls, that's not exactly protocol. I'm just wrapping up my bit of the investigation here before I head back to Pitney, and I realized I'd forgotten to reach out to you. So…" The Detective offered the sort of warm, unpretentious smile that only a deeply savvy operator can manage. "I really wanted to make sure I caught up with you before I left town."

Looking over the detective's shoulder, Kira saw an unmarked Crown Vic, parked behind a windowless van dressed in the splashy graphics of Neirmouth's own Team Time News Action Weather at Eleven News Team van. The woman whose smile blighted the side of the van was leaning against her enormous face and talking urgently to a cameraman, who had his lens trained on the Trecothik house. They were stood as near to the property line as they could be, without actually trespassing.

"What is this?" Kira demanded, racking her grimace from the news team to the detective.

Dresselhaus rolled her eyes. "I'm sorry, they're not for here for you. I lucked into a break in the case, and they've been following me ever since." She threw her thumb over her shoulder, without looking to see where it was pointing (but, Kira couldn't help but notice, it was pointing *directly* at the lady with her face splashed on the side of the van). "She's got it into her head to make one of those murder documentaries everybody loves so much. And listen to this, she asked me to interview for it, and I said no, and then she asked me to help *finance* it. I said, go to your network, why are you asking me? I tell you, the nerve of th-"

"What was the break in the case?" Kira wondered, innocent as could be.

"Ah, yes. May I come in?" Detective Dresselhaus asked with a smile.

Blinking so slowly it would have been more accurate to say she'd simply taken a very quick nap, Kira said "…"

"If now's not a good time, perhaps tomorrow morning might work? I am winding things down here, and I'd re-"

"Now works," Harlow said from just behind Kira.

Kira jumped slightly.

The detective, unless Kira was very much mistaken, noticed.

"Certainly," Kira agreed, stepping back and opening the door wider. "Please, come in. We're happy to help however we can."

Detective Dresselhaus expressed her appreciation and stepped inside. As Kira closed the door, she looked at the news team in the street. Now the camera was most definitely trained on her.

HARLOW WAS PACING. Like somebody with something to hide. Like a guilty person.

Or like a hungry young actor, just as the house lights were going down.

"Okay Mr. Trecothik," said Detective Dresselhaus. "Perhaps you might lead the way."

Harlow squinted at her as though she were speaking in hieroglyphics. "Where?"

"The living room," Kira suggested curtly from behind the detective.

Curling his nose, Harlow turned to his wife.

She shrugged aggressively at him.

So Harlow led the way to the living room, at which point Dresselhaus took an initiative she was tired of pretending she hadn't already taken. She passed Harlow, waddling to a chair in the far corner of the room. It was one whose placement was universally agreed to be poor, tucked right under the left side of the TV as it was, but apparently had all this time been awaiting a detective with questions; wall at her back, clear view of the entire room. "If you two would be so kind as to take a seat," she said, scooting the entire chair – not a small chair, mind – forward with one hand grabbing a fistful of cushion, the other hand pulling a pen and notepad from her pocket,

"I only have a few questions. Simple as can be. Won't take more than a minute of your time."

"Ask away," Kira challenged in as friendly a manner as she could muster. Still on her feet.

"Please," the detective reiterated, "if you could take a seat." She waved a hand around the room, as though she was trying to sell Kira her own furniture.

Glaring, Kira took a seat on the sofa.

Harlow perched himself on the arm of the loveseat next to the sofa. When there was plenty of room on the sofa, next to Kira.

Eyes on Harlow, the detective said "I heard the girls mentioned to you that I wanted to speak with you."

"Young women," Kira corrected her.

"Oh. I'm glad you know exactly who I'm talking about."

Kira hoped she'd manage to keep her displeasure hidden, as she vowed to tread more carefully. "They're always in our thoughts here," she covered, gesturing between Harlow and herself.

"Yes, of course. At any rate, the *young women* relayed to me that they mentioned I wanted to speak with you."

"They did."

"Did they mention why?"

"No."

Dresselhaus nodded, and leaned forward. "Well, there are a few details about this case we're keeping close to the vest for now. So…I'd appreciate it if you didn't share any of what I'm about to tell you, with anyone."

"We won't," Harlow answered for the both of them.

"Excellent." The detective leaned back in her seat again. "We have a witness to the murder who overheard the entirety of the act. Actually *saw* the tail end, but *heard* it in full. And in her telling, the victim *greeted* her attacker. In such a way, the witness believes, as to indicate that the victim knew her assailant."

Bullshit, Kira very nearly blurted out. Nicole hadn't greeted her. She'd turned, and she'd smiled uncomfortably at the sound of her own name, but she hadn't *greeted.*

Fortunately, Harlow had his own bone to pick with the detective's telling of the crime: "the *victim* has a name," he grumbled.

"Yes," Dresselhaus nodded. "I am aware of that."

"So…?" Kira tried *very* hard to keep her voice at an indoor volume. She'd give the effort a solid B-. "What is this? What are you…are you asking us…?"

"The *young women* informed me th-"

"Why are you saying that sarcastically?"

"I'm not…" Dresselhaus sighed, slicing her hands in front of her. "I'm sorry. You're right. My mistake. It's part of the job, the…standoffishness. You just sort of hit the jump at speed. Can start you off on the wrong foot sometimes. I'm sorry. Can we start over?"

"Please."

"Okay." The detective took a deep breath. "We're operating under the assumption that whoever murdered Ms. Nicole Ligeti was known to her. *Well* known, in fact. And trusted, well enough to keep Ms. Ligeti from running, even as her assailant sprinted towards her in a poncho and balaclava."

Kira shifted nervously. Part of the whole point of her getup, beyond the functionality of it, had been to draw attention to itself. To stick in the memory enough to keep people from noticing anything more useful, as far as identification went.

All the same, it was terrifying to have her costume recounted to her by a detective. Impossible to think of it as a *good thing*.

Dresselhaus clapped her hands softly in front of her, then held them out as though to tell the Trecothiks she'd caught a fish about *yea big*. "The young women, Ms. Madeleine Encomb and Ms. Zoe Cottrell, informed me in the course of my conversations with them that you had something of a relationship with Ms. Nicole Ligeti. Through the heroism of your late daughter. And I am so sorry for your loss, by the way."

"It's alright," Harlow replied, a touch too quickly, and *far* too casually.

"We appreciate that," Kira added. She shimmied in her seat a bit, trying and failing to not stare death at her husband, then said "so you're wondering if we might know something."

"Some*one*, to be specific." Dresselhaus only now returned her hands to her lap. "It's a long shot, of course, but, to the best of your recollection, did Ms. Ligeti mention any…unsavory acquaintances? Perhaps there was a…bully at school taking too keen an interest in her, or someone at h-"

"You aren't considering that it has something to do with the Firestarters Massacre?" Harlow volunteered.

Kira couldn't even *try* to hide her anger this time.

Dresselhaus proved to have a much stronger poker face. "We've been considering everything. We simply have no reason to disproportionally direct our efforts down one path or another, at present."

"I'm trying to remember," Kira blathered, just making noise so that Harlow wouldn't, "if Nicole said anything to me that might be useful…hmm…you know, we didn't really have the sort of relationship where she would…be telling me all kinds of stuff. And, really, almost every time we met, the girls were th-"

"Young women," Dresselhaus corrected, the faintest whisp of a smirk on her face.

"Yes, I know, the young women were there, with us. So I don't know if I could offer anything that they couldn't."

"They both informed me that you and Nicole had something of a rapport. Moreso than you had with the two of them."

Harlow didn't quite flinch, but he did turn his gaze on Kira with an obnoxious herky-jerk urgency.

Kira felt her brow falling. "This is starting to feel a bit like a grilling again."

Dresselhaus kept that loathsome little smirk on her face and shrugged. "It's just my demeanor, I suppose."

"Well…I don't appreciate it."

"Noted." She glanced towards the ceiling. "I'd like to zero in on the conversations that you and Nicole had bef-"

Harlow pointed to Kira. "She did it."

Kira made an involuntary *ahlp* sound. Quiet, it had been. But probably not quiet enough.

The detective's expression remained expertly cemented in place. Her eyes didn't even flit towards one or the other Trecothik; she kept on staring at the ceiling, hands hovering just a few inches above her lap.

Kira only realized how tightly her fingers were digging into her knees when she broke the skin through denim.

"There," Harlow grunted, "my wife murdered Nicole Ligeti. When I found out, I helped her get rid of the evidence. Mystery solved. Case closed."

Dresselhaus peeled her disapproval off of the ceiling and showed it to Harlow. "Sir, please."

"I'm serious. The knife she killed her with is in the kitchen. Still in the chopping block. We washed it, but I'm sure we missed a spot. Maybe down where the blade joins the wood. It's hard to get down there with the sponge wand, you know?"

"Do you think you're being funny right now?"

"I think you're being obtuse. I'm confessing."

"Alright," Dresselhaus sighed, pushing herself to her feet.

Harlow shook his head, pointing at the detective's center of gravity. "You don't wanna write this down anywhere? You don't have a little book you can write it down in?"

Dresselhaus ignored Harlow, instead looking to Kira as she reached into her pocket and pulled out not handcuffs, not a gun, but a business card, which she thrust into Kira's trembling hand. "Two wrong feet is a bad way to start. If you feel like *actually helping*," she sneered with a frankly unnecessary nod towards Harlow, "or you think of anything I should know, call me. Even if I'm back in Pitney, I'll know who to connect you with here. And, you know, I'm only an hour away." She nodded silently at Kira, then added, "I want to catch this bastard. For Leigh, as much as Nicole."

A low blow, conscripting Leigh's name into service like that. That, more than anything, put Kira on edge: seemed like it'd be quite a bit harder, to outmaneuver a detective unburdened by a moral compass.

"Ok," Kira replied, nodding as she took the card. "I will."

She showed the detective to the door, then out of it. Once the investigator was on the other side, Kira closed and locked it. Pausing for just a moment, to watch (with some poison-tipped delight) as the news team rushed towards Dresselhaus, and Dresselhaus visibly deflated at their approach.

Hand slipping off the sweat-slicked doorknob, Kira took a deep breath, then stormed back into the kitchen, where Harlow was standing, waiting.

"What the *fuck* was that?!" she growled at her husband.

"She left," he fired back, "didn't she?"

He sounded disappointed.

HARLOW FELL ASLEEP STRAIGHT AWAY. The moment his head hit the pillow. Zonk. Goodnight.

Kira lay on her side, glaring at the back of his head,

boring a hole into it with her fury. Watching the peaceful rise and fall of his shoulder.

Had he really wanted to turn her in? Or had he known that would be a quick way to get the detective out of their home? Oh, but surely that was giving him too much credit. There were a hundred and one other ways to chase Dresselhaus off, all far less dangerous than *fucking confessing*.

No…that had been a game of Russian roulette. Only whether the bullet wound up in the chamber or not made no difference to Harlow. It wasn't his head the gun was pressed against, after all.

Kira thought for a few more moments, then jabbed Harlow hard in the back of the neck.

He flinched, groaned quietly, and rolled over. "Hrn?"

"We're taking that money from the settlement," Kira decreed, "and we're going to Portland."

"Okay," he grunted, rolling back over.

Kira couldn't be certain, but it sure seemed like he'd fallen straight asleep. Again.

She took one final look at the back of Harlow's head, then rolled over, turning her back to his. One long weekend should be enough, she reckoned. Enough time to get clear on what mattered. There was so much that had come between them since the Firestarters Massacre, but it was all bubbling away *right there,* just below the surface.

It wouldn't take much to yank it into daylight. A long weekend was *more* than enough.

And what if she didn't like what she learned, in the

course of this weekend, in the process of getting clear?

She bit down on the comforter as the tears came. Hurting Harlow wasn't an option – to even consider it was more than she could bear. How would she explain his absence to Leigh? How could she bear the loneliness of this home, before she managed to bring Leigh back to her?

And, bringing up the rear of this contemplative parade: how would she be *able* to hurt him? Even if he didn't love her anymore…Christ, she hoped he'd been lying when he'd said that. Speaking from a place of fury, rather than truth. Because she still loved him. Desperately. Even as she absolutely *despised* him, she loved him. The two were not mutually exclusive. The one had a way of feeding the other, in fact.

So what *would* she do, if Harlow should be determined to turn her in, or at least to stop her from finishing what she'd started?

Well…the long weekend wouldn't be for a little while yet. So she'd have to leave herself enough time to get clear on *that*.

She had to hope that any amount of time would be enough.

NO SURPRISE HERE: arranging that long weekend away fell entirely to Kira. Harlow wasn't as committed to mopey stoicism as he had been, but reintroducing speech into his repertoire hadn't actually improved his communication skills much. His new go-to was passive aggressive agreement, in the vein of "if you think so," or "whatever you want." So it went for everything Kira proposed, from what music to listen to, to what to have for dinner, to where to go within their Portland getaway. She tried her best not to exploit her husband's agreeability, making choices she thought he might enjoy as much as she. Why she was going out of her way to placate him, when she wouldn't get so much as a parody of gratitude in return, she couldn't say. Oh, well, she could say. It was because she loved him. Fool that she was.

At her suggestion, and by his limp accord, Kira took their two-grand windfall and reserved an entire cabin in Gray for a weekend in mid-October (peak leaf-change season would come about a week later, but apparently you've gotta lock that shit down ten years in advance). Gray being just about thirty minutes outside of Portland, yet so dense with nature as to feel like the middle of nowhere. But in a romantic way, not in the way that Neirmouth was *truly* the middle of nowhere.

She squirreled the rest of the money away, to be put towards visits to restaurants a cut above their usual go-tos, along with some fancy steaks to cook up their first night in the cabin. Having charted out the *easiest* bits of that long weekend, the Trecothiks entered a kind of domestic holding pattern as the heat of late summer gradually gave way to a blustery fall.

In all that time, little changed. Harlow warmed to Kira again, bit by bit, volunteering a "how was your day" here, or a "what are you up to tomorrow" there. All in Gregorian monotone, all small talk, as though he was taking their relationship from the top…but really, that wouldn't have been so bad. If that was what he needed to do, then Kira was happy to play along. It was so nice to be able to talk to him again, be that talk small or otherwise.

The manhunt for, well, Kira, was sputtering out. Publicly, at least. She was hearing less and less about the FBI's involvement in the case – she wondered if they'd ever been more than just a tactic to make the murderer, er, *her* panic and make a mistake. More concretely, the media had clearly long since lost interest, so keeping abreast of the case required more and more proactivity; the announcements of a new lead and/or a dead end now dribbled out onto the metaphorical page six, or even further back. But they were still there. And they painted a picture of a frustrated police force shunting the case towards cold storage, where some colossal percentage of these things wound up. They'd cycled through two suspects (both cleared, Kira was both relieved and ever-so-slightly disappointed to hear), five seemingly auspicious breaks (only one of which truly worried her, that being the cell phone footage one of the bicycle house bozos had taken of Kira's flight from the Conservatory parking lot – thank god they hadn't had an angle on her getting back into her car), and only one truly substantive witness. That had indeed been Gillian, she of the Conservatory, she who had overheard Nicole's cry for help and popped her head out the front door to scream a bunch. The closest her testimony had gotten the authorities was, very indirectly, delivering Detective Dresselhaus to Kira's front door.

So…no one wants to jinx these things, there's no

upside in articulating the thought, or even allowing it to coalesce into a fragment of language within the mind, but, even still…

It really looked like Kira was going to get away with it.

She was going to get away with murder.

Which wasn't something to be *proud* of, she knew. Obviously. Murder was bad, and being good at it was… not good. All the same though…it was kind of remarkable, wasn't it? That she had thought it all through *just* enough to stymie the authorities? She couldn't help but take a horrible satisfaction from that. Not so much that her insides didn't turn to liquid every time she thought about doing the next one, but hey. She'd aced the first. That was nothing to sniff at.

It'd have been a stretch to say that things were *looking up* as the year ticked away, but Kira certainly felt better about, yes, *things*, than she had in quite some time. If there was tragedy behind her, and more still to come, she could at least appreciate this little oasis of something resembling peace.

At times, she found herself doing more than appreciating. Might be more accurate to say she *caught* herself. Each time she found herself breathing a bit too easily, felt a smile alighting too quickly on her face, she tried to remind herself that there was still work to be done. Things were not back to normal, they were not okay, not by a long shot.

But it wasn't the worst thing in the world to, maybe, why not, *enjoy* those little pockets of relief along the way, was it?

By posing the question only to herself, in her own head, the answer could be anything she wanted. And so it was.

THE TREES STARTED TO SPLASH THEMSELVES RED around the same time Leigh would have been going back to school, but held off on the full autumnal bloodbath. By the time the solstice rolled around, almost all of the trees still had their leaves, most of which were still as green as could be.

Kira found herself more on-edge than usual for that first week of autumn, but as she knew from brutal experience, red exorcised red. As crimson bled into the canopies one leaf at a time, Kira felt able to return to whatever passed for a baseline temperament. If, of course, anything did. She and Harlow were still quite obviously tiptoeing around one another, and it was furthermore apparent that each knew that that was what the other was doing. Harlow was fearful of setting Kira off – or so Kira suspected – and she herself was nervous of frightening Harlow away, be it to another room to call that detective, or (somehow worse) back into his hole.

Not that he was fully out of said hole yet. But there was at least a snout wriggling towards sunlight. Progress that could be lost. It was such a deep hole.

During all this time, the investigation into who might have killed Nicole Ligeti chugged to a final standstill. A surprise arrest had been made, yet drew forth no conviction (for obvious reasons). Nicole's mother still appeared semi-regularly on TV – on local networks rather than nationals now – her appeals for anyone with information to come forward growing more and more muted each time. Harlow always left the room for those. Kira forced herself to watch. She felt, in some demented way, like she owed it to poor Mrs. Ligeti. Or maybe it was pure, stupid self-flagellation. Hey, why not both? Grief certainly left room for both.

At any rate, apparently poor Mrs. Ligeti's grief led her to make a deranged, last-ditch appeal to *Ruthger Gully* of all people – the perpetrator of the Firestarters Massacre – for information. The thinking (which the mass murderer did nothing to dissuade at first) being that Gully had accomplices, acolytes skittering about in the shadows, tasked with killing those who had survived the initial massacre. Gully ultimately had no light to shine on the investigation (again: obvious reasons), and so returned to the anonymity of wherever the fuck they kept him as he awaited his trial.

And then, as far as Kira could tell, the investigation officially ran out of steam. Yet another mass shooting fully captured the public's attention. Detective Dresselhaus went back to the city that had shared her. That news van with the reporter's face on the side was…well, Kira still saw it from time to time, but in places where it made more sense. Like the grand opening of a dog salon, or a sack race at the Harvest Fest.

Which meant…it no longer seemed as though Kira was going to get away murder.

It meant that she *had gotten away with it.*

On the day this fact finally shouldered its way past the velvet ropes of terror and guilt and incredulity and paranoia, to reach that VIP lounge in the back of Kira's brain where all of her beliefs talked incessantly about themselves as they snorted serotonin off of each other's thighs, Kira felt nearly crushed by relief. Made dizzy by it, made *ill* by it. Which she didn't know was a thing, but, wow, apparently it was! Assuming this was relief she was feeling. This sickness. It only stood to reason that it was belief, right? *Relief,* rather. Not belief. Ha.

That night, as Kira was reaching to turn off the light, Harlow, already tucked tightly under the covers, his back turned to her, asked in his tiniest voice, "are you proud?"

Kira knew immediately what he was referring to. She wondered how he'd come to the same conclusion as she had, on the very same day – it wasn't as though Pitney PD released a statement saying that whoever killed Nicole Ligeti did a really good job and was totally off the hook now – but it didn't really matter. She knew what he meant, just as she recognized there was nothing goading or judgmental in his tone. He was simply curious. And that was enough.

"Yes," Kira replied in a voice half the size of her own, "a little."

She turned and looked down at the back of her husband's head. Tried to recall the features on the other side of it. Imagined what sort of face those features must be forming. What such a face might signify was happening, in that skull of his.

Slowly, he rolled over. From this angle, Kira propped

up on an elbow, Harlow flat on his back and revolving, his features struck her as…incorrect. It was like watching strange alien topography crawl over the horizon; the peak of his nose, the roll of his lips, the crevasse of his philtrum leading to those two caves of despair held open by a clear Breathe Right nasal strip…

The eyes were the last thing Kira beheld. Those were unmistakable. Impossible to imagine being other than what they were.

And what they were was…interested. In her.

Gone were the contempt, the fear, the confusion, all of those terrible shadows Harlow had been trailing for so long.

Was this forgiveness? Acceptance? Gratitude?

No, no, and *certainly* not.

But they were *interested,* those eyes.

Kira had to imagine this was an expression well-known to any apex predator that had been airlifted out of their natural habitat and dropped into a zoo.

Before she could question the wisdom of it, Kira acted on an impulse: she leaned down and kissed Harlow. A single smooch, passionate, yet polite. The sort that closes out a tremendous first date.

She leaned back and studied her husband with, yes, *interest.*

He hadn't moved. Still wasn't. Not scooting over for a little more sugar…but not recoiling, either.

Progress.

Kira smiled, then leaned over and turned off the light.

Click. Goodnight.

MID-OCTOBER CAME ON HARD, temperatures plummeting in concert with Kira's paranoia. Day by day, she forgot her fear, let it fall away with the ever-reddening foliage. What did she have to be afraid of, after all? She'd gotten away with it. She'd won.

Won the first round, at any rate.

At long last, the weekend of their two-grand getaway arrived. So Southward ho went the Trecothiks, striking out in Kira's spiffy new Focus (the old one had been damaged beyond repair, and so specialized were the parts required for replacement, the galaxybrains at State Farm determined that buying Kira a new model would actually be cheaper for the company than repairing the old), loaded down with meat and mead. Well, technically wine, but allowances must be made for euphony. Aesthetics matter. Example: trees were better at red than Kira was, that was for damn sure.

The cabin was as isolated as promised, plopped on a hill that rolled upon itself in three steep tiers. A bit like squatting on top of a snowman with chlorosis. In, it must be said, an adorable little log cabin. The view it afforded was stunning; sit on the front porch and witness arcs of autumn leaping off to stage right, higher still in the opposite direction! Slope and blushing swell, sweetly perfumed by heath aster and woodbine! The spectacle of a wood tending towards the skeletal was all the more beautiful for the knowledge of what was to come: palsied death, grey and angular. But no sense dwelling on that. Sit on the front porch, and witness. Or, when one is all witnessed out, play cards. Or read together. Just *be* together, prior to the coming of the grey and the angular. Sit on the front porch, until the sun goes down.

So they did. Starting on chairs at either end of the deck, ultimately finding themselves sharing the same porch swing. Who could say how such a teleportation act had been accomplished? It had simply happened, as had the little smiles deforming their faces as their eyes met, at first accidentally, then less so. In each of these glances, Kira would have sworn she saw the man with whom she had once, long ago, gotten stoned and lain in the back of a borrowed pickup truck. For just a single, solitary instant at a time. Like scanning the beach for bubbles as the tide rolls out. That's where you want to dig, to find a sand crab. If finding a sand crab is something you want to do. Watch for the bubbles.

If you know what you're looking for, they're easier to spot than you might expect.

As night fell, and moths launched vain assaults on the porchlights, Kira and Harlow retired to the living room of the adorable and, it had to be said, poorly designed cabin. Harlow sizzled the steaks in a skillet with butter and a few flavorless green garnishes. Kira poured the wine and got a head start, a bibulous distance Harlow announced his intention to close just as soon as the meat was done. He didn't wait that long, naturally, and so the meat got more done than perhaps it ought to have. It still tasted heavenly, though, and when they were done they sat back out on the porch, ignoring those insects braving the cold for blood, watching the stars' careful procession across the heavens. Not a pickup truck, and their minds had been made swirly by a different substance, but it would do. It would do just fine. Before long they were cold beyond comfort, and so they headed back inside. Finding the bedroom was a full-contact sport, the chief opposition coming from the disorientation of the cabin's baffling layout (the only way into the bedroom was through the bathroom), as well as the dizzying delights of Bacchus and his nectar. Victory was ultimately theirs, and as the most devious of their clothing's latches and levers and gizmos had been disengaged in the course of this lately concluded struggle, their vestments proved a far more quickly-dispatched sort of villain.

They helped one another get undressed, each peeling off the other's trousers. Laughing all the while. God, it was wonderful, wasn't it? They were young again. Drunk and young and in love. And nothing that had happened since the back of the pickup had actually happened. Just a dream. A dream that had been mostly beautiful, yet dissolved into a nightmare at the end. Thank god they were awake now. Awake, drunk, young, in love.

Less dreamy were Harlow's difficulties in the dingus department; each time Kira checked, it got softer. Which somehow seemed to fly in the face of one of the laws of thermodynamics, or something. How could it just…*keep getting softer?* Harlow blamed it on the wine, which was true in as much as was saying the Hindenburg got blown up by a spark. True, true, but the explanation made little sense if one failed to consider all that hydrogen. Fortunately, there were precious few comparisons to be made between the disasters; Harlow quickly righted the ship, and if there were any outbursts along the lines of *oh the humanity,* the delivery was quite different than that known to history.

"I love you," Harlow wept into Kira's sweat-glazed shoulder. "I love you. I don't know what's happening to us."

"I love you too," Kira whispered up to the ceiling. She wrapped her right arm around him, her palm making a wet *slap* against his sweat-glazed back. "We love each other. That's what matters."

"I'm so fucking confused."

"Me too, baby."

"I'm really scared."

"It's gonna be okay."

"I want to do it!"

"…I thought you did?"

"No, not….that's not what I meant."

"…" Kira snaked her trembling hand under Harlow's shoulders and bench pressed him until she could look at his face. He was *bawling,* silently leaking, his face swollen like one big bee sting.

All of the air left her lungs. The thoughts left her head. The bones left her body.

"…what do you want to do?" she asked.

"I want…" Harlow grimaced and turned his face from Kira's. "I want one last day with her." He turned back to Kira, eyebrows upturned and shoulders hunched, as though anticipating rebuke with equal parts fear and hope.

Kira studied his face, his puffy, drunken, post-coital

face. What was she looking for? Bubbles in the sand. Balloons dropping rope.

Red. She was looking for red.

"You understand what that means," Kira asked in a way that was just short of a question. "What we have to do."

"Yes," he nodded. "I do. That's why I'm so fucking…" He took a deep breath, getting his voice back under control. "She can't die scared. The way she looked in the car…that can't be the…the end."

Kira's eyes ran frantic loops around Harlow's face, seeking the slightest crack in the mask.

She saw a few.

Through them…she saw what she was looking for. Heard a small voice, whispering. Carrying a tune.

"I want us to talk about this tomorrow," she said carefully. "I really do. Tonight, I want to focus on each other. Is that okay?"

Harlow nodded.

That night, they focused on each other.

The following morning, they started to focus on someone else.

TEN

YOU DO WHAT YOU CAN

RID OF RED

MADELEINE ENCOMB STILL HAD NIGHTMARES about Knot Hedge. Each time they were precise recreations of the actual day, the boost over the log from Leigh Trecothik, the impatient *THUTHUTHUTHUTHU* of the bullets hitting the other side, the sound of Leigh's body hitting the ground, all of it. She longed for some fantastical embellishment, a ghoul or a goblin, something, *anything* to cut the reality of it all. What she got was nothing, nothing but what it had been. Her nocturnal visitors (she thought of them thusly, as *intruders,* for to consider them now a part of herself was to open the door on a much darker vision of her future than she could bear) naturally cast shadows into the daylight hours. Twice-weekly therapy and a small arsenal of medications brought Maddie back from a terrible precipice, one upon which she hadn't recognized her toes' having trespassed. Going outside was a challenge for her; she was liable to be triggered by the slightest unexpected stimuli. Sudden, loud noises set her off, of course, but the sight of a fallen log on one of the nature walks her therapist had suggested she go on could prove just as deleterious to her psychological well-being. Withdrawal and aversion weren't strategies, that was what people told her. But those were people who hadn't been on Knot Hedge, who hadn't gone over the log, hadn't heard the high-caliber tapping against the far side (and the muted reports of the bullets stopped by Leigh's body). Though she didn't wholly believe this, it struck Maddie as impossible that anybody who hadn't gone over that log could ever understand what it was that she was going through.

Lucky for her, there were two other people who had.

It had been mere days after the event when Maddie, Zoe, and Nicole had arranged to meet up and discuss just what they were going through. Nicole seemed to be handling it the best of the three of them, but that was hardly a surprise. Hers had been a troubled upbringing; in particular, she had a father who was either absent, or prompting his wife and children to really wish he were. He was a mean drunk, striking more often by the word than the deed (though the hand did rise now and again). One could bend beneath these blows and present the back as a canvas, or one could stand tall and play defense. Nicole Ligeti had, unlike her prostrate siblings, selected the latter course. Consequently, she possessed a strength no one as young as she was should ever have to. It wasn't that she hadn't been affected by what had happened to them on the island – that would require a detachment tantamount to sociopathy – but as far as Maddie could tell, Nicole had found a way to slot back into her old life and relegate her grief to scheduled appointments.

Zoe was, as far as coping went, the baseline. She evinced a greater level of disease (er…*un*ease) with what she had been through than Nicole did, her despair falling upon her at times, and to degrees, that could be neither predicted nor prepared for. Example: in the aftermath of the Massacre, the Firestarters reconvened as a group to discuss what had happened, and to offer subsidized psychological support for the survivors. All three of them attended that meeting, none of them prepared for what the Firestarters leadership would later admit was the poor-taste decision to hire a dozen highly conspic-uous armed guards to patrol the auditorium in which the meeting was being held. Good guy with a gun, and all that. Not a few of the kids saw the goons with their Red Dawn arsenals and ran from the room in tears. Zoe and Nicole followed their distressed contemporaries out, shaken but not quite traumatized. Nicole recovered almost at once; Zoe needed a day. Whereas…

Oh fine, just own it: Maddie was one of the ones who'd bolted out of that auditorium, nearly blind for terror. She was, without a doubt, the most poorly equip-ped of the three to handle what had happened to them. Not just because she was getting triggered by men with guns; she couldn't even handle a spotting a fucking log in the woods.

Only Zoe and Nicole truly understood what Maddie was going through. Not just the terror, the anguish, all of that…no, there was also the weight of that unfulfillable obligation. They were alive, the three of them, because someone else wasn't. Leigh Trecothik had quite directly given her life to save theirs. How to repay that debt? It was impossible. By steps, they had attempted to build a relationship with Leigh's parents (a charge led by Nicole, of course, she being the strongest of the three). Mixed results, all told, but they would keep trying. They would never be able to make the Trecothiks whole again, but they each felt a strange obligation to try, to do their best.

Nobody else who'd been on the island that day wholly understood what that felt like. At least, no one that Maddie spoke to. So, perverse though it was to look at any of this under a rosy lens…Maddie sometimes wept, for how fortunate she was to have Zoe Cottrell and Nicole Ligeti in her life. To help her carry this weight, this terrible weight. Even when they didn't speak of it directly; they so rarely spoke of it directly. Did it make sense to say that not speaking of it made it easier to discuss? Of course not, but Maddie didn't think that made it any less true. That day had not been lived by word. Language could never rise to an account of it.

They also never discussed just what they meant to one another. That didn't need to be said. It was a known fact. To dwell upon it would have been akin to sitting around and pointing out that, when you dropped an object, it always went *down*, never *sideways*. And somehow, it seemed dangerous to put it into words. As though what they had built was fragile, a bashful scaffolding that might collapse beneath a kind word. So keep it private, then. All Maddie knew was she couldn't imagine going on without Zoe and Nicole, without their support, their friendship; she hoped she was able to give back half as much as they gave.

When she found out Nicole had been murdered – *brutally* murdered, stabbed *nineteen times* by some lunatic in the parking lot of the music school she went to – Maddie passed out. Fully lost consciousness, dropped the phone in her hand, plummeted to the floor. Her dad had been standing close enough to rush in and catch her before she hit the ground, tearing his bicep in the process. When she awoke, that injury he'd sustained for her upset Maddie more than it did her father. Which only made her cry more.

Yet the next time she saw Zoe, Maddie forced herself not to cry. For much to her surprise, Zoe had come completely unraveled at Nicole's murder. Eyes watering, mouth open wide in a silent scream, clutching the fabric of her shirt and wringing it in two tight fists. Pure despair. Whatever relative composure she had maintained in the aftermath of the Massacre was now completely exhausted.

Zoe's fortitude had always been a front, Maddie only then realized. Just as her own consoling, caretaker demeaning now was. For she recognized a great need in her friend, and however difficult it was for her, she wanted to meet it.

"It's okay," she whispered to Zoe one night, as they

sat in the dark of Zoe's bedroom. They'd come up here to sit in front of her laptop and stream the first episode of some splashy, slapdash Netflix documentary about the Massacre. Morbid curiosity. Five minutes in, it started showing real footage from the day. Just silly videos taken by the kids before things turned. Still, it was too much. So they'd closed the laptop, and the room became dark. And almost at once, Zoe had begun to cry. And Maddie had said, "it's okay."

"I just wish everything would stop," Zoe sobbed. Curling against Maddie, clutching frantically at her shirt. Like a newborn.

"I know," Maddie whispered, fighting the quiver in her chin. Refusing to give in.

As she so often did, Zoe fell into an eye in the storm, a moment of lucidity between tearful fugues. She leaned back slightly, not quite managing to meet Maddie's eye, but getting close. "The world is an awful place. We live in such an awful place."

Maddie could only reach out and wrap Zoe in her arms, pull her friend's face back into the port of her shoulder. She never knew how to respond, when Zoe said stuff like that. Which always broke Maddie's heart. She wanted so desperately to help her friend. But she never, ever knew what to say.

Nothing ever stopped. Autumn rolled on; Maddie suddenly found herself unable to occupy confined public spaces, also known as *rooms*. She discovered this new fact about herself at the same time as the rest of her third period US History class did. "You just flew across the room," her friend Ty told her when she later asked what had happened. She didn't remember, of course. She didn't remember all but flipping her desk and sprinting towards the door, not to open it but to slam into it, slide down it, and lapse into unconsciousness. The most unsettling part, Ty had explained, was that Maddie's doing this was completely unprompted. Whatever had set her off was something that had happened in her head, nowhere else. What was more, she did all of this in complete silence. No crying, no screaming, no nothing. Silence.

So Maddie left school. They'd try again next year, her parents and the administration all agreed. In thusly halving the amount of time she got to spend around Zoe – around *anyone* else – Maddie came to realize just how vital her pretending to hold it together for Zoe's benefit had been, in the project of actually holding it together. Now alone, her low points got lower, cost her that much more to climb out of them when she did go see Zoe in the afternoons. Yet climb she did, because Zoe needed her. By Zoe's own account, she was able to wear the mask of her composure at school, but in Maddie's presence, no amount of effort could keep it on. This touched Maddie in a way she would never have even tried to articulate. To be so trusted by someone, regardless of the situation…there was strength in that, too. So if Zoe could be strong for Maddie, then Maddie would be strong for Zoe. In this way, they learned to support each other. Just the two of them.

Sometimes she thought about going to see Nicole's

parents, the way Nicole had built a bond (however tenuous) with Leigh's parents. But then, she remembered the stories Nicole had told of her father. Given how short their friendship had been – Maddie had hardly known Nicole's name before they were united by Leigh's sacrifice – Maddie had to assume they hadn't even heard the worst stories about him. Seemed safest to keep her distance, then. Besides, there was always that little suspicion she nursed, had never mentioned to anyone, not even Zoe: *maybe Nicole's dad did it.* Oh, it somehow felt a betrayal, keeping small secrets like that in the face of Zoe's incredible openness, her vulnerability. Yet Maddie didn't know what else to do. Didn't know how else to be tough, how to help her friend, whom she had come to love as she imagined siblings learn to love each other, later in life.

Were there times when Maddie dreamed of complete disconnect, wondered if her life might not be improved not by strength but by perfect porousness, by feeling nothing at all? Yes. Of course. Were there a surgical procedure that could sever the heart from the brain (metaphorically, of course), she would several times have been tempted – particularly as fall tipped towards the dark of winter – to sign herself up. But, of course, if she lost her empathy, she'd be the sort of person who saw a stranger, a *neighbor* in need, and drove right on by. And that wasn't the sort of person Maddie wanted to be. She was alive thanks to the selflessness of one friend. She was strong thanks to the need of another. It was unthinkable, to take those gifts and embody their opposite.

So she reminded herself, on a particularly bleak and unremarkable late afternoon in early-November, as she was driving out to visit, who else, Zoe. The year's premature cold had deepened, but no snow had as yet fallen. Snow would have made it all a little more bearable. Maddie couldn't remember ever longing for it so desperately.

In the meantime, here was a car with its hood up, parked on the side of the road. A lonely road, a single-lane that traced the eastern edge of the barrens. Far from picturesque, hemmed in by thick cedar trees that would have looked less imposing with a lovely little dusting of winter. Not a good place to break down, this unnamed slash of pavement, not when it was this cold out. For all the times Maddie had taken this road – it was the shortest route to Zoe's house, so she'd taken it quite a lot lately – she couldn't remember ever seeing another car on it with her.

So it fell to her to help, then. Ok, ok. It was situations like these, when Maddie was still glad of her heart's more expansive qualities. Made even larger by imagining what her friends might do here in her shoes. Leigh would have stopped to help. She surely would have.

Maddie guided her car into the tilted stretch of gravel that passed for a shoulder, nosing up a few yards behind the rear bumper of what appeared to be a fairly new Ford Focus. As she approached, the passenger of that car got out.

It was Mrs. Trecothik.

Maddie gulped. She hadn't really spoken to Leigh's mother since…what had happened to Nicole happened.

Nicole had been the one to really bring them all together, after all. Without her…oh, was it bad to have not kept in touch? Would Mrs. Trecothik be mad? It was bad that she'd lost touch with the mother of the person who had saved her life, wasn't it?

Already, Maddie felt anxiety tightening its grip around her neck. What would she say to Mrs. Trecothik? She didn't know what to say. She never knew what to say.

Taking a deep breath – unintentionally loosing a low, anxious hum – Maddie parked her car, turned it off, and got out.

Mrs. Trecothik smiled at Maddie.

Such a warm smile. Instantly put Maddie at ease.

So she took a breath and waved to Mrs. Trecothik. "Hi!" she called, as she stepped around the front of her own vehicle. Her voice trembled a bit. Ah, so she was still nervous. Her body was, at least, even if her mind wasn't.

"Oh, hey!" Mrs. Trecothik called back. She planted one hand on her hip and pointed with the other. "…*Madeleine,* isn't it?"

"Uh, yeah!" Maddie cocked her head slightly. She'd had dinner with the Trecothiks. Did Leigh's mom really not recognize her? "I just go by Maddie."

"Maddie?" called a voice from behind the raised hood of the Focus. Mr. Trecothik's head poked out from around far side. "Say, aren't you one of the girls that Leigh…"

For some reason, Mrs. Trecothik whipped around towards her husband.

"...yeah," Maddie replied. Feeling a bit lost. The whole reason she'd *gotten* that dinner with the Trecothiks, and with Zoe and Nicole, was *because* of what Leigh had done for them.

She *had* gotten dinner with them, right? They were acting like they'd never seen her before. She hadn't imagined that meal, had she?

As though thrilling to her own potential delusion – finally, something concrete to be nervous about! – her heart started to beat faster.

"Mhm." Both Trecothiks grew quite still then. In contemplation of their daughter, perhaps.

"So," Maddie ventured in the silence, doing her best to seem – and so, who knew, maybe feel – calm and composed, "you guys need help with your car?"

"Yes," Mrs. Trecothik finally said, "and we're glad you stopped. Even more so than we would have been if you weren't, you know...*you*."

"But you *are* you," Mr. Trecothik noted.

"...right," Maddie replied.

"Yes," Mrs. Trecothik allowed. She sounded slightly annoyed. She and her husband must have been arguing just before this. That seemed like a thing married people did, right? They argued about things that couldn't be helped. So Maddie assumed, anyway. She'd never even been in a relationship. Not like, not a *real* one.

"Okay." Maddie zipped up her fleece, which she'd had open while she was driving. The car had heat, after all. Unlike these lonely woods. "So, I'm sorry I don't know much about cars and stuff. But I can give you a ride somewhere?"

"Oh yes," Mrs. Trecothik scoffed with a dismissive wave towards her husband, "he's having a grand old time, making *zero* progress. I think if we could just get a ride back to town with you, that'd be perfect. I assume that's where you're heading?"

"Um…do you mean, like, the garage in town?"

"Yeah."

Torn between gainsaying an adult and the facts of geography, Maddie cocked a thumb over her shoulder. Back the way she'd just come from. Back the way they'd *both* come from, given the direction the Trecothik car was facing. "The garage is back that way."

"Oh, thank you *so* much. Harlow!" Mrs. Trecothik called over her shoulder.

"I'm ready!" Harlow shouted from behind the hood of the Focus.

Mrs. Trecothik seemed startled by this response. She shot Maddie a quick, appraising look, then once more spun back around towards her husband.

For her part, Maddie didn't see what was so strange about that. Mr. Trecothik was ready for a ride into town. Ready to quit fiddling with his engine and get into a car with heat.

And then Mr. Trecothik spotted whatever expression his wife was sending his way, straightened up, and said, "I mean, yes, dear?"

Which was weird. Very weird.

Then again, they were cold, and agitated, and probably pretty shaken up from breaking down on such a rarely-traveled road.

Mrs. Trecothik nodded at her husband. "We're getting a ride with Maddie here. Grab your bag and let's go."

Harlow shut the hood of the car delicately, as though trying not to wake a baby, and walked around to the rear door on the driver's side. He opened it, leaned in, and grabbed a massive duffel bag. The way it folded, the way he flung it around with such abandon…it looked completely empty.

This, too, was weird.

Maddie didn't say anything, though. Because she was just a teenager. These were adults. She'd always been a bit awkward around adults – well, she felt pretty well defined by social anxiety around *everyone,* but adults were a special case. Adults knew things. They knew their business. Their floppy duffel bag business.

Once again slamming his door, Mr. Trecothik walked the bag over towards Maddie. Smiling like he was expecting to have his picture taken. "I'm ready," he repeated, chuckling this time.

Maddie smiled, even as something about all of this struck her as wrong. The Trecothiks coming over, to get in her car, for a ride back to town…what was wrong here?

She looked from Mr. Trecothik to the Focus, and back again, then saw it. Ah, yes. "Don't you want to lock your car?" she asked him.

"Oh, wow!" Mrs. Trecothik laughed stiffly. "Yeah. Don't forget to lock the car!"

"Yeah, alright," Mr. Trecothik grumbled. He turned

and trudged back to the car, then squeezed a little button on the tailgate.

BEEP BEEP! the car trilled.

"I didn't forget," he continued as he trudged back in Maddie's direction. "I just didn't think anybody would steal it here."

"Better safe than sorry," Mrs. Trecothik said. "Right?"

"Who's gonna steal it?" Mr. Trecothik snapped. "A moose?"

"Easy," Mrs. Trecothik ordered her husband. "Relax."

Something about the way she said that – *relax* – tipped beyond the merely weird. It really unnerved Maddie. That hadn't been a lover's rebuke. It had been the person on belay, coaching a climber after their rope had just snapped.

Maybe…this didn't make any sense at all, but maybe this particular feeling wasn't *just* your garden variety social anxiety.

Which meant it could be any of the myriad artisanal, *executive level* social anxieties.

Or, of course, maybe it was something else entirely.

Maybe. Who knew. All Maddie knew was that she didn't want to be here anymore. For whatever reason. She wanted to get off this road. Right now.

She wanted to get away from the Trecothiks.

But she couldn't. And what anchored her to the spot was the flipside of anxiety: pure social propriety. There was no excuse she could generate that would be sufficiently urgent to justify leaving two middle-aged folks – particularly the parents of the girl who had given her life to save Maddie's – alone on a cold, lonely road hardly anybody ever…

…

Thoughts crashed around her skull like wrestlers bouncing off the ropes. None of which made any sense. They all served to underline how very much she wanted to get the fuck out of here, though, and that was good enough for her.

So many times, in so many words, her therapist had told her to trust her feelings. And Maddie was nothing if not a good listener.

"So, um," Maddie said, reversing towards her car behind her, trying and failing to keep her voice from wavering, "I actually just remembered, I've really gotta get going, in the way I was already headed, which is *that* way…since you're going the other way, would it be okay if I just went ahead and called you a ri-"

"We're ready to go now," Mr. Trecothik smiled, by now within high-fiving distance.

"We really appreciate it," Mrs. Trecothik added, as Mr. Trecothik reached, and then passed, Maddie.

"The inside of my car is also….um," Maddie scratch-ed at her forehead, "it smells. It's kind of embarrassing, but I haven't had it cl-"

"That's alright," Mrs. Trecothik assured her, stepping towards her. Voice dropping as she got nearer.

Maddie forced a chuckle, taking another tiny step backwards. "Do you mind if I ask where you were heading? Just so I c-"

"That's alright," Mrs. Trecothik repeated. Nearly subaudible.

Maddie felt herself whimper quietly. She couldn't hear it, but she could feel it. The familiar way it shook her skull.

This was just how it had felt, between hearing the first shots on Knot Hedge, and learning what had caused them.

Mr. Trecothik opened the trunk to Maddie's car – she was standing close enough to it for the key fob to unlock it – and pointed inside. "Can I put my bag on this?"

Maddie, now perfectly between the two Trecothiks – Mrs. in front of her, Mr. behind – could only keep her eyes on one of them at a time. She elected to turn around and look at the latter just long enough to ask "what's that?"

"This here," he repeated, jabbing a finger at the trunk.

She fought her breath as it got faster and faster: the trunk of her car was empty. She knew that for a god-damned fact. So what was he talking about?

"What is it?" she asked, unable to keep her voice from trembling.

"I don't know. You kids and your gizmos," he mono-toned. As though reading from a script.

Leave, Maddie told herself. *Jump in your car. Run into the woods. Just get out of there.*

Yet, how could she? That would have been *rude*.

Mr. Trecothik popped his head up over the top of Maddie's car, studying the street before him. He winced, kept his eyes shut, and said "yeah."

"Yeah wh-" was as far as Maddie got before she heard Mrs. Trecothik's footsteps come up behind her at a run.

Maddie was just about to turn around when the woman's arm swung through the bottom of her field of vision, out from behind her, stretching in front of her, then swinging back t-

Mrs. Trecothik clamped Maddie's neck in the crook of her arm.

Like a choke-out.

Scratch that: not *like* a choke-out. The pressure applied to either side of her neck as Mrs. Trecothik flexed her arm, trying to crack Maddie's windpipe like a walnut, made the intention clear.

She was getting choked out, on the shoulder of a lonely road, by Leigh's mom.

"WHAT THE FUCK?" she managed to croak. Reflexively, she reached up and clawed at Mrs. Trecothik's hands. There was thick leather over them. What do you call 'em. *Gloves*.

Mr. Trecothik lunged forward and grabbed for Maddie's hands. She used Mrs. Trecothik for support and kicked at the husband as hard as she could. "Stop!" he shouted absurdly.

"Jesus Fuck!" Mrs. Trecothik screamed. "Come on!"

"Put your other hand behind her head!" Mr. Trecothik shrieked. He swiped at Maddie's legs as she kicked.

"I am!"

"It said you have to put your other hand behind her h-"

"I'M DOING IT, HARLOW!"

Finally, Mr. Trecothik caught one of Maddie's kicks. He yanked her leg, lifting Maddie to an elevated horizontal.

Mrs. Trecothik lost her grip. Not entirely – just enough to let Maddie suck in some air as her upper body swung towards the street, her feet a fulcrum in Mr. Trecothik's hands.

The back of her head *cracked* on the pavement.

Blind. Maddie was blind. She needed to get up, she knew. The only thing she knew. She tried to move her body, but it was fused to the pavement. She was concrete.

Mrs. Trecothik's hands slipped roughly beneath her shoulder. Lifted her up.

"Bend from the legs," Harlow instructed.

"I *am.*"

Mrs. Trecothik wrapped her arm around Maddie's neck again. Placed the other hand on the back of her head.

Maddie tried to fight, but her legs were air, they were evening. Without substance. Tending towards something else.

Wait, she tried to say as Mrs. Trecothik's arm got tighter, tighter, so tight Maddie couldn't believe her head hadn't just popped off. "Hllg," was all she could manage. *"Hllg."*

She tried to lift her arm and pull Mrs. Trecothik off. Away. Get. Go. She tried. She tried.

"Just stop," Mrs. Trecothik told her. "Please."

434

No. Sunrise. Maddie found her hands again and reached up, grabbed Mrs. Trecothik's arm as hard as she could. Right where forearm met windpipe.

She felt Mrs. Trecothik tighten her stranglehold.

"Fucking...come *on,*" Mrs. Trecothik whined. As though she was making great points, and Maddie just wasn't getting it. "Stop it!!"

Maddie kicked at the ground.

Felt the soles of her feet land flat on the pavement.

Felt the strength in her legs. Three years of field hockey.

She rolled forward, forcing Mrs. Trecothik to come along for the ride, like a backpack with the straps too tight.

Mrs. Trecothik tried to pull her back down to the ground with just her bodyweight. Too bad she hadn't done three years of field hockey.

Maddie tightened her core, ignored the black spots boiling in her vision, and put every ounce of power she had into her legs. Did her best to squat Leigh's mom.

It worked. She felt Mrs. Trecothik get heavier on her shoulders as she bore more and more of the woman's weight. As the ground bore less and less.

"Help!" Mrs. Trecothik called to her husband.

Mr. Trecothik walked directly up to them, bouncing softly on the balls of his feet a mere foot or two from Maddie and shouting "I don't know what to do!"

"Grab her feet!"

"Okay!" he replied, then lunged forward and grabbed Maddie's ankles.

Grabbed and pulled.

Maddie's feet flew out from under her.

She crashed back to the ground. Landing on Mrs. Trecothik.

At the moment of impact, Mrs. Trecothik's deathgrip eased up. Just a bit.

Maddie took a gasping breath.

The arm immediately slid around her neck again. Tightened.

Mr. Trecothik collapsed to his knees, leaning on Maddie's shins, holding her legs.

It occurred to Maddie that she might well have just taken her final breath.

"Please just…*stop,*" Mrs. Trecothik sobbed. Mr. Trecothik was crying, too.

Maddie slapped at Mrs. Trecothik's arm. Didn't have the strength to dig her fingers in, nor the breath to plead she ease up. All she could do was throw weak little slaps. *Slap. Slap slap. Slap.*

Mrs. Trecothik made some non-verbal noises of frustration, using her elbows to check Maddie's attempts to hip-bump her way to freedom. "How long is this supposed to take?!" she mewled.

"I think it should be faster than this," Mr. Trecothik replied through tears.

"I don't know what I'm doing wrong."

"I can try if you want."

Mrs. Trecothik said nothing to that. Maddie could only imagine her face. Except she couldn't. She couldn't think of anything that wasn't precisely what she was looking at. Which was a constellation of colorless orbs, no two alike and yet each indistinguishable.

Mr. Trecothik swallowed loudly and wiped his nose with his right sleeve. "It looks like she's...like it's working."

Probably because it was.

Vision was the first thing to fail. Starblind, swallowed whole. White and black, both at once. Sound abandoned her shortly thereafter, dividing and fleeing to either extreme in the spectrum, to a shrill ringing high, to a deep muted rumble.

A burning spear plunged through her throat. Sorry. Her throat *was* a burning spear, solid metal brought to a glow, furious, sorry. So sorry. They kept saying sorry.

Maddie's arms no longer heeded her commands. Lift, she bade them. Slap. Nothing of the sort transpired. They were sleeves of cool disobedience. So she kicked. Tried so hard to kick. But the man was on her legs, and he was so heavy. What was his name? What was his name? What? What?

Something came apart. The feeling was so clear. Close. Right there. When the thing was together it made a mind, and that mind could know more than pain. But the thing had come apart.

One voice: "Finally. Jesus."

The other: "It's okay. It's okay."

The thing apart couldn't focus. Mentally or physically. There was a difference, it knew. There were two bodies of blur, a spread of white behind them. Right behind them. Her hands were so heavy.

There were hands. That was coming back. The blur and white were gone, conquered by black. But the hands had returned. As had the mind. It was her. Maddie. She was Madeleine Encomb and she didn't want to die. She didn't understand. How could she? Her head was so heavy. Not for long, though. It was emptying into the rattle and bounce of the place her body occupied. How m…

Maddie tried to lift her hand. She couldn't. There was a cloud in front of her. A cloud with the skin of a lizard. She was inside the cloud, its scales scratching her flesh raw. How weak she was. Was her flesh. In front of her. Knees racked against the chest. Fetal.

She took a rasping breath. Air! It stung, stale with sweat, but sweet all the same. Her throat rattled.

"Hn…uh…" she tried to speak but could find no words.

Words: cloud. Dragon. Nonsense. What. Legs. Shoulder. Contact. Movement. Huffing. Crackle. Snap. Wh…

Focus. Think. *Know.*

Bag.

The duffel.

Zipped inside Mr. Trecothik's duffel bag. That empty bag, now full of her. She was inside the bag…inside of something that was moving. Driving. In the trunk of a car. An empty trunk. *Her* car?

Awareness went, and came again. Now they were carrying her, one at her hips, one at her shoulders. No. They were carrying the bag. Maddie just happened to be inside of it. They carried the bag, grunting and huffing…

through the woods? Shh. The dull hush of wind through trees. Crackle. Snap. Dead branches under foot. No one spoke. Where were they taking her?

Did they know she was alive?

Carefully, she reached for her pocket. Tried. Scales stitched into her arms. No. Shed and molt. This was possible. This was possible.

Maddie took as deep a breath as her burning throat would allow, then used her fingers to take her hand for a walk. Forefinger, middlefinger, again, again. Doot-de-doot-de-doo. One finger, then the next. Down her hip, to her pocket.

Her phone. It was still there.

They thought she was dead. Had to.

Had to call someone. Or she was dead. Would be.

Snaking one finger into her pocket. Trying hard not to move the rest of her body. Not any more than she had already.

"Nng," escaped her throat. So loud. They would hear her. They would hear her and kill her. A tear raced down her cheek. She was so scared, because now she had hope. Hope that she could call for help. Hope that could be crushed. Her mouth was full of blood, was bone dry. "Hlng."

"Stop," her feet said. No. Mr. Trecothik, down at the feet.

"What?" her head. Above. The Mrs.

Maddie froze. Not her tears though. They were liquid. They rolled on.

Breathing was automatic. Not a choice. Deafening.

Couldn't stop it happening.

Maddie sniffed.

Feet fell. "She's alive!"

Shoulders came down more slowly. Respectfully. Why bother.

zzzzzzzzzIP! The bag opened. Maddie blinked. Blinding. Blinded. White. Right. Behind.

Two heads. One shook. "Oh, honey." Mrs. Trecothik. Talking to her. Maddie. "I'm so sorry." Hands from the white. Right *and* left. One over her mouth, the other pinching her nose. "Hold her." Flat. Said and done.

Fingers still on the phone. In Maddie's pocket. *Her* pocket. Not ready to let go. Just needed to call. Someone. Anyone. Help.

Needed air to call. Feet kicking on their own. Left hand flailing. Keep right in the pocket. The right. Tried. Failed. Flailing. Burning. Lungs on fire, throat on fire. Fire fire. No light though. All fire no light. Heat without light. Then cold. Then dark. Then *pdldldl*.

Chk.

Maddie *GASPED*. She tried to stretch. Couldn't. The universe had established boundaries. Blue boundaries.

Still in the bag. She was still. There. Curled. Fetal. *Pdldldl.*

Chk.

A voice from above: "Stop!"

Yes. Stop.

Maddie tried to roll onto her side. *Pdldldl* from her chest to the ground.

Dirt. On top of her, sliding off as she turned. Some

still on her. More below.

Dirt below her. Dirt on top.

How?

Oh. Of course.

A hole. Buried. She was being buried. In a hole.

"She's still alive!" Mr. Trecothik screamed.

Mrs. Trecothik replied: "Oh, for god's sake!"

Silence. Hush. Wind through trees. But deeper. Deep down. Six whole feet.

Maddie *howled.* Not a human noise.

She noticed the birds overhead, far overhead, by their sudden silence. Then she tried to roll. Couldn't.

So she screamed. Tasted blood. Kept screaming.

She wasn't screaming. Thought she was screaming, but wasn't. Wasn't making much more than a gusty hiss.

"What do we do?"

"We have to…" Mrs. Trecothik gave a staccato sigh. "We can't bury her…like this."

Shh. Rattle. Deep.

"Maybe," Mr. Trecothik whispered, "it was just the wind I heard." His voice shook. Shaken by the wind. Like dead branches.

Three people crying. Two above, one below.

"Hhhh!" Maddie choked. "Nnnnl!" Words wouldn't come. "Nnnlmh!"

Chk.

Pdldldl.

More dirt. Back to burying. One shovelful at a time. It was only the wind they'd heard, after all.

Reaching for her phone. Still there. One finger on it.

Now two.

Chk.

Pdldldl.

Pinching it between two fingers. "Hnng." Trying to lever it out.

Chk.

crrrrOSH, a bowling ball of dirt, splitting on her head. "Nnnnnno!" Loud as she could. "NO!"

Phone out of the pocket.

Crying from above. Cry your hearts out. Heartless.

Chk.

Crank the neck to see screen. The screen. Just a screen. No button. Touch no good. Need to see.

CRRROSH. Another bowling ball cranked the neck further. Too far. Left shoulder popped. "AAH!"

"Kick some in." So saith the angel.

PlmplmPLPLPLPLmmmmmmplmplm. Quick trickle of dirt.

Chk.

PlmlmLMLMplmplm.

Pdldldl.

A clump knocked the phone from her hand.

Her jaw unlocked

"NOOO!" Maddie cried, at full voice this time. "PL…PLEASE!"

A bed of even pressure rising to halfway up the bag. Half-buried.

More dirt falling all the while.

Chk.

PlmplplplMMMplm

Pdldldldl

PLMLMMLMplplpl.

Maddie reached beneath her body for the phone. Gone. Somewhere down deep. Buried.

"LEIGH!" she shrieked.

Chk.

Silence.

Maddie gasped and sobbed. Felt the words she'd found. "Leigh saved me! Please!"

They listened. Above, they listened.

She shifted in the bag, lifting her head as far as she could. Not far. But maybe enough. "She died so I c-"

The moon crashed into her head. It shuddered. Metallic.

Not the moon.

The head of the shovel. Swung down at her head.

It came down again, hard. *CRACK.* A break to match the back.

Maddie turned her head further. Coughed blood into the bottom of the bag.

Pdldldl

Plmplmplmplm

Chk

She felt the dirt rise over her head. Dirt muted dirt. More felt than heard.

ck

hwwww

hwwwmmmmm

She screamed and cried for as long as she could. Until there was enough dirt on the bag to press the fabric

443

against her body. Her face. Form-fitting. Trapped in a vacuum.

hwwww

ck

Then all she could hear was the sound of her breath. Shallow, wet. Fighting. Boggy. A swamp. A morass. Quicksand. She sank into it. Deep, down, deeper. There was nowhere else to go. The weight above her grew heavier, heavier. Crushing from all sides. Breath was a blessing. All blessings are withdrawn.

She lived for so long, down there.

ELEVEN

AS I LEIGH DYING

"COME ON!" Leigh screamed at her friends. She crouched, ground her right knuckles into her left palm, and held her hands out just below hip level. "I'll give you a boost!"

"What about you?" Maddie asked, shouting to be heard over the din of terror and gunfire.

"I can climb up after! Go!"

Nobody asked any follow-up questions. Maddie planted her foot in Leigh's hands. This wasn't a maneuver Leigh had ever performed before, boosting somebody over an obstacle like this, and it turned out to be harder than they made it look in movies. Maddie's weight tilted Leigh forward a bit, but she righted herself quickly enough to get Maddie up and over the fallen log without needing to take a second stab at it. Quite a lot of that undoubtedly fell to the largesse of adrenaline.

"You!" Leigh called to, what was her name… *Nicole.*

No questions: Nicole took the boost and scrambled over the top, clipping the back of Leigh's head with her shoe as she thrashed her way over.

Note to self, Leigh thought, *give her shit about that later.* What a laugh that would be, an oasis of levity in a day of unmitigated horror.

Last up was Zoe, who didn't need to be prompted. Friends for so long, they could say so much with just a look. Which they did now. Just a look.

Then Zoe planted a muddy boot in Leigh's hands. The booster boosted her boostee, then turned to face the fallen log which had necessitated the boosting. Zoe straddled it, left leg holding her in place as she proffered her right hand down to Leigh.

"Come on!" Zoe screamed.

Leigh reached up to take her hand. Then her body ignited as the log in front of her laughed itself pink. No, red. No, black.

She fell to the ground, gaining a termites-eye view of a busy little ecosystem, no doubt oblivious to the human-sized horrors playing out above them. All these bugs. Just scuttling around like kids weren't getting chewed up by heavy weaponry. A fuzzy little caterpillar scooted across a young fern only just poking up from the peaty earth. Maybe this caterpillar would be a butterfly one day. Or a moth. Or maybe nothing. What did it matter. It had no idea what was really going on.

Leigh wondered if these creepy-crawlies didn't study the strange giants, these creepy-clumpies who had invaded their territory, and think very similar thoughts.

A crash.

A car.

She was sitting in the passengerseat of a car, looking through the windshield at a dark parking lot.

"The fuck?" she wondered. Fair question, she thought. Context clues revealed that whatever car she was in was parked in the lot of a Wal-Mart Supercenter. Boy, just how wrong *had* all the world's religions gotten it?

"Oh my god." Her mom's voice whispered from over her left shoulder. "Leigh."

Leigh's blood ran cold. More to the point: it ran *in* her, as opposed to *out* of her.

She whipped around to the backseat to see Mom sitting back there. In her lap was the box of a board game, covered in Jenga blocks. "Mom?" So if Mom was there…Leigh tucked her hair behind her ear, and turned to investigate the driver's seat. "Dad?" There he was. Looking back to Mom. "How did I…I was…"

Was what? Dying? *Dead?* How did she know she still wasn't? Wasn't *this is just a loopy death dream* by far the most logical explanation for how she'd gone from lying in a pool of her own blood on an island to sitting in the parking lot of a Wal-Mart Supercenter with her parents, half-buried in board games, in the blink of an eye?

She studied the car for otherworldly details that might confirm this as a final pre-death hallucination. Wasn't that a thing? Leigh seemed to recall reading about that theory in AP Psych or something. That the brain spins out fictions as it closes up shop for the rest of time. Some people believed that life as we knew it *was* the deathdream. Far out, man. There's just no way to know.

Of course, there's no harm in asking.

"Am I dead?" she asked her mom.

"Oh God!" Mom lunged forward, knocking what remained of the Jenga towers off her lap. The blocks clattered to the floor. They sounded like gunfire.

Leigh started to gasp. Hardly had the chance.

Mom wrapped her tight and squeezed, as though trying to wring her out. Oh, more cold, ice cold. Leigh shivered. Her mom seemed no more convinced that Leigh was alive than Leigh herself was.

Because she was dead. That was the only explanation.

All at once, she became aware of something sitting in the seat directly behind her. Like suddenly realizing one is sat at the precipice of a sheer cliff face. Tremendous peril, completely impersonal.

A demon. A devil. Or whatever passed for it in the Scriptures of the Supercenter. The Greeter at the gates of Hell. Take a frowny face sticker. Enjoy your eternal torment.

Leigh didn't turn to look at it. No want, no need.

"Mom!" Leigh cried. "I died! I think I'm dead! I don't know what's happening!"

"It's gonna be okay," Mom told her, planting her hands on Leigh's cheeks. "Look at me. Listen. It's going to be okay. Are, um…where are you? Where do you go, when you're…when you're not here?"

The blocks on the floor rearranged themselves. Bang bang bang. Leigh imagined her own body hitting the ground, as it had just seconds ago. She heard it, *felt* it all over again.

"What do you mean?" Leigh asked. "I don't know what you mean!"

"It's okay. It's okay."

"Dad," Leigh gasped, extending her hand. "Hold my hand."

Dad just blinked at her. No, not even at her. At nothing.

"Dad! I'm scared! Please!"

He reached out a hand and grabbed Leigh's. "I love you so much."

"I love you too," Leigh replied. "Mom. I love you."

Mom tried to say something back to her, but couldn't.

Then she did, from across the living room.

Mom and Dad on the loveseat. Sunlight shining through. All the lights were on, even though it was the middle of the day.

Leigh stood before them. Just a few feet away. On a beautiful morning. On her own two feet. In her home.

Just a minute or two after being shot and killed on an island, she was home.

"Oh, Leigh," Mom cooed through tears.

Not having much of coherence to offer, Leigh planted her hands on either side of her head and whimpered. Until something inside of her snapped and spasmed. Like a worm cut down the middle.

"What's happening?!" Leigh gasped, breath scratching at her lungs. "What's happening to me?"

"Nothing!" Mom shouted, rushing forward to embrace her daughter.

"You're confused," was all Dad had to contribute from his spot on the loveseat.

Leigh pushed her mom away and staggered backwards. It wasn't something she had either intended or even considered; reflex dictated the retreat as surely as it did her response to the stooped pillar of stone into which she backed. Slowly, Leigh lifted her gaze to find a face locked in cold magma, leering down at her.

The demon.

A picture slid down the wall. A pillow fell over on the couch. A lamp toppled off of a table against the far wall and shattered.

"We know," Mom snarled at the demon.

The demon nodded, turned, and lumbered to the front door. It reached out and used the doorknob. The absurdity of seeing it grasping the little brass bulb and turning it was enough to stop Leigh whimpered and start her wondering.

She looked down at herself. She was wearing precisely what she'd been wearing yesterday morning. Or…perhaps she'd have been on firmer ground to simply say *the morning she'd left for Knot Hedge.* Because she *wasn't* wearing what she'd been shot in. What she'd died in.

She had oh so many questions. Most of which she had to imagine were splashed across her face.

"We have a lot to explain," Dad understated, with a distant smile and nervous look to Mom.

"We do," Mom agreed. "But…" She made a sharp *honk* noise. A half-second sample of either laughter or lamentation. Perhaps both at once. Or neither. It wasn't a noise Leigh had ever heard before. "Are you hungry? I could make…some flapjacks, maybe?"

"Uh…" Leigh wasn't sure she could eat. Nor was she sure in precisely what sense she meant that. "I think I'm ok."

Mom's face looked as though it was stretched across smile-shaped scaffolding. "I made sure we'd have Bisquick, though. I bought s-"

"That's alright," Dad interrupted, "if you don't want flapjacks."

"Yeah. Right." Mom lifted her spirits as though by petard. "Are you hungry at all?"

Leigh gave this question solemn, searching consideration. "I don't know. I just wanna know what's going on."

Her parents nodded, glanced nervously at each other, and returned to their own private thoughts. Finally, Dad thumped the space next to him on the loveseat with his palm. "You should take a seat."

That sounded like a swell idea to Leigh. She did as was suggested, crossing her legs, folding her arms and hunching her shoulders. Committed to proper posture though she ordinarily was, correcting poor form was more than she could manage just now.

Dad squirmed in his seat, but said nothing.

Mom approached from the window and sat in the chair across from the loveseat. "This is very difficult for us to say, and I'm sure it'll be even harder for you to hear."

"I died," Leigh helped her along. "On the island. I got shot and killed."

A long, sandpaper sigh. "That's right."

Leigh lifted her right hand and rubbed at her left shoulder. "So…are we all dead?"

Mom shot a glance to Dad, who quickly turned his face back towards the ground before Leigh had a chance to make a study of his reaction.

"We brought you back," Mom mumbled at her knees.

Leigh very nearly asked if that ambulatory gargoyle had had something to do with that, but that would have been a pretty fucking stupid question. More worthy of articulation, however choked: "How?"

Mom started to point towards the window, through which could be seen the stone giant galumphing down the street like there wasn't a neighborhood watch in the area.

"You want to know what it cost," Dad filled in.

Leigh nodded.

Another freighted glance passed between her parents.

"Nothing we weren't willing to pay," Mom said.

Dad chuckled at that. Though *chuckle* might not have been the right word for it.

"We, um…" Mom rubbed at the knuckles of her left ha…woah.

"Mom, what happened to your hand?"

"Hm?" She started at the old scar bubbling across the top of her left hand, like it was news to her too.

Leigh rushed forward and knelt before her mom, taking her hand and examining the scar as though she envied this evidence of trauma. Only then noticing that she had another, smaller scar on her right hand. Still,

Leigh stayed focused on the left hand. "Was this part of how…was it like a blood pact?"

"This is just…no. This is something else."

"Cooking accident," Dad explained, as one tells a child how teeth under pillows become quarters.

Mom wiped at her eyes. "I don't know how to tell you this, sweetie. Uh…what we did, it was enough to bring you back for one day. Twenty-four hours from now…" Never before had Leigh heard someone's voice snag in quite the way her Mom's did. It was like hearing the flesh of a bare thigh catch on a thorn, a sharp *shrk* from deep in her chest.

Once again, Leigh to the rescue: "I go back to being dead. After today…I'm just, dead. Forever."

Sobbing and nodding from both parents.

Leigh found such emotional extremes inaccessible. It was too much, too fast, for her to process. "How long… what…" She looked out the window again. Buck-naked tree branches. "What month is it?"

"November," Dad gulped.

Christ. Just about half a year, she'd been dead.

Leigh flumped backwards into the loveseat. "It was just a few seconds ago for me. That I was…" she poked at herself in the places where phantom pain still lingered.

Dad sobbed, just one loud honk.

"We want to give you the best day," Mom forced through her tears. "Anything you want. We'll go any-where, do anything. Whatever. Anything. What do you want?"

Leigh couldn't comprehend the offer, any more than

she could make sense of what motivated it. She was dead. She had been murdered on Knot Hedge. This was just a twenty-four hour time-out. A time-in, rather, before being cast back to the eternal time-out. How to explain to her parents that she was still on Knot Hedge, still watching the creepy-crawlies go about their little buggy business, marveling without the least sense of disgust or violation as the more adventurous ants rushed forward to drink of her blood? She was still sinking into insensibility, seduced by release, by a ringing darkness in which resonance was a fact unto itself, independent of cause or capsule. No room for gutshot agony, no time for heartache. Blessed insensibility. Come. Carry. Sing.

And then she's in the parking lot of a goddamned Wal-Mart Supercenter.

And then she's in her goddamned living room. And it's November.

What sort of a day could she possibly have, burdened with that kind of psychological lodestone? A long life into the next century might be enough for her to *begin* unpacking everything she'd been through, in what felt like a sequence of mere moments. A day? One fucking day?! What the fuck did they expect her to say? *Let's go to Six Flags?* She didn't want to do anything with her one fucking day. Knowing what was coming at the end of it, how could any of this matter? God, only now did she realize that she'd never truly considered the fact of her own mortality. Even as she'd been bleeding out on the island, she'd been too shocked to wholly wrap her head around what was happening. Now, though…how the fuck was she supposed to use this day for anything other than hours of unbroken contemplation on her own imminent non-existence?

The thought of it hollowed her out, filled her with unendurable dread. Jesus Christ. She just…she wanted the day to be over. She wanted to go back to being dead. Better the long goodnight should come now, than to suffer through this 3AM stagger-to-the-bathroom of a day, only to wind up in precisely the same place.

She very nearly verbalized this when she wrestled her attentions from her own navel and realized something that was all but tattooed on her parents' foreheads.

This wasn't for Leigh. Whatever they'd done to bring her back, they might have justified to themselves by thinking they were doing it to give Leigh her Make-A-Wish day…but this was for *them*. A chance for *them* to say their goodbyes, to make *their* peace with what had happened. And just as Leigh knew one day would be entirely insufficient for coming to terms with her own death, the two of them likely knew, *must* have known, somewhere deep down, that it wouldn't be enough for them either. Yet they had managed to convince themselves that it would be enough for *her*.

So…alright. In a way, this made things easier.

Leigh could convince them that this day was enough. She could put on a brave face for them. At the very least, it might help them cope and, ultimately, someday, move on. Which would certainly make Leigh feel a bit better than she did now, right? Wouldn't it?

Maybe not. But hey, she wasn't the one who was

going to have to keep on living.

This was doable. Leigh would play along, spend the next twenty-four hours smiling as best she could, do her best to leave her parents looking to the future, not the past. For their sake. And then the sleep, the release, the song.

"Well," Leigh said quietly, "actually, maybe I will have some flapjacks."

Mom grinned so wide, it was a wonder the top of her head didn't roll clean off.

LEIGH FORCED THE FLAPJACKS DOWN and, more remarkably, *kept* them down. This was less a comment on the message than the medium, specifically *her* medium, which still hadn't quite made its peace with being large as life again. She expected chewed-up flapjack to come spilling out bullet holes in her midsection, was regularly stunned to look down at her lap and *not* find a pile of syrupy mush. Such thoughts were the ones that nearly stopped her flapjacks in their flaptracks and returned them whence they came. She soldiered through, though. And as it quickly emerged, soldiering would be the order of the day.

"Do you remember," Mom asked for the twentieth time, choking up just as she had during the prior nineteen reminiscences, "the first time you swam in the deep end of the pool? You were so scared, but you were so brave too, and you did it. I was so proud of you."

To this, Leigh responded as she had to all the other little memories: "I remember." A lie. Yes, there were some swirls of color and sound on a bed of chlorine that might be the remains of that memory, but in truth, Leigh was having a hard time with the past right now. Yet that was all her parents wanted to talk about.

Well, mainly Mom. Dad stayed quiet. Nodding softly, either staring too hard at Leigh or at the table in front of him. Not hard to understand why: most of the recollections Mom pulled out to admire, he hadn't been present for. He'd spent so much time at work.

Still, he got a few in: "I remember the first time you rode a bike without training wheels. We went to Abner Lane, and it such a beautiful day…"

"Um…" Leigh scratched her neck nervously. "Yeah. Can I ask you guys a question?"

"Of course," Mom replied at once.

"On the, on that day, right before…it happened, I helped a few of my friends over a fallen l-"

"They didn't make it," Mom interrupted.

Dad sputtered, coughing as he choked on a sip of coffee.

Leigh couldn't keep a brave face on for that. "What?!"

"I'm sorry, honey," Mom replied, brushing invisible crumbs from the table. "Yeah. Do you mean those three girls? We heard about that. They didn't make it, though. Unfortunately."

Leigh's mouth went so dry, she had to spit a bite of flapjack out into a napkin. Dead. Of course, it hadn't just been her. So selfish to forget that. "How many people?" she asked in a hushed voice.

"Almost forty," Dad replied in kind.

The coffee pot bubbled and chuckled from the kitchen counter. Bubble bubble chuckle. So hard for Leigh to not hear strange malice in it. "What about the guy who did it?"

"In custody," Mom informed her. "Expected to go to trial next year."

Leigh struggled with the thought that popped into her head. It wasn't the sort of thing she tended to find her mind spinning out…but, well, it had. So she said it: "I wish *he* was dead."

"Me too," her parents replied, at once and in unison.

Leigh looked upon what remained of her morning repast and sighed. "I don't know if I can eat anymore. It was really really good, I'm just…"

Mom smiled and took Leigh's hand. "It's ok."

"I feel like I can't even finish sentences," Leigh said, taking a dry run at levity, "let alone breakfast."

"It's ok."

Bubble bubble chuckle.

AS LEIGH PUZZLED not over what she wanted to do with her final day, but what her *parents* probably wanted her to want to do, she quickly realized that what they wanted most was to not leave the house. The reason went without saying. Still, Dad took a crack at saying it.

"Neirmouth's just so small," he mumbled, seeming more bashful than anything. "If somebody saw you, it'd be…it'd just be…"

"I understand," Leigh said to fill his silence. Another half-lie, which made it a half-truth too. Yes, she could appreciate that if somebody spots the girl who's been dead for half a year, that'd make the rest of her parents' lives fairly difficult, for at least a little bit. And the whole point here, for her at least, was to take her parents by the hand and lead them where she couldn't follow, hopefully sending them off feeling at peace with leaving her behind. Assuming they would ever truly know peace again.

Still, she convinced them to take her on one last drive around town. To say goodbye to Neirmouth, a place she could only truly appreciate now that she knew her own sell-by date. But also to kill some time. Hopefully make the day go a little bit faster. This, she had arrived at via negotiation: at first, she'd wanted to do the drive on her own. Mostly to have some space, a private moment to process what was happening. But Mom and Dad didn't seem inclined to let her out of their sight. Greedy and possessive, sure. But their greed was love. It could be such a fine line.

She had to imagine her parents felt themselves owed her time. Not that they would ever say as much. But, well, they had yanked her back to the land of the living by communing with an evil entity. And god, despite being (for now) living testimony to this having happened, she still couldn't imagine it. Her parents! Mom, who'd once gotten mad at a six-year-old Leigh for even *asking* what marijuana was! Dad, who sometimes tutted unhappily when music with foul language played in family restaurants! She truly could not imagine the two of them canoodling with the devil, surrendering their pound of flesh or whatever had been asked of them, to earn their daughter another day above ground. And yet, clearly, this was what they had done. It was insane. Might have been funny, in another world. In another life.

Oh, she was so curious. She was, ha ha, *dying* to know. What *had* they done, to bring her back? Just another question she didn't want to ask, knowing it would upset them. Knowing the answer must be truly terrible. A question she *did* feel like she could ask – one she felt she was entitled to know the answer to – was, *where is my body?* She didn't even want to get into the metaphysics of her predicament (that word seemed apt to her), whether or not this corporeal form she inhabited now was in any sense *hers*. She was just interested to know what they'd done with her remains; it wasn't like she'd ever gotten to pick between *burn* or *bury*. And even if she had, lots of people get to plan what they want to happen to their body. Nobody ever gets to know for sure.

She would ask them in the car, she decided. Maybe it'd be easier for them to answer a question like that, if they weren't looking at her. For she'd sit in the back, of course. The rear windows in Dad's car were tinted.

She decided she wanted to change before they set out on their drive. Her final drive around town. The wardrobe change filled more time, yes, but also, what she was wearing was a bit…itchy. Even if these weren't the clothes she'd been murdered in, they were what she'd worn to the island. She didn't want them touching her anymore. So she headed upstairs, and got changed.

And as she was getting changed, she heard the

doorbell ring. *Ding dong*, a cheery tinkle followed almost immediately by footsteps thudding, at just short of a sprint, towards the door.

"Fuck!" she heard Mom say.

Huh.

Leigh crept from her room, down the hall, to the stairs. As she sometimes had as a kid, when Mommy and Daddy had been having one of their Loud Conversations. Leigh crept to that familiar spot on the hallway side of the banister, in earshot, out of sight.

Just like old times. Except this time she wasn't afraid of encountering monsters in the darkened hall; real monsters, it turned out, didn't bother hiding.

She heard the door open.

"Mrs. Trecothik," the visitor blurted out hastily. A female voice, probably middle-aged, but vital, sharp. Not a voice Leigh recognized.

"Now's not a good time," Mom snapped at once.

Leigh heard a *thunk*. Her Mom trying to close the door, perhaps. The visitor using their foot to keep it open. Perhaps.

"I'd just like to speak to you," the visitor said, "just a mo-"

"Come back tomorrow. I've got nothing but time tomorrow."

Another *thunk*.

Followed by Dad's footsteps, hustling down the hall. His voice came on quickly, and loudly. Too loud. "Can we help you, detective?"

Detective?

Leigh reached out and gripped the banister. Squeezed it tight enough to *pop* her knuckles.

What was going on? Had someone seen her, somehow? No. What a stupid thought. It's not a crime to come back from the dead.

"No," Mom answered for the detective, "we can't. Not today."

"We are quite busy," Dad concurred.

"Are you two aware," the detective asked, "that the second girl your daughter saved has g-"

WHAM. The slamming of the door severed the sentence, but what Leigh had heard dangled. She could see the words swinging before her eyes, dripping with something viscous.

The second girl your daughter saved has g-

The *second*. What did that mean? Implied a sequence. Beyond that?

Wait a second…*saved?*

Leigh wondered how best to pose all these new questions to her parents when, to her astonishment, she found herself storming down the stairs, rounding them at speed (catching a glimpse of a dumpy unmarked car outside, and a dumpy woman in a black coat heading back towards it), and charging towards her Mom.

"What the hell was that?" Leigh's mouth demanded without her brain's consent.

"Huh?" Mom turned. "What was what?"

Dad nodded and hustled back towards the kitchen.

Leigh didn't fail to notice the look Mom shot him as he left. She had to imagine she herself looked somewhat similar. "That…was that a detective? Why was she here?"

Mom thought hard enough to flex a vein in her forehead. *"Oh,"* she finally erupted, "that. Oh yeah, yes, that was a detective. She's been so invasive. She's trying to just dig up old nonsense. Not that it's…I mean, it's just, she's out of line. She always wants my opinion about, uh, whatever."

"Why did she say the second girl?"

"The what?"

"She said *the second girl*. That I *saved*. Why did…why would she say that? What was she starting to say?"

Mom laughed nervously and glanced back towards the kitchen, where Dad was hard at work washing the dishes from breakfast, with the hunchbacked intensity of a man who wanted very much to look like he wasn't hearing any of this exchange. "I don't know why she said that," she chortled, unconvincingly. "I'm not her."

Ding dong.

Mom's face fell hard enough to make a dirty-laundry-down-the-chute noise. "Go back upstairs," she demanded. So much for the breakfast bonhomie.

"Why is she back?" Dad couldn't stop himself from moaning.

"I don't *know*, Harlow." Mom turned to Leigh and repeated the order: "go back upstairs."

Leigh did not go back upstairs. She remained precisely where she was. Planting her hands on her hips now. "I want to hear what she has to say."

"You only have a day. Why ruin it with this…" she

flapped her hand in the air. It was either a dismissive gesture, or she was trying to shake off a moth that had landed on it. "…crap?"

"She wants to tell you something about my friends," Leigh replied. "She called them the friends that I *saved*. But you told me…"

Ding dong.

Mom grimaced, eyes darting from her daughter to the door to her daughter to the door.

"You open it," Leigh insisted, "or I do."

A sharp inhale through the nose. "At least stand where she can't see you. And stay there. No matter what you hear, this lady absolutely *can not* see you. Okay? Can you please promise me that?"

Ding dong.

"Please?"

"Ok," Leigh allowed. She stepped behind the corner leading from the kitchen to the front hall, leaned against the wall, and listened.

The door opened. "Ah," the detective said to Mom, "Might as well schedule some time to chat tomor-"

WHAM!

Leigh frowned and popped her head out from around the corner. The door was shut. Mom's voice was raised from the other side.

Staying at a half-crouch for reasons she couldn't quite work out (it felt contrary to some natural law, to be crouching like this whilst nearly blind with consternation), Leigh crept her way to the bay window and peeked out from around the corner, gazing through the leftmost panel that gave her a glimpse of the porch.

Mom was contradicting the friendly doormat, standing astride it, stance wide, arms crossed. *Welcome*, the mat declared in threadbare cursive, whereas Mom might as well have been wearing a shirt that said *Ask me about my low center of gravity*. The detective spoke quickly, saying something Leigh couldn't hear. The glass in the window was far from soundproof, but it muddled the precise clip of the detective's forceful cadence enough to make her unintelligible.

"You. Are. Trespassing," Mom thundered (Leigh could hear *that*). "Get off of my property and leave me alone. My husband and I are going through hell, and we don't need you here accusing us of…something, I don't even know!"

"Nobody is accusing you of anything," the detective said, louder and slower than her initial, in hindsight clearly prepared, opening gambit. "I'm just trying to g-"

"It's a coincidence! It's a terrible coincidence. I don't know."

"As long as we're talking, I w…" the detective swung her gaze towards the bay window.

And locked eyes with Leigh.

Leigh froze.

Despite having never seen that woman before in her life…that expression on the detective's face sure looked like *recognition*.

The detective pointed at her. "Who's that?"

Leigh dropped to the ground.

Shit. Shit.

She didn't know what was going on with her parents, or, hell, with *anything*. But it was clear enough she'd just made all of it, whatever *it* was, infinitely more complicated.

"Who's what?" she heard Mom ask. Oof. The Oscars are calling, Mom. It's a cease and desist order.

Who's what was the last of the Doormat Showdown that Leigh heard. Staying low, this time for a very good reason, she crawled her way through to the kitchen via the scenic route of the "dining room" (more of a fancy plate museum, as it was only ever used for dining on holidays).

Dad stood in the kitchen, frozen at the sink, holding a coffee mug upside-down in one hand and a soaked-through dishtowel in the other, watching impassively as his dead daughter crawled into the kitchen on all fours. Leigh looked up at him. He looked down at her.

They both smiled nervously. There was no other way to respond to a situation like this.

ShhhWHAM.

Mom's clomping footsteps announced her return from the front porch.

Leigh stopped smiling. Then Dad did. Replaying her entry to the kitchen in her head, Leigh realized that she had smiled, and *then* Dad had smiled.

Not that that mattered.

Leigh shot to her feet just as Mom stormed into the kitchen. "Mom," Leigh said.

Mom paced and shook her head. "Not right now, honey," she growled. Distant, for the first time today.

"Then when?"

"*Later.*"

"Mom."

She stopped pacing but kept shaking her head.

"*Mom.*"

The head stopped shaking, its face a gnarl of cracks and crevasses. *Erosion* was the word that popped unbidden into Leigh's mind. Ah, behold, the process in progress: tears sliced down Mom's cheeks. She ground the meat of her right palm into her forehead, brayed once, and retreated. As she slipped by the front door to make for the stairs, the door *ding dong*-ed, as though to mock her passage.

Leigh turned to her father. "I want to know what's going on," she demanded, voice nearly lost in the gap between reach and grasp.

Dad blinked hard, holding his eyes closed for just an instant too long. He replied, "we all do."

Ding dong.

THE DOORBELL RANG INTERMITTENTLY throughout the morning. So did the phones, though those were more easily silenced.

"I warned you about this," Dad reminded Mom cryptically.

She silenced *him* with a *tst*.

Leigh put her foot down. Quite literally – she stomped on the carpet in her parents' bedroom, the intended effect undercut by the high piling. "The second girl. That I *saved*. So they survived? What does that mean? The *second* girl. The second to do what?"

This, too, was gobbled up by the carpet.

From down the stairs: *ding dong*.

"Just one day," Mom sacrificed to the floor. "That's all we wanted."

Leigh knelt before her mother, slouched over the side of the bed as she was. "Tell me what's happening or I'm going outside."

Mom lifted her eyes but not her head, looking at her daughter through her eyebrows. She looked…angry?

"Are you mad at me?" Leigh asked, tilting her weight back slightly, as though preparing to spring up to her feet at a moment's notice.

"Oh, no! Of course not." Mom shook her head, casting off the fury that had unmistakably darkened her features, if only for a moment. "Not at you." She flinched at nothing. "I just wanted us to have a day together. One last day."

Ding dong.

"We still do," Leigh pointed out. "I'm still here."

"Not the way I wanted."

Well at least you had a say in it, Leigh very nearly retorted. She held her tongue, though. Whatever the fuck was going on, it was clearly going to have consequences for her parents long after the day ended, taking Leigh with it. There was no sense rubbing salt into wounds her parents had likely inflicted upon themselves to bring her back. Or, well…maybe it made a little sense, but only according to a cruel sort of logic. That wasn't what Leigh wanted. That wasn't how she wanted to leave them.

That didn't mean she wasn't going to figure out why the fuck a detective was *ding dong*ing at their door though, asking her parents about the friends whose lives she had tried to save. And, apparently, succeeded in saving.

Why had they lied to her about that? Unless the *detective* was lying?

The questions couldn't wait anymore.

She rose and turned to her father. Specifically him. Much as Kira hated to admit it, he was more liable to break. She had always known this about him. "Tell me my friends died on that island," she demanded.

He choked.

"They did," Mom was quick to answer on his behalf.

"I'm asking Dad," Leigh snapped.

Still, Dad said nothing.

"Harlow," Mom prompted.

"Are they actually dead?" Leigh pressed.

Harlow, her father, her dear old fucking dad, whispered "not all of them."

"Harlow!"

He threw his arms up. "What do you want me to say?" He thrust two upturned palms toward Leigh, still looking at Mom, and made a face to match the question.

Ignoring the way they spoke of her as if she weren't present, Leigh took a step towards her father. "Did they die on the island?"

"Yes," Mom supplied with a speed and force ill-suited to the truth.

"Okay," Leigh nodded, "so that's a no."

Dad closed his eyes and practiced his pranayama.

Ding dong.

There was a decision to be made. Much as Leigh wanted to play at having a happy last day on Earth, leave her parents feeling somewhat good about their daughter's final moments…well, the questions couldn't fucking wait anymore.

Leigh swallowed hard, turned to her mother and planted her hands on her hips. "I'm done with this. You tell me what happened to my fri-"

"It was the only way," Mom told the carpet.

"…what was?"

Mom, mother dearest, gave her head a hard jerk towards the stairs. "The fucking…detective," she mumbled. Leigh could tell it was a separate thought from the last. So she held her peace, waiting. Finally, Mom sighed and heaved herself upright. "Did you see Uisch?"

"Did I see who?"

"The big stone th-"

"Oh, yeah. I did. For just a second, but, yeah."

"Well," Mom explained, "it's called Uisch. It just came walking up to the house not long after you…that day. Middle of the day, just right up the walk." A quick breath, in and out. "It made me an offer."

Ding dong.

"And I…" Mom continued, "I made a choice. Because I love you. More than anything. Because you mean more to me than anyth-"

"What did you do?"

"We love you," Dad averred, attacking from behind with a cold embrace.

472

Juking to avoid the postmortem affection, Leigh applied conscious effort to drawing breath enough to speak. "What did you guys do?"

No answer.

"What the fuck did you do?!"

Ding dong.

"Listen to us!" Mom shouted, rising from the bed.

Shoulder to shoulder, Leigh's parents approached like the undead. Arms out, brows furrowed, mouths drawn.

Leigh backpedaled to keep away from them, reversing into the wall behind her. Her parents, she couldn't keep herself from noticing, were between her and the exit.

"TELL ME WHAT YOU DID!" Leigh shrieked.

Ding dong.

Thnk. A picture fell from the wall, its nail popping out of its own accord.

KRSSHHH. The frame shattered.

CreeeePLNK. A tie rack toppled over, its throat-throttling charges slithering across the floor.

Mom looked to the ceiling. "Oh, *STOP!*" She looked down to her daughter, softening her features as she did. "Not you, honey!"

In these ever-shrinking redoubts of things unsaid, Leigh saw something come into focus. A great shape shifting, more felt than seen.

The second girl.

Your daughter saved.

"Did you…do something to my friends?" Leigh sobbed. "Was that the deal this thing made?"

"Not *all* of them!" Dad offered somewhat impatiently, as though Leigh were willfully seeing the casket as half-empty.

"*HARLOW!*" Mom shouted.

"Who?!" Leigh demanded. "What did you…who?"

Dad appeared to consider his next words carefully, but appearances can be so deceiving. "Maddie is still alive!"

"Zoe!" Mom growled. "Maddie was the…you're thinking of *Zoe.*"

"Right, *Zoe* is alive." He cleared his throat. "The deal was, one of them gets us a min-ute with you. The Wal-Mart parking lot, you remember. Two of them gets us the day. Today."

"What do you mean, one of them, two of them, what…?"

Dad just sighed, and said, "all three would get you back for good." His voice so low, Leigh could barely hear it.

And somehow, that made her understand.

Her legs quit. No notice, not even a warning. Their resignation was swift and decisive. She flopped backwards, landing hard on her ass. On the floor. On her ass on the floor. Not the ceiling. Remarkable, when you considered all the backflips the universe was doing.

Her parents were murderers.

Her parents had communed with a golem, struck a deal, and murdered her friends.

Her parents had murdered the friends she had died to save.

Oh. Ok. Of *course.*

Shaking her head, Leigh chuckled, the compartmentalized *ha, ha, ha* of someone laughing gamely at their boss' off-color joke. "I get it," she giggled. "Very funny." She extended a quivering finger and whizzed it around her head, encompassing the entirety of the room. "I'm dead. I'm dead and this is Hell. I get it."

The Kira- and Harlow-shaped hellspawn before her exchanged demonic glances, evilly, and so forth.

Leigh flopped flat on her back, arms splayed above her head. She wasn't laughing anymore, but at least she got to keep the smile.

Ding dong.

They stared back at her. Mom had dropped her arms to her sides. Dad still had his raised. "This isn't hell," he informed her, as though he were just now hearing about it himself and hadn't yet had the chance to vet the information.

"You're alive, honey," Mom claimed. "For the day. We did what we did because it was the only way. *They* were supposed to have died. It was meant to be. You could have jumped over that log, and you should have. But you didn't. So all w-"

"We all died," Leigh insisted, lowering her head back to the sweet, sulfurous embrace of the sound-swallowing carpet. "And now I'm in Hell."

Ding dong.

"This isn't Hell," her father insisted, a bit more confidently now.

"Oh, yeah?" Leigh pointed towards the windows facing the front of the house. "Then how do you explain him?"

She watched her parents follow her finger to the thing they called Uisch, standing in the corner of the room, backlit by the grey of the early afternoon.

HhhTTn. A dresser drawer opened and closed.

Dnn. The humidifier in the corner popped.

Hhhhnnnnn. A pile of laundry slid off of a chair.

MMmeeeeee. The door to the closet creaked.

It, Leigh understood the room to be saying. *And don't mind me.*

"I bet you're fucking *loving* this," Mom snarled at Uisch, "aren't you?"

Uisch said nothing. Didn't have to.

Ding dong.

"DOESN'T SHE EVER QUIT?!" Harlow erupted. Jerking his arms as though only just aborting a plan to thump his chest like a gorilla, Leigh's father stormed out of the room and down the stairs. Leigh, Kira, and maybe even Uisch, briefly united by their incredulity, listened as the front door swung open and *WHAMMED* shut. They could hear Harlow outside, screaming something, but the words bled together. Leigh suspected he was hardly more intelligible to the detective.

"You're not in Hell," Mom grumbled. "You're not dead. Not for today, at least," she added with a trembling breath. "You're here. You're alive. And however that's come to be, you need to enjoy the goddamned day. You have no idea what we've sacrificed to give it to you."

"Yes I do."

Mom's nose twitched. "You really, really don't."

They stayed just as they were, Leigh sitting on the floor, Kira standing before her, for what felt like nearly a half an hour. A portion of the day. Time they would never get back. All the while, they listened to Harlow screaming outside. Even after Leigh was certain she'd heard a car starting up and driving away, Dad was still screaming.

"JUST STOP!" Mom kept shouting at her. "You're being…*so* ungrateful!"

At first, Leigh had responded to that preposterously tone-deaf accusation with a sharp look and pinched lips. When that proved insufficient to stave off subsequent broadsides, she opted for a more vocal, proactive approach. "How can I be ungrateful?!" she returned fire. "That would mean you did me a favor and I'm taking it for granted or whatever! You didn't do m-"

"We gave you another day!"

"You killed my friends!"

"Not *all* of them," Dad sighed from his perch on the dirty laundry in the corner. It had taken no small portion of snarling and snapping on his part to chase off the detective – particularly since she now had such *specific* questions about who she'd seen staring back at her from the bay window – and the effort had plum tuckered him out.

Mom threw a glance at her husband as though it were a spear. "That's not helpful!"

"What the fuck do you expect me to say," Leigh demanded, *"thank you?!"*

Foolish with rage, Mom said "well...it wouldn't kill you, would it?!"

"You're *fucking* insane!"

Dad became one with the laundry. "Come on, now."

Leigh turned on her father. "Look at you! You don't even believe in it!"

"In what?" he said to the space between himself and his daughter.

"In what you did!"

"...what do you mean? Of course I believe in it. I have to."

"No, you don't!"

He smiled a thin smile. "I do. Because you're here."

"Well, I wish I weren't." With that, Leigh left the room, largely to avoid the look of hurt she knew her comment had chiseled into her parents' features. She paused at the top of the stairs, glancing down at the front door. Getting a load of that tall rectangle of wood, resting languorously in its frame, beckoning her. Come hither, that door to the outside seemed to coo. I can show you better places to spend your last day.

Leigh turned away from it and continued down the hall to her bedroom.

It was absolutely trashed. Another gift from Uisch, no doubt. Oh, nevermind the carnage. She closed the door behind her, locked it, and sat against it.

Why shouldn't she go outside? She didn't give a good goddamn about her parents' emotional state anymore. So why shouldn't she spend her last day taking a final spin around Neirmouth? In fact, why shouldn't she go to the police and tell them who she was, what her parents had done?

Ok, how would that work? March down to the precinct (which was all the way in *Pitney,* mind) and say "guess what, I died but got better because my parents made a deal with spooky rocks and killed some kids," and then disappear long before she had the chance to testify to that effect? What evidence did she have, anyway, besides her own existence? She had no clue how Nicole and Maddie had been killed, which of her parents had killed them, where the murders had been conducted, or where the bodies had ultimately wound up. So, then… what? Perhaps there would be no legal repercussions, but her parents deserved to pay for what they had done.

God, it made her sick to think of herself as having spent her life raised by people capable of this. Of killing innocent teenagers. For whatever rationale, towards whatever end…it was stomach-turning.

Her parents deserved to pay. They deserved to face consequences. If not legally, then morally. They deserved to suffer.

No, she recognized as she forced herself to get her breathing under control. That would be letting the rage win. Letting the red win. All her life, she'd wrestled with a temper. Hacked heroically at those tendrils of red forever curling in from the edges of her vision. Hard to be sure, but she was fairly certain she came by that honestly. Felt like she'd seen a bit of that red behind her parent's eyes, from time to time. Particularly Mom's, yes, but Dad's too.

Wherever the red came from, Leigh had refused to let it run her. Always had. Now should be no exception. To let it win, in fact, would be to compromise herself. It would only make her feel worse, in the end. Whenever that end should finally fucking arrive.

So stop thinking of how best to hurt her parents. Think, instead, of Zoe. God, it was almost perverse of them to have saved her for last. Leigh's best friend, since time out of memory.

No. Not for last.

Whatever might be the most effective rebuke of her parents – sitting and sulking, letting them know just how much she *hated* them for what they'd done to bring her back – that only set them up for still greater feats of self-delusion. *The problem was that one day wasn't enough for her to understand,* they might well find their way to thinking. *If only we could give her more than one day…*

This was about more than whatever petty retribution Leigh could dream up, about more than her parents' brittle little feelings.

Zoe's life was at stake.

Should she warn her? No: sneak out of the house to go find her, and her parents might well kill her just to solve a problem of Leigh's creation. Call her in secret? Easier said than done: the eldritch compact by which she'd been brought back apparently had a *no cell phones* policy, and much though she hated to admit it, she didn't actually know Zoe's number by heart. Reaching her had always been just a button on a phone screen.

Zoe's life is at stake, she thought again, with an even

more forceful topspin. Her life was at stake because of Leigh's parents. God. Dear god. It was more than she could stand, to know that her own flesh was of such disreputable issue. Had they always carried the seed, the potential for this inside of themselves? Or had they just lost their fucking minds?

And if they had…

No. That was the red talking. The part of her that was *them*. She had to listen to the part that was *her*.

She needed to go back to square one. Play nice, make believe that everything was fine. Make her *parents* believe. But not for their sakes, god no. For Zoe's sake.

Pretend to have a good day with her parents. Pretend she wasn't disgusted by the sight of them. Pretend to make peace with what they had done, and to forgive them for it. Demonstrate to them, or rather, *simulate* for them that she had made peace with her own death. Then die, having made clear that she was happy, that she was ready, that she *didn't want to come back. Ever.* That would be the most foolproof way to save Zoe's life.

And in the process, make her parents believe that everything they had done had been worth it. That was what broke Leigh's heart the most. Emotionally speaking, morally speaking: she had to let them get away with it.

Leigh collapsed onto her bed, buried her face in pillows, and screamed until she tasted blood. It didn't really get anything out of her system, but it clarified a few things. She could only hope that, once she opened the door and began the goddamned simulation, she might figure out what those things were.

A SIMULATION. Yes. It was easiest to think of it in these terms, in the very language her laptop-happy mother might use when discussing apps of whatever the fuck with her clients. Input and output, process and result.

Input: As you step into their bedroom once more, Mom looks at you as does the lead of a bomb squad when approaching a roadside IED, and says "I know it's a lot to take in, honey. Um…how are you?"

Process: Don't look too eager to backpedal into agreeability. That'd be implausible, suspicious. Display your actual dismay, but smother it so it registers as something softer, like mere reticence. As though a great internal monologue has played out in the ruins of your room, and the result is tending towards – but not yet achieving, though it will in time – acceptance, even embrace.

Output: You crack your lips into a sunnier shape and say "I'm processing."

Result: Mom's expression loosens. Dad deigns to rise from the crater of filth into which he'd been slowly sinking. In other words: optimal.

Input, output. Process, result. It was only this level of detachment that allowed Leigh to face what was left of the day before her, to look into the eyes that must have met Nicole's and Maddie's in their fearful final moments. Sometimes Leigh could imagine her friends' faces reflected, warped, in those dark little marbles her parents called *eyes*. Oftentimes she imagined not only horror, but *recognition*. For they knew Leigh's parents. Well, Maddie had at least. What must she have thought, for her final thoughts on Earth? She couldn't ask, for these were simply reflections, projections.

When she saw her friends in her family's eyes, it was a simple matter of suppressing her humanity, of imagining herself as a solid state consciousness. An animatronic version of herself. Steady, solid. Input, output. Process, result.

The Trecothik doorbell went mercifully unrung for the remainder of the day. They didn't have a drive around town though, needless to say. They didn't go out at all. Too dangerous now. Needless to say. Instead, Leigh sat with her parents and talked. Sometimes about things, most times around them. What did they talk about? Hard for Leigh to say, with any specificity. But the outputs were strong enough to make for an optimal result, that was all Leigh knew. Each time she said something to bring a smile to her parents' faces, every time she chose tender words instead of the more precise, pointy ones she wanted to use, her estimation of herself dropped one inch, then another, then another. Buoyancy was to be found in remembering Zoe. This was for her.

Yet Leigh's retributive impulse, a fleshy protrusion into her self-conception she'd never before noticed, throbbed and chafed at her every attempt to salve the outrage. Her parents ought to face what they had done, be *made* to face it, free from any pretense of acceptability afforded by the ends it effected. They deserved to be called to the mat. They ought, in short, to feel bad. Worse than bad. They had done evil. And they should never be allowed to forget it.

But Leigh couldn't be the one to remind them. She could only stop them from doing more.

Input: Dad entertains a fantasy of being *cool* by suggesting they "take a big risk" and have that little fucking drive-about. "Go see your school, check out your favorite, uh, playground…" and then the suggestion just fades out, mid-sentence.

Process: You realize how little your father, so often consumed by the work that granted you your cushy upper-middle-class existence, actually knows about you. This makes you feel a tiny bit resentful, but in larger measure sympathetic towards this sacrifice he had chosen to make for the sake of your mother and you. Sympathy towards your father would only complicate the manipulation you are attempting, however, so you narrow in on the resentment and try to puff it up like an air mattress.

Output: You tell your father, after an overacted moment of deliberation, "no, it's okay, I don't want to make you run risks. I'm happy to just hang here."

Result: Your parents look at each other with an expression that doesn't often pass between them. As such, you cannot interpret it.

That kind of opacity became the chief characteristic of the day. Leigh caught the scrutiny with which she observed and parsed her parents' every move bubbling up to appear on her face from time to time, and if she wasn't very much mistaken, she recognized *their* recognition of said bubbling. Likewise, she would periodically catch a similar expression on one or the other of their faces, but never at times that seemed to warrant the suspicion. For instance, in the kitchen, reaching for the paper towels to sop up the bacon grease that had splash-ed on the countertop (Dad was busy slicing store-bought tomatoes and staging leaves of iceberg lettuce on whole wheat bread, so Leigh could have her favorite acronym for lunch), got Leigh one hell of a stinkeye from Mom. Later, Dad seemed similarly skeptical of the way Leigh shuffled her cards as they were setting out to play Go Fish. Go Fucking Fish! Whatever. Today was apparently just a day to spend scrutinizing each other. So Leigh let it slide, instead turning her mind from the means to the end: Zoe.

One of her dearest friends. Always the first person Leigh invited to every party she had ever had. A friend so close they'd only ever fought about things that didn't matter, little grievances that only irked them after they'd spent a week straight together, when the tiniest infraction was made to feel immense by its emptiness, its capacity being precisely right to store the whole of their affectio-nate discontent. The only person to whom Leigh had ever, and now *would* ever admit that she wasn't sure she had a sex drive the way so many of her classmates seemed to, didn't quite understand the way the world at large seemed so fixated on the act, and what did that mean, was she just a late bloomer or was there something wrong with her? Zoe had known what to say then. She always did. She knew precisely what one needed to hear to feel better, which was quite often (at least for Leigh) distinct from what one *wanted* to hear. Zoe also knew when to come by with soup when Leigh was sick. Soup! Who the fuck *actually* comes around with soup?! Only this wonderful young woman called Zoe Cottrell, that was who. The young woman her parents wanted to kill, like they had killed Leigh's other…no. Stop. Input, output. Calm down. Carry on. This was the only way.

Input: For the fifth time, Mom drolly wonders if they shouldn't bring the clock over to the table, so that you don't have to keep craning your neck to watch it.

Process: A panoply of zippy retorts are dishonorably discharged to clear the ranks, that a more polished response may ascend.

Output: You say "sorry Mom, I'm just kind of…" Then a squeaky little boo-hoo noise happens. You don't plan for that, you are in fact more than a little distressed by it, but it's worth it for the

Result: Both parents converge on you, their daughter. The day teeters towards dusk, after all, and you, their daughter, will be turning back into a pumpkin sooner rather than later.

As the time of her second death approached, Leigh found herself thrumming with a tension she'd managed to dull by focusing on subterfuge and the future. It wasn't *her* future she had been considering thus far, of course. So it wasn't until night fell that Leigh began to think about what lay ahead for her, how short and predictable a path it was. In a way, the predictability was the worst part. Youthful and privileged as she'd been, her life had been defined by possibility, by potential. She was bright. She was (moderately) athletic. She was (she sometimes allowed herself to think) pretty. Most importantly, she still hadn't chosen between the three or four career paths she'd been entertaining. Something socially engaged, perhaps law or political science. She'd planned to apply to NYU, Harvard, Yale, all the big brainiac places, and perhaps naively felt she'd had a decent chance of getting in to one (or more) of them. Yes, hers had been a life of opportunities. Of glorious unpredictability. Anything could happen.

Now, of course, very few things could happen. She had hours left to live, and what was more, she *knew* it. Even if she decided to surrender discretion and go absolutely bananas, stealing her parents' car, driving it through a pet shop, releasing the puppies and becoming their Queen, she'd only lead her canine commandos halfway up the steps of City Hall before she re-pumpkinized. Only it wouldn't even be that dramatic; more likely, she'd probably just vanish.

How many hours did she have left? She hadn't paid close attention to when she'd arrived (she had been, to put it mildly, a little fucking preoccupied), but it had been morning. Right now it was night. Quarter past seven, to be (approximately) precise. Maybe twelve hours, then? Should she try to stay up all night, as her parents would almost certainly want to? Or should she insist on going to sleep, hastening the end, maybe even sleeping through it? Er, there was nothing on the other side for her, so maybe it made more sense to say sleeping *into* it? There was temptation in that sort of surrender, but all the same, pondering her personal conclusion so concretely was too disturbing to manage for more than a moment or two at a time. How easy it was to think magnanimously of personal sacrifice, when the moment of action was still a day away!

Input: nothing material, merely the realization that the end is coming on quickly.

Process: You realize that it doesn't have to be the end. You could, at any point, simply ask your parents to do what is necessary – no, not even that, you could just…fail to discourage them from doing the necessary thing. And they would do it. You know they would. They would do the necessary thing, and you would be back. This is an option. You hadn't even considered it before, but now that you've touched the idea, you find that it sticks to your palm. To accept the done deal of death, when you're gutshot on an island, that's one thing. To actively *choose* it, to *choose* to let yourself slip into nothingness just to save the life of someone else, for a *second time?* That's difficult. That's a struggle. That's impossible. And yet:

Output: You take your parents' hands in your own and lie to their faces. "I'm so happy," you tell them. "Thank you. I really…this just feels right. I want this to be the end."

Result: Optimal. Your parents smile. It's not a happy smile, but it's a smile. A happy smile would have been suspect, anyway. This isn't a time for happy smiles.

Mom shifted in her chair and squeezed Leigh's hand. She didn't say anything. She didn't have to. She was wearing the question.

"Yes," Leigh told her. "It's okay." And wouldn't you

know it, she started crying. Leigh did. She hadn't imagined herself to be the sort of person who shed tears of self-interest, but she felt she was entitled. Given the situation. The highly unusual situation.

Mom and Dad were crying too, but that was to be expected.

Not wanting to reclaim a paw from either of her parents, Leigh hunched her shoulder to wipe her cheeks dry. "Yes," she repeated. "I'm happy with this. I want it to end here. It's okay."

Her parents nodded. On this, all three of them could agree. It was okay.

LEIGH DECIDED SHE WANTED TO SLEEP THROUGH, er, *into* it. Her parents convinced her to at least let them sit with her as it happened. She couldn't imagine just lying in the ruins of her bedroom as her parents stood over her, watching, weeping, so, for lack of better alternatives, she asked if she could die in front of the TV. Absolutely not her first choice; it was such an…*American* way to go.

Mom and Dad said yes (they weren't in much of a position to say no), so Leigh brought blankets and pillows downstairs and ensconced herself on the recliner in front of the TV. Mom sat next to her, Dad pulling up a chair to cover the other flank. They flicked through some movies – all too dramatic for Leigh – and burned thirty minutes scrolling through various streaming menus. How to choose the last thing you see before you die? Even in this, Leigh struggled to take such an active role in programming her final moments. So they flicked back to the cable menu, and discovered one of those endless marathons of the game show in the taxi on GSN, and that would be good enough. Leigh watched as a balding comedian puttered around New York, picking up strangers and asking them questions and handing them money or else kicking them out. Everyone was always so excited. Leigh saw their delight, and wept, for she would never know what it was like to be in the Cash Cab. Among other things.

She drifted away to the sounds to New Yorkers pretending to be surprised. It wasn't the way she'd ever imagined taking her leave, but it was definitely a step up from being splayed over a rotten log on Knot Hedge, ears ringing and gut leaking. This was painless. This was comfortable. There was love here. It was a sick, poisoned love, but there was solace to be taken from the knowledge that the poison *was* the love. A fatal overdose, that had proven fatal not for Leigh but for the people she had tried to save. For Nicole. For Maddie. Mom and Dad, Kira and Harlow Trecothik, so loved their only daughter that they gave two of someone else's daughters. Gave them to whom, to take them where? To wherever Leigh was about to go. Back to the absence. Oh well. Absence denied evil, at least. Evil borne of love. Evil that touched far more than its two victims. Nicole and Maddie's families, both immediate and extended, touched. Evil that spread, love that shrank. Love that touched only one person. Love that took. Hey, if you spell *love* backwards, you get *evol.* That sounds kind of like *evil.* No way, man. And if you spell *evil* backwards, you get *live.* Man, if she'd gone to college, she'd probably have gotten really high and made a whole night out of that. But she was just a kid. A kid who'd never smoked weed, or gotten drunk, or done any of that stuff.

Oh well.

She only realized her eyelids had begun to grow heavy as she flinched herself awake. For an instant, she feared the worst – that she was back again. Which would have meant that Zoe was dead. But no. She was still on the couch. The Cash Cab was still on the move.

Her parents were both watching the television. Faces slack.

Leigh smiled at them.

She hated them so much for what they had done, even as somehow, in some hideous way, she loved them for having been willing to do it. Both feelings at once. They contradicted each other, yet they weren't mutually exclusive. How odd. How impossibly odd. It was the sort of thing that might be a worthy topic of study, had she the long life she'd always imagined having in which to study it. Maybe she would go to one of those fancy-ass Ivy Leagues for psychology, or neuroscience, or whatever it was that would let her study those things.

Would have. Not would. *Would have* gone.

She giggled softly. She couldn't help it. Going to college, and then graduate school, and then maybe *another* graduate school…that all sounded like a lot of work. And here she was, tired and cozy. What a relief, she wouldn't have to do any of that work! It was an absurd thought, yes, but the world was well-suited to such thinking.

"It's okay," Leigh mumbled to her parents one last time. They said something to her. She wasn't listening, though. She was riding in the Cash Cab. She was in. She was winning. "I love you," she told them, as sound and image merged and faded, cranking into a deep dark, deep down, a well with no bottom. There was no bottom and she could hear black water lapping at the stonework. It's okay. Down. I love you. Deep. It's okay. Dark. I love you.

Light.

Leigh flinched herself awake.

TWELVE

YOU'LL AFTER DO BETTER THAN THAT!

LEIGH VANISHED WITHOUT FANFARE. Had both her parents not been watching her so carefully, they would have missed the moment her blankets silently drifted down to rest onto the recliner cushions. But they had been, and so they each made soft sounds of acknowledgement to fill the now-empty space between them.

With great solemnity, Harlow turned off the *Cash Cab* marathon.

That was it. It was over. Leigh was gone. But they had been able to say goodbye, at least. They had given her a good last day. At least.

It was impossible for Kira to look at that empty space and *not* think about the last one. Zoe Cottrell. It wasn't because Kira had the least intention of doing anything to her; Leigh would be furious. Plus, you know, the whole business of committing yet another murder. No, Zoe would be receiving no visits, clandestine or otherwise, from the Trecothiks. But that wasn't to say Kira's mind wouldn't be turning towards Zoe, for as long as they both lived. That sort of thing was impossible to guard against.

Kira wondered if maybe she should scoot over, into the space Leigh had lately occupied. To be closer to her husband. Only that didn't really make sense, because he was sitting on a chair *next* to the doublewide recliner. *He* should shift over, so that they were both on the comfier of the two seating options. But he didn't. That didn't necessarily mean anything, though. It wasn't as though either of them were moving. It wasn't as though either of them would move – or speak – for hours.

IT WAS A POST—FUTURE WORLD into which Kira and Harlow rose. The myopia required to get those two killings done had precluded any real consideration of what the After would look like (beyond Not Going To Prison, of course). Kira hadn't really considered that not having Leigh here would be a possibility. She'd imagined that, once begun, she would see the work through. She would have her daughter back, and Leigh's return would stitch the Trecothik family back together again. You'd always be able to see the seam, run your finger over it and feel where it had torn, but the stitches could make it stronger than it had been, strong enough to never tear again. Maybe. Such had been the extent of Kira's forethought. Particularly as regarded her own relationship with her husband.

It wasn't much, but it beat out her hindsight, which only now recognized that most of those rips and tears had been incurred in pursuit of the mending.

Kira slowly lifted her eyes from the hole in their home that Leigh had left. Harlow met her displeasure in kind.

"What do we do now?" he asked.

Kira fought the urge to avert her gaze once more. Mostly successfully. "We see if we get away with what we did."

Harlow nodded. Cleared his throat. "Did she seem…happy to you?"

"…no. But I think *happy* was off the table as soon as she heard…what we did."

He sniffed. Nodded again. "Maybe Uisch can change her memory."

"…"

"If…*could have,* I should say."

"Yeah."

"I just…" he glanced behind himself, as though to sit back down, but ultimately remained standing. "I wanted her to be happier."

"I think that's off the table," Kira sniffed. Christ, she wasn't going to cry now. She *refused*. "She said she wanted it to end here. She doesn't w-"

"What I was saying," he interrupted timidly, "is maybe Uisch could, *hypothetically,* when, or *if* we brought her back for good, change her memo-"

"We're not inviting that fucking thing into our daughter's head, Harlow."

He turned and looked out the window. Nodding once, twice. "Mhm," was all he had to say. Right up until he said, so softly it was scarcely audible, "I don't regret it."

"Neither do I," Kira replied at once.

"We tried."

"We did."

He took a deep breath. "I feel like I *should* regret it. But I don't."

Kira said nothing to that. Because much to her astonishment, deep down, under layers and layers of justification and rationalization, there thrummed a tussock of… something unhappy. Maybe not *regret,* maybe not *guilt,* but something quite similar to both. She'd had such a clear vision of what she needed to do, what having done it all would mean for her and Harlow, how it would all feel.

It was only now that she realized just how little thought she'd given to how *Leigh* would feel about all of this.

Allowing the thought to uncoil sent Kira crashing backwards onto the recliner behind her. She hit it with enough force to *pop* whatever mechanism held the leg section down. It flipped up as the seatback tilted, *slamming* Kira into compulsory comfort. "Fuck," she grunted as she flexed her hamstrings to lever the leg section shut again.

Somewhere in that slapstick routine, her face had snuck out a few tears.

She sat forward in the chair, elbows on her knees,

head in her hands. Unable to stop those tears from coming, sure, but that didn't mean she had to let Harlow see them.

"Leigh," she grunted into her hands. "Oh, god."

"Come on, now," Harlow cooed, sitting himself beside her. He rubbed her back reassuringly. "You did...*we* did what we did because we love her."

"Then why didn't I..." Kira slipped into nonverbal sobbing for a few seconds, then reemerged to finish the thought. "Why didn't I think she might not *want* it?"

"It's a confusing time. Everyone's confused." Harlow grunted, satisfied with his summary of the situation. "We're all confused."

There was no hiding the tears anymore. Kira bawled into her hands, while a stone-faced Harlow rubbed her back. Until he grew tired of that, and rose to see to other things.

Kira stayed where she was, as she was, until the sun went down again.

CONSIGNING LEIGH FULLY TO THE PAST was a torture twice over. Not only was it akin to receiving the news of her daughter's death all over again – and Kira was in no mood to unpack the ways in which that statement did or didn't make sense – it also left her facing a life run through with a million tiny tears, most of her own making.

The following day, life just kept on going. Harlow had to go to work, Kira had a dentist appointment. And this was their life now. The hope of having Leigh back – then

Kira's *certainty* that she would do what it took to make that happen – had sustained Kira in a way she only now came to appreciate. Now that she was here. Living her life without that hope. The rest of her life.

Such reflections could only be sustained in a moment of relative calm, of course. So maybe it was for the best, that the calm be so short-lived.

Astoundingly, it was only at the dentist's office that Kira fully absorbed the implications of Detective Dresselhaus' return to the Trecothik household yesterday. She was halfway through a routine cleaning, lying back on that cream-colored, plastic-covered slab, mouth agape as the dental hygienist scraped at the base of her teeth with that little silver hook, filling her head with a gravely *skrrrk skrrrk skrrrk,* like fingernails against the inside of a coffin lid (or a duffel bag, who knew), when between the *skrrrks* she heard an older man in the waiting room scoffing to the receptionist about "city cops." Then the *skrrrks* resumed, and the rest of that conversation was lost. Kira, of course, was unable to demand more details, what with having a relative stranger sticking sharp objects into her mouth. But she went home, spent approximately two minutes on Google, and had her suspicions confirmed.

Madeleine Encomb's body had been discovered in the barrens. Unclear how, or by whom. Within an hour, though, besuited newscasters were painting a much more colorful picture: young Ms. Encomb had been throttled, beaten, stuffed into a bag, and buried in a shallow grave. The autopsy had yet to be performed, but preliminary reporting indicated that the girl had likely been buried alive. That latter surmise was one Kira could not accept, flatly *refused* to accept. What the hell did *preliminary reporting* even *mean,* after all? Just sensationalism, that was. That was all. Granted, such a mental bulwark was harder to defend once the eventual autopsy confirmed that *preliminary reporting,* but by that point Kira'd had time to reinforce the castle walls enough to fight off any fact thrown at them.

Despite Maddie's dispatch being arguably just as gruesome as Nicole's, and despite this now being the *second* survivor of the Firestarters Massacre to have been murdered in less than a year (in a town with a typical *murdered-girl-per-annum* tally of, well, zero), this case didn't attract a national spotlight the way Nicole's had. Sure, just about every network in the country ran a story about it, but most of them were simply recycling reporting done by local affiliates rather than sending out their own teams the way they had the first time. Best as Kira could tell, even the FBI couldn't be bothered with this one.

Yet the local police seemed to be taking this one even more seriously than the last. So it appeared to Kira, at least, though that probably had something to do with Detective Dresselhaus materializing so quickly on their doorstep. Yesterday, when Leigh had been here, Kira had only thought of the detective as an obstacle to be removed. Now, though…it got her thinking. Worrying. Why *had* the detective come straight to the Trecothiks after the discovery of Maddie's body? Obviously that was the most obvious connection between the two victims, the fact that Leigh had saved both of them…but still, why bother the parents of the slain hero?

By sheer force of will, Kira decided to view this as a useful development. In the wake of Leigh's final departure, that familiar, terrible silence had once more fallen on the Trecothik household. Wordless meals, quiet times getting ready for bed. Maybe a common threat would unite them. Like in movies, whenever aliens attack, and humanity sets aside their differences to shoot missiles up instead of sideways.

"What do you think the detective knows?" she asked Harlow one night, from across the dinner table. Profaning that familiar hush.

Harlow paused, stared at his spaghetti, then asked "do you mean what does she *suspect?"*

"I guess both. Why did she come here?"

Slowly, he lowered his fork to the table, then let his hand slide into his lap. There he sat, staring at his half-eaten Italian, for nearly a full minute. At the end of this meditative interval, he burped quietly and took up his fork once more. "I don't know."

So much for the common threat.

Kira took a sip of water, then sighed. "Do you think we should talk about that?"

He *clinked* his fork down onto his plate, hard. "What do you want to talk about?"

She flinched, then furrowed her brow. "Don't snap at me like that."

He shrugged down at his food. "Sorry. I just don't see what you want to ta-"

"I thought you might want to hash it out given how you handled her last visit."

"I handled it," Harlow mumbled. Hard to say whether that was repetition or response.

She very nearly asked Harlow what was wrong, but didn't bother.

As time went on, she didn't bother herself overmuch with making sense of her husband at all. His behavior continued in the direction it had already been heading; erratic, swinging wildly between overly solicitous sentiment, prickly standoffishness, and an encore of his mute surrender to introspection.

"What's wrong?" she couldn't help but ask him at intervals.

"Nothing," came the reply, with a delivery dependent upon his mood at the time. On those rare occasions when he deigned to elaborate, he managed to do so without actually clarifying anything. "I'm just sad that things happened the way they did." That was as near to specificity as he ever got.

Kira supposed that turnabout was, indeed, fair play. Had she not presented herself in precisely this manner to Harlow, between learning of Uisch's offer and fulfilling the first of its three requirements?

That wasn't a pleasant parallel to draw; it only raised the question of what *Harlow* was wrestling with, what courses of action he was deciding between.

Only…no. Perhaps this was simply wishful thinking, but Kira didn't believe Harlow was steeling himself to commit some irreversible idiocy. Her beloved husband had simply been hollowed out. No, not quite so passive: he had hollowed *himself* out. Hollow Harlow, hiding himself away from the fact of what he'd done, what it had amounted to. Had he tucked his essence in some far corner of the attic, to be retrieved at a later date? Or had he buried it with Maddie? Kira didn't know. She wished she could find it for him, restore it to its former glory, remake the man as he had been…but, on the other hand, Hollow Harlow was harmless. Whereas a more…fully constituted version of the man could well prove dangerous. He knew details about the murders that had never, as far as Kira could tell, been made public. If he ever got serious about turning himself and his wife in, he could simply give Detective Dresselhaus a ring and walk her to precisely the location where the cops had found the body, just past the spot where that tree had fallen a few years back, prompting an intercounty dispute as to whose responsibility it was. He could tell her precisely what sort of bag Maddie had been stuffed into. Describe the dimensions of the shovel which had paused in its intended task to smash the girl's skull in. Any or all of these things would take minutes to convey, minutes to verify, minutes to ruin his and Kira's life forever.

But he never did it.

Coward, Kira caught herself thinking now and then. The thought made her smile. It made no sense. But what did?

Before long, her hollow husband started avoiding her entirely. If he saw her in the living room when he got home, he'd make a beeline for the stairs. Were she upstairs, she'd come down to find him sitting in front of the television, or at the table. She never bothered him. Never knew what to ask him, without already knowing the answer.

It sounded a bit like a children's book. *Hollow Harlow Has The Heebie-Jeebies*, by Kira Trecothik. It had a nice ring, didn't it? Except for that last bit, maybe. *Trecothik*.

And that was next logical question, which Kira had to imagine Harlow posed to himself about as often as it occurred to her: why stay married? Why not divorce, move on, try to put this dismal chapter of their lives behind them? To see each other, however irregularly, to constantly pass through a house that was still now as it had been, when it had lodged three occupants rather than two…it was agonizing. A reminder of how good they'd had it, a deepening of misery's contours, rendering it all the more horrible in unrelenting relief. And maybe that was the answer. Maybe they felt the ceaseless screw-turning was their earned lot. Perhaps this was the only sense in which the Trecothiks could be spoken of as a bloc. Self-flagellation. Woe is me, good for me. Were we back to that? Possible, but Kira wasn't convinced, not for her part, anyway. The more she thought about it, imagined a different sort of After, one with no Harlow, no Neirmouth, no past at all while she was at it…the more she came to appreciate the danger in that fantasy. Breaking from her past would give her the distance to put it under glass and study it. Peel off the emotion and poke at the ethics, weigh *this* cost against *that* benefit. And maybe, in so doing, she might forget how truly abominable the decisions had been, the sounds those girls made as they were dying, the choking and shrieking and gurgling and *hlllng*ing, the smell of blood soaking into wet, freshly turned Earth, the sights the sights the sights. The rattle of the handle as the shovelhead struck the face of the girl in the hole. Maddie. Her name was Maddie. Had been. See? She could forget. Kira believed that was an option. And, she felt, it was a selective jettison she could effect. No Uisch necessary. Simply lose the awful memories but keep the sunny ones, the ones of Leigh returned to them, playing cards and watching *Cash Cab*. Yes, those had been tension-choked affairs, but that was a detail that could be thrown overboard with the other shitty bits. What would be left was the sun without the shadow.

And if that were the case…Kira could very easily imagine herself making a compelling argument, to herself. The thrust of which being, *what's one more kid, anyway?* The first had been the hardest. The easiest of the three turned out to be anything but. Meanwhile, the one Kira had imagined being the most difficult on a purely psychological level, by dint of Zoe's having been closest to Leigh in life, could well turn out to be the easiest to off. Psychologically. Hypothetically.

Ugh, see? She was thinking about thinking about it. Next thing she knew, she'd be thinking about it, full stop. Soon after would come thinking about *how*. Then bang, you're killing another kid. And then Leigh's sticking around forever.

And hating you, forever.

Maybe not, though. If Kira could forget, why couldn't

Leigh?

Goddamnit! Why did her brain insist on thinking like this? Bad brain! Cut it out! There would be no more killing of her daughter's friends. There would be no forgetting, no disengagement between the past, the present, and the future. And thus, no divorcing of Harlow. And thus, any children's books that Kira Trecothik happened to write would bear her taken name. But she wouldn't be writing any children's books, of course. Why would she? The fuck did she know about kids? She'd only given birth to one.

She had killed more than that.

ONE NIGHT THAT AUTUMN, Kira and Harlow accidentally had dinner together. Well, *dinner* was all a matter of perspective. Kira (having become something of a night owl, for reasons she didn't investigate too carefully) was having breakfast, Harlow dinner, so split the difference and call it lunch. They were having night lunch together. By accident. Though that, too, was a matter of perspective.

Kira had been sitting and eating an omelet she'd prepared. Eggs (natch), cheese, bacon, mushroom, some sautéed spinach. Nothing fancy. Just breakfast. Just night lunch.

Harlow made his typical entrance: swinging the door open, bending over to pick up the suitcase he'd inexplicably put on the ground next to his feet before opening the door, and falling across the threshold head-first. He looked, every night, as though he were angling for a face-plant but lacked the nerve to follow through. Never had a lovable supporting character on a multi-cam sitcom had such a distinctive, reliable entrance. *Heeeeeere's Harlow!* Laughter, applause. And what was this? A prop? A grease bag from McDonald's? The situation whence tonight's comedy. Applause.

The grease bag wasn't the only deviation from routine on this particular evening. Where Harlow would typically spot his wife at the table and steer clear, tonight he marched right over, sat himself on the chair next to Kira (thus, being close to her without looking at her), pulled a napkin out of the grease bag, tucked it in his collar with a courtly flourish, and started plucking rogue fries from the branded bag. The smell of it overpowered the taste of Kira's omelet. She wasn't entirely mad about that.

Harlow nudged her softly with his elbow. Kira looked to him. He nodded down at the grease bag. Tilted the aperture towards her and wiggled it. Kira felt a dim smile creep across her face. She reached into the bag and rescued a cold fry, to consign it to masticatory oblivion.

They finished the fries in silence. Kira couldn't stop herself smiling. This was probably just another swing in mood, sure…but she would let herself enjoy it. Did she still love Harlow, as he was now? It was getting harder and harder to say. But in this moment, she was making him smile. And that felt good.

Actually…she didn't know if Harlow was smiling or not. His reflection on the glass-top table was warped too far from true. Another matter of perspective.

RID OF RED

KIRA FELT HER HAIR SHIFTING. What woke her from her first halfway pleasant dream in recent memory was not the sensation itself, but the thought that recognizing such a subtle sensation through the wall of sleep was, hm, what was the word…unlikely? Odd? Not *impossible*, but close.

So the thought woke her, restoring to her just enough consciousness to hear what her hair, along with the gentle rustling of bedsheets beneath her, was whispering into her ear.

No language came to her. Yet she sensed the intent.

Gripping the sheets in a vain attempt to keep them from shifting, Kira raked the darkness with a fulminant glare, searching vainly for the hunched immensity of Uisch.

She didn't see it.

What she did see, though, was her husband sleeping beside her, on his side, facing her.

More to the point: she was almost positive she saw his eyes close the moment her gaze met his.

Kira stared at him for quite a while. Trying to work out if she'd imagined that or not. She was almost positive she hadn't. Same went for the shifting of her hair, the rolling of the sheets.

She was certain Uisch had spoken through her as she slept.

But not *to* her.

She kept watching Harlow, but he didn't move. His breathing seemed deep, slow. Though that was easy enough to fake.

Lowering her head back down to the pillow, Kira kept her eyes on her husband until she couldn't keep them open anymore. But that wasn't to say she slept.

THIRTEEN

SMATTERS OF PERSPECTIVE

RID OF RED

"FOR FUCK'S SAKE, ANDREA."

Immediately, Andrea Dresselhaus – *Detective* Dresselhaus to anyone who didn't outrank her – shrank into herself a bit, mumbling "I know, I know" at Chief Greider. This sort of shrinking from conflict wasn't her style at all, but she was, for once, having a hard time taking her own side here. She might have managed it were Chief Greider a bit more of an asshole, but unfortunately his frustration was born of genuine concern for Andrea Dresselhaus' career, to say nothing of her mental well-being. And she couldn't blame him. God, what had she been thinking, telling him what she'd seen? How else was he *supposed* to react?

Greider weaved into Andrea's half-cubical, crossed his arms and nodded at her computer. "Can I see it?"

Only now did she think to close out of the spread-

513

sheet. Flushed with rage at her own embarrassment. "Call it deep background," she offered limply.

"I'd just like to see it."

"I'm not doing it on department time," she assured him.

"You're doing it on department *resources*."

Andrea looked to the ancient desktop that could only be considered a *resource* in the Pitney PD precinct. "Fine. I'll do it on my laptop."

"Do you identify yourself as a detective when you interview these people? Do you drive up in one of th-"

"I'll use my own car. It's fine."

Greider wrinkled his nose into the distance. He scratched the back of his head and scooted an inch or two further into the cubical, nodding at the computer again. "Let me see."

"Aaaah…" Andrea's grimace self-actualized. She shook her head, shrugged, and keyed Excel back open.

A spreadsheet of names, belonging to all the parents in the greater Pitney area who had lost children in the Firestarters Massacre, dribbled down the y-axis. Along the top, questions in the x:

Believe?	Felt?	Seen?

Beneath that, an X or an O in each of the boxes corresponding to a given name. For Jill MacFadden, it was XXX. For Ryan Mack, OOX. For Jodie Howell, OOO. And so it went.

Andrea looked at the screen, but she *saw* Greider's taut disapproval. It was a look that had been seared, lightly but undeniably, into her vision, sort of like how old TVs could be branded by a static image held for too long. It was belittling but warm, a look that said *I know you can do better* and daring you to meet the implicit challenge. It was the only expression capable of making Andrea feel like she *was* nuts.

She wasn't, though. She knew what she had seen in the bay window of the Trecothik household. *Whom* she had seen.

Leigh Trecothik.

A dead girl.

Which was impossible, of course. Obviously. And yet, she'd seen it. Seen *her*. If she closed her eyes she could *still* see the girl in the window, with such clarity that no amount of logic could convince her she hadn't.

How ridiculous she felt. She wasn't superstitious, wasn't spiritual. All her life laughing at the cranks claiming to have communed with the dead, thinking them either grifters or gullible.

And yet and yet and yet. She had *seen* Leigh Trecothik in the window. Which completely changed everything. It had to, by virtue of rewriting the laws of the goddamned universe as Andrea understood them.

Two of the three girls Leigh Trecothik had given her life to save had been viciously, inexplicably murdered. And now Leigh Trecothik was alive again.

What the fuck. That was something, right? That couldn't possibly be nothing.

More critically, as far as living in a lane with the metaphysical bumpers up: how could she convince her colleagues that the dead could live again, without them thinking she'd absolutely lost the plot? She'd only tried with Greider thus far, and that had *not* gone well.

Naturally, Andrea's first thought was: *make a spreadsheet.*

She collected the names of those parents bereaved by the Firestarters Massacre. Knowing perfectly well how delicate this all was, she began slowly, carefully, as tactfully as she could, to reach out to them. Tell them she had a few questions that might help the investigation (to her surprise and relief, only two or three actually thought to ask, *what investigation?*).

These were unusual questions, Andrea would warn them, best posed in person. Ideally at your house. So you don't have the luxury of hanging up or storming out. Andrea never said that last bit, of course.

At this point, she'd schedule a face-to-face meeting. They'd sit down, no coffee for me thank you, just three quick questions and I'll be out of your hair.

First: do you believe in ghosts? Strange question, I know, please just bear with me. I promise this is pertinent to the investigation. Once they finally got their head in the game and answered, Andrea wrote their response in her notebook, to be transferred to her spreadsheet at the end of the day, an O for yes, an X for no. Very good, very good. *Next question: have you ever* felt *a ghost?* Many people asked for clarification as to what she meant here, which she offered by way of repeating the word *felt*, pronoun-

RID OF RED

ced in italics and preceded by a *you know*. O for yes, X for no. *Last question: have you ever* seen *a ghost?* Almost everyone asked if that wasn't covered by the *felt* question. Andrea insisted that it wasn't. Well, alright then. O or X.

What Andrea typically got out of this was OOO, XXX or OOX. What she was looking for was someone who responded XXO. As in, people like her. People who didn't believe in ghosts, didn't feel they had ever *felt* a ghost, yet insisted that they had *seen* one. She'd even have settled for OXO, as seeing is so often grounds for believing. What she wanted, in short, was an answer without logical integrity. Such an answer might imply there were more kids killed in the Massacre who'd come back than just Leigh Trecothik. Instead, though, Andrea got responses that fell into categories that, if you accepted the premise of the initial X or O, all too often made sense. As in, they had an *internal* logic by which they made sense.

Driving to and from these fruitless interviews, Andrea felt like an absolute loon…but also, like a proper cop. This was the way she'd always imagined it being as a kid, seeing something that no one else could, chasing down the truth with her reputation on the line. People probably thought Woodward and Bernstein were crazy, but who was laughing now? Einstein didn't believe in quantum theory, and now he was dead and string theorists were playing cat's cradle with the laws of the universe. Which, granted: not a cop, our dear friend Einstein. Nor were the Watergate boys. But the point stood. Even brilliant people got things wrong. Which was actually a different point from the one she'd been making with the

517

Woodward and Bernstein allusion. But fuck it, she was looking for things without logical integrity, right? At any rate, she felt sane in the driver's seat. She never imagined herself to be even the least bit batty.

She *always* felt batty when Greider was checking her work. It was that *I know you can do better* face. The one Andrea could see without looking at it.

"This looks like everybody," Greider observed, "yes?"

Andrea cracked her neck, *crk* to the left, "All the *parents,*" CRK to the right, "oof."

Greider huffed his frustration like a dragon. "So what does that mean, all the *parents?*"

"Means I interviewed all the parents."

"It means you want to interview people *other* than the parents?"

"There are other people who might have seen something. I'm thinking the cleanup crew on the island. Somebody had to go in and collect the bodies, right? And we had people on the island. Maybe they saw something. I know McCall was there, I'd like to talk t-"

"They probably saw a lot of things. I bet that was a traumatic job."

"And you're implying what?"

"I'm not implying anything. I'm stating a fact."

"You don't say *I bet* when you're stating facts. You don't say *I bet Wednesday comes after Tuesday.*"

Greider sighed and shook his head at the computer screen. "Listen, you're off the clock, you do what you want. But don't use the car, and don't give anybody the idea that you're talking to them in your capacity as a detective." He turned to leave.

"You're gonna eat crow when I figure this out!" Andrea shouted, even in the moment recognizing, *man, I sound batty.* "I'm gonna write a book about this and win the Pulitzer!"

He spun around, smiled, and granted "good shot at a Hugo award." He thumped the top of the cubical wall twice, *thump thump*, and walked away.

Andrea frowned at his back, then spun in her spinny chair and frowned at her monitor. "A Hugo award," she mumbled unhappily to herself.

She sighed. Perhaps this indirect approach was all wrong. Stop fishing for other people who *might* have seen something. Go find someone who absolutely *would* have seen something, had there been anything to see.

There were two people who fit that bill. And Andrea had a pretty darn good idea which would be the easier nut to crack.

She smiled softly, her gaze drifting to the X's and O's on her screen. For a split second, her brain interpreted them as calligraphic shorthand. Hugs and kisses, kisses and hugs, all beneath the names of parents who had lost their children.

She shuddered and pressed the power button on her monitor, sending it to sleep.

HARLOW DIDN'T UNDERSTAND why he hadn't lost his mind yet. Maybe he wanted it too badly, longed for sweet senselessness in an overly rational way. You couldn't reason yourself to madness. Maybe that was the problem.

Still, he did what he could to nudge himself over the edge. He watched violent movies on the weekends while Kira was still asleep, horrible movies about gun massacres and killing people with power tools, all the things he imagined would finish him. They upset him mightily, yes indeed, but failed to occasion any descent into gibbering insensibility. Rooted to the real world he remained.

That wasn't all bad, he supposed. Reconciliation with his wife was measured in millimeters, but it was slugging along reliably enough. The break demanding reconciliation was harder to identify, as far as its particular cause went. The first girl had been a gruesome act of *Kira's* doing. The second had been a group effort, but *his* idea. The third they were choosing to leave be, *together*. It was a *they* choice. A *them* choice? *They* or *them*, one of the two. Or was it *their*? A *their* thing?

Ah, *there* it was! Madness, approaching in the guise of grammar! Come, come, carry me off!

Madness, averse to commitment as ever, shrank from Harlow's hunger. Thus he was left, standing in the middle of the grocery store, both hands on an empty cart.

Huh. Grocery time, then. He looked in the little navel-height basket for a list. No list. He opened up his phone and checked the notes. No list. He was in a grocery store with no list, and no real memory of why he'd come here, or how he'd arrived. Ok. *That* seemed crazy. Good. He would take his madness where he could.

"Mr. Trecothik?" Someone behind him asked.

"That's me," he replied, somewhat surprised, without

turning around. What was he surprised about? Still reeling from the lost list, maybe.

"Mr. Trecothik," the voice repeated, confidently enough to spawn a body from Harlow's peripheral vision. It was the detective. What was her name? Something that sounded like a German synth band from the 80's. "Funny bumping into to you here!" she said.

Harlow checked what aisle he was in. Crackers and chips. Not a particularly funny aisle, to his mind. "Is it?"

"You're shopping light today, I see."

"Huh?" Harlow's eyebrows sent each other distress signals in morse code. He looked down at his cart. Still empty. "I can't find my list," he offered, more as apology than explanation.

"I was thinking about th-"

"Can you hear me?"

The Detective hesitated. "…yes?"

"Oh."

"Why do you ask?"

Harlow rested his hands on the handle of his cart. "You just weren't acknowledging that I was saying anything."

Nodding her head as though manually rewinding the tape of the last minute, detective…whatever, the detective shrugged and said "sorry about that."

"It's alright," Harlow allowed. He pushed his cart and followed it further down the crackers and chips aisle.

"Mr. Trecothik!" Ugh. The detective was following.

Harlow turned to look at her again, eyes grazing the bags of chips…he gasped. "Dresselhaus!"

"Yes?"

Lifting his hand from the cart, letting it drift unattended – not fast, not far, but alone – he pointed to a bag of chips on the shelf, the bag that had brought her name back to him. Humpty Dumpty chips, of the All Dressed variety. "That's your name. I couldn't remember it, but I just did."

"Mr. Trecothik, are you alright? You seem…odd."

"You don't know me well enough to say that."

"I got the impression th-"

"See," Harlow said, planting a hand on his hip, "you're doing it again."

"Doing what?"

"Not acknowledging that I've said something. It seems like a bad thing, no offense, but it seems like a, *not great* thing for a detective to do."

"How would you like me to acknowledge that you've said something?"

"I don't know. Like a normal person would." Harlow was taken aback by how *not* taken aback he was by his own passive aggression, directed at a law enforcement officer no less. It made sense, though. He'd been behaving uncharacteristically for so long, it had become characteristic of him to do so.

"You don't know *people* well enough to say that," Dresselhaus replied, doing a poor job of suppressing a grin.

"Ha, ha. I have to go. Nice to see you, De-"

"I think you want to tell me something."

Harlow made a show of considering her assertion, the

lip-pursing, chin-scratching spectacle of a mind already made up. "I don't think so. No." He put his hands on his cart and pushed.

Pushed right into Dresselhaus, who had zipped around in front of him. "Do you remember what you said to me, the first time we met?"

"Mmm…no, I don't remember."

"You told me your wife murdered Nicole Ligeti."

Harlow took a deep breath. "We've…had some rough…you know, losing a daughter…uh…I was just not…myself."

"I can't imagine straying far enough from myself to accuse my spouse of murder."

Harlow's eyes darted down to the Detective's hand. No ring.

She clearly noticed, amending her statement with "or accusing *anyone* I love, rather."

"Do you have children?"

"No."

"Then you don't have the first fucking clue about how far there is to go."

That time, the detective seemed to hear him. This, he gathered only from her expression. "I believe you were trying to tell me something. That you're keeping a terrible secret. That you could breathe again, if only you could get this horrible, heavy thing off your chest."

Splaying his fingers out and patting his pecs, Harlow tried to ignore the sting in his heart where her comment had struck, and smiled. "Nope. Nothing on my chest."

"Tell me about Leigh."

Harlow sighed, unable to suppress his hurt now, but still retaining enough control to keep it at arm's length, like a tall man holding off a pugilistic child with a hand on the forehead. "What about her? She was…everything. I can't just sum her up. It'd be impossible."

"Just tell me something about her. Anything."

"I…she…" he shrugged. "I wouldn't even know where to start."

"Tell me about the first time you spoke to her after she died."

Harlow's hands went numb. He stared at the detective, watched her face crack and go runny like an egg. There were words of denial, derisive phrases with which to deflect the patent idiocy of what she'd just said. Those things definitely existed. Harlow just couldn't find them. They were on the grocery list.

He saw the look on her face, her reaction to whatever face *he* was making. Her expression spoke without words.

Oh god. Kira had been right; Dresselhaus had seen Leigh through the window. And despite what both of them had hoped, the detective hadn't managed to reason herself into doubting the impossible, true thing she'd witnessed.

And the fact that she was here, asking Harlow about it…oh, god. What did *that* mean?

"I, uh," he tried, better late than never, "I have no idea what y-"

"This is me acknowledging what you're *not* saying," Dresselhaus cooed in a voice that inspired and invited confidence in equal measure.

All at once, Harlow wanted to tell her everything. That was how fucking good that voice was. He wanted to *confirm* it all for her, because that voice said it already knew everything. But there was no way she could know everything, was there? Unless Uisch had paid her a visit and drawn her a diagram, all she could have right now was a vague hunch that the Trecothiks were seeing ghosts. That wasn't a crime, was it? To see ghosts?

…was it?

"Leave my family alone," Harlow said, only realizing as he was storming away from his cart and the aisle and the store that *family* was an odd word to describe just his wife and himself.

PART OF BEING A GOOD DETECTIVE was precision. Identify someone's weak point and find a way to poke it without breaking the skin. The husband, Andrea had identified, was a weak point. His confession on the first day she'd visited the Trecothik house had initially registered as little more than dismissive provocation of the kind any detective is well-accustomed to. After the sight of Leigh made clear that something was very much *up* in that household though, the husband's confession came to seem more like a cry for help. She still couldn't quite scale the mental hurdle to take at face value that Harlow and his wife had killed that girl, hadn't honestly reflected on what he'd said as much as the significance of what his having said it might be…but the more she thought about it…thought about him standing in the grocery store, going white as a haddock filet at Andrea's question…

There was a deranged elegance to it. A simple, straight line, so easily traced that Andrea was inclined to dismiss it out of hand. To say nothing of its utter absurdity, which was embraced easily enough – she'd crossed that line some time ago.

Imagine the Trecothiks had made a pact with the devil. A deed to bring their daughter back, signed in blood. Just not *their* blood.

Andrea puttered the oversized milk jug she called a car up to the red light, and felt a bubble of acid laughter inflating at the base of her throat. A bit like when you have to sneeze, but can't. Whatever the equivalent of that was for dread.

When the light turned green, she tore through it, turned off onto a side street, and parked. Safest thing to do, when you start feeling dizzy behind the wheel.

What the fuck was she doing? What was she thinking? The thoughts swirling around her head belonged to somebody making a horror movie, not a detective trying to solve two murders. These thoughts were worse than foolish; they were insane. Indicated more than a few loose screws. She could appreciate this.

And yet, she'd seen Leigh. Harlow Trecothik had all but confirmed that she had. His full muscular lockdown upon Andrea's asking him about posthumous visits from his daughter, the way his eyes seemed to lose their light as they contemplated an unthinkable expanse, that *endless* moment of perfect, heaving silence, between her asking the question and his lame attempt to deflect it…

Andrea would never, ever, *ever* forget that moment.

She'd wanted to press him further, strike while he was exposed and see what he might spill. But she, too, had locked up.

So…was that all it had taken to make her believe? To move forward with the understanding that Leigh had come back from the dead? And from that, maybe, hypothesize that her parents had done terrible things to make that happen?

Not quite, Andrea granted herself. But it was enough to make the idea stick.

She sighed and let her head flop forwards, brow landing on the top of the steering wheel. Smartest thing to do, assuming one lived in a world with wheelin', dealin' devils, would be to tail Zoe Cottrell. Make sure nobody in a big blue poncho tried to pay her a visit. Unfortunately, impish intrusions to one side, this remained the real world. Things were still expected of Andrea, professionally speaking. Yes, she could surrender all of her personal time to this project, but…

She lifted her hands to her temples and pressed, digging in with the heels of her palms. God, she could practically hear thoughts grinding against each other, feel the friction radiating down to her jaw.

She was *absolutely* convinced that the Trecothiks had found some way to bring their daughter back, by killing the three girls she'd saved.

She was also *absolutely* convinced that that was the most ridiculous shit she'd ever heard in her life, that whatever was going on had a perfectly rational explanation. Seeing Leigh Trecothik in the window had a perfectly rational explanation. Everything in the universe had a perfectly rational explanation.

If it didn't, then Andrea Dresselhaus was in the wrong line of work.

Groaning unhappily, she threw the car back into drive, and hit the road once again.

Split the difference. One foot in the real world, the other in nightmare fantasy land. She would continue a proper investigation, following that as far as it took her...but she would also try to swing by the Cottrell house, at least once or twice per day. Just to keep a look out. Maybe she'd put in a request to send a few expendable beat cops up from Pitney, too. The worst they could say was no.

If they said yes, though...that'd free Andrea up to swing by the Trecothiks' place, every now and again.

HARLOW HAD TO PULL OFF onto the shoulder so he could hyperventilate. Pulling off onto the shoulder made him think about the last time he'd pulled off onto a shoulder. On a long, lonely road through the barrens. That sure didn't help his heartrate much.

The detective knew. She knew everything. She had to. Right? To ask a question like that? What was going on? How had she found out?

Nope. Okay. Deep breath. She didn't know *everything*. If she knew *everything*, it would have been an entire SWAT team – or at least a few more officers with big jackets and guns – cornering him between the crackers and the chips.

The detective was rattling the cage. That was all. That had to be all.

"FUCK!" he shouted, slapping the steering wheel. He added, "ouch."

He wanted this to be over. That was all he wanted. And getting caught would be a great way for this to be over. But then, he'd spend the rest of his life rotting away with regret. Wouldn't he? Maybe. He might. He had so much regret for what he had done.

Imagining himself in prison, tasting the reality of it in a way he'd managed to avoid thus far, almost *feeling* that stale air in the cell block stick to his skin…it made him realize that there was more than one kind of regret.

One could, after all, regret things *not* done. Just as easily as those done. And getting caught would plop him before the double-barrel discharge of both types of regret at once. For the rest of his life. Bang. Bang.

For good measure, he slapped the steering wheel a few more times.

HOW DO YOU THROW OUT A SHOVEL?

Kira stood in the garage, staring at the spade hanging on the wall. It had dug a hole, smashed a girl's face through a duffel bag, and buried her.

Had Kira known Maddie was alive when she'd…? Well, hang on. One question at a time.

Her first thought was, either absurdly or brilliantly, to bury the shovel. Two questions following close behind made clear that brilliance had no part in the idea: *how would anybody ever dig it up again*, she caught herself wondering with satisfaction, *but then, come to think of it, how would I fill in the hole?* Ok. Dumb questions, dumb idea. Nevermind. Still, she didn't want to just drop it off at a dump. She'd scrubbed the thing down, drenched it in bleach, and re-dirtied it by turning some soil in the garden. It looked like a regular, unbloodied shovel from here. Even under a microscope, you'd probably never guess the thing had a body count. But Kira couldn't get any further on that score than *probably*. She didn't know. She *couldn't* know. And she didn't want to take the risks necessary to find out.

She also didn't want that fucking thing in her garage anymore.

KRA-Chhhh the garage door screamed as it shuddered to life.

From the other side of the door, a car revved its engine. *rrRRrrr, rrrrRRRrrr*. Like the start of a street race.

Kira backpedaled towards the door to the kitchen.

As the garage door rose, Kira could see it was Harlow's car on the other side. Obviously. Less obvious was why he was pumping the pedal like a church organist ripped to the tits on communion wine.

Kira hopped up onto the step leading to the kitchen door, clearing a path for Harlow to come roaring into the garage. He stopped his car so suddenly Kira thought he might have smashed into the rear wall.

"What was all that about?" she asked him as he swung open the door and nearly tumbled out.

"The detective knows," he gasped, scrambling upright and charging towards, then past, Kira.

Kira stood fast, struggling to wrest her attention from the shovel on the wall, now half-obscured by Harlow's car. She snapped herself out of it and followed him into the house. "What does the detective know?"

Harlow grabbed a glass from the cupboard. As he held it beneath the spigot to fill with water, Kira noticed how much his hand was shaking.

"What does the detective know?" she asked again, in a much punchier tone.

Harlow chugged half the glass and put it back beneath the faucet to refill. "That detective found me at Hannaford. Detective Dresselhaus. She must have followed me. How did she find me? She *cornered* me."

Kira processed this as Harlow tried to drown himself at the counter. "The detective cornered you at Hannaford?"

"Yeah*,*" Harlow grunted between glugs. "In the crackers and chips aisle."

"Take a deep breath. I'm not following what you're saying."

Harlow, even in his affective extremity, made a big *AAAAAH* noise after he finished drinking. He slammed the glass down on the counter and said "she asked me when did I talk to Leigh after she died."

Kira felt the whole world *jerk*. "Fuck."

"The detective, she looks at me and she says, I think her exact words were, um, *when was the first time you saw your daughter after she died?* Something like that."

Kira gnawed on her upper lip. Slowly, her head started bobbing. "She was fishing. She doesn't actually know anything." A pause. "We knew she saw Leigh in the window when she was back. She took a flyer on that. We knew this might happen." Another pause. "What did you say to her?"

"…"

"Please tell me you didn't say something…you didn't do something like you did last time."

"I…" His eyes traced nervous circles in their sockets, then finally settled back on Kira, committed to indecision. "I might have done the wrong thing."

Kira took a deep breath of her own. "Honey…when someone asks if you've seen a dead person, you just laugh at them. Or call them crazy."

"…yes."

"…"

"…"

"So *what did you say?*"

Harlow looked at the glass of water in his hand as though it had just starting singing the national anthem. "I'm not even *thirsty*!" he shouted at it.

"Hey!" Kira stepped forward and snapped her fingers in front of his face. "What did you say?"

"Nothing! Nothing. I just sort of walked away."

"*Sort of?*"

"I did. I just walked."

Kira shook her head and just sort of walked away. She made it halfway down the front hall before turning around and storming back towards her husband, who remained deeply disturbed by the glass of water he had poured himself.

"Dresselhaus comes up and asks you about your daughter's ghost and you…you…"

"I know," he mumbled to his beverage.

"You basically told her she was on to something!"

"I know. I'm sorry."

"It's okay," Kira assured him reflexively. "I just… you need to…" she sighed, threw her arms up, and let them fall back to her side. "Okay. Well, I mean…what's she gonna prove though, right? Unless they're gonna call Uisch to take the stand, they'll never work out motive. And I feel like they're not even gonna have…how are they gonna know what to look for if they can't figure out why we'd have done it?"

"Just like a regular case, maybe."

"That's not helpful."

Harlow shrugged.

Kira sighed and folded her arms, unfolded them, put her hands on her hips, moved them towards her pockets, and ultimately folded her arms again.

Harlow wriggled his left hand into his pocket, while the cup-clutching right hung awkwardly at his beltline. "Listen, um. I was thinking," he ventured with an apprehension that primed Kira to say *no* to whatever was coming, "if we go to prison…"

"We're not going to prison," Kira insisted, staring vacantly at the empty space between them.

"But if we do, or if it looks like we're going to…we'd never get out, right?"

"Maybe we could get some kind of insanity plea or something."

Harlow shook his head. "I doubt it. We premeditated."

"Well, we might get out. Murderers get out eventually, I think."

"It wouldn't be for years. If ever. Can we agree on that?"

"Sure."

"Okay." Harlow put down his glass and stared into the middle distance, holding his hands out in front of himself at chest-level. Conductor at the podium, ready to lead the orchestra. "So, what I guess I'm getting at is, if we're in prison for the rest of our lives…there will be… and I'm just sort of saying this because it was something that I was thinking, well, that I *thought* about. But… there'll be things we can't do in prison."

Kira squinted at her husband. "Yeah. Prison's pretty well known for that."

"Don't be that way."

"Well I don't know what you're saying, Harlow."

"I'm saying…" he huffed, then leaned back against the counter, folding both arms across his chest. "There are things that we might feel one way about now, when it's an *option,* that we might change our minds about after it's not. In the whole…" he unfolded his arms and waved his hands in front of himself, an invisible accordion solo. "…span of…*time.* The fullness of time."

Kira felt winter sweep down her spine. A memory asserted itself without her needing to go look for it: the feeling of her hair shifting in the night, the bedsheets swirling around her. Harlow's eyes, closing the moment they met hers. "…Harlow."

He kept his gaze vague, far from Kira, far from the kitchen here. His hands jittered their way through a few gestures that had no clear connection to what he was saying. "And if we're probably going to get the worst punishment they can give us *anyway,* then…*maybe,* that would help her…well, anything else we do, they can't make it worse for us. So, if w-"

"You better be telling me you wanna rob a bank or something stupid like that."

"If we chose to do it *now,*" Harlow continued, as though Kira hadn't said anything, "to do what we might, in the future, *wish* we'd done…she would be furious at us." Finally, he turned his head to look at Kira. "But we would be in prison. We would be *paying* for what we'd done." Reconnecting with the words, Harlow's hands hardened into *we're number one* pointer fingers and jabbed in Kira's direction. "And that would mean she could have a second chance. At *life.* She would…see us, being in prison, and she'd decide that she could mo-"

"You want to kill Zoe," Kira snapped.

"No," Harlow replied with a greater conviction than Kira had heard from him in quite a while. "I want to bring Leigh back."

Fuck.

Fuck.

How to put this gruesome toothpaste back in the tube? Even if she managed to talk him down here and now…who was she kidding, no one could have talked her down after she'd made up her mind to start all this.

Only now that Harlow had come to occupy that terrible territory did Kira realize she'd ceded it.

Yes, of course, there was still the voice in her head saying *do it, do it, have your daughter back*. But it was smaller than it had ever been, further off, deeper down.

What had silenced it was the thought of Leigh herself. Not the hole she had left in the world, but the beautiful way in which she'd once filled it.

Leigh didn't want to come back. Not at the cost of her friend's life. She'd made that clear, Kira felt. Though the more Kira reflected on their last day together, the more she wondered how much of that was just a panto-mime of happiness, for their benefit…but that was irrelevant.

Yes, Kira still wanted her daughter back, more than anything. But she couldn't. *They* couldn't.

So get Harlow off that goddamned hill. Talk him down.

"Wow" was all Kira could think to say.

Harlow blinked. "What's the *wow*? Have you thought about that too?"

"…no."

"I don't believe you."

Kira just shook her head. "That's a change."

"From…what?"

"You saying you want to *kill Zoe.*" She made sure to hit the words as hard as she could. Success: Harlow flin-ched. "It's just…that's a hell of a change from how you thought about this whole…the whole thing. Before."

"Things are changing."

536

"Things always change."

"…right."

"…"

"What are you saying?"

"I don't know."

"Then can you…*react* to what I'm saying?"

Kira rubbed her face with her hands. "Aaaah…" she let her hands fall. "I understand where you're coming from. But…at a certain point, we just need make a choice and be okay with the consequences. Even if it is forever."

"…that applies to what I'm saying too."

"Okay. I don't think we should do it, Harlow. We *can't*. Leigh doesn't want us to."

"Didn't. At the moment."

Kira grimaced.

Harlow held her gaze. "And I don't remember her saying that. Specifically."

"She said she wanted it to end there. That's saying it."

"Well, she didn't say she wanted to come back in the first place. That didn't stop you before."

"Why would she fucking say that in the first place? We didn't even know this was…it was a completely different situation!"

"That's still beside the point." He heaved himself out of his lean, standing straight on his own two feet. "There was just as much reason to imagine she wouldn't have wanted you to kill Nicole, before any of this started."

"You're right. I made a mistake. I fully admit that. I made a deal with the devil, and that's on me."

"So why did you?"

"Because I missed my fucking daughter," Kira explained, voice and heart breaking in concert. "I didn't think it was possible to hurt as much as I did. And I...I was just...I don't know, I was seeing red. I wasn't thinking. So I j-"

"That's bullshit."

Kira flinched. "Excuse me?"

"You were *absolutely* thinking. You were thinking about how you could do it without getting caught. You were thinking about who to kill, in what order. You were thinking enough to follow those girls to learn their lives and find the best place to do it. You were thinking non-fucking-stop. We both were. And we still are."

"*You* are. I'm telling you, I want to honor Leigh's wishes. We need to...and I hate this too, but we need to let her go."

"I don't think that's it."

"Harlow, if you're trying to say something then just fucking say it."

Lower the temperature, another small, oft-ignored voice in her head counseled. Harlow wasn't likely to be persuaded of anything in an argument, and if she wasn't able to persuade him to drop this...she'd need to find other ways to frustrate his Zoe-annihilating objectives.

"I'm sorry," she added hastily, holding her hands up in soft surrender. "I'm sorry I raised my voice."

He flattened his lips. "All I'm saying is, you weren't seeing red. Not really. That's just a thing you say, so you can feel better about being an angry person."

Oh, how wrong he was. Kira was seeing red right

now, red in the place where her husband used to be.

"I'm saying," he continued, in the tremulous growl of a man trying to convince himself he's being logical, "that we need to make a sober, considered, *rational* decision for this last one. No more passion, no more emotion. Recognize what we're doing, and do it because it's the right thing to do for our daughter."

"I couldn't agree more. We need to be *rational.*"

"Okay. We're agreed."

"Yes," Kira confirmed. "We need to take a deep breath…and realize…that coming back, is not what Leigh wa-"

Harlow scoffed, shook his head at Kira, then turned and stomped out of the kitchen.

"Hey!" Kira shouted.

Harlow spun around. "You said we were going to be *rational!*"

"I'm *being* rational!"

He thundered back into the kitchen. "No, you're not!" He chopped the air with his hands. *"Think* about it! For all we know, we have a day, maybe two, to bring our daughter back. After that, we're gonna get arrested, probably, and th-"

"How is it rational to just *assume* we're getting arrested that soon?! You just pulled *one or two days* out of thin air! And we don't even kn-"

"Why else would Dresselhaus have asked me that question in the crackers and chips aisle?"

"If she had any real evidence, she wouldn't have *asked* you anything! And the only rea-"

"If she *didn't* ha-"

"Let me *finish,* Harlow!"

"No! Listen to m-"

"Let me fucking finish!"

"No!"

From the outside in, Kira's vision burst. Pure red poured in through the cracks.

She rushed forward and shoved her husband. He staggered backwards, bumping his glass of water on the counter and knocking it to the floor. It exploded, a giggling crash of glitter and liquid. Neither of the Trecothiks flinched. "What changed?" she demanded. "What changed?"

"Don't push me," Harlow warned her.

"What changed?"

"I don't know what you're talking about. Honestly."

"What changed between when you're crying on top of me, saying *oh, we've gotta do this even though it sucks because we've got to give our daughter a nice last day,* to now, you not giving a shit about what your daughter wants because hey, if we're going to jail, might as well kill another kid on the way, huh?" She shoved him again. "Was it easier than you thought? You get a taste for it?"

"I don't know what moral high ground you think you have," Harlow rumbled, suddenly seeming his full five feet and ten inches tall, "but you need to pump the godda-" Another shove halted him mid-word. He gave a frustrated tough-guy chuckle.

In that moment, Kira hated him. She couldn't articulate why. But really, did she have to? Red was red was red.

No. Goddamnit, *no*. She didn't hate him. This was terror, on his behalf.

Because if she couldn't knock him off of this goddamned hobby horse he'd welded himself to, well…Harlow would learn how wrong he was, about what ground Kira imagined herself to be occupying.

None of this was moral. It never had been. It had always been for Leigh. Still was.

So if Leigh wanted to stay gone, wanted Zoe unharmed…and Harlow was determined not to honor that…

That wasn't something Kira could even contemplate. So she took a deep breath, banished the red, and said "that's not what this is about" as calmly as she could (which was still *not very*). "There's no *moral high ground* for either of us. I'm not trying win an argument. We're talking about an innocent girl's life."

"Yes, we *are*."

Kira frowned. "Leigh is dead. Zoe isn't. I hate saying this, I *fucking hate* saying this, but…there's only one *life* there."

"Yes," Harlow replied, his voice like an oncoming train, less heard than felt through the track, "there is."

Kira hesitated. Studied the unmoving callous his brow had become. Keeping her gaze there because she couldn't bear to let it fall to his eyes.

She'd seen so much in those eyes. Not all of it good, to be sure. But most of it. More often than not, she saw warmth and kindness and compassion and *love* when she looked into those eyes.

Not now. Not today. She had never known those eyes to look at *anything* the way they now bored in to *her*. Seeing them in the corner of her vision was enough to make her wonder if she hadn't spent the entire latter half of her life in the grip of some fearful delusion. For a man capable of looking the way Harlow now did could never be capable of warmth, nor kindness nor compassion, *certainly* not love.

It terrified her. On both of their behalves.

She wasn't going to convince him. Without a shadow of a doubt, she knew that to be true. Whatever fucking bee had crashed into his bonnet at the first mention of prison had been busy indeed, building a hive and stuffing it into the skullspace where Harlow's fucking brain used to be.

He wasn't going to do anything right now, though. Because he needed Kira's help to do it. It was she to whom Uisch had appeared, after all.

Yes. Of course. The safeguard. His stupid, songless grief.

"You can't do it without me," Kira sighed, unable to hide her relief, *really* hoping she did better with the smile she felt threatening to break. "Uisch appeared to *me*. It made the deal with *me."*

That cranked Harlow's glare into a different gear. Something quicker, yet colder. He said nothing.

That was victory, Kira knew. Unless…unless Uisch really *had* spoken to him the other night. Had given him the high-sign. Maybe that was what had triggered this change of heart.

She didn't think so. His was not the face of a man concealing a wonderful secret. He looked beaten.

What better place to leave him?

"I'm going to bed," Kira mumbled. She turned and trundled towards the stairs.

"It's the middle of the afternoon," Harlow noted, sounding vaguely disappointed. And why not? His playmate was taking her toys and going home.

"Yes," Kira replied, as she turned and heaved herself up the stairs, "it is."

It was the work of both hands on the banister to get her up to the second floor. Once there, she didn't so much walk to her bedroom as fall in its direction and manage to get her feet beneath her, over and over again. She crawled under the covers without removing a single item of clothing. She simply hadn't the energy.

There was not a single iota of energy she could spare right now. Assuming *iota* was the best unit of measurement for energy. It might have been better to say…no, see, shut that down. Those were wasted iotas, or whateverthefucks.

She needed to put everything she had into fucking *thinking*. Was Harlow desperate enough, terrified enough, to try to go through with it anyway? As long as he was convinced he and Kira might be going to prison, he was a threat to Zoe. So…how do deal with that? Er, how to deal with that in a diplomatic way?

How to stop herself from thinking of all the many, many, *many* ways to hurt a person?

She put everything she had into that. Into stopping

those thoughts. Putting in everything, she was left with nothing.

And so, she fell asleep. In the middle of the afternoon.

HARLOW SPENT THE FIRST HOUR after Kira went upstairs just waiting for her to come back down. He had more to say, and he suspected that she did too. Why was she being like this? He'd imagined he would come home, tell her what he'd been thinking about, and be met with something to the effect of *funny you should say that, that's exactly where my head's at too, and as it happens I've done a bit of brainstorming on next steps.* It hadn't honestly occurred to him that Kira would fight him. He might have handled himself better, he conceded, if it had occurred to him. Alas.

Actually, no! *Not* alas! He'd handled himself as well as anyone could have, upon being confronted by such… *audacity.* That was the only word for it. Who the hell was Kira to be so dismissive? He could well have shouted *I learned it from you!* right in her face.

After an hour of waiting, Harlow got the message: Kira wasn't coming back down. At least, not any time soon. Which, it was not lost on him, was the most sure-fire way to filibuster Harlow's proposal.

Did he know for a *fact* that Kira needed to be the one to kill Zoe? That if he drove over to the girl's house right now and shot her in the face (he didn't own a gun, but, you know, broadly speaking), all he would succeed in doing would be forever closing off Leigh's only avenue of return to this world?

No. He didn't know that for a fact. But that wasn't something he could roll the dice on.

He thought hard about the other night again. When he'd been so sure Uisch was speaking to him, through the sheets, through the curtains, through Kira's hair just a few inches from his face. If that had indeed been the demon though, he hadn't understood it then. And he could make no more sense of those sounds now.

So…he went about his day. And what an unremarkable day it was. The first task of which was finding his half-completed grocery list on the counter by the landline cradle. He picked it up and looked at it, until a voice in his head urged him to *throw it out*. Which was odd. He'd looked for it so he could go back to the store (what were the odds the detective would still be waiting to ambush him there for a second time?) and actually get what he needed.

But there was something persuasive about that voice. Something so effortlessly logical. There really wasn't any point in getting groceries, was there? Doing that seemed to imply that this time next week, he and Kira would be cooking food together, to eat together, here in this home they lived in, together.

Somehow, the odds of that felt…low.

So Harlow crumpled up the grocery list, walked it over to the trash, and disposed of it. That done, he leaned against the counter and cried. Which rather set the tone for the remainder of his day.

When said day was done, capped with a lonely meal of reheated leftovers (a chicken-centric something or other, Harlow couldn't remember what it was but could remember all too well what life had been like when they'd had it, how the air between Kira and himself had finally begun to feel as though it were clearing, the way they'd been able to offer tepid little smiles to one another between silent bites of this…fucking…whatever), Harlow lumbered upstairs, lingered outside the door to his own goddamned bedroom for a moment…and went inside.

Kira was sleeping in their bed, naturally. The bed in the room that was, alright, *theirs.* Together. Still, it irked him that she'd just come right up and crashed into bed here, in their room, as though she'd just *assumed* he was going to go sleep on the couch. And *sure,* she hadn't actually *told* him she wanted him to sleep on the couch. But it seemed implied, didn't it? Right?

Well grumble grumble grouse then, that was fine. If Kira wanted him to sleep on the couch, he would sleep on the couch. If there was any hope of changing her mind, or bringing her on board to finish what *she herself* had started, and you better bet he would remind her of that fact, much more forcefully than he had during their argument earlier today, which was not forcefully enough, not at all…*anyway,* if there was to be the least possibility of making her see the light, it would only come when she'd calmed down enough to drop her defensiveness and listen to reason.

Which meant playing nice. Hence the grumble, hence the grouse.

Back downstairs in the living room, he grabbed a thick woven throw blanket from the chair beside the TV, collected the pillows from every seat, and did his best to construct a comfy catafalque on the sofa for the evening.

Within minutes, he determined that his first attempt had fallen short of the goal; sharp pain in the neck, dull pain across his upper back, a fiery little chomp at the base of his spine. It was intolerable, so Harlow rose, rearranged the pillows a bit, and moved the goalposts to *tolerable.* Again, his construction couldn't meet the bare minimum. New pains in the same places.

There followed two more attempts to make a bed and lay in it, each meeting with failure. Aches, pains, the little agonies of getting older. Man, it really snuck up on ya, huh? There'd been that two-year stretch in his late teens he'd spent sleeping on the couch of one buddy or another. Nary an orthopedic complaint. Hard to believe this was the same body.

Harlow tossed, turned, then opened his eyes and stared at the ceiling. The windows down here didn't have blinds, so he could see the whole room clearly in the royal velvet of moonlight. He considered turning on the TV to take his mind off of…well, he'd have been happy to have it take his mind off of him entirely, like a pickpocket. No doubt there were some stern academics who would have insisted that this was *precisely* what that damned television did, but they were wrong. Harlow knew from experience. Fill the mind's bilge tanks with enough poison, and even the good old television will want nothing to do with it.

Still…sleep wasn't going to come. So Harlow swung himself up to a seat, then rose from the sofa and padded into the kitchen. Grabbed a glass from the cabinet (half-knocking it over in the process; there were fewer windows to illuminate the kitchen), and filled it with tap water from the sink. No doubt he'd come to regret this when he awoke in a few hours needing to piss. Another tally for the *getting older* column. But hey, if he did, that'd mean he'd gotten to sleep in the first pl-

Hrlw. A dish towel tucked into the handle of a drawer beside the sink slid free and fell to the floor.

Speaking his name in the process.

Harlow froze, staring at the towel on the floor, water glass halfway to his face, tilted far enough to splash a bit of water onto his toes. The water said nothing as it fell.

Slowly, he peeled his eyes from the towel on the floor, scanning as much of the house beyond the kitchen as he could make out in the gloom. No titans of stone, that he could see.

Which meant nothing, of course. Save describing one of the many, many things he couldn't see at present. Also in that category: Mount Rushmore, and Jupiter, and the Taj Mahal. Harlow was unable to see most of the things that existed. Okay. Good to have that clarified.

Yet he was sure Uisch was here. It was just like the other night, when he had been so sure Uisch had woken him, was speaking to him, yet he couldn't understand, he'd been so *close* to understanding…

Harlow put down his water glass, bent down, and picked up the towel. He threaded it back through the loop of the handle.

"Are you there?" he whispered.

RID OF RED

The drawer slid out.
Silverware rattled.
And this time, he understood.

FOURTEEN

BYGONES BEGONE

RID OF RED

KIRA AWOKE TO FIND HARLOW MISSING. She glanced at the clock – 5:33 AM – then reached out and rested her palm on the mattress where his body should have been.

Cold. Flat. No depressions, at least none that the memory foam could recall.

She grunted herself into a mermaid pose, torso teetering on her arms as she took in the room. Slashes of blue dawn highlighted a space precisely as Kira had left it yesterday. No piles of clothes on the floor, no closet or bathroom doors swung wide. No sign that Harlow had been in here at all.

She rolled herself off of the bed, then turned around and made it. Pulling the sheets taut, tucking them in, then yanking out the wrinkles in the comforter. Hardly the most pressing task of the day, but habits were hard things to break. And every day since time out of memory, when

Kira woke up, she made her bed. So that was what she did, and that was why she did it.

It occurred to her, in the making of the bed, that she actually couldn't remember the last time she'd done this. Probably the day Leigh had been killed. Yes, why not say it had been then. There was no way to disconfirm that, at this distance.

She savored the clarity of this whole process. Making the bed, reimagining her past. Thrilled to its purity. And then released it, for there would be no more of that today, she feared.

Out the door and into the hall she went, then down the stairs. She called "Harlow?" just as she touched down on the ground floor. No response then, nor when she said it again in the kitchen.

This was all fine. Him not being here did not necessarily imply anything beyond his being elsewhere. It did not, for example, mean that he was off to go do something he could never take back. Kira had convinced him that he couldn't. That *she* would have to be the one, to finish the job, as it were.

Having no idea if either of those things were true, of course. Her being the one, Harlow being convinced.

Kira considered playing it cool. Making a pot of coffee, maybe even fixing breakfast, waiting for Harlow to simply reappear. She considered this, and ultimately released it, along with clarity and purity. Today did not seem like a day to play it cool.

"Harlow?!" she shouted as she stomped into the living room. Here, too, was a space that was perfectly itself.

Nothing out of place. The remotes, the pillows, the blankets, everything was as Kira remembered them being yesterday.

"HARLOW!" she demanded of nearly every room in the house, as she made an increasingly frenzied tour of the space. The mud room? Nothing. The office? Nada. The downstairs bathroom? Niente. The basement? Nichts.

Eventually, there was only one room left for Kira to check. One outside of which she now stood, staring at the doorknob. The more things changed, huh?

"Harlow," she growled at the door to Leigh's bedroom.

The door did not answer.

She reached out and touched the knob. Turned it. Opened the door. Didn't step through, but pushed it hard enough to get a look inside.

Leigh's room, too, was as Kira had last left it. An absolute shambles, in other words. Wh-

She blinked, then stepped across the threshold, treading lightly through the dust-sprinkled wreckage.

Just a few feet in front of her, flush against the wall across from the window, reposed a pile of stakes and splinters that had once been Leigh's bedframe. In the center of which lay her mattress. Flat on the floor. Which couldn't be possible, surely. At least *some* of the bedframe would have been pinned by the mattress, as the former collapsed in service of a hateful vow. Oh, no, sorry – an *exchange*.

Kira knew who had lifted the mattress and kicked

aside that wreckage beneath it, of course. She could still see his indentation in it. Kneeling down and placing her hand where her husband had slept…she felt his warmth. Even still.

Revulsion, here and then gone. To sleep in your dead daughter's bed, for even just one night…it was obscene.

Speaking of here and gone: Harlow couldn't have left long ago. So said that body heat Kira could still feel on the foam.

But it was a Sunday. No work. Day of rest. So where had he gone? And *why?*

A drowning feeling flooded up from her feet. Waters, rising. Hot salt water, rolling in to drown her. Glug glug, motherfucker.

No. She was letting her panic do her thinking for her. Harlow wouldn't go after Zoe yet. Wouldn't risk killing her without knowing whether or not Uisch would honor that as a contract fulfilled. So take a breath. Take a breath, and believe it. Don't do anything stupid.

She left Leigh's room, closing the door behind her.

Kira called Harlow while her oatmeal was in the microwave. He didn't pick up, and the call went to voicemail. Kira didn't leave one. Then the microwave beeped, and it was time to eat.

She opened the silverware drawer to take out a spoon. And froze.

The drawer was a mess. You'd think the little plastic tray they'd bought to organize the cutlery was just for show. Inverted forks in with the knives, the potato peeler in the spoon trench, a few of the smaller serving utensils floating free on the bottom of the drawer beside the tray with the can opener. Anarchy.

As though the drawer had been shaken. Furiously, by something hungry for syllables.

Kira glanced around the rest of the kitchen. Checked a few other cabinets. Had Uisch been here again? Used the kitchen to speak to Harlow? She saw no further evidence of concord through chaos. But then, Harlow could have cleaned the rest up. He could have just forgotten to tidy up this one drawer here. Out of sight, out of mind.

She took a deep breath, and reminded herself not to jump to conclusions. Sure-fire way to do something stupid, that was. Instead, she sat down to endure her now-cold oatmeal.

Fine by her. She wasn't hungry. She just mushed her breakfast around her bowl with her spoon, ultimately forcing herself to choke down a few bites, washed away with water. She didn't waste time making coffee. Her heart was already pounding. Add any caffeine to the mix, and her spinal column was liable to pop out the top of her head like a bottle rocket.

It was somewhere in this period that the idea occurred to her. Probably came to her from staring at the space in the living room where they'd spoken to Detective Dresselhaus, the first time. Where Harlow had shown his entire ass, in an attempt to expose Kira's. It struck her as the best approach to frustrating Harlow's aims, this idea of hers, by virtue of being the only approach she'd thought of thus far. It wasn't a very good idea. But it was something.

Assuming it became necessary. Assuming she believed that Harlow really was off to hurt Zoe. Which she was slowly, unintentionally convincing herself he was. With every second that passed, her own inaction disturbed her more. Which could only mean one thing. Theoretically.

She tried calling him again while she got dressed. Sensible clothes today. *Functional.* A long-sleeve shirt and jeans. The call went to voicemail just as she was slipping on a belt.

Should she be worried about him? As in, *for* him? Were it not for their argument yesterday, she'd have been worried about him. It was still possible that concern was the rational response to his absence. Maybe he'd just gone out to clear his head and gotten hit by a…

Moving quicker than she had all morning, Kira leapt down the stairs, dashed to the *actual* last room she hadn't checked yet.

Harlow's car was still in the garage. Wherever he'd gone, he'd gone on foot.

To make it harder to find him? Possible. Certainly possible.

One last try: Kira took out her phone and called Harlow again.

Vrrr-vrrr. Vibration from the table where the landline lived.

Kira stepped to it slowly, continuing her approach even after seeing precisely what she knew she would: Harlow's phone. Here. With his car. But not his person.

All at once, she remembered seeing something on a cop show about how people's whereabouts at any given

558

time could be sussed out using their phone. Something about cell towers. Whether or not that was true, she was fairly certain she'd watched that show with Harlow.

I wish I'd remembered about the cell towers, came a pathetic little thought.

"Fuck," Kira told the phone. Whatever Harlow was up to, whatever he had planned…well, he hadn't set off on foot without his phone to ensure an uninterrupted spree of kind acts.

So she'd have to go with the only idea she'd had. The not very good one.

Which meant passing over a point of no return. For the both of them.

Not her fault. His fault. He had done this, by leaving the house without his phone.

Before she set out, though, Kira had another idea that she granted herself was half decent: she changed the disarm code on their home security system. It took Googling the instructions, but wasn't hard once she got those up. She changed it to 3418. Completely arbitrary numbers. They didn't matter. What mattered was that Harlow didn't know the new code. So whenever he came home, the alarm would go off, and keep going off, until the security company called the number they had on file to ask for the verbal disarm code.

The number they had on file being for Kira's cell, of course.

It wasn't the same as knowing where he'd gone…but it'd be good to know when he came back.

That done, Kira engaged the delayed arming option

for the system, shut the panel of the console, and left before the beeping countdown hit *zero*.

SHE BARRELED THROUGH INTERSECTIONS, took turns at speed, and still stopped at stop signs because old habits died hard, oh yes they did, which was one thing they had over humans.

As she drove, she kept her head on a swivel. Looking for her husband, as though he'd be strolling merrily along on the sidewalk. Not likely – Harlow was clearly at least putting some thought and effort into his disappearance – but it made her feel good to be *doing something* in each moment, however vain those little somethings were.

Now and again, she snapped her eyes up to the rear-view mirror. Again, old habits. Safety first.

Had she not been in such a paranoid lather, she might well have missed the fact that someone was following her.

It was a dumpy, anonymous car, driven by someone Kira couldn't identify through the rearview. They were doing well to keep nearly three blocks' worth of distance between Kira and themselves. Not hard to tail someone through Neirmouth, given how little traffic there was. Unfortunately for them, it was easy enough to spot a tail for the same reason.

After a few more turns, trying to work out just who it was behind her, the chase car got close enough for a positive ID.

Kira laughed out loud. Couldn't help it.

Detective Dresselhaus. Just who she was about to

drive all the way to Pitney to go see!

She pulled off onto the dirt shoulder of the long road to Graham's Landing, parked beneath an autumnal inferno of trees at long last ready to dump their leaves (how unusual, that these boughs had held on to their modesty for so long – Kira shook off the unnerving sensation that they'd been waiting for her) and got out of the car.

Dresselhaus nosed in right behind her. Joined her on the shoulder. Out in the open air.

"I need to talk to you," Kira called, stomping towards Dresselhaus. One footfall occasioning a *crunch,* the next a *squish.* All the leaves still falling around them died different deaths, it seemed.

"Okay," the detective said, as though this were all standard procedure. "Talk."

Once they were within handshake distance, Kira paused. "Why were you following me?"

"What do you want to talk about, Mrs. Trecothik?"

"…okay. Fine. I…" Kira opened her mouth to speak. Her tongue was sandpaper. Boy, what she wouldn't do for a glass of water right now.

Only no, don't think like that. There had to be *plenty* of things she wouldn't do for a glass of water.

She licked her lips. This accomplished little beyond making her lips dry too. The category of things she wouldn't do for a glass of water shrank.

Okay. God, she had imagined she'd have the whole drive to Pitney to work out how to start this conversation. How to conduct it towards the desired conclusion. But…well, she didn't. No sense dwelling on how things *could* have gone. Meet them as they are.

"You ambushed my husband at Hannaford," Kira opened. "Why did you do that?"

Dresselhaus visibly deflated. "Is that what this is about?"

"Not entirely. I just want to know why you did that."

"I had a question for him."

"Shouldn't you have called him in, or whatever? I've never heard of cops ambushing people in the grocery store."

"I was buying groceries," the detective bluffed. "I had wanted to speak with him, and just happened to see… don't make that face."

Kira only then realized that she was, indeed, making a face, and one that could be fairly described as *that*.

"It was just a coincidence. A funny coincidence."

Kira made *that face* again. "Please be honest with me. Please. It's important."

The detective studied Kira for a long, silent moment. Then she crossed her arms and gazed up at the kaleidoscope overhead. "Alright," she finally admitted, widening her stance slightly, once more looking to Kira. "There were…I'm gonna have to be kind of broad here, but *details* were brought to my attention that made me feel as though I ough-"

"Details were *brought to your attention*."

"Yes."

"By whom?"

"I'm not at liberty to say."

"Okay. What details were they?"

Dresselhaus's expression fell. "Excuse me, ma'am, but I'm not the one being interrogated here."

From above: a flash of red. "I'd say the one being interrogated is whoever answers more than they ask."

A vein on Dresselhaus' forehead inflated.

Kira blanched. "Sorry. I'm sorry. I really do want to tell you something. I just…I just *react* sometimes."

Dresselhaus paused, then shrugged agreeably. A magnanimous de-escalation. "What do you want to tell me?"

Kira sighed. Glanced down the long, lonely road behind the detective. Tried to stop her mind from making any associations. "I just…um…" She returned her attention to Dresselhaus. "You asked my husband about seeing my daughter after she died."

Dresselhaus said nothing.

"Ah…and I believe you saw her too. Yourself, through the window."

"Lot of believing there," Dresselhaus noted, tilting her head slightly. "Have *you* seen her?"

Kira closed her eyes and cut the truth. "No," she said. "But I…after my husband joked when you came to our house the first time, when he said what he said about how I…well, I *thought* he'd been joking. Making a horrible joke. But, so, then I starting talking to him, and poking around the house…"

She sighed and took a final moment to consider what she was about to say. It'd have been hard to walk back the ground she'd already covered here, but it was still possible. Whereas the upcoming clause was a Rubicon.

Yet there was nowhere else to go. Not really.

So she finished her thought: "…and I'm scared that he might not have been joking, entirely."

Dresselhaus' eyes ran laps up and down the road before finally reaffixing themselves to Kira's. "Is this a confession?"

"No, I w-"

"Because his *little joke* was to name you as the murderer of Nicole Ligeti."

"That's why I'm saying *entirely*," Kira replied. "It was so ridiculous to say that I was involved, I think he did that to throw us off." She laid that *us* on as thickly as she could without being obvious. "Like, if he'd just said that *he* did it, maybe I'd believe it because he's been acting so strangely lately. Erratic. Or it'd at least get me thinking, the way I am now. Would have gotten me talking to you sooner, I should say. But by saying that *I* did it, he w-"

"I just want to be *abundantly* clear, you're talking about the murders of Nicole Ligeti and Madeleine Encomb, right? When you say *it?"*

"That's right."

The detective removed her phone from her pocket and fiddled with the screen. She held it out towards Kira with the Voice Recorder app open and running. "Do you mind if I record this?" she asked.

"Um…" That was a curveball headed straight for Kira's nose, but not one she could dodge with any modicum of grace. Should have seen it coming. Alas. "Sure."

Dresselhaus nodded and leaned forward again. "Sorry, if you could start from the top. For the record."

"Yes, of course, I'll start again from the top." Kira

leaned towards the phone, and the unblinking red orb on its screen. It took her by surprise. "So yesterday, after Detective Dresselhaus harassed my husband at the grocery store regarding my daughter's ghost, wh-"

Dresselhaus shook her head, fixing Kira with a truly gratifying *the fuck are you doing* face. "Uh-uh. That's not the top." She leaned in to the phone and assured it more directly that "that's not the top." Leaning back, she frowned at Kira and jutted her jaw out to the right. Her left, technically. Not technically. Her left, full stop.

"Sorry," Kira said, meaning it. "It's just reflex."

"Start at the point where you suspected your husband's mock-confession, which," she clarified for posterity, "can be found detailed at length in my summary report from August twelfth." A permissive wave signaled that it was Kira's turn. "Start at the point where you suspected."

Kira took a deep breath. "W-"

"Sorry, sorry." To her credit, Detective Dresselhaus *did* look sorry. "Could you state your name for the record?"

Biting her lizardscale tongue to keep it from running, Kira fumed at the phone and said "Kira Trecothik."

"And Mrs. Trecothik, you are here speaking to me of your own free will, correct?"

"I am."

"Okay. From the actual top, please."

"Sure." Kira took a deep breath. "I…have reason to believe that my husband is behind the murder of those two girls."

"Nicole Ligeti and Madeleine Encomb."

"Yes. That's right."

"…both?"

"Yes."

"And you believe this why?"

"Well, like I mentioned before you were recording, he made a weird joke to you."

"Which was?"

"The first time you came to visit, he told you that *I* had murdered Nicole. Only, it s-"

"Ligeti. Nicole Ligeti."

"Right. And it sort of made me start thinking that, maybe it wasn't a joke. Entirely." And so Kira spun a yarn that, while nowhere near the whole truth, had at least been unraveled from it. Oh, sure, there were a few synthetic threads knit into the tapestry, primarily ones which exculpated Kira as best she could manage. But in the end, there remained what Kira thought was a believable number of plot holes and shaggy bits. No good trying to stitch things up *too* tightly – the less wriggle room she left herself, the more likely a tear in the near future.

The punchline of all this: Kira presented what she thought to be a plausible, albeit almost entirely circumstantial, case for Harlow's guilt in both murders. She mentioned details of both cases she didn't believe were public knowledge, attributing *her* knowledge of them to Harlow's boasting. For yes, in this telling, he was something of a braggart, a vain monster of a man who had been bottled up in his unassuming human form for far too long, finally loosed upon Neirmouth. God, every white lie she told, every new adjective she piled on, it all cost her. Even now, she couldn't quite reconcile these dishonest means with the virtuous end. But this was the only way she could think of, to stop Harlow, to protect Zoe. To save her life.

The more guilty she felt, the more she tried to convince herself that the Harlow she described to the detective was the one she had married, lived with, loved for all these years. Mixed results, which she put down to being painfully aware of the effort.

But hey. She could work through her disgrace later. What mattered now was that Dresselhaus believe her; on that score, Kira was optimistic. The detective had only met Harlow once…er, twice. And nothing Kira said contradicted those glimpses of the man that the detective had gotten. As far as Kira knew, anyway.

All in all, it was a terrific performance, if she said so herself. Which she did, mentally allowing for an applause break here, a standing ovation there. Yes, she was doing terrifically well, right up until the end.

"Thank you," Detective Dresselhaus said. Not sounding the least bit surprised about any of what Kira had just said. *That* was concerning.

"You're welcome," Kira replied, not knowing what else to say.

"So, Mrs. Trecothik, do you have any idea why on Earth your husband would be murdering the girls your daughter gave her life to save?"

Just as Kira was about to give the only answer she

could, *no, of course not*…she felt the words catch on a most uncanny sensation. Something about the way Dresselhaus had asked that question, the angle of her head, the rollercoaster of her tone…it was as though she knew. Knew about Uisch. Knew about its offer. Knew something, somehow.

She's figured it out, Kira realized with a start. All it took was one glimpse of Leigh through the bay window, and the detective had put it together. Gleaned the shape of it, at least.

To Kira, that shape was a lever. Something she could pull.

"I don't know," she said, shrugging theatrically, wincing at how unconvincing she sounded. "Um. I just feel like…he's been very…lately, he's been very…I don't want to sound crazy."

Ah, what luck: this was clearly what Dresselhaus had been waiting to hear. For the first time in the entire conversation, the detective looked truly *open* to what Kira was saying, ready and willing to suspend her disbelief. "What do you mean by that?"

Kira played for time by frowning down at the phone in the detective's hand, still recording.

Without breaking eye contact, Dresselhaus paused the recording. Good aim with the thumb there. "I won't think you're crazy. I promise you, whatever you tell me, I won't think you're crazy."

Kira tapped her natural anxiety about being honest, let that inform her performance. Running both hands through her hair, she turned away from the detective for a moment, then turned back. "Did you see Leigh through the window?"

"I believe I did," Dresselhaus responded at once. Stepping out on the tightrope. "Am I right? You tell me if I'm nuts or not."

Wincing at the word *nuts,* Kira took a long, deep breath, then practically whispered, "you're not."

The release Dresselhaus must have felt in that moment was practically audible, the slow crash of a great wave upon a breakwater. Her posture softened, eyes brightened. A smile trembled across her face, like a flame at the very end of the wick. "So *what the fuck is going on?*"

"Something evil."

"Where is Leigh now?"

"I don't know," Kira responded, hoping the sudden honesty in her response didn't put paid to all the little lies she'd told. "My husband…I don't know exactly, but somehow…" Kira shook her head. Considered describing Uisch, but that would have been a waste of time.

Now that she had Dresselhaus on her side, every moment not spent tracking down Harlow was a waste of time.

So she cut to the chase: "he's doing evil things, and we need to go arrest him. Right now."

The detective's face changed yet again. The pinching of the lips, the wrinkling of her undereye bags. She'd retreated once more into wariness. The fuck?

Kira wondered if she wasn't the only one pulling on levers here.

"No," Dresselhaus replied, really wringing every drop

of skepticism out of the word. "I can't just arrest your husband. We need a lot more than ju-"

"He's dangerous," Kira pressed, despite herself. Glancing down, she noticed that the detective had restarted the recording. When had she done that? "He said, uh…" she quieted an objection lodged by one of the more sentimental bits of her brain. "…he wants to hurt me."

The detective sighed. Not, perhaps, the response Kira had hoped for. "Has he hurt you before?"

"…no." That wasn't something she could bring herself to lie about.

"Yet you feel he poses a credible threat to you now?"

"I don't know. Theoretically, sure. He's stronger than he looks."

Now it was Dresselhaus who was making *that face*.

"You have to lock him up," Kira ordered. "You have to. As soon as possible, you've gotta…even if it's just temporary, until you can find something that sticks. You've gotta lock him up."

"…as soon as possible."

Kira cleared her throat. "Yeah."

"Is there something else you want to tell me?"

"Um…yes, actually." Kira scratched her nose. Even as she said the words, she regretted them: "He told me he was going to kill Zoe Cottrell today." Was it her imagination, or had that red circle on the detective's phone gotten bigger and brighter, started emitting a shrill whistle as it swelled to devour the impossible silence around them?

"Well," Dresselhaus finally said, pausing the recording once again, "off the record, Mrs. Trecothik, maybe you should have fucking started with that."

DRESSELHAUS MADE KIRA ride in the backseat, which she didn't appreciate. She'd wanted to follow in her own car, but the detective had insisted, in a way that felt unwise to gainsay. So Kira left her car where it was, and climbed into the backseat. Like a child. It felt a bit less humiliating when she imagined the detective to be her chauffeur, ferrying her about town. It wasn't *entirely* inaccurate – Dresselhaus had, by all outward appearances, bought Kira's story enough to do her bidding, calling Pitney to send a few more units up to Neirmouth. She didn't mention Harlow by name in so doing, but referred only to a suspect who was "potentially armed and dangerous," which unnerved Kira, even through the red. She didn't want her husband killed. There was no need for it. All the same, she couldn't well dispute that description.

This being a weekend, there was nowhere Zoe was *supposed* to be, nowhere they could easily find her. Dresselhaus placed a call to Zoe's parents asking after their daughter's whereabouts; the elder Cottrells had started panicking immediately. Kira had wondered from the backseat (Dresselhaus didn't have the call on speaker, but her phone was nonetheless loud enough for the other end of the call to reach Kira) why outright panic had been their first response…but then realized the only answer that made sense.

They absolutely had to have been aware that Zoe was the final part of a trio that was two-thirds gone. In which case, it struck Kira as breathtakingly irresponsible that they had ever let the girl out of their sight.

But on the other hand…what was the alternative? Zoe would have to leave the house eventually, if not for school than for something else. That's what you raise children to do, after all. Leave.

"Can you call Zoe directly?" Kira asked Dresselhaus after the latter hung up with the Cottrells.

The detective looked up to the rearview mirror. "Do you have her number?"

"…I don't, no."

"You don't know?"

"No, I don't, *no*. I don't, *comma,* n-"

"Ah."

"N-O."

"I'm with ya." The detective thought about that. "You don't have it in your phone, even?"

"I think I have it written down somewhere at home. But I…never put it in my phone."

"…wasn't Zoe basically your daughter's best friend, or something?"

Kira shrugged aggressively. "It's never been an issue before."

"Hm."

There was an accusation in that little harrumph. "Do you have kids?" Kira snapped.

"No. Never wanted 'em. Too much hassle." The detective darted her eyes up to the rearview.

Kira could see the faintest glimmer of shameful realization in those eyes. Good. She considered twisting the knife a bit – *yes detective, such a hassle to have your heart ripped out of you* – but let the look suffice.

"Anyway." Dresselhaus grunted. She made another call on the radio mounted to her dash. This one had a bit more police jargon in it, letters and numbers and whatnot. But at the end of it, Dresselhaus looked back into the rearview mirror and asked "do you know how to get to the Cottrell house from here?"

That, Kira did know. With a *k*.

"HI," Zoe's mom said in a daze when she opened the door, because she was still home.

"We need to find Zoe," Kira couldn't stop herself from announcing. She added, "hi."

Mrs. Cottrell took a staggering step backwards. What was her first name? Kira was drawing a blank. For as close as Leigh and Zoe had been, Kira hadn't ever had much interaction with Zoe's mo…oh, Sherri! That was it.

Anyway, Sherri took that staggering step back into her house, lifted a pointing finger towards Kira, and shouted "she's here!"

Kira and Detective Dresselhaus exchanged looks, then turned back to Sherri. "What?"

"HELP!" Sherri screamed. Stumbling over her feet and falling backwards onto the floor.

From behind her, the rumble of heavy shoes approaching at a clip.

Instinct sent Kira into her own clumsy retreat.

Detective Dresselhaus reached into the pocket of her

jacket, and pulled out a billfold wallet. Officious in the face of danger. Great.

From behind Sherri, three uniformed police officers emerged, hands on the holsters of their firearms.

"Down on the ground!" the big one in front shouted.

"Detective," a smaller one behind hollered, "get away from the suspect!"

"I'm not the suspect!" Kira shouted.

"HANDS ON YOUR HEAD!" the third one shrieked.

How disappointingly demure Kira's reflex turned out to be: her hands *flew* to her head, of their own accord.

"Help me please!" she implored Dresselhaus.

"Okay, okay." Dresselhaus lifted her palms and flapped them towards the ground. The universal sign for *let's dial it down a bit*. "She's with me. So let's all take a breath."

The biggest cop tapped the smaller one on the back, prompting the little guy to rush forward towards Kira.

"She said take a breath!" Kira whimpered, hands still planted on her head.

The detective reached out and caught the smaller cop by the arm as he tried to rush past her. "Hey. Buddy. Cool it."

"Let go of the officer, detective," the big one boomed.

Dresselhaus did as requested. "You wanna bring me up to speed, then?"

The smaller officer stepped behind Kira, grabbed her wrists, and forced her hands down behind her back. "Ow!" Kira screeched. She added "HEY!" when she heard – and *felt* – the handcuffs going on.

574

Detective Dresselhaus seemed thoroughly unruffled by this. She simply stared at the officer cuffing Kira as does a resigned babysitter, upon discovering that their charge has, once again, shit themselves.

"Put her in the car," the big officer ordered.

"I DIDN'T DO ANYTHING!" Kira shrieked.

"Ask her where my girl is!" Sherri roared from behind the cops, arms folded against the cold. "ASK HER!"

"Okay, *stop.*" Dresselhaus commanded, her voice low and sturdy.

For a wonder, everyone did.

In the relative calm, Kira noted the identification on one of the officer's shoulder patches. These guys were from Pitney. But Dresselhaus had only just put in the call for them to come up…

The guys had already been here. The detective had been playing Kira. Come to think of it, when she'd 'called Pitney for backup' in the car, Dresselhaus hadn't given them an address. That had been a code, to get ready. Gah, so stupid to not put that together sooner!

But that look of credulity, that crash of relief she'd seen on the road…

God, she was getting dizzy. Whatever was happening, it was all out of her control. Already.

"We're here because we're *looking* for your daughter," the detective explained to the Cottrells. "You know that."

Sherri pointed to Kira. "She's lying to you! She wants to kill her!"

"No," Kira countered, "I fucking *don't!*"

"Yes you *do!*"

"NO, I DON'T!"

"Her husband *said* she would do this!"

"My hus…he was *here?!*"

"He came looking for her too! And to *warn us* about you!"

"About *me?!* He's the one wh-"

"Alright," Dresselhaus cut in. "Let's dial it d-"

"Harlow is the suspect!" Kira shrieked, jerking as she felt the small cop slap a hand on her shoulder. "I'm not the susp-"

"Put her in the car," the big one repeated.

The little one dropped his hand to grab Kira by the tricep.

Kira snapped her torso to the right – which ended up hurting her back a *hell* of a lot, she really wasn't flexible enough to have her hands cranked behind her like this – and stepped towards Dresselhaus. "I'm not the suspect! Tell them!"

"Things have changed," the detective explained patiently to the officers. "It's *Harlow* Trecothik I'm most worried about now."

Kira stomped her foot. "See?!" Belatedly, she noted the implication of what Dresselhaus had said. Specifically that word, *changed.* "Wait, what?"

"Officer McCall," the big one thundered.

Kira felt hands return once more to her upper arms.

"No! I'm not the fucking sus-"

"It's precautionary," Dresselhaus interrupted her. "Cool off, and let us sort this out."

Kira boggled at the detective for as long as she could, before Officer McCall pulled her away, leading her off the porch, down the yard, around the corner…and towards two patrol cars parked on the curb which she'd managed to not see on the way in. Another sign that Kira wasn't paying attention. Jesus, what *else* was she missing?

"I'm not the suspect," she mumbled.

Officer McCall said nothing. Simply reached out, opened the back door, and stuffed Kira inside, warning her to "watch your head" as he did.

"Don't push me," she couldn't stop herself from snapping.

McCall slammed the door shut, then turned and sauntered back up towards the house.

Kira twisted around to get her knees up on the leather seat, maneuvering her hands to feel about for a handle inside. Nothing. Just smooth plastic. Figured.

She glanced around the cop car. Her first time in one of these. The front seat, on the far side of this metal mesh grating, was a veritable Circuit City's worth of Cold War-era electronics. A big clunky monitor sat on what appeared to be an entire Dell desktop. Next to it, a walkie-talkie – one of those small square ones that truckers used – mumbled numbers and letters to itself in a variety of different voices.

Here in the backseat, there wasn't nothin' but nothin'.

Kira wriggled her legs back out from under her and stared back towards the Cottrell house.

Sherri had fully stepped out onto the porch now, having unfolded her arms to wave them furiously at

Detective Dresselhaus. The officers were perfectly positioned and posed, like supermodels on the cover of *Deli Meat Monthly*. Hands on their belts, hips popped to one side or the other, listening intently to Sherri's fulminations. Then, as one, they turned to Dresselhaus. Kira couldn't hear what was being said, of course. She couldn't hear anything beyond the beeping and murmuring from the walkie-talkie up front, or the crinkling of the leather bench beneath her.

She scooted herself towards the window to rest her head against it.

Drnntwrr, the leather creaked.

In a way that sounded a lot like *do not worry*.

Kira froze. Cranked her head around, glancing out every window she could. Struggling to get her legs under her once more, she peered out the barred-up rear windshield.

She spotted Uisch halfway down the street, doing a poor job of concealing itself behind a tree.

Slowly, it lifted an arm and waved at her.

Kira only became aware of just how wide open her mouth was when her lower gums started getting cold. She glanced back towards the Cottrell house, to the unnervingly sedate discussion happening up on the porch. Gone were the gesticulations; everyone was pretty well locked-in now.

Kira glanced back out the rear windshield.

Uisch was gone. Obviously. Kira didn't know why she'd even bothered to look a second time.

"The fuck are you doing here?" she asked to the

578

empty space where Uisch had been.

Receiving no answer, she turned back to the house in time to see Officer McCall, his large colleague, and Detective Dresselhaus all traipsing down the slight hill towards the car.

Kira heaved her feet back into the well of the seat. Studied the faces coming her way, doing her best to read their expressions. She was pretty certain those weren't *here we come to release you* faces.

Detective Dresselhaus took the last few steps at a jog, so she was first to the car. She opened the door (unlocked from the outside, it seemed), and then stood in its place. Blocking Kira from getting out.

"Excuse me," Kira said, scooting towards the door, gesturing to the world past Dresselhaus with a nod of the head.

"I want to explain what's going to happen," Dresselhaus informed her, with a calm, level tone. "You're not in trouble, alright? I want make that clear."

The top of Kira's field of vision collapsed. Surely the hardest scowl she'd ever pulled.

Dresselhaus didn't fail to notice. She sighed, rested an arm across the top of the open door, and spun her hand lazily from the wrist. "We've determined the best course of action *for everyone* is that you are taken into a kind of protective custody, until we can sort th-"

"Fuck no."

"I can't be your chaperone."

"I don't need a fucking chaperone."

"Okay. Let me rephrase." She pinched the fingers of

the hand hanging from the door. "You can *only* fuck this up. There's *nothing* that you can contribute here."

"I don't think *that's* true, but whatever, I'll g-"

"Trust me. It's true."

"Fine. Whatever. Then I'll go home."

The big cop leaned down to get a clear view of Kira from over Dresselhaus's shoulder. "That's not an op-"

Dresselhaus took her hand from off the door, then turned and waved a softly-extended pointer finger at the cop.

The big cop grunted, and backed away.

The detective put her hand back on the top of the open door. "I'll reiterate. This, uh, protective custody is the best course of short-term action…*for everyone.*"

Kira glanced from Dresselhaus to the cops behind her, back to Dresselhaus. "I'm not the suspect!"

"We just want to figure out what's going on."

"I…I thought you were on my side!"

Dresselhaus's expression softened into one of genuine confusion. "Why?" she asked.

Kira took a moment to process that, scanning the various arms of authority arrayed outside the vehicle. There was no winning here, she determined that quickly enough. There were only various degrees of losing.

She pinched her eyes shut, then opened them and asked "can they at least take the cuffs off? I'm not very flexible, they really hurt."

Dresselhaus considered that. For several seconds. Finally, looking quite displeased with herself, she rose to standing and summoned Officer McCall with a single crooked finger.

McCall sighed at the demeaning gesture, but did as bidden. He pulled a key off of his belt and half-crawled into the car.

Kira turned her back towards him and tilted forwards. "Ay," she grunted as McCall tried to lift her hands for easier access. "Careful."

"Sorry." McCall crawled further into the car, planting a knee on the bench beside Kira to get the key in the lock. Eventually, he got it, saying "sorry" once more as he undid the cuffs and took them with as he backed out of the car.

Dresselhaus was quick to reinsert herself into the open door. "This is really just a formality," she insisted. "We want to keep everybody safe, until we understand what's happening."

"Zoe isn't safe until we find Harlow."

"Until *we* find Harlow," Dresselhaus said, gesturing to the officers around her. "Yes. And we will. Don't worry." With that, she slammed the door shut, and thumped the roof of the car twice. *Thump thump.*

Kira stared at everyone's torsos as the law had a conversation just outside the car. She couldn't make out what they were saying. But they seemed tense.

Then they all broke formation, Dresselhaus and the big cop heading back to the house, McCall circling around the back of the car, to the driverside door. He opened it, got behind the wheel, and closed it. "I don't wanna talk," he said at once, "okay?"

Kira leaned forward, threading her fingers through

the grating between the front and back of the car. It only occurred to her now, as McCall threw the cruiser into drive and nosed it away from the curb, to ask "can I sit in the front seat, actually?"

"I'm sorry, but no."

"What happened there? My husband showed up here earlier?"

"I said I don't wanna talk."

"I just want to understand. Was Zoe there when he showed up? Did they call the you guys after he left, or were they…when did you get there? Tell me wh-"

"Ma'am…" McCall glanced at the rearview mirror. "Come on."

"This is stupid. I can help you."

"I'm not stupid."

"I didn't say…I said *this* is stupid. The situation."

McCall steered them onto Saffron Street, a long, gentle slope of a road leading down to…whatever the cross street down there was called. Kira couldn't remember just now. "Let's just not talk," the officer suggested, reminding Kira of herself, when she would look in the rearview at a very unhappy young Leigh in her car seat, all but begging her to play the Quiet Game.

Kira sighed and folded her arms. Leaned back against the vocal upholstery. Tried to think. She needed to do something. Whatever the detective did or didn't know, Kira didn't trust her to find Harlow before he did something irreversible. Dresselhaus didn't know him well enough. Didn't know what he was capable of.

Then again, Kira was worried that she didn't either.

She felt the car lurch slightly, as McCall applied the brakes a bit more forcefully than necessary. It wasn't all that steep of a hill.

Rrr, groaned the chassis from under the car.

Nnnnt, the roof of the car added as it puckered gently.

Rhhhhr, the window beside Kira sighed as it warped ever-so-slightly in its frame.

Dur, the brakes concluded with a squeal.

Kira listened very carefully to that. Waiting for the sounds to arrive at meaning. She waited. And waited.

Her phone rang.

She looked down at it.

It was a number she didn't have in her contacts. But her iPhone was smart enough to suggest who it might be.

A security company.

The security company, whose system was meant to protect the Trecothik household.

The alarm at their house had gone off. And since Kira had changed the disarm code…

Harlow couldn't shut the alarm off. Harlow, who was back at their house.

McCall's eyes darted up to the rearview mirror. "I don't think you're allowed to answer that."

"I'm not arrested," Kira reminded him, hands shaking for reasons she couldn't quite explain to herself. "I'm in *sort of protective custody."* She answered the phone.

"Don't answer that."

"I already did."

"Hang it up."

"Shh, I'm on the phone." To the phone, she added,

"hello?"

"Password," was all the voice on the other end of the call said. Brusque, but that was what they paid for. If the alarm system in their home was triggered, and the (correct) passcode not entered into the system within a certain amount of time, the designated number in the account would get a phone call from one of the company's reps, asking for a predetermined verbal password. Saying the password would signal an all-clear. Saying anything *other* than the password would trigger an immediate call to the police. Either way, the rep would say nothing on this call other than "password" at the beginning, and "thank you, goodbye" at the end.

So…did she want the police going to intercept Harlow without her, assuming he hadn't turned right back around and left the house after failing to shut the alarm off?

No, she decided. Harlow in custody sounded mighty dangerous to her. As in, *for* her. He knew way too much, and might well decide to be more fully truthful than she had.

So she said the real password: "Varnish."

And then she wondered what the fuck she'd thought the alternative to the police was. It's not like she was well-positioned to go after him herself.

So she added: "fuck me."

"Thank you," the rep on the other end said, "Goodbye."

Click.

Kira stared very intently at the grating in front of her,

for several long, silent seconds. Seconds during which Harlow had time to accomplish whatever it was he'd returned home to do. Or get. Or hide.

Or anything.

"Varnish, fuck me," Officer McCall repeated thoughtfully.

"Inside joke," Kira grunted. She leaned forward, threading her fingers through the grating between the seats. "Listen, we need to go back to my house. Urgently."

McCall divided his attention between the rearview mirror and the road before him, the mirror, the road. "I can't do that."

"If I'm going to be in protective custody, I need...that doesn't mean I can't pack a bag, right?"

"Until we sort all of this out, we're just gonna go back to the station."

"I'm going to be...*very unhappy,* if we can't go back to my house right now."

Remarkably, that seemed to find *some* purchase with the young officer. He bobbled his head from side to side for a few moments, then tapped an unfortunate store of fortitude. "We can't do that."

Kira leaned even further forward, so that her face was nearly (but not *actually,* yuck) pressed against the grate. "Listen to me. *My husband* is at my house."

"...okay."

Kira waited for McCall to realize what she was saying, to slam on the brakes and crank the gear shift and screech through a one-eighty in a very exciting way.

She kept waiting.

Then she said, "my husband is Harlow Trecothik."

"I know."

"We're looking for him! He's the one we're looking for!"

"I know. But I'm supposed to take you to the station, just until w-"

"What station even? We don't have a station."

"Yes we do."

"No, we don't."

"Yes…oh, right. Well, *Neirmouth* doesn't. But Pitney does."

Kira gawped wordlessly for a moment. "You're taking me to *Pitney?!*"

McCall just shrugged. "Yeah."

"My husband's at my house! Go to my fucking house! You're gonna be so fucked if he does something horrible, and you have the chance to st-"

"Ma'am, *stop talking.*"

Kira felt her eye twitch. No matter what phrases she auditioned in her head, she couldn't imagine any of them getting her any closer to home. *I'm serious, this isn't a joke, this is a matter of life and death.* What would any of those mean to this fresh-faced follower of orders?

But the more pertinent question: what could Harlow be going back home for? Could he be…was he after the shovel? Kira had done her best to exorcise whatever, uh, evidential qualities that thing had, but she was fairly certain somebody with a microscope and an axe to grind could find something on it. That, and maybe the knife. Evidence. He could be going for evidence, to fink on

Kira the way she'd tried to fink on him.

Only…no. He was trying to commit another crime. The *last* thing he'd do would be to tangle himself up with the police.

So what the fuck, Harlow?

McCall steered them into the intersection at the bottom of Saffron, then turned left. Onto the street Kira couldn't remember the fucking name of. And she'd forgotten to check the sign as they turned onto it. Oh well.

She sighed and once more sank into the seat. Looked down at the phone in her hands. This had to be useful, right? Was there a phone call she could make to get out of this? Her lawyer! She'd call her lawyer! Granted, she didn't have one of those. But she did have access to the internet. So she pulled up Google, then searched for "best lawyers Maine." She was just checking out the yelp reviews of the top result when her phone rang again.

This number, she had in her contacts.

Home. The landline.

Harlow.

"Please don't answer it," McCall requested limply.

Kira ignored him. Just stared at the phone. Why was he calling? To taunt her? Try to win her over from a distance? What kind of cut-rate mindfuckery was this?

She answered the call and said "what the fuck are y-"

The scream that came from the phone turned every inch of Kira's skin to gooseflesh. Her body froze, her face flushed. The unbreaking, high-pitched keen was the most horrible, heartwrenching sound she had ever heard.

It was a teenaged girl's voice.

Zoe's voice.

"The hell is that?" McCall asked nervously. So he could hear it from the front seat. And the phone wasn't even on speaker.

Harlow had called to make Kira listen to him killing Zoe. *Torturing* her. He'd fucking cracked. Jesus.

"DON'T!" Kira shrieked into the phone. She didn't know what else to say. What to do.

"What's happening?" McCall demanded.

The low end of the girl's howl was starting to shred, the voice coming apart like a poorly built space shuttle reentering the atmosphere.

Kira *smacked* the grating in front of her. "HARLOW! STOP!"

Slowly, the same way Uisch could stitch a dozen little mishaps into speech, Kira recognized that the unthinkable sound in her ear had a word hidden in it.

That word was *why*.

And that voice, she suddenly realized, wasn't Zoe's.

It was Leigh's.

Kira longed for the days of cold limbs and warm cheeks. Now she couldn't feel anything. Not a goddamned thing.

"What…oh God…" she gripped the phone so tightly that it *cracked*. Or maybe that was just her knuckles. "He did…I wasn't…oh, fuck…"

"WHY AM I BACK AGAIN?!?" Leigh cried through the phone.

"What's going on?" McCall asked from the front seat.

Kira put her hand on the receiver. "Go to my fucking

house," she ordered McCall. "Right now."

"What's going on?!"

"I don't fucking know! Just go!"

"No!"

From the phone: "I TOLD YOU I DIDN'T W-"

Kira flinched. "Listen to me, Leigh! Your father did this! I tried to stop hi-"

Leigh screamed once more, moving beyond language, into the realm of sounds without form, noises which could only mean precisely what they meant.

Then she hung up.

Kira stared at her phone for however long it took for the screen to flick to black. Which wasn't long at all.

Seeing her face reflected in that deep-well darkness was like glimpsing thirty years into the future. She looked so old. That was the face of someone on their deathbed.

God, she needed to get home. Needed to see Leigh. Was so desperate to see her again. Even as she knew that she would be completely incapable of in any way making this hurt go away. If anything, her very presence might only further dismay and enrage her daughter; she was, to a large degree, the cause of the hurt. And there was nothing she could do to change that, she knew. There might never be.

As a parent…how could that be anything other than absolute failure?

In the darkness, Kira saw her face beyond the deathbed.

Then she thumbed the phone on again.

"Go back to my house right now," Kira warned Mc-

Call, only noticing her anguish in the clogged quality of her voice.

He snapped his eyes to the rearview. "Are you talking to me?" The question was sincere.

"Yes." Kira looked up the number for the Pitney Police Station. "This is your last fucking chance."

"…is that a threat?" Again, wholly earnest. Just asking.

"I just need to get to my house." She pressed the number, then lifted the phone to her ear. "I need to get to my fucking house."

"Who are you calling?"

A voice in the phone said "Pitney PD, how may I direct your call?" A real person, not a recording. Proof that Pitney still wasn't a real city.

"Hello," Kira said to them, fighting to sound as casual as she could. "I have an urgent tip for Detective Dresselhaus. She gave me her card and told me to call, but I lost it." She felt herself losing her grip on that even tone. "Um…would you be able to connect me with her?"

"To her personal line?"

From the front seat, McCall said "hey, come on, don't call her."

Kira ignored him. "Whatever number was on the card. I think she said it was her cell? I need to speak with her *urgently.*"

"Uh," the police station operator replied, "Yeah. Sure. I don't have that number available off-hand. Hang…" the woman's voice retreated deeper into the phone line. "Huey! Do you have that detective's number?"

"I don't work for her," McCall groused from the front seat. "She can't get me in trouble. She's not even technically…she doesn't work for us. I don't think."

Lucky for Kira, she'd never stopped frowning at McCall. So she didn't need to start doing it again.

"It's for this lady!" came the half-throttle cry on the other end of the phone. "The lady on the phone!"

"I'm just doing my job," McCall whined.

Kira heard the woman on the other end of the line say "hang on, I c-" before what sounded like a pile-up of plastic matchbox cars heralded the arrival of a man's voice, grunting "-st give me the phone." And then, nothing.

Kira shook her head slightly. Wiped the tears from her eyes. "Hello?"

"Yeah ma'am," the gruff newcomer rumbled. "Gonna forward ya to her cellular. In a minute…in… what button to I press?"

A loud *beep*.

"No," Kira heard the first woman say. "This one."

"This one?" the man asked.

"Yeah."

"Okay, here it is. Call forward. Bye now."

The call *clicked* to silence, followed shortly by the cyborg gargle of a ringing phone, as heard from the inside.

"Dresselhaus," the detective answered almost at once.

Kira took a deep breath. It didn't feel real until she said the words out loud. Oh, she tried to savor that final instant of precious unreality. And there it went. Bye now.

"Zoe's dead," she informed Dresselhaus. "Harlow

killed her."

"…he told you this?"

"…yes."

"He killed the girl, and then he called you, and he told you that he killed her."

"Yeah. Basically. But listen, I need to get back to my house. I think…I don't think he's there anymore, but I think he *was* there. My alarm went off, and th-"

"Are you still with Officer McCall?"

"Yeah. He won't take me back. I keep te-"

"Okay. Do me a favor, put the phone on speaker so he can hear me."

Kira pulled the phone away from her face, clicked the circle that set it to speakerphone, and held it up, so it was level with both her head and McCall's.

"Can you hear me, Officer McCall?"

McCall leaned back and to the right slightly. "I can, ma'am. But listen, the only reason I didn't t-"

"You're doing the right thing. Take her to the station and book her."

"WHAT?" Kira screamed, after a speechless interval.

"Accessory," Dresselhaus continued. "We need t-"

Kira hung up the phone. Slapped it face-down onto her thigh. Glared at McCall through the grate.

The officer slumped over himself slightly. Shoulders rolling in, elbows sagging towards his lap. Eyes firmly on the road.

"Let. Me. Out," Kira commanded.

"I can't do that," McCall practically whined, as he turned on to French Street. A slightly quieter little avenue, this was, which would take them to Dunscomb. Then they'd hit ME-116, which you could ride nearly all the way to the interstate.

If she had any hope of getting out of here, it needed to happen before ME-116. Before he opened it up to sixty miles an hour, and set the cruise control.

So call it three minutes of escape time left.

Kira glanced frantically around the interior of the backseat. Looking for some weakness. A crack of daylight, a needle poking out of the upholstery. Something she could turn to her advantage. Something she could use to *get out of this fucking car.*

Nothing. Obviously.

She leaned back, pressing herself into the seat, and did her best to get her foot high enough to kick at the grating. Perhaps a younger Kira might have pulled that off. Alas.

"AH!" she shouted, as hot agony winked in her low back.

"Just stop!" McCall shouted at her, sounding almost as distraught as she was. "It's gonna be fine! If you're innocent, we'll figure it all out. And if you're not, I mean, then…you know, this is also fine."

Kira bunched her right hand into a fist and scooched towards the window behind the driver's seat.

"Don't punch the window," McCall cautioned. "That's gonna h-"

Kira punched the window.

She'd never broken a bone in her life before, so she couldn't say for certain that what she felt in her wrist now was a broken bone. But she could say this much: it hurt *quite* a lot more than most of the other injuries she'd sustained in her life.

"AAAAAAH!" she concluded.

"Jesus Christ! Calm down!"

"Fuck," she tried to add, folding over herself, holding her left hand over her right as though the latter were warming the former. As she bent, her subsequent oaths were choked beyond intelligibility.

"What?" McCall asked.

Kira tried to repeat herself. Once again failed. Or, she supposed, succeeded, seeing as she failed in precisely the same way as she had the first time.

"Hey," the officer simpered, "talk to me."

And goddamnit if he didn't sound just as earnest, sincere, genuine, whatever word you like, as he had before Dresselhaus had called Kira an *accessory*.

Poor Officer McCall was, it seemed, one of that impossibly selective group known as *the good ones*. He was one of those.

And as Kira had been learning over and over this year: goodness was a tender underbelly.

She picked her phone up off the seat where it had fallen during the scooch, and opened up the browser. It didn't take long to find the site she was looking for. Her phone seemed to have remembered it, from when she'd looked it up some months back. Even though she'd thought she'd deleted her history.

Hopefully her muscles had remembered all this too.

There was only time for a quick skim of the How To Perform A Chokehold page this time, but she felt like she did remember most of the important bits. Bicep and forearm pinching the neck, hand on the back of the head. Oh yeah. Got it.

That done, she locked her phone, put it back in her pocket, and threw herself back into the seat as hard as she could. Needed to look good, after all. She winced as her head *thwapped* back over the top of the headrest and *snapped* forward again.

Pain ripped through her neck. Which was fine. She could use that too.

Kira rolled her eyes into the back of her head and vibrated as quickly as her long-neglected twitch muscles would allow, sputtering and stammering as she did. Almost certainly nothing that would fool a doctor. But a nervy rookie catching her reflection in a narrow piece of glass from the far side of a metal grate? Different story. Almost certainly.

"Hey! What's wrong?!" McCall squeaked. "What's happening?!"

More sputtering, even sharper stammering. God, she hoped the kid was gonna pull over soon. She couldn't keep shimmying like this forever.

As luck would have it, *soon* came even quicker than Kira had imagined. McCall cranked the wheel so hard the tires yelped, coming to rest at the curb just in front of what appeared to be, through Kira's quivering half-squint, a sky-blue adobe shack. Which it surely wasn't, of course. That was just what it looked like to her right now.

"Unit 331," McCall quacked into the walkie-talkie on his dashboard, "requesting *immediate* medical existence on, uh, on the corner of French and Dunscomb! In Neirmouth! I'm in Neirmouth, is there an ambulance in Neirmouth?" The radio started to squawk its answer, but McCall didn't wait around for it; he swung open the front door and tumbled out of the car.

Medical existence, he'd said. Not the brightest bulb, this one. Frustratingly, Kira found that oddly endearing.

Further evidence of the man's dimness: McCall swung open the door just behind his and leaned into the back-seat. "Tell me what's happening!"

Kira pushed herself even harder, jerking her shoulders in and out forcefully enough to launch her torso an inch or two off the seat with each spasm.

"Aaaaah…" McCall glanced up French, and down it, then made a mockery of what little training he must have had to go through to get that badge.

He climbed into the backseat of the car. With Kira.

"Should I CPR?!" he shouted from his half-kneel over Kira, one knee planted on the seat beside her now-nearly-prostrate body, the other propped like a kickstand in the seat well. His face was less than a foot from hers. He'd had fried onions with his lunch.

The only reply he got was Kira kicking his extended leg out from under him.

He plopped down, hitting the edge of the seat with his face. Lucky for him about the padding, then.

Kira rolled off the bench, following him down into the well of the seat. Not exactly roomy. But she could get her arms up and around his neck, so it would do.

She pincered his throat in the crook of her left elbow.

Bicep pressing on one side, forearm on the other.

Her right hand pressed forcefully into the back of McCall's head. The window-punching hand. The pain of it, the absolute, excruciating *redness* of it, was nearly enough to knock her out cold.

But she held on. And she squeezed Officer McCall's neck in her arm. Squeezed as though she meant to jimmy his head right off.

McCall struggled, naturally. He bucked and jerked and slapped at her arms. But he didn't have much room to maneuver down here. Kira had used up all the room.

"Okay," Kira grunted. "It's okay. Stop."

As McCall fought, the car rocked. This way, then that.

McCall made a thumbs-up gesture with his right hand. *Launched* it back over his head. Towards Kira's face.

His thumb jabbed her right cheek, just an inch south of her eyeball.

"HEY!" she gasped, shifted her weight for a better angle on the man's neck. Tried to hide her head behind his. She flexed her left arm harder, willed her right hand to push straight through the back of the silly bastard's melon.

The thumb came back again. And again. And again.

Kira tried to dodge the ballistic digit, jerking her head wherever the thumb wasn't.

On one thrust, she and McCall each jerked in the same direction, at the same time.

The car lurched *hard* in that same direction.

Inertia brought Kira and McCall back, then rolled them in the other direction.

The car followed suit.

And goshdarnit if that wasn't just the way the car needed to move, and with just the right amount of force, to swing closed the door through which McCall had come back here.

Clunk, it announced. Once more locking Kira in the backseat.

"FUCKER!" she screamed into McCall's ear. But one thing at a time, though. That's all you can do.

She squeezed harder, harder, harder. Her left elbow *popped,* then went numb. Something snapping out of alignment? She wouldn't be surprised. But she could still squeeze with it. That was all that mattered.

Her right hand had started bleeding. She didn't know how that was possible, unless a bone had poked through somewhere. Which *was* possible. She wondered if McCall could feel some shattered bit of her skeleton, tickling behind his ear. As she pressed. Harder. Harder.

Kira kept on screaming. McCall kept on fighting. Until he didn't anymore.

She kept on squeezing though. Kept screaming. Couldn't risk him waking back up before she found a way to get out of this goddamned backseat. No way she'd be able to get the jump on him again.

So she kept on squeezing. Only letting off the pressure once the red receded, and she remembered that she couldn't stay here forever. She needed to let him go. She needed to get up.

Slowly, cautiously, Kira eased the pressure on McCall's neck, threading her left arm out from under. She lifted her right hand from the back of his head.

The officer's head teetered forward, hanging at an angle that...worried her.

Refusing to fear the worst, she crawled up onto the seat, lying flat out across it, then reached down and shook McCall's shoulder. "Officer," she whispered.

He didn't move. Didn't react.

Which was good. That was what she wanted. It was unspeakable idiocy, to try to wake the man up while she was locked in the back of a patrol car with him.

So instead, she reached down and held her finger under his nose.

Where she felt nothing. No little tingles of air coming or going.

Kira almost slid off of the seat. She shimmied herself further towards the edge and cranked her shoulder enough to let her get two fingers on McCall's neck.

Where she felt nothing. No little thum-thum or rum-pum-pum of a heartbeat.

Oh for two on the vital checks.

"Oh," Kira whispered to herself. She did not add *for two*. No need.

She reached down and shook his shoulder again.

Same result.

So she rolled onto her back, looking up at the ceiling of the car, and took as deep a breath as her aching ribs would tolerate. McCall must have cracked her a few times there with his elbow. Her pain was his legacy. Fair enough.

She didn't let herself wonder about his having a

family. Tried to remind herself that this was the *third* life she'd taken. It wasn't anything new. Ho hum. Another murder, you say? And not even a child this time? Ho the fuck hum.

But this one was different. Because it didn't *need* to have happened, in the way that the others had *needed* to.

Or so it had seemed at the time.

Deal with this later.

She pulled herself up to a seat and glanced around outside the car. Saw nothing to be concerned about. Nobody on the street. No curtains hanging back at suspicious angles. No cars coming her way.

That was what she needed to focus on. Not the man in the well of the seat down there. She would have the rest of her life to wring her hands about him, along with Nicole, and Madeleine, and sure, maybe even Zoe. Even though that last one hadn't been her fault. Not directly.

She gave the door at her feet, the door through which McCall had come crawling, a spiritless little kick. Just a formality. Just like the final survey of the interior she made. She didn't really expect it to amount to anything. Which it didn't.

Okay. Okay.

Keeping that emptiness of the street outside in the front of her mind, she rolled back onto her belly and reached down towards the body in the seat well. Started to reach for his gun…then changed course and grabbed his nightstick. Billy club. Whatever the hell they called it. She undid the leather thong holding it on the dead man's utility belt (after a tremendous amount of fumbling, but nevermind that), then pulled it up as she heaved herself onto her knees. Noticing as she rose that he had no ring on the relevant finger. Trying to be at least a little relieved by that.

She turned around and kneelwalked along the seat towards the passengerside window, the one facing the sidewalk. Worse for keeping an eye out for *witnesses*, she supposed, but the idea was to be through the window in the very instant after the truncheon managed the feat. Sidewalk was the only way to go then; she didn't want to launch herself out, only to tumble into the path of a big rig. Not that this street looked like the sort that had ever seen a vehicle with more than four wheels. But still. The point stood. And Kira kneeled.

Once she was nearly flush with the door, she sat back onto her ankles, experimented with a few grips on the cudgel before ultimately settling on pressing her right hand (which she was still pointedly refusing to look at) against the bottom of the hilt bit, then using the left to grab just shy of the center…and *ramming* the truncheon against the window, as hard as she could.

The sensation was akin to shaking hands with a ringing church bell.

Every bone in her body jiggled in their sleeves of sinew. Even with her muscles fully tensed, it took a full second for her insides to settle back down.

"Fuck," she grunted. She squared her shoulders for another go.

From all around her, a familiar set of sounds:

Rrr.

Nnnnt.
Rhhhhr.
Dur.

This time, unlike last time, Kira understood those sounds at once. The difference-maker, she feared, must have been McCall's body on the floor. Improved the acoustics.

You need to try harder, Uisch encouraged her, in the voice of the car.

Kira used her left forearm to wipe tears from her cheek. The forearm smelled like a sarcastic fruit bowl. Aftershave, surely. McCall's. Surely.

She shook her head. "I'm trying as hard as I fucking can," Kira assured the car.

The car said nothing to that.

Regaining her grip on the baton, she tried to imagine that the window wasn't there. That was the trick for breaking wooden boards, right? At least according to karate movies. Pretend the board isn't there. Punch through it.

So Kira glared through the window, and jammed the club straight out, as though the glass wasn't even there.

The glass objected to this. Reminded her that it was *very fucking there.*

"COME ON!!!" Kira screamed, hammering the club against the window a few more times, her technique much less considered. She kept this up until the pain in her right hand locked it up, at which point she lost purchase on the rod, and her hand slid forward along the club, into her field of view.

She pulled it back before she got *too* good a look at it,

but…oh yeah. She'd seen a flash of bone there.

Movement outside the car caught her eye.

A mother and son, the latter on a little plastic tricycle, the former trailing along behind, her arms crossed, shoulders hunched. Well, perhaps one oughtn't assume they were a mother and son. They could be strangers. The lady could have abducted the kid. Or the other way around. Who knew. Anything was possible. Except, of course, for opening the rear doors of a Pitney PD patrol vehicle from the inside.

The woman and child were heading this way. The former staring at Kira. The latter oblivious, giggling at nothing, just loving this strange new thing called life.

Kira laid the club at her right side, lay her bloody right hand on top of it, and waved at the woman with her left. She smiled, then realized that being beckoned by a woman grinning from the back of a police car might not have the desired effect. So Kira frowned. Which…didn't seem an improvement.

"HELP ME!" she shouted, overenunciating enough to crack her lips at the corners of her mouth. She pointed to the space on the door where the little lock nub would have been, in an ordinary car. "I CAN'T GET OUT!"

The woman paused. The kid kept on riding towards Kira. Until the woman said something to the kid. Something that made him stop, look back at her, then laboriously turn his plastic tricycle around.

"I'M IN TROUB…I'M…" she gestured to the car around her. "THIS WAS A MISTAKE! THE POLICE MADE A MISTAKE!"

JUD WIDING

The woman pulled her phone out of her purse, dialed a very short number, and put the gizmo to her ear.

"Goddamnit," Kira muttered.

The pile of electronics in the front of the car fell apart, in precisely the way they needed to to say *ask for help.*

Steeling herself against the pain, Kira took up the baton once more and resumed whaling on the window. "I FUCKING TRIED!" she thundered as she did.

From the end of French Street: sirens.

Kira paused. Hell of a response time. But hey, the cops were already in town. Just a few streets away.

But hey again…to be coming from that end of French…that couldn't be the cops.

The Neirmouth volunteer fire department's ambulance proved her right by yodeling its way off Dunscomb and onto French.

Oh. Of course. Here came the *medical existence.* Too late for McCall, alas. Unless…hey, maybe he had a few braindead years left to while away as a glorified external hard drive, powered by heart-pumping paraphernalia beyond number. If that wasn't *medical existence,* then what was?

The woman on the phone glanced down the street, then stuffed the first finger of her free hand into her ear.

The kid on the plastic tricycle took his feet off the pedals. Stared blankly at Kira, his mouth hanging open an inch or two. Couldn't have been more than five or six years old.

Too young to see a dead body. But who wasn't.

Kira frowned down at what used to be Officer

604

McCall.

Not her, the car purred.

Glancing up once more, Kira looked to the woman on the phone. A mother, yes. Assume she is a mother, by the hand draping gently over the boy's shoulder, by the subtle comfort he seems to take from this.

Ask for help. Not her.

"Then who," Kira demanded. "…you?!"

Ask, Uisch ordered, by knocking the rearview mirror to the floor. The way it clattered as it fell sounded unmistakably like laughter.

Kira frowned. Fuck no. Uisch had done this. All of this, yes, but especially *this*. Given Harlow the green light to kill Zoe, no doubt. And so, as a result, gotten Kira locked in the car. That was its fault. *McCall* was its fault. She didn't want that thing's help. She wanted nothing to do with it, ever again.

And yet, if she wanted to reach her daughter…what choice did she have?

What choice had she ever had?

The ambulance had closed half the distance to the car already. Volunteer EMTs weren't trained for this kind of thing, were they? Whatever *this kind of thing* was?

Probably not. But they were bound to be strong. Kira didn't like her odds there.

Ask.

Kira's pride made a good faith effort (maybe dragging a few principles along by their hair) to insist that she didn't need help, especially not from Uisch.

Those principles of hers were no match for what they

argued against.

"Okay," she mumbled, "open the door. Blow out the window. Whatever."

The door to the glove compartment flipped open. More clattering, more laughter. *Not the right step.*

"...the fuck does that mean?" She slapped her left palm against the window. "Come on!"

I live to lead.

The ambulance screeched to a halt on the opposite curb, just a few yards away from the police car. Two EMTs leapt out, a guy and a gal, both from the cab of the vehicle.

The mother, now between the cruiser and the ambulance (but much nearer the former), turned around to wave over the paramedics.

The boy just kept on looking at Kira. Mouth still gawping open.

Kira didn't have to think too hard about what *help* from Uisch looked like. And why the demon might not like the idea of being told what to do. Being limited to opening a door, or breaking a window.

"Tell me how you want to help me, then."

I only show. Never tell.

"I'm...not going to let you. Until you t-"

Let me, the car cackled as it collapsed around her.

"No."

Let me. Not laughing this time.

Kira took another glance down towards McCall's body...then said "no." Wishing she felt as confident as she sounded. Assuming she sounded as confident as she hoped she did.

A thoughtful silence from the vehicle.

Followed by what remained of the dashboard constr-uction finally *crashing* down onto the center console, roll-ing off into the driverside seat well.

LET ME.

"Wha-" was as far as Kira got, before all four of the doors on the police car *snapped* off at once, clonking onto the ground in their own time.

Learn, they said to her.

However incensed she was to have her will gainsaid, however distressed she was to realize that more and more of her choices were being curated by Uisch, how-ever much she *didn't* want to be learning whatever dance that fucking monster meant to lead her in…Kira wanted out of the car. And she got it, leaping through the sidewalk-facing door in a many-leggéd scramble.

"Ma'am!" one of the paramedics, now speaking with the woman and her son, called across the street to Kira. "Stay right there, ma'am!"

She made the mistake of turning to look at him. And so failed to mark just how high the curb on French Street was.

Her right toe caught on said curb, which was very high indeed. Kira managed to get her feet under her for another two steps, before crashing onto the sidewalk, landing on her right shoulder.

The instant she landed, Kira spun to look at the paramedics.

They were sprinting towards her, full-tilt. The one on

the left looked like he had some muscle.

Kira planted her hands on the grey pavement beneath her, regretted that *instantly*, and did her best to push herself to her feet using just her left hand.

She got her right foot under her, heaved herself halfway to standing.

Then the paramedic on the left, the one with the muscle, screamed.

The naked terror in the cry got Kira upright fast enough to throw a muscle between her shoulder blade. Which she promptly paid no mind.

Because the oncoming paramedic on the left was bleeding from the crown of his head.

Then splitting, like a pair of old jeans in a deep squat.

Like the skunk in the park, so long ago.

Kira made a soft *uh!* sound. It meant nothing.

The top of the paramedic's head unfolded, peeling like a skunk in a park. Blood rolled down his perfectly, almost *artfully* exposed musculature, like red velvet down the tiers of a fondue fountain. But inertia was a hell of a thing: even as the paramedic on the right stopped on a dime, the one on the left kept on running, running straight for Kira, even as he was flayed alive by an invisible hand. Even as his terminal striptease reached down to the shoulders, tearing through his shirt, sections of his former face flapping against his chest.

His eyes, bulging and unlidded, remained firmly fixed on Kira, his lipless teeth locked in a grimace. Gore bubbled from the flat cavities of his nostrils. And still, he ran towards Kira.

The jaw opened and closed, opened and closed, as though attempting to speak. No words emerged, only groans and gurgles. But he kept on coming, at a full sprint.

His tongue slid out from between his lips. It slapped onto the street, and his teeth tumbled out after to applaud its technique.

His fingers detached from the hands detached from the wrists detached from the arms, leaving the bones to dangle on a string of loose meat, clicking together like joyless windchimes.

Kira screamed, and so was mercifully spared the sound his eyes made as they slid from their sockets, one dangling from its nerve, the other detaching and landing on the ground, to be promptly boot-crushed like a grape.

Once the ribs started to unsheathe from the torso, it was pretty much over.

Finally, at the end of that eternity, the meat and bone that had until recently been a paramedic (and, one assumes, more besides) stumbled to a halt, dragging a tail of its own flesh, before finally flopping to the Earth, sloshing onto the curb, half in the street, half on a lawn.

Whh. The tendons of his neck coming loose, flapping like tentacles.

Dhdu. The hips splitting in half, draping the spine limply over the still-pumping organs.

Thock. The skull cracking, as though under immense pressure, creating a little fissure for the brain to dribble out.

Meaningless. Nothing. Just death.

Kira stared down at the manmess. Lifted her gaze to the other paramedic.

The poor kid was terrified. And she was just a kid, that other paramedic. Like Officer McCall. They were all kids.

Help, Kira heard Uisch say, with a chuckle.

Kira flinched. The word had seemed to arrive as itself. No other sounds it could have been, that she…

Ah. Of course. That had been the sound of the other paramedic's scalp, splitting.

"NO!" Kira screamed.

"Something's wrong with me," the paramedic had time to say. As though she didn't know exactly what was about to happen. As though her partner hadn't just shown her. Then she switched to screaming, which was a sign she'd probably worked it out in the end.

Kira shook her head, not even bothering to look for Uisch looming in one of the shadows thrown by the houses. "This isn't help!" she cried to the afternoon. "Stop! I don't want this!"

The paramedic followed her partner's lead, splashing not-so-face-first into the spreading pool of his blood.

"ELI!" the mother in the street screamed.

Kira looked up, to the child on the tricycle. In time to see him shriek and paw uselessly at his head. As it bloomed like a flower.

The boy's mother shrieked, until she, too, opened to daylight.

"WHY ARE YOU DOING THIS?" Kira roared.

Behind her, she heard the sound of laughter. It was only after she recognized it as laughter that she noted it was, incidentally, the sound of tiles sliding off of a roof.

Kira spun around to behold the house in front of which two paramedics, a mother, and her son Eli had just gotten the worst haircut in human history.

There was an older fella standing just outside the open front door of that house. A looky-loo. "Jesus," he said.

"GO BACK INSIDE!" Kira screamed. As if that would make a difference.

Run home, Uisch giggled, as more tiles slipped from the roof and shattered on the ground.

Run home, the top of the older fella's skull sighed at the touch of open air.

"STOP…FUCKING *STOP! PLEASE!!*" Kira screeched, forcefully enough to taste blood.

Run home, she heard from the next door neighbor's front stoop. Kira didn't need to look to know there was another curious member of the community unspooling over there. But she did look.

Run home.

Then Kira turned and ran. Ran as hard as she could. Uisch was killing anyone who looked at her, she was fucking certain. Killing the witnesses. Protecting her. No. Saving her not *from* something…but *for* something.

She realized she was running the wrong way.

Run home, she heard in stereo, from either side of the street at once.

"I'M GOING!" she panted, as she turned around and ran back towards the *scene.* That was how it would be described. Assuming Uisch left anyone in this fucking town alive to come look at it.

Run home in triplicate, from the car that puttered past her, crashing hard into something in her wake.

Run home twenty times over, from the busy playground she passed.

Run home.

FIFTEEN

RED

RUN HOME.

Kira ran. Each time she heard those words, spoken through the rending of flesh, she tried to run faster, but she couldn't. She wasn't in good shape. She was – or rather, had been and apparently was now again – a mother, a woman raising a child and working a job and living a life that left no time for galumphing along on a treadmill or picking up heavy objects only to immediately set them down again. Had she gone to seed a bit? Sure. Alright. Guilty. But how could she have known how profoundly she would come to regret this, how her *entirely justified* idleness would cost so many good people in Neirmouth their lives?

Run home.

She wished they would just stop looking at her. Stop making themselves *witnesses,* to be unzipped by Uisch.

But how could they not look? Who in this sleepy little snowglobe of a town, where nothing happened except for sometimes young women being murdered, could fail to have a gander at the gone-to-seed middle-aged lady gasping her way down the street, her face no doubt red as a beet and shimmering like the oiled buttock of a model in a perfume advertisement?

Run home.

Being less conspicuous wasn't an option, though. For she couldn't slow down without coming to a full-on *stop,* as she'd done four or five blocks back. She'd stumbled to a halt, then bent over and planted her hands on her knees, sucking air with the same ferocity she brought to the little pull-cord when she was trying to get the goddamned lawnmower to *start.* All that wheezing and panting drew just as much attention as running did, ultimately. As a well-meaning young man from that two-story house over yonder discovered to his cost.

Run home.

Better to draw attention going to where she needed to be. Where the goddamned demon *wanted* her, at least.

Run home.

Run home.

So Kira *ran home,* her vision fully bleeding out, leaving only the red. Which wasn't to say she couldn't see anything. She knew where she was headed, didn't slip off of any curbs or trip over any mailboxes. Yeah, she could see well enough. But somehow none of it seemed to penetrate. Not in a way that mattered. There were no shapes, no boundaries between objects. It was just color. It was all the same. It was so much noise and shadow between where she was and where the devil needed her.

Finally, Kira turned onto Hamlin. Her street. Fighting for an especially deep breath, she pinched her mouth shut, ducked her head, and pushed herself as hard as she could. She didn't want to kill her goddamned neighbors, some of whom had lived here before the Trecothiks, had known Leigh from the day she was born, had b-

Run home.

Had paid their respects after sh-

Run home.

Whose names and faces and lives she knew, at least in passing.

Run home.

"STOP!!!" Leigh screamed again. As if Uisch was liable to listen *this* time. Yes, the first thirty times hadn't been persuasive, but thirty-one, that was the ticket.

Run home.

That last one had almost surely come from the Carters' across the street. Where Wanda Carter lived. Wanda, who had left a truly gorgeous homemade cake (chocolate and spongey, with a caramel ganache thing on top) on the Trecothik's porch two days after Leigh's murder, with a note that simply said *call if you want to*. A touching gesture, that had been, particularly as the Trecothiks and the Carters had never known each other much beyond the pleasantries. Kira had never called, of course, and it had been quite odd to eat a slice of (er, half of) a cake and have to hold the thought *this is absolutely delicious* in her head at the same time as *I am only eating this cake because my daughter is dead.*

Well, Kira noted solemnly as she turned onto her own driveway for the very last push, it sounded like she would need to leave a cake of her own on the porch at Chez Carter. No chance it would be anywhere near as good, though. For a number of reasons.

Kira puffed up to the front door of her home, grabbed the knob, and turned it. The knob turned, but the door didn't budge.

Locked. Huh.

So she pulled out her keys, found the one to the front door, and used it. For the first time in years. Maybe ever. She'd always entered her home through the garage, or left the front door unlocked as she stepped out of it, knowing she would be back just a few moments later.

She stepped through the door and entered her house as would a guest. As had Uisch.

"Okay!" she screamed. Well, tried to. *Wheezed* struck closer to bullseye.

Her legs decided they'd supported her for long enough, and fucked off without so much as a note, let alone a cake.

Kira tilted forward, grabbing a little accent table as she fell. Unfortunately, the table wasn't any more interested in holding Kira up than her own legs were; it tilted right along with her, the framed photos of Trecothik vacations gone by sliding onto her head as she landed, hard, on the floor.

With her ear to the ground as it was, the footsteps coming on fast from the kitchen roared like cannon fire.

Like a semi-automatic cannon. Like a…that wasn't a thing. Scratch that.

Kira couldn't muster the strength to push herself up at present, so she simply rolled onto her side for a better angle on the kitchen.

A furious teenager came stomping through into the front hall. Only belatedly did Kira recognize the girl to Leigh.

She had never, *ever,* seen her daughter so furious. Not even when Kira had told her she couldn't go on the band field trip (not after the previous year's band field trip had been rock n' roll enough to earn a few column inches in the paper). Not even when Kira had grounded her daughter for a week after calling another girl at school, whose name escaped Kira just now, a *squiddley-bitch,* even if that was a really funny thing to imagine someone earnestly snarling in the heat of an argument. Not even when…well, when Leigh finally realized just how her parents had managed to bring her back the first two times.

For the shorter stays.

As opposed to this one. Which was for keeps.

Leigh was back. By both hook and crook, Kira's daughter had come back to her.

Kira couldn't help it: she smiled.

Correction: *now* Kira had never seen her daughter so furious.

Leigh kept on coming. And coming. Until it was clear she wasn't going to quit swinging her feet just because she'd reached her mother.

"Wait!" Kira whimpered as she swayed back up to bipedalism, "listen, your fa-"

Leigh made a fist and used it to *thump* Kira on the right shoulder. Hard. Clearly not as hard as she could. But still. Hard enough to hurt.

Kira jerked backwards. "Woah – *hey!*"

"WHY DID YOU DO IT?!" Leigh cried. Sounding just as she had on the phone some ten minutes ago now. Hadn't done much cooling off in the interim.

"I didn't do it!" Kira blubbered, trying again and again to plant her hands on Leigh's shoulders, even as the latter kept slapping the affection away. "Dad did! I tried to stop him. I tried to save her, honey. I really did."

Leigh made the fist again, this time only waving it in the air a few times as she grimaced at Kira's shoulder, like a golfer practicing their snot. Sorry, *shot*.

Kira reached out and used the back of her hand to wipe her daughter's nose.

Leigh slapped the hand away again. "They were my friends, Mom."

"I know." Kira risked her hands on her daughter's shoulders again. Was pleasantly surprised to find Leigh receptive this time. "I'm so sorry. I'm so sorry."

Tears positively *bubbled* in the corners of Leigh's eyes. She pulled her fist into her own chest, and thumped the bone over her heart. The entire lower half of her face trembled.

Kira wanted so badly to pull her daughter to her and hug her. She wanted to hug her baby. Tell her everything was going to be alright. But she knew she needed to take it slowly. Leigh was fragile. She w-

Leigh practically bodyslammed Kira, so forcefully did she move in for an embrace.

"Oh!" Kira gasped.

Leigh buried her face in the shoulder she had only just struck. Wept silently. Kira felt her daughter's tears seeping into the fabric of her shirt.

She wrapped her arms around Leigh. Squeezed her as hard as she could. "I'm so sorry," she repeated. "I'm so sorry."

"Oh…" Leigh groaned. She gently peeled herself free of her mother's affection.

Kira had to work hard to let Leigh go. Even just enough to step back a few inches.

"How long am I here for?" Leigh asked quietly. "Am I…?"

"Uh…" Kira's voice rattled itself to bits. She cleared her throat, swallowed, and said "yeah. Forever. You're here, sweetie. You're alive." She once more reached out for Leigh, but forced herself to hold back. She didn't know if she'd have the strength to let her go again. "You're alive."

Leigh's face cycled through a range of emotional extremes. Every muscle above her neck flexed and trembled and slackened by turns, her nose running, her eyes leaking, her teeth chattering periodically. "I'm alive," she repeated in a sigh. "Oh god." The pace of her breath quickened. She placed a hand on her chest. "God. Fuck. I'm alive. Oh. Oh."

"It's okay. We're okay. We're g-"

From outside the front door: familiar footsteps pounded up onto the porch. Followed shortly thereafter by the jangle of keys pulled from a pocket.

"Go upstairs," Kira told Leigh at once.

"Is it Dad?"

ker-CHHNK. A key slid into the lock of the already-unlocked door.

Kira said nothing.

"Why do you want me to go upstairs?"

"…I don't know."

"Then I'm staying here."

Kira considered that, then nodded. "Okay."

The door opened. Harlow stepped through.

Kira could tell, simply by his blanched, drawn face, that he'd been subjected to the same *run home* nightmare as she herself had.

He spared not even a sour look for his wife, though. "Leigh," he wheezed, opening his arms for a hug and rushing forward.

Leigh took a step back.

Harlow froze. Frowned.

"You killed Zoe," Leigh asked, in the form of a statement.

And suddenly Harlow had eyes for Kira again. They were sharp, beady little things. "I brought you back," he told Leigh, looking back at her for the latter half of the sentence. "And now we're a family again. So it's fine."

The words hung about in the air, like teenagers outside a corner store hoping someone will buy them beer.

It was, needless to say, not fine. Kira struggled mightily to focus on how needless that was to say, because she wanted to very desperately to *say it.* Among other things.

But then, now wasn't the time.

"So it *is* fine," Kira finally allowed, hoping to put some time back on the clock before the bomb needed defusing, "but all the same…we should probably…you know…pack some bags. And get out of here, right now."

"Right," Harlow concurred. "We sh-"

*ooooo*OOOOOO

Kira and Harlow looked to each other. "Wait here," they said to their daughter in unison.

They both hotfooted it to the bay window looking out over their front lawn. Which also looked out over the street, and so, onto three police cruisers screeching to a halt outside.

Backup had arrived from Pitney then. Christ, how fast had they been driving to be here already?

Harlow delivered the more pressing question: "How did they know we're here?"

Kira wondered the same thing, right up until Detective Dresselhaus stepped out of the passenger seat of one of the cars. Which reminded Kira of her (incorrectly) telling the detective about how Harlow was back at their house. And once reports of all the, uh, *unfolding* around town hit the scanners…well, it made sense to send cops here, to their house.

For the sake of brevity, Kira said "I don't know."

Harlow nodded. Reached out and took his wife's hand. Squeezed it.

"I love you," he said.

623

After a *very* brief, but *very* freighted pause, Kira said "I love you too."

He leaned in, kissed her on the cheek, then turned and walked confidently towards the front door.

"Harlow…"

Harlow put his hand on the knob, then turned and smiled sadly at Kira.

"Dad," Leigh said cautiously, echoing her mother. "What are you doing?"

He turned to Leigh. "I'm doing what's best for us. You should hide somewhere. For now. They won't know what to make of you."

Kira took a step towards her husband. Her legs still shaky beneath her. "Harlow…are you…?"

Rather than repeat himself, Harlow turned back to the door, opened it, and stepped through.

Kira rushed forward a step. Not quite to the threshold, but close.

Outside, the police drew their weapons.

Detective Dresselhaus crouched sharply, crabwalking back towards the cars.

Harlow kept walking forwards, his arms raised in surrender.

"We need to go," Kira hissed to her daughter, stepping backwards, trying and failing to pry her eyes from her husband's idiot heroism. "While he's distracting them, we can sneak out the back door."

From beside her car, Detective Dresselhaus lifted a palm and shouted "STOP RIGHT THERE!"

Harlow raised the pointer finger of his left hand and,

without lowering it, gestured back towards the house. "SHE'S INSIDE!" he screamed. "MY WIFE IS INSIDE! SHE DID IT! SHE KILLED THE GIRLS!"

"Oh you *fucker,*" Kira growled to herself, as she backpedaled away from the door.

As Leigh stepped closer to it.

"Hey!" Kira snapped at her. "Get away from th-"

Leigh *shrieked* out the open door.

Kira followed her daughter's gaze out the door, to… ah. Of course.

The various law enforcement officers outside their home were unfolding. Much to Harlow's evident frustration.

If Kira wasn't very much mistaken, Detective Dresselhaus locked eyes with her through the open door, in the moment before her face fell away in three beefy strips. After that, the eye contact became *truly* unbroken. So Kira did what Dresselhaus could no longer do: she blinked. Then looked away.

"MOM!" Leigh blubbered. She turned to her mother. "Mom! What's happening?!"

After the last of the cops fell to the ground, Harlow shrugged angrily, turned around, and trudged back up towards the house.

Kira watched the first two steps of his return, then hustled to the kitchen.

"What is HAPPENING?!" Leigh demanded, following her mother.

"I'm doing what's best for *us,*" Kira replied, as she hurried to the counter, pulled her favorite, flesh-flaying knife from the block, and turned around to meet her husband at the door.

LEIGH HAD DECIDED she wanted to sleep through, er, *into* it. Her parents had convinced her to at least let them sit with her as it happened. So she'd brought blankets and pillows downstairs and ensconced herself on the recliner in front of the TV. Mom sat next to her, Dad pulling up a chair to cover the other flank. There'd been one of those endless marathons of the game show in the taxi on GSN, and that would be good enough.

She'd drifted away to the sounds of New Yorkers pretending to be surprised. It wasn't the way she'd ever imagined taking her leave, but it was definitely a step up from being splayed over a rotten log on Knot Hedge, ears ringing and gut leaking. This was painless. This was comfortable. There was love here. It was a sick, poisoned love, but there was solace to be taken from the knowledge that the poison *was* the love. A fatal overdose, that had proven fatal not for Leigh but for the people she had tried to save.

"It's okay," Leigh mumbled to her parents one last time. They said something to her. She wasn't listening, though. She was riding in the Cash Cab. She was in. She was winning. "I love you," she told them, as sound and image merged and faded, cranking into a deep dark, deep down, a well with no bottom. There was no bottom and she could hear black water lapping at the stonework. It's okay. Down. I love you. Deep. It's okay. Dark. I love you.

Light.

Leigh flinched herself awake.

Leigh had frowned into the light. It was supposed to be dark. It had been dark. The end came in darkness. But this was light. Therefore, it wasn't dark.

Therefore…

"No…"

Morning.

"No…!"

No. Afternoon. Smack in the middle of the day.

A beautiful autumn day.

Leigh had been brought back to her empty home. And for a few disorienting minutes, she had been able to convince herself that this was the afterlife's antechamber. Started easy, the heavens did, reflecting the recently departed's earthly home. How considerate. What finally banished that delusion was opening the back door to step outside, and being deafened by the *BEE BEE BEE BEE BEE* of the home alarm system. She'd tried to shut it off, but the code wasn't working. Hard to imagine the angels bothering with a low-stakes prank like this. So, either she wasn't dead…or she wasn't in heaven.

Nothing that happened after that served to rule out the latter conclusion.

Now here she was, backing impotently into the staircase as Mom, armed with a goddamned kitchen knife, charged towards the door that Dad was about to walk through.

"MOM!" Leigh shouted at her.

Mom paid her no mind.

"STOP!" Leigh reached out and grabbed Mom's arm as she passed.

That had *some* effect, at least; Mom flinched, like a Labrador awoken from a dream. "We can't all be together," she said in a daze. "Someone has to take the blame."

Leigh pointed to the knife. "That's not *blame.*"

Mom considered that for a moment, then shook her head and said "you'll understand when you're older."

Dad stepped through the front door.

Mom turned, lifted the knife, and charged.

"NO!" Leigh screamed. She reached out to grab Mom again, but wasn't fast enough.

"Shit!" Dad shouted, staggering back but missing the door, instead bumping into the doorframe.

No, Uisch weighed in, via the blade of the knife snapping free of the handle.

Mom drove what was now just a small rectangle of wood at the center of Dad's chest. It connected with a dull *thump.*

The blade giggled as it clattered to the floor.

Dad and Mom both looked down at it. Then looked up at each other.

"You tried to kill me," Dad marveled.

"You tried to turn me in," Mom explained.

"You tried to turn *me* in."

"You were trying to kill Zoe."

"I was trying to bring Leigh back."

Rather than reply, Mom turned to Leigh. "See? I told you, I tried to stop him."

"I did what had to be done," Dad added towards

Leigh. "For you."

"Which she *asked us* not to *do!*" Kira reminded him.

"She didn't *explicitly* ask us not to, technically!"

"It was *obvious,* Harlow!"

"Well, I disagree, Kira!"

Leigh looked from Mom, to Dad, to Mom, to Dad, taking one step of retreat with each turn of the head.

"She couldn't have been more clear!" Mom hollered. "You should have known what she wanted!"

"She's still a child, she doesn't *know* what she wants!"

"I didn't want this," Leigh whispered. Backtracking into the kitchen now.

Mom shoved Dad, hard.

Dad shoved back.

From deeper into the kitchen:

Hhhhsmp. A framed graphite print of a rock that looked like a heart slipped its nail, slid down the wall, and thumped onto the floor.

crrrrONK. The wooden drying rack next to the sink trembled, creaked, and collapsed in on itself.

CSSHSHH. The glasses that had sat on the rack fell and shattered.

A shard soared across the room and sliced at Leigh's thigh. She felt a runlet of blood trace its way down her leg. Her gaze never dropped to investigate, though.

She was fully preoccupied by the nine-foot-tall demon hunched in the far corner of the kitchen. The very same creature she'd seen before. First in the car. Then waddling out the front door.

Leigh refused to say its name. But she thought it.

Which was bad enough.

She turned around to look at her parents.

They were locked in a frieze. Fisticuffs in the Foyer. Mom had Dad's lapel bunched in her right hand; Dad had Mom's left wrist in a deathgrip. Both, though, were looking past their daughter. To the creature.

"Uisch," Mom said.

Leigh turned back around.

The demon was barely two feet away from her; it had closed the distance in perfect silence.

Every impulse in Leigh counseled retreat, yet that would send her back towards her parents. Which didn't seem much of an improvement at all.

Uisch bowed its head, bringing its horrible mask closer to Leigh's face. Again, it moved without making a sound.

It occurred to Leigh that perhaps this *thing,* which made its thoughts known through destruction, had no other means of communication. Perhaps it was incapable of making any noise on its own. How sad that would be. How lonely.

All the same; how fitting.

"Get away from her!" Mom boomed at the beast.

Ha, the house giggled as the top hinge of the door to the garage popped off the wall.

Ha, it continued, as the loosely-screwed top spun off a bottle of olive oil on the counter.

Haaaaaaa…

Leigh looked up, towards the source of the final, rumbling titter: the ceiling.

Mom and Dad stepped cautiously into the kitchen, glancing up for a better look.

The ceiling above the door to the garage *exploded*, caving in as a hole to the second story tore itself open, depositing an entire five-drawer dresser onto the kitchen floor, mere inches from Leigh.

Not incidentally, the crooked wreckage of the dresser in the threshold served as an imposingly splintered barricade between Leigh and her parents, fully blocking any means of easy escape through the front hall. It didn't block Leigh's view of Mom and Dad, though; the inverse must necessarily have also been true.

As the dresser and its contents settled, they spoke: *so many dead.*

"HEY!" Mom jerked herself free of Dad's grip, then stepped towards the dresser. Shouting at the devil now alone with their daughter in the kitchen. "We're done with you!" Kira tried pushing the dresser to one side of the hall, earning nothing for her effort save a four-inch splinter in her palm. "We did what you asked," she grunted, almost perfectly indifferent to the shard of wood, yanking it out without looking at it. "We did it, and you brought Leigh back, so…it's done! It's done! Go away!"

Not done, Uisch insisted by way of the cupboard doors. *But almost.*

Mom turned herself sideways, to slide past the dresser and into the kitchen.

Krrrrrr, the dresser squeaked as it slid, seemingly (but obviously not) of its own accord, to fill the gap Mom was trying to squeeze through. "AH!" she exclaimed as the furnishing *thwunked* against the wall.

Mom tried to pass on the other side. This time, a portion of the dresser detached and swung towards Kira. Brandishing a crooked, rusty nail. One she only just avoided taking in the chest.

She turned around to Dad. "Help me!"

Before Dad had a chance to answer, the kitchen resumed disassembling itself.

So many dead, Uisch told Leigh, *for you. So many lives, for one.*

Leigh shook her head. Sniffed. "I didn't ask for any of this."

Oh. Sing to those left behind. You did not ask for this. All is forgiven. The sneering, sarcastic tone came through loud and clear, in the shrill shattering of springs and coils in the fridge.

Leigh turned to grimace at her parents. "This isn't my fault," she whimpered.

"That's right," Mom told her, still trying and failing to find a way to scale the bloodthirsty wardrobe. "You didn't do this. *We* did."

Yet, Uisch informed her, going further into tearing apart the house around them, pulling pipes from the walls, popping nails and staples from the furniture, *I offer you the most wondrous gift. Leigh.*

"Don't say her name!" Dad shouted, sounding appropriately pathetic.

Leigh shook her head. "…what gift?"

"What the fuck is this?!" Mom demanded. Receiving no answer, she tried to climb over the dresser, planting her hands on the top of it to lift herself up. The timber beneath her hands shifted – and a stake perfectly sized for the heart of a vampire *rrrRIPPED* through her right hand, goring it from below, punching out through the scar of the squirrel bite.

Mom *screamed*.

"Oh, fuck!" Dad contributed.

Mom tried to pull her hand free of its mounting, but couldn't. Even Leigh could see, the stake was notched like a fishhook. Not by chance, no. This was design. All design.

"Fucking *help me!*" Mom snarled at him.

Dad just boggled at Mom's hand, the color draining from his face.

The entire second story of the house *groaned*. Displeased at having been picked at. Who wouldn't be.

Uisch turned its sedimentary smile towards Mom and Dad. *This is the funny part,* spake the ruins in progress. *Watch.*

Dad snapped out of whatever stupor had gripped him; he took a running leap at the dresser, hitting it with his shoulder. Trying to knock it flat onto the ground.

"NO!" Mom screamed in agony, having become one with the dresser. "STOP!"

Dad didn't stop. So Mom kept screaming.

All of the kitchen cabinet doors swung open at once.

Everything in them that could shatter, did. Glass, porcelain, wooden cooking utensils. Shards and splinters, all.

And wouldn't you know it, one particularly thick, many-pointed chunk of a glass bowl slid to Leigh's feet, halting just an inch from the toe of her left shoe. A needlessly expensive glass bowl.

The gift is a choice. Always a choice.

"Hold it steady!" Leigh heard Mom shout. "Every time I try to pull my hand off, it fucking moves!"

"I'm gonna be sick," she heard Dad whimper. "I'm gonna be sick."

Leigh bent down, slowly. As though guided. No: *guided.* The choice was clear. Clearer to her than the reflection of her own face in the broken glass.

Her knees *popped* in unison. She couldn't recall them having ever done that before. Seemed like she was a bit young for that to be happening. Alas.

"Hold it steady!"

"Okay! Okay! I'm trying!"

With a trembling hand, Leigh reached out and took hold of the shard. It was roughly the size of a drink coaster, with one side in particular tapering to an unmistakable point.

The point, unmistakably, was to be used.

She heard Mom scream. Primal, wounded, furious. Oh, what she would have given to have never heard anyone she loved scream like that.

A deafening *CRASH* shot Leigh back to her feet. Bringing the fragment of glass in her hand with. She looked to the front hall just in time to see the ceiling above the front door collapse. Insulation and wiring preceded the wall-mounted television in Mom and Dad's room, as it all came tumbling through from the second story.

Mom and Dad spun around (the former, still palm-gored, clearly regretting it), shrinking from the new chaos behind them.

Watch your daughter. You may soon be made proud.

That comment grabbed Mom by the shoulders and spun her head back around. "I'm already fucking proud of my daughter!"

HAAAAAAA, the ceiling over the kitchen sneered.

Leigh flinched at a splash of pain in her hand. She looked down to find blood dribbling from between the glass-gripping fingers. Even still, she couldn't manage to loosen her hold on the little bloodletter.

The gift is simple. Uisch bowed its unmoving mask down, as though studying the glass in Leigh's hand. *Take your own life. Those dea-*

"NO!" Mom screamed.

"LEIGH!" Dad bawled.

Those dead on your account will be made whole.

Leigh couldn't feel the Earth beneath her feet. She was floating. Falling. Sinking.

The glass in her hand cast no reflection, she suddenly realized. It never had. Not that it should. It was not that kind of glass. Still, she wished it might show her something other than the gashes it had opened in her flesh, the blood pooling beneath it in her palm.

"...everyone?" Leigh repeated.

Yes. Your friends. The unfortunates of today. All those lives. Made whole.

With a sound a bit like a someone spilling water on a leather jacket, Mom *yanked* her hand free of the stake on top of the dresser. She did this silently, apparently not even registering the pain of it. "LEIGH!" she called, as she once more tried to climb over the obstruction.

Before she had a chance, the *SSSHHHRRRRR* of something heavy sliding across the floor upstairs terminated in her parents' bed crashing down through the yawning hole in the ceiling, only to catch on some electrical wiring and dangle in midair. Further impeding Mom and Dad's progress into the kitchen.

And yet, still leaving enough space for them to see. To watch.

Leigh watched Mom's head pop out from beside the dangling bed, watched as her face flushed with the vain effort of leaning her shoulder against it. "PUSH, HARLOW!"

Dad's face popped out from around the other side of the obstruction. Tears streaming down his face. "Don't!" he shouted at Leigh.

I live for this love, Uisch snickered through the floorboards buckling and cracking at Leigh's feet. *Show me. Show me. The love. Ten.*

Leigh flinched. "What?!"

The choice. Nine, the window nearest the kitchen table shattered.

Leigh turned to her parents. Mom was screaming at Uisch, shouting something that didn't sound like language. Dad was suddenly nowhere to be seen.

They both must see the gift. Eight. I make no one whole, if the ones who love you do not see. Seven.

Wherever Dad was, he started screaming too.

Leigh let go of a breath she hadn't realized she'd drawn. Her heart didn't seem to be skipping beats so much as taking on too many. How was she still standing? How was she still holding this glass in her h-

Six, announced something sliding down the stairs behind her parents.

It was only then, with six seconds to go, that Leigh grasped the unspeakable, immense power this creature commanded. It took and gave life, whenever and wherever it wanted, on a whim. Somehow, being the one brought back had made the implications of such a resurrection impossible to wholly absorb. Yet to see it from the outside…Uisch pulled human souls from the clutches of eternity with a shrug. With a giggle.

Imagine if a less malignant entity possessed such power! Oh, but perhaps that power left no room for good intentions. It was not the nature of tyrants to be benign.

Nor was it their nature to offer their subjects choices. For this wasn't a choice. Even if the demon had presented it as one.

Leigh looked up towards her parents. More than anything, she felt pity for them. Which surprised her. The anger and affection and even hatred made sense. But the pity…well, she supposed that tracked as well.

Perhaps this was just the guilt that every child ought to feel. Parents upend their lives to raise children. This was not the first time Leigh-faced obliteration had touched the senior Trecothiks. They had throttled so many of their own passions and ambitions to raise their daughter; what, in the face of that small annihilation of the ego, was visiting obliteration upon the glorified strangers to whom Leigh had never even properly introduced them? Nothing. Nothing at all. This had all been what her parents had always done, which was: what they thought was right for Leigh. And this was what had come of it. Glass in her hand.

In the end...it didn't matter. People hurt each other. Love breeds suffering. News at 11.

"Look at me," Leigh demanded through tears.

Mom already was looking; but she fell silent now. Dad's face failed to materialize. He was busy screaming somewhere behind the mattress on which their daughter had been conceived.

Five.

"Hey," Mom blubbered to Leigh. Her voice gentle, so horribly gentle. "Don't. Don't."

Four.

Leigh took a deep breath. Tightened her grip on the glass again. No sense worrying about cutting herself now. "I need you to look at me, Dad."

"I can't," his voice came back, small and wounded.

Three.

Mom stared at Leigh, no doubt studying whatever she saw on her daughter's face. Whatever that was, it caused Mom's expression to...settle. As a shipwreck does, at the bottom of the ocean. "Look at your daughter," she commanded Dad.

"It won't bring anyone back if you don't look," Leigh managed with a trembling voice.

Two.

Dad shook his head. "I can't!"

Leigh lifted the glass to her neck. "If you fucking love me, *LOOK!*"

He looked.

Leigh wanted to tell them that she loved them. Even if it wasn't entirely true in that moment. It would just be something to help them live with themselves, with what they'd done, with the meaningless suffering they'd tacked on to their end of their daughter's life.

But the words caught in her throat. Maybe because they weren't entirely true, in that moment.

Unfortunately, there were no more moments left.

So Leigh drove the sharp end of the glass into her neck.

Her parents both screamed.

The house laughed itself to bits.

Leigh sawed the serrated glass through her skin, feeling the flesh stretch, then split like latex. She cut deeper into her throat, all those muscles first crowding her hand, urgent and warm, only to yield as she sliced them in two, fiber by fiber. Blood poured from her lips, onto her hand. It lubricated the edge. Made the work easier.

Pain washed down her spine, up into her head. Like boiling water filling her skull from the bottom. The deeper she cut, the more the full sensory experience lived only in her head; the pressure and progress of the cutting edge radiated through that chunk of bowl that had once upon a time been used to mix flapjack batter, up into her hand, through her arm, to her head. All she was was this skull now, which she fought to separate from the rest.

Everything else vanished into molten contraction.

It was with a kind of clinical disinterest that she felt the muscle and sinew in her neck fraying one layer at a time, old rope under a dull blade. A girl tied to an anchor, sinking into the deep. Cut me loose. Cut me loose.

She felt hands on her, probably Mom and Dad's. Must have made it through that barricade. Uisch must have *let* them through, now that it was too late. A final twist of the knife. Classic Uisch.

They fell upon her. Screaming, crying. Hands on her shoulder, on her cheeks, fighting to wrest the glass from her hand. But she fought them off and tuned them out. As she did, she heard the gash in her throat, the sound of glass on tendon, speak to her. They were words she didn't understand, spoken by a voice, by a *mind,* with which Leigh was perfectly unfamiliar.

Uisch nodded, though. Uisch knew what spake through Leigh Trecothik, and it agreed.

A muscle to the left of Leigh's windpipe *snapped.* It was apparently a load-bearing something or other, as it sent her head flopping down and to the left. The weight of her skull stilled the blade in her throat for a moment, but she pushed through, sawing and sawing and sawing, wondering when it would be over, when would she just fucking die already. Sawing and sawing and sawing, no doubt more blood on her clothes and at her feet than in her veins. Cut me loose. Cut me loose. Cut me loose.

The agony lasted a lifetime. No mercy until the end. At which point, there was nothing. Certainly not mercy.

No. Nothing.

SIXTEEN

GOOD RIDDANCE

LEIGH FELL BACKWARDS ONTO THE GROUND. Or rather… her body did. Because Leigh was gone. A single look at what had once been her face made that abundantly clear.

The house stopped laughing. Save the hush of settling rubble, it fell absolutely silent.

Harlow threw himself down and curled up into a ball next to Leigh's body, embracing her remains and wailing into her shoulder.

Kira simply collapsed. No aim or direction. Just straight down, a controlled demolition.

She could feel Uisch drinking in their agony. Taking, taking, taking, radiating an inhuman satisfaction. Only, no. She knew this feeling. It was that crackle in the air you feel in the theater, watching a great comedy with a sold-out crowd.

This was what Uisch had wanted. The whole time. It

had been driving them towards this. The whole goddamned time.

For minutes, hours, who knew, they were trapped where they were. Harlow crying, cradling Leigh's body. Kira catatonic. Uisch getting precisely what it had wanted, whatever that was. Until, without another word spoken, in destruction or otherwise…Uisch turned towards the door to the garage. The other two hinges rocketed off the wall. The door fell almost as heavily as Leigh had. Saying nothing.

Uisch turned, gave the Trecothiks one final wave, then swaggered through the door and into the garage.

Ch-KRRRRUHKUH, the garage door rumbled as it began to open, only to snap free from its rail and *smash* to the ground.

Kira let her head loll in the direction of her husband. Watched as his entire body trembled, so violently that he seemed to be scooting himself sideways along the floor.

It was impossible for Kira to imagine life beyond this. Even one moment into the future. How could she ever push herself to her feet? Pry Harlow from their daughter's corpse, to help him up to standing? How could she step back into…only, no. She wouldn't be stepping back into her old grief, that morass into which she'd sunk immediately following the Firestarters Massacre. What a privilege that would be, to return to that.

What lay before her now was an altogether deeper pit. One in which there was only light enough to study her hands, reflect upon what they had done, how she had used them to utterly undo herself, in the service of suffering. Suffering for herself, her husband, her friends, her neighbors, her town, and most of all, her daughter.

In the end, the only thing she had accomplished, in everything she had done, was to make her daughter suffer.

She knew there were tears to cry over this. Yet they didn't come. They, too, wished to punish her: crying was catharsis, after all.

From outside the house, she heard a scream.

Kira lolled her head past the obstructions and towards the front door, whence that high-pitched squawk. Made no moves to investigate, though. Had no interest in knowledge.

The second and third cries were enough to more fully command her attention, at the very least.

After the fourth distinct voice she heard raised in terror, Kira tilted forward, planted her hands on the floor, swept them from side to side to clear a launch pad among the rubble, then used that to push herself to standing.

The many-headed howl outside grew a few new voices. Surely half a dozen people, at least. All screaming outside the Trecothik house.

Slowly, Kira snuck back through the hole she'd clawed in the mattress, tripping over the same plank in the bedframe which had caught her foot the first time through, and steadied her gait just as she reached the shrieking front door.

She put her hand on the knob. Forgetting her right hand had one hell of a hole through it. The knob slid part way into her palm. She pulled her hand back, though not for the pain. She'd felt nothing.

Still, she paused.

Then turned and considered the bay window just a few yards to her right. She didn't have to open the door. She could see what all the screaming was about through that window. She didn't have to let them in.

…

With her left hand, Kira turned the knob and opened the door.

Outside were at least twenty people. No, more than that. Standing in the middle of the street outside the Trecothik's home, standing in the driveway, standing on the lawn. Quite a few were screaming. Including Nicole Ligeti and Madeleine Encomb. They were embracing each other, crying with laughter. Relieved laughter, which only redoubled as Zoe Cottrell shouldered through the scrum to meet them.

As they celebrated, Madeleine spotted Kira. Pointed to her. The other two girls turned to look. Their faces dropped in unison.

Oh. So they remembered.

Also present and accounted for were all of the cops whose cars were, of course, still scattered about in front of the house, gumdrop lights still turning. Along with Detective Dresselhaus and Officer McCall. The former tried vainly to placate the latter, holding her palms up to his full-throated ululations.

Then McCall looked up and saw Kira. That shut him up *real* quick.

Dresselhaus blinked at his sudden silence, then turned

to follow his gaze.

As those few fell silent, others in the group looked towards their suddenly mute streetmates, perhaps wondering what had caused them to clam up so suddenly, perhaps feeling insecure about now being one of only a few screaming voices. The mother and her boy, Eli. Wanda Carter. So many people Kira didn't recognize, who she could only assume numbered among the peeled people. One by one, sometimes in pairs, they all turned to grimace at Kira Trecothik.

From the back of the crowd, a squirrel darted in one direction, while a skunk chundered in the other.

Kira stood on her front porch, staring down at the faces arrayed before her, as they stared up at her. All silent. None moving.

She wanted to say something to them. Something that would help them understand what had happened. Why it had happened. But she couldn't think of anything to say.

So she stood.

And they stood.

Staring.

None moving.

All silent.

SEVENTEEN

HOPE

MAINE ATTORNEY GENERAL FORSTER threw the file across the room for the sixteenth time. *This* time, she wasn't going to go pick it up. Definitely not. It was a bullshit case and she was one hundred percent on a hidden camera show. Had to be. If she wasn't, the world had gone fucking insane.

As after the previous fifteen throws, she picked the file back up while patrolling the room, searching in vain for the wink of a lens peeking out from behind a vase, or maybe through the grating of a vent. As with the previous fifteen times, she found nothing, and so walked the file back to her desk. She didn't sit back down until she'd had a chance to refill her glass of brandy, which had developed a nasty habit of emptying itself.

Forster's intercom beeped. One of its buttons lit up

and flashed. It took Forster back to her professorial days, to the teachers pet who would wave their hand around, all but shouting *pick me pick me*, like they were fuckings toddler. Th-

No. *Teacher's pets. Fucking toddlers.* Ever since joining the esteemed ranks of the United States Attorneys General, she'd begun to suffer a bit of a pluralization impediment. Oh, how she longed to have this case off her goddamned desk, so she could go back to having elementary grammar being among her largests problem.

Until then, the intercom. *Pick me pick me pick me*, the button begged, and so Forster obliged. "They here?" the Attorney General demanded.

"Yuuuup," replied the intercom. There was a person on the other end of it, or so Forster had been told. She knew nothing about them, least of all their name.

"Well, send 'em in."

"Okay."

Almost at once, a plump, greying old biddie Forster couldn't believe was a detective waddled into the office. "Uh…" Forster asked, "you're Detective Dresselhaus?"

The Detective nodded. "I am, Madam…General?"

"If you like."

A larger man, who looked more like his rank, followed Dresselhaus in and closed the door carefully behind him. Chief Greider needed no introduction, and Forster wasn't in the mood to extend the pleasantries any further than they needed to go. Or, for that matter, even as *far* as they needed to go.

She dropped a flat palm on the file. Muscle memory

nearly took over and sent it off to the far wall, but fortunately the highers faculty were on the job. Gah! "Would you care to explain to me why…uh, why?"

Dresselhaus smiled politely. "We're happy to explain anything you like."

Forster narrowed her eyes. "Are you aware of what this…this stupid fucking folder here says? On the inside?"

"I am."

"Well then first order of business might be to quit smiling, how about that?"

Dresselhaus complied. "Sorry, Madam General."

Ordinarily, Forster wouldn't have allowed the detective to stand on ceremony like that. Made her skin crawl, personally. But a bit of deference to authority wouldn't go amiss here. She turned to the Chief. "You know you can't keep innocent people locked up without cause. I shouldn't be having to deal with bullshit like this. This is Law Enforcement 101."

"With all due respect," the Chief explained to Forster's desk, "they're not innocent."

Forster caught herself snarling, just a bit. She put her teeth away and once again successfully kept herself from frisbeeing the folder across the room. It was a near-run thing though, a matter of *when* rather than the other one. Chekov's folder, this was. She leaned back and steepled her fingers, the universal sign for *I'm definitely still listening, but to save time I've already decided I don't like whatever you're about to say.*

Detective Dresselhaus cleared her throat. "Um…they

killed three young girls."

"Oh," Forster grunted, "that all? Because, and maybe I'm a little fuzzy, I've only read this thing about sixteen fuckings…fucking times, but I seem to recall in your statement on November nineteenth, you saying something to the effect of your *also* being a victim of the Trecothiks' reign of terror. Along with thirty-three other individuals from across Neirmouth, all of whom *also* gave statements that they had been killed. *Skinned alive,* some of them said." She picked up the folder and forced herself to put it down again. "I'll defer to you two, I assume you've still got more experience with this stuff than I do. I was but a humble securities litigator. I never saw murders. But the impression I had, you know, maybe I just got this from TV, but I was really under the impression that murder victims *typically* didn't testify at their killer's trial."

"Not usually," Chief Greider replied.

"So we can all agree, that it's *pretty fucking weird* that you're trying to charge a couple with the murders of three dozen people who are all *very much alive?* One of whom is in this goddamned room?"

The detective nodded. "Sure, b-"

"And can we also agree that it's not a good look for the state to have hot-shot Hollywood lawyers swooping in and taking the defendants' case pro-bono, sending appeals to *my* desk – which is already fucking insane because there wasn't a *trial*, so what are they even *appealing* – with the threat of kicking it to the Supreme Court if I don't swat it down?"

Greider chuckled. "They can't take it to the Supreme Court. It's not a real ca-"

"No," Forster shouted, "it really *isn't* a real case, *is* it?!" Ah, shit. That would have been a great time to throw the folder.

"Which lawyer is this?" Dresselhaus asked.

Forster laughed. "Some detective you are."

Chief Greider smirked at that.

Dresselhaus noticed. Instead of frowning, or something of the sort, she rolled her eyes and smiled a little.

Forster grimaced at the two of them. You couldn't cut the sexual tension with anything much weaker than a chainsaw. "Eric Tillman."

"Never heard of him," the Chief declared.

"And you're the Chief, huh? He's an LA guy. Big deal out there. Wants to be a big deal over here. Every once in a while makes a noise about running for President, like a goddamned, fucking…remember, uh…." Forster snapped her fingers three times, then pointed at Greider. "Avenatti. Remember that guy?"

"No."

"Well." Forster flopped the folder in her hand. It very nearly escaped her grasp, but she wasn't about to waste a good folder-throwing opportunity. "I'm not looking to give anybody easy headlines, you understand?"

"I have a confession," Dresselhaus whined.

"You made this all up? Yeah, I know."

"No, I *obtained* a confession…" the detective produced her phone from her pocket. "From Kira Trecothik, I have her *on the record* implicating her husb-"

"Implicating her husband in the murder of *living people.* Do you get that that's the hurdle?"

"But we *know* Nicole Ligeti and Madeleine Encomb were killed! It was national news!"

Forster pinched her eyes with the thumb and forefinger of her right hand. "I know. I heard about that. But, fucking *again,* here's that tricky little detail – *they're alive now.* That's all the defense has to say! Call the victim to the stand, point to them, and say *what murder?"*

"The body, then," Detective Dresselhaus mumbled. "How do you explain that?"

"What body?"

"Leigh Trecothik's body."

Forster smiled and set the folder down on the desk. She leaned forward, planted her elbows on the table, and interlaced her fingers. "Not my fucking problem."

"I'm just asking you how you account for the dead daughter appearing at the house and all but beheading herself," Dresselhaus tapped the folder, "which the coroner confirmed, as I'm sure you saw. It w-"

"Sixteen times, I saw it. All sixteen times, you know what I said to myself?"

"So how do you square that with Leigh Trecothik's *confirmed* death *months before* in the Firestarters Massacre?"

"Not my problem, that was what I said. All sixteen times. Not my fucking problem. Because that's not the case."

"And," Greider submitted, "we still can't figure out how the h-"

Dresselhaus threw a halting palm up at Greider. "One

thing at a time, Chief."

"Right you are, detective."

Forster scooted back in her chair and peeked under the desk. Remarkably, the two people sat across from her *weren't* playing footsies down there.

Dresselhaus thumped on the folder again. *"Well?"*

Forster scooped her gaze off the floor, smeared with all of the shit these two yokels tracked in. The full fury of said gaze, she directed to said yokels.

"Sorry," the detective was smart enough to say.

"Taking *not my fucking problem* as read," Forster asked, "what would you hope to hear me say right now?"

"That you believe us, that these two people are criminals that n-"

"Okay. You want me to believe that something magical happened in some no account little town, and that these Trecothiks murdered three dozen people, most of those murders being full-on fucking *flayings* that occurred in the span of just a few minutes, *all* of those murder victims being people who are still alive. Which means you want me to turn around and announce, publicly, that I'm upholding what by sane, real-world standards is an unlawful imprisonment. Which means you want me to all but call up Tillman and tell him I've got a notch I'd like to help him put on his belt."

Dresselhaus darkened. "So this is about not letting a west coast lawyer get a win, is it?"

"No, it's about keeping Neirmouth, and Pitney, and *you* from becoming a fucking laughingstock, or a…haven for conspiracy cranks, or some shit."

"We can at least get the woman on assaulting an officer," the Chief volunteered.

Forster shook her head. "McCall? That one?"

"Yeah."

"...have you read his testimony? Not only does he claim he died like everybody else, at the end he goes off on this riff about there being a monster on Knot Hedge that he didn't see, but *knew* was there. That's your guy?"

"...well, we could ask him to recant that part, maybe."

Forster squeezed the bridge of her nose. She took a deep breath and let it out in double-time. "There's no world in which I don't tell you to free these people yesterday."

"Because they didn't commit any crimes," the detective sneered.

"Correct. None we could possibly prosecute."

Dresselhaus nodded. "Well...what if there were a way for th-"

"Stop." Forster held up her hand. "Just for the hell of it, I'm going to choose this moment to remind you how...*colossally* fucking foolish it would be to even *think* of suggesting a frame job to the Attorney General."

"Hm. Well, if I should return here sh-"

"Further, on a causeless whim, I'm gonna point out that having perhaps intuited the possibility of a frame job, I'm now duty-bound to be particularly vigilant as to...uh, that possibility." She leaned forward. "Let them go."

"Aw," Chief Greider frowned. He had the good sense to wilt under the twin glowers of Dresselhaus and

Forster.

"You're making a mistake," the detective declared.

Forster forced herself to smile again. "Hey, if they kill you a second time, you come let me know, and I'll *really* let 'em have it." She pointed to the door.

After the two emissaries from Pitney, a town Forster kept forgetting even existed, left the room, she realized she'd plum forgotten to throw the folder during that whole damn meeting. That was frustrating enough to send the paperwork across the room for the seventeenth time.

"THAT DEFINITELY COULD HAVE GONE BETTER," Greider noticed as they walked back to the car.

Dresselhaus shrugged. "Maybe a little. She was never going to let us keep them locked up forever. I was hoping for at *least* another, I don't know, week or two though. Enough time to figure something out."

Greider circled to the passengerside of the car and tried the handle. Locked. "You worried they're gonna skip town or something?"

"Why wouldn't they? Their house is half-destroyed. Chances are the insurance will come through, give 'em a hell of a lot of fun money." She unlocked the car. Greider tried the handle at the same time.

"My side's still locked."

"Stop trying the…*stop*." Dresselhaus unlocked the car again. The two of them climbed in. She sniffed and pulled out her phone. "Not to mention," she added as she opened a new text message window, "their friend circle's shrunk a hell of a lot. Everybody in town knows what they did, even if we can't…prove it." She started the car. "Everybody outside of town's gonna know, too. Whether or not they believe it."

Greider squinted at Dresselhaus. "How's that?"

"The dashcam footage. From McCall's car. That woman and her son…"

She only realized she'd zoned out again when Greider reached out and touched her shoulder, softly. That was a step in the right direction: he'd at least stopped asking her what it was like, to…*unfold*. Because she could remember. She had a hard time *not* remembering.

"There's other stuff too," she resumed. "I'd wager a year's salary that somebody out there had one of those camera doorbells. I'd wager they caught something in one of those."

"Detective…"

"And there's just the *testimony,* Chief. All that testimony! So many people…what we all went through, it's… you couldn't fake that."

"I don't know if th-"

"Just because we can't get them legally doesn't mean we c-"

"*Andrea.*"

Dresselhaus flinched at the sound of her first name, coming from her Chief's lips. It rang like profanity; had he *ever* said her name before?

God, he looked so *sympathetic.* It was awful.

"What is that face?" Dresselhaus said.

"I don't have a gentle way to say this…this is going to

ruin you if you don't let it go."

"…let it go?" Dresselhaus adjusted herself to more fully square her shoulders to Greider. "Are you fucking kidding me? I got…I got *skinned alive,* goddamnit! I got…" the word that came to her was *peeled*. She couldn't get it out, though, for the knot of emotion in her throat.

She couldn't cry in front of him. Absolutely not.

"Stop looking at me like that!" she demanded.

"Like what?"

"Sympathetic!"

"I don't know how else…I'm just looking!"

"Well, stop!"

Greider shook his head, then looked to the rearview mirror outside his door.

"Are you saying you're not gonna help me?" Dresselhaus demanded.

A thoughtful pause. Then: "I think it's best for everyone in the long run that this just…goes away."

Just to have something to do, Dresselhaus threw the car into reverse. "Unbelievable," she grumbled. Cranking herself around to look out through the rear windshield. Taking her foot off the brake.

Chief Greider just kept on staring at himself in the side mirror. Or maybe he was nodding back at his reflection. Hard to tell in her peripheral vision, but it looked like he was shivering.

"IT WAS MY IDEA," insisted the lady sitting on the stainless steel bench across from Kira.

Kira said nothing. Which was as much encouragement as she'd given this lady.

Nonetheless, the lady continued: "I guess that's my point. I mean, it was in the Diane Keaton movie. I forget what it was called, but you look up *Diane Keaton Apple-sauce Movie* and I'll bet you'll find it. You're sure to find it. There can't be more than one. But to do it for *real,* that was my thing. Then this lady's on the TV show with it? Flavored applesauce? You've gotta be kidding me. You've just gotta be…be *fucking* kidding me, sorry about the language. I've always loved applesauce. So flavoring, that was my idea. I've had raspberry applesauce. Strawberry. Even vanilla. I made it, I mean. Va-"

One of the day officers walked over to the station lockup. "Trecothik!"

After just a moment's pause, Kira rose from her bench and walked to the bars.

From the next cell over, her husband did the same.

The day officer stuck his bulbous little toadstool key in the lock to Kira's cell and turned it. "You're both up, good. It's the both of ya's."

Kira stepped out of her cell. Stared at the far wall, as the day officer locked it up behind her, then stepped over to Harlow's.

The wall was painted two different colors. From the floor to about three feet up, it was a sickening grey-green. The rest of the way up, a white made filthy with history.

She heard Harlow step out of his cell, then the *clang* of the day officer locking the gate behind him. Only then did she turn to look at her husband. Staring more at his neck, not quite meeting his eye.

Shivering, at the sense that he was looking right at her.

Quick as could be, she snapped her eyes up to meet his. Only he wasn't looking at her. Not directly. Seemed to be aimed at her shoulder.

They walked out of the holding area together. Kira wondering where they were being taken. Indifferent to wherever it might be. Because it didn't matter. It truly didn't.

The officer walked them closer and closer to the intake window, then turned and blinked at them. "You don't wanna know where you're goin'?"

No response from either.

He shook his head, shrugged, and walked away.

So they were probably free to go, then.

Alright. Fine. It made no difference. Kira headed for the exit, trusting that Harlow would be following close behind. It was, she knew, very probably the last thing on which she would ever trust him.

Without a word spoken to one another, they collected the belongings they'd had on their persons upon being dragged from the wreckage of their old lives – the once-happy home that had become the final resting place of their daughter – and got a Zyp car back home. The moment they returned, they walked directly to Harlow's car, got in – Kira behind the wheel – and drove. Where to, they didn't know.

Which made sense; there was so very much that they didn't know. All Kira knew was that they were driving away. Into the unknown. There was nothing good in the known, after all. Whereas, in the unknown…

There was one certainty, of course. Or at least, one thing that Kira believed so strongly as to make it indistinguishable from fact.

She knew, for reasons she couldn't articulate, that she and Harlow would never be rid of each other. Nor would they ever truly try. Nothing on that needed to be said, could be said, least of all with words. They deserved each other. They would get what they deserved.

That was bedrock, at an impossible depth.

The only known thing.

FOR HOURS, THEY DROVE, not *to*, but simply *away*. Never speaking, never discussing. Just driving.

Whenever Kira pried her eyes from the road and looked into the rearview mirror, she expected to see her daughter back there. Blood pouring from her neck, finger raised in accusation. But that, too, would have provided a kind of catharsis. To be haunted was to pay penance. It was to be repaid with suffering in kind. She had forced her daughter to choose death, for a second time, in a fashion far more grisly and undoubtedly painful than the first time. She had done that to her beautiful baby girl. Harlow had helped, yes, but it was Kira who had opened the door. If only she hadn't let Uisch in. If only she had ignored its offer. If only a million things.

She wondered where Uisch was now. Not just because she wished to warn whomever it was the devil appeared to next. But also because, even still, even now, she wanted another chance to bring Leigh back. Oh, how she wanted to bargain with the beast one final time.

Harlow for Leigh. I'd do it in an instant. Just give me back my daughter. Let me do it.

Kira looked to Harlow. He was looking at her, but averted his gaze when it collided with hers.

He was thinking precisely the same thing, she knew. He would kill her to have Leigh back. Easily. Happily.

So there were two known things, then.

Perhaps the second known thing explained the first. Accounted for why they would never be able to part from one another, why they would live out the remainder of their lives together.

There was always the chance that Uisch would return. There was always the hope that a deal could be struck.

Kira pulled her eyes away from her husband, and looked to the road ahead of them. An uncommonly straight one for the backwoods of Maine, this was, slicing through cedar and balsam fir all the way to the horizon. The only path open to them.

Kira wondered if they were still in Maine. Couldn't be sure.

After a time, they switched places. Harlow driving, Kira not. She closed her eyes and tried to sleep. Tried and failed. Despite being absolutely shattered by exhaustion, slumber eluded her. Each time she seemed to drift close to it, a dreadful anticipation snapped her awake. The certainty that at any moment, she would feel a cold, blood-slicked finger touch the back of her neck. The thought of that touch terrified her. Yet she longed for it, at the same time, to the same degree. It was the only thing that could free her from this awful, gut-twisting, heart-rending apprehension.

But it would never come.

ULSCH WOULD, of course. And did. It returned to the Tre-cothiks countless times throughout their long, long lives together. But only by night, only in secret.

Only to dance.

EPILOGUE

TO THOSE SQUASHED BY THE WHEEL

ZOE HAD NO IDEA WHAT TO SAY to her friends. Nicole and Maddie had been through things that made the Firestarters Massacre seem like…well, not like *nothing*, but like a slightly smaller thing than it was. And they remembered all of it. Nicole remembered being stabbed again and again, remembered the feeling of the blade clicking against her ribs, sliding into the tender underside of her jaw, over and over and over. Maddie said she had to sleep with the light on and the covers off – and even then, she sometimes felt the fabric of the bag collapsing onto her face, heard thick payloads of dirt landing atop her. On the really bad nights, she said, she felt the flat head of the shovel against her face. So, Zoe supposed, in a very real way it didn't even make sense to say that they remembered these things. They simply re-experienced them.

Zoe didn't re-experience anything. It seemed that she had somehow managed to avoid experiencing her own death at all. She'd gone out for a walk that morning, just to enjoy the autumn air, and also, alright, to get away from her increasingly overprotective parents. The winter was due to be brutal, and Zoe found it hard to clear her head indoors. Well, she found it hard to do outdoors too, but at least without walls she didn't feel like she was suffocating. The world, after all, had been closing in around her. So she went walking down the street, until she was suddenly standing outside of the Trecothik's house, along with a whole bunch of other people, many of whom were screaming, *screaming*. Including Nicole and Maddie. It was only later that she learned that Harlow Trecothik had killed her; what disturbed her most about this was that no one could say how, or even where, for certain. There had been no witnesses save the murderer himself. The man had been on foot at the time, that much was known. Presumably he had attacked her from behind, then dumped her body somewhere. But whatever the means of resurrection that had visited Neirmouth, they involved a mystical refurbishing of corpses. Plucking some from the ground, sealing holes in the skin of others, or in Zoe's case, pulling her from whatever shrubbery Harlow had tossed her into, to plop her down in the middle of Hamlin Drive. So she would *never* know what had happened to her.

Zoe's last memory before said ploppage had been

of walking past the Bruner house on Sycamore. Yet a search of the area turned up no bloodstains on the sidewalk, no Zoe-sized divots in any back gardens.

Sometimes, Zoe envied Nicole and Maddie their certainty. Which was stupid, she knew. But still. Stupid was sort of the watchword that year.

To wit: some stupid little documentary about everything that had happened had gone live last night. On Vimeo, natch; hard to imagine even the most desperate no-name streaming services wanting to touch it. The piece had been posted anonymously, but Zoe knew precisely who had spearheaded it: Detective Dresselhaus, whose requests for interview Zoe and her two friends had declined more times than they could count. Zoe likewise declined to watch it, but by all accounts it was a deeply surreal piece of 'reporting,' one that was almost universally lauded in Neirmouth, and apparently either mocked or (more overwhelmingly) ignored the world over. And who could blame those folks from away? The film featured interview after interview with self-proclaimed murder victims, about their own fantastical murders. Even if two of the resurrected (whose refusal to take part in the film certainly didn't lend it any credibility) had made noise on a national scale when they'd been murdered…well, it was fake news. And/or a cheap Blair Witch-style gimmick movie that wasn't even made well. From what Zoe had heard, there were already breakdowns explaining how the effects work with the (oft-grainy, obliquely captured) footage of the unfolding people had been accomplished. All quite rudimentary, it was believed. Easily dismissed, easily forgotten.

This was what Zoe had been told, at any rate, during the many, many conversations she had with Nicole and Maddie, as the three darkened the corners of their respective bedrooms and attempted to make some kind of sense of what had happened to them. What had been *done* to them. And every day (for that was how often they met), Zoe tried to say things that might reassure them, help them understand that she was in their corner, on their side, had their backs. Nothing came out right. It always sounded trite, or forced, or… just dumb. Because despite their having nominally suffered the same fate…their experience was so profoundly different from her own.

Still. Nicole and Maddie always acted appreciative of Zoe's pabulum, even if nothing she said actually helped. That was obvious. What wasn't clear was what she *should* be saying.

After weeks and weeks of these meetings, Zoe realized why her inability to say the right things to her friends bothered her so much: she felt as though she was being left behind. She had grief too, goddamnit! She'd been traumatized in the massacre – lost fingers in it – and more to the point, death had swallowed her and spat her back out just as it had them! Maybe she hadn't been *as* violently murdered, at least not in a way that she could remember, but that didn't mean her trauma wasn't worth talking about! Trauma was trauma, right? Why should she have to sit there and be a sponge for other people's, without having the opportunity to exorcise her own?

But that made her sound petty. She wanted to be there for her friends. She just wished their meetings hadn't become *her* listening to *them* all the time. She just wished they could be there for her, too.

It was in just such a low mood that the night spoke to Zoe, in her own voice.

They are, it said to her.

Oh, don't give the night so much credit. She'd said that to herself. And she had a point.

So the next day, Zoe screwed up the courage to tell Nicole and Maddie about her struggles. She did a hell of a lot of qualifying, but after a two-minute clearing of the throat, she started to unburden herself, and with considerable candor. She told them of feeling left behind, of feeling traumatically outclassed by orders of magnitude. She told them about how sometimes when she first woke up, especially from a nap, she would forget where she was for a moment and become *certain* that she was dead again. Sometimes those thoughts ignited a deranged, tearful fit of laughter. *Dead again.* She told them how it was hard to not think of this second life as a pointless intermission in oblivion — which she supposed all life was, it just hadn't ever *felt* that way to her before. She told them about how she couldn't hang out with her friend Jack anymore, at least not at his house, because he lived on the road that the fire-trucks used to get from the station to the main road. The sirens were more than she could handle – they reminded her of the way everyone had screamed, upon being brought back. She told them about how she'd started to hate herself for being unable to face these triggering stimuli, how she'd read plenty about cognitive behavioral therapy and immersion therapy and all the other fucking therapies that say *don't run from it, face it, conquer it*, but she couldn't do that, couldn't stop running. And she hated herself for it.

She told them all of this. And even though this was chump change compared to what they had been through, they listened. And they tried to say all the right things to Zoe. And Zoe smiled, even though none of the things they said did much to make her feel better. Which wasn't to say they weren't helping. It was their listening that made her feel better, the moments when she didn't feel like a problem her friends were trying to fix.

After that night, they all did a lot more listening, even on those evenings when no one did very much talking at all.

The night never spoke to Zoe again. Not in her own voice, or anyone else's.

IT SPOKE TO RANDALL, THOUGH.

Young Randall McNichols, all of eleven years old,

didn't know enough about the world to make sense of his mother's death. He was old enough to know that the two little twins sharing a crib in the corner of his room were the reason she was gone. He was also old enough to know that the voices he was hearing in the wake of that tragedy weren't real. Dad told him so, his talking doctor told him so, everybody told him so. The voices weren't real. They were in his head.

But then one night they stopped. Like someone had said *shhh*. And the voices had listened.

Then the next night, there was just one voice, and it came from outside of his head. Only it wasn't a voice. It wasn't his new brother, or his new sister. It was his room that spoke to him.

Dn. One of his softball trophies fell off the shelf and onto a pile of clothes.

Beep! His awesome waterproof stopwatch asserted itself.

Sssssk. A poster his Mom had tacked to the wall just two days before she went away slipped loose on one corner and slid along the wall.

Red. That one wasn't even a sound – it was his nightlight, flashing red, for just a moment. Randall's head filled in the syllable though, completed the thought.

Don't be scared, the nighttime had whispered to him. But Randy wasn't scared. He was listening. And the nighttime was speaking.

Even though he was only eleven years old, he knew

enough not to tell Dad about what the nighttime had told him, about the amazing things it had said it could do. He played it cool when his Dad blew his top about what a mess Randy's room was the next morning. That was alright; he'd make it up to his Dad. He'd make it so he wouldn't have to cry in the middle of the day anymore. He'd make his family be how it was supposed to be, instead of how it was now.

Randall would wait until tonight. Then he'd make the night-time laugh.

END

Also by Jud Widing

Novels
Doragha
Down The High Tomb
Jairzinho's Curbside Giants
The Little King of Crooked Things
A Middling Sort
Patience, Ambrose
Westmore and More!
The Year of Uh
Your One-Way Ticket To The Good Time

Samuzzo D'Amato
Go Figure
The Whole Branzino

Stories
And Now, Destroy The Room
Identical Pigs

60963165R00404